For Linda! (My Agent! LOL)

Joani Lacy

SORRY'S RUN

SORRY'S RUN

Joani Lacy

iUniverse®

SORRY'S RUN

This is a work of fiction. All of the characters, names, incidents, organizations, and dialogue in this novel are either the products of the author's imagination or are used fictitiously.

iUniverse books may be ordered through booksellers or by contacting:

iUniverse
1663 Liberty Drive
Bloomington, IN 47403
www.iuniverse.com
1-800-Authors (1-800-288-4677)

ISBN: 978-1-4917-9297-1 (sc)
ISBN: 978-1-4917-9298-8 (e)

Library of Congress Control Number: 2016904776

Print information available on the last page.

iUniverse rev. date: 04/20/2016

DEDICATION AND DISCLAIMER

Sorry's Run and its inhabitants are clearly a fictional idea, created out of my own sense of wonderment and fun. I hope my readers will forgive the license I have taken, because Greenup County is real. My made-up town might be very hard to place for local residents, because in my love of the "neck of the woods" from where my family hails, I have glamorized things just a bit. And I must admit that the Underground Railroad most likely never traveled the route I have described. And though my people are not of Scotch-Irish ancestry, this rich European heritage is real to Kentucky, and I honor that. And I thank my friend, Joni, for the notion.

The healers in this story are perhaps an exaggerated extension of my grandfather, T.C. Clay, who was a natural herbalist and medicine man in his own right. But in truth, I have my Uncle Soc to thank for the inspiration for this novel. The story didn't go where I initially intended, but still, it was Soc, who is a gifted storyteller, who flamed my desire to set my characters down in a place that will always feel like home to me, though I have never lived there.

With all that said…

This book is dedicated to the CLAYS OF GREENUP COUNTY.

TO MY EDITORS:

Levan Burgin, A.R.E. National Outreach Coordinator, my sister and soul partner. I thank you for your constant help and undying support in my projects. I pray that we are not done yet.

Todd Wesley Burgin, talented writer and editor. Thank you for coming on board and getting involved with this book. And thank you for my back cover copy. You share in my love of language and storytelling, Nephew. You are just beginning.

Nicole Vieth-Clayton, CEO of CJV Reporting Co. I think your dad would have been proud of our collaboration. I thank you for everything! (The list is too long!)

Jack Heffron, former senior editor at Writer's Digest Books and Story Press, and author of several nonfiction books, including "The Local Boys: Hometown Players for the Cincinnati Reds." Without your encouragement I doubt this would have become a printed book. Thank you for your much-needed advice in this daunting publishing world. You are such a blessing.

And Special Thanks To:

Donna Lucas, publisher of "Video Watchdog." I couldn't get here without your technical help. Your patience is as precious to me as your brilliance. Thank you, my friend.

Jan Perry, writer and blogger, who helped me become a better writer.

Joni Templeton-Skinner, renowned Kentucky paralegal and Zumba goddess, and her beautiful daughter, **Liz Shinkle.** Thank you both for the Scotch-Irish inspiration. What fun I had in thinking on all you shared of your own heritage. I think it's you who allowed me to love this book more than I ever could have.

Detective Bruce McVay, of the Boone County Sheriff's Department. Thank you, my friend, for your help, especially with the deputy's oath of office. Even though "my cop" is more fiction than the real deal, your guidance was invaluable.

Lea Nolan, of the Hamilton County Public Library. Thanks for your continued help with promoting my work. What would I do without you?

Sheree and **Ann**, "Always and Forever." 'Nuff said.

As always, I thank the love of my life, **Robin**, for the rock 'n roll ride. "*The Beat Goes On...*"

And finally, to my readers! Without you I would have had no reason to publish again. I kept many of you close in my mind's eye as I plowed through this work. I thank you and hope you have a fun escape with my latest effort.

"It ain't nothin' but a party!"

Bring the fairies
Circlin' 'round our head.
From the wee ancient ones
We all will be led…

PROLOGUE
KENTUCKY 1940s

MARTHA MAGGIE MCBRIDE lay perfectly still on the scratchy feather comforter that served as her bed in the tiny loft. She listened hard to the grownups down below in the one-room cabin.

"I heard it, I tell you. I heard the rocks on the roof," her father's usually booming voice cracked.

"I think I heard it, too, Sean. Three rocks. The fairies is circlin' closer. You can feel it," her mother whispered.

Seven-year-old Martha trembled in her rough bed. She was so afraid of the fairies. She knew her granny was real sick, but she didn't want the fairies to take her. Her mama always told her the fairies would come and take Granny's soul back to Ireland when it was her time, and it was the dreaded Banshee who would do the warning. Martha didn't want Granny to go. She loved her too much. But Granny was always talking about the old country and how she missed the green of the land she had grown up in. Little Martha would look out the window and see the pretty green hills of Kentucky and she didn't understand.

"It's different, child. Ireland is a mystical land and it's full of wonder. It's not just the green color of the grass, it's what lies 'neath the grass that makes it a magical place. Fairies roam the land and look out for our souls in Ireland. I hope and pray they will find me here when it's time for my passing over. I am so far away. I hope they will find me."

Martha remembered her granny's words and it made her feel better. Granny wanted the fairies to take her soul, so it must not be a bad thing. Martha just couldn't figure out what a soul was.

"Your soul is your God light, girl. It's what makes you shine." Granny would grin, showing her pink gums.

"But Granny, do I have one? A soul, I mean? I want to shine, too."

"Of course, lass. Everybody has the God light. It's just that some people be tendin' to turn it off." She winked at her grandchild. "Don't worry, wee little one, you are going to shine so bright!" Granny held her skinny arms high up over her head and Martha believed her. She believed she would shine.

And now her granny was lying below her on the only mattress in the cabin and she was making terrible noises. Martha was very sure her granny wasn't shining. She just hoped her soul wouldn't leak out some way or get lost.

There was a knock on the door. Granny was always saying three knocks on the roof meant that someone was about to pass. Martha didn't understand where you passed to, but it sure made everybody sad. She hoped a knock on the door wasn't the same thing.

"Come in, Joel, Sandra. Come in. Her time is close."

Martha heard different voices below her as more and more people crowded into the small cabin. The voices were muffled and hushed and then it got really quiet. An awful choking sound rose up from her granny, like a gurgling rattle. *Granny?* The little girl felt a cold chill.

She heard her mother speak in a hoarse voice, "Get the priest quick, Joel, before her soul takes its leave. She has to have God's blessin' first and then the fairies can take her. Hurry quick now."

Then a wail broke out from someone and soon everybody was wailing. Martha pulled the sticky blanket over her head to try and block out the awful noise, but there was no keeping it out. It just got louder and louder. She crawled out from under her blanket and rolled over to the spot where the boards didn't match up in the floor. There was a crack big enough to see downstairs. She could make out the heads of her mother and father bending over granny. When they pulled back, there was a sheet over granny's face. All the women gathered around her mother and held onto her as one of the men left to go outside.

Her mother stood straighter and moved over to the stove, where she and the other women tended to a big iron pot and began kneading dough to bake bread. The smell was wonderful and Martha knew there would be good eating later. She remembered when her baby brother had gone with the fairies. There had been so much food. More than they ever had before. Her mother had always said they might live poor, but they were rich in blessings. Martha liked that. She liked thinking about blessings. She pictured the little fairies as blessings. Now she hoped the blessings were making sure wherever the little baby had gone was the same place her granny was passing to on her way back to Ireland. Surely the fairies knew the way.

It seemed like somebody was always passing.

She watched her father as he reached for a big bottle shoved to the back of a high shelf. It was filled with golden water and the men started handing it around and drinking from it. The priest came and it got quiet for a while as he murmured words over her granny. But as the night wore on, there was much singing and dancing and much crying and shouting. Nobody checked on the little girl and she was free to watch her granny's Wake until the sun came up.

Martha's tiny limbs trembled from staying in the same spot for so long, but she didn't want to move. She wanted to see the fairies. Granny had been gone all night and she hadn't seen them. *What if they were lost?* The little girl whispered a prayer over and over, "Please help the fairies find my granny so when she gets back to Ireland she can send me her God light. I want to shine like her. Granny, please, send me your God light!"

CHAPTER ONE
NEW YORK 2015

"THAT'S A WRAP!" THE ART DIRECTOR looked smug as he said the magic words. A collective sigh of relief went around the hot studio and a weak applause came from the models who had survived the all-day shoot.

"Did he really just say that?" Shelby Jean looked over at her attractive photographer and asked again, "Jack, seriously, did I just hear what I think I heard?"

"You did, Shelby. We all did. Will you ever forgive me?" He smiled sweetly and she melted, just as she had for the fifteen years he had been photographing her in the brutal modeling business in New York.

"Jack, you know you're just too good-looking for your own good."

"That's what they tell me."

"How come you're always behind the camera?" She grinned.

"Because it allows me to stare into those outrageous green eyes in that perfect face of yours for hours without being arrested."

"Oh, yeah, charmer? Or should I say pervert?" she asked and giggled. "Whatever. Don't push it. That was still an agonizing eight hours." She punched him in the arm and grabbed a towel to wipe off her makeup before adding, "Now I am convinced. I am finally and completely too old for this shit."

"Not true, Shelby Jean Stiller. Definitely not true. Girl, you look as good as ever. No, that's not true. You look better. Healthier, you know?"

She punched him again and demanded, "So you're telling me I'm fat?"

He laughed and shook his head. "You girls never change. But seriously, I had no idea this director was such a dick. I swear I would never have put you through this."

"It's okay, Jack. I enjoyed it." She hesitated and then added, "No, that's a lie. I didn't really enjoy it. And yes, the director is a dick, and yes, I am too old for this shit. Next time don't call me, I'll call you."

"Come on doll, I'll get you a cab."

"Thank you, Jeremiah." Shelby tipped the tall, uniformed doorman her usual as he opened the door of the taxi for her in front of the high-rise.

"Ah, Shelby Jean, I thought we made a new rule. No more tips. The Christmas bonus is plenty. You live here. It's my job. Gratuities is just plain tacky."

"Well, then, darn it, give me back my twenty." She tried to grab the money back.

"No way! This one is mine. New rule starts next time." He stuck the bill into his pocket.

They both laughed and hugged. It was a game they had played for years. She took care of him and he took care of her.

"How was it?" He asked.

"It sucked. Never again."

"Okay, then, Ms. Shelby. Never again."

He opened the massive front door and she walked into the lobby of her home, a posh high-rise apartment building in the Upper West Side of Manhattan. As always, all eyes followed her as she entered the elevator. And as always, Shelby was oblivious to the stir her beauty created.

"Caitlin?" Shelby yelled as she unlocked the door to her 14th floor apartment and tossed her purse onto the closest chair. It was getting dark outside and through the vast windows of the apartment the city lights lit up the night like earth-bound stars. The smells coming from the kitchen made her mouth water. She realized she hadn't eaten all day. "Oh, no, not the garlic soup again?"

A stunning tall brunette came into the living room with an apron wrapped around her waist and a glass of red wine in her hand. "What, you're complaining about my soup? You want something else? Hot dogs? Hamburgers? Bologna?"

Shelby took the wine and laughed. "Uh-uh, roomie. You will bring me garlic soup and bring it now!"

"That bad, huh?" Cait smiled.

"No. Way worse. What was I thinking? I don't need the money and I sure as hell didn't need the aggravation."

"Well, Jack will see to it you're plastered all over New York again. You'll be famous."

Shelby took a sip of the French wine. "Oh, Cait, I don't care about that. I seriously don't. And it was no fun. That art director was insane. And besides, all the fuss was about selling hairspray. Ain't nothin' to write home about. So, is anyone coming for dinner?"

"No, but Tommy may stop by later. I think he might have had another breakup."

"Oh, no. Not again."

"Yeah, afraid so. But he's better off without Gregory, if you ask me. Not that Tommy would ask. His heart is too fragile right now. But Shelby, you need to sit down and relax after the day you've had. And speaking of something to write home about, here's something that will make you smile." She picked up a letter from a stack of mail on the table and handed it to Shelby.

Shelby looked at the envelope. It was addressed to her from Sorry's Run, Kentucky. "Grandma Mart?" She smiled the best smile of the day and took a seat at the table next to the windows that overlooked the City. Cait went back into the kitchen and left Shelby alone to read the letter from her grandmother. The handwriting was the usual pretty cursive, but this time the letters were uneven as if written in a shaky hand. Shelby's breath quickened as she read:

Dear Shelby Jean,

Hon, I need to ask you somethin. I know you have a wonderful, busy life in New York, but your daddy isn't doin so good and I think he could really do with a long visit from you. Actually, I could really do with a visit as well. I am gettin old, Shelby Jean. I feel it and I need you to come and help with your daddy's care. I know it's a lot to ask. I know how you feel about Kentucky and I know how you feel about your daddy. But Wesley is not gettin any younger either. Would you please think about it, hon? Would you please think about comin home? I love you so much. I need you.

Love, Grandma Mart

That was all there was. The letter was just one paragraph, and it was enough to shake Shelby to her core. Her grandmother had written her many times over the years, but she had never asked anything of her. They had had a wonderful relationship, much love and no demands. But this sounded like a demand. Shelby put the letter down and drank her wine, reflecting on her grandmother. Martha had grown up dirt poor in an old cabin in Sorry's Run. The McBride clan had been steeped in Scotch-Irish folklore, and Martha had clung to the old stories like they were gospel. Shelby had heard all her life about Irish fairies and the awful Banshee. It had all been so much fun and a little scary. But her grandmother had been her constant joy.

Caitlin came out from the kitchen. "Is it bad, Shel?"

"Yeah, it's bad. Grandma Mart is telling me to come home."

CHAPTER TWO
HOMECOMING

"SHELBY JEAN, HON, I DON'T LIKE DRIVIN' that far, but I can get one of my friends to pick you up. Bella wouldn't think a thing of goin' to Huntington."

"It's okay, Grandma, my flight was so early I arranged for transportation to bring me to Wesley's."

"Well, okay, then. If that's the way you want it. But Shelby, I do insist on takin' you to church Sunday mornin'. I've been braggin' just a bit, and I wanna show you off." Martha giggled on the phone, and added, "I am so anxious my own self that I'm afraid I might blow a gasket. I love you hon, and have a good flight. I've pictured my sweet fairies holdin' up the wings of your plane and bringin' you safe. And Shelby, thank you."

Shelby smiled as she thought of the conversation they had had the night before. Grandma Mart had sounded like her old self, no urgency in her voice. Maybe she was just lonely for her granddaughter. It had been a long time since Shelby had visited. She gazed out the backseat window of the airport van. A mist lay on the Ohio River and the early spring had already brought some green to the hills. *I bet Ireland looks something like this.*

Shelby liked remembering all the "tall tales" she had heard since she was barely big enough to run through the waving, high grass in the field behind her parents' Kentucky farmhouse. Everybody always said her Grandma Mart could spin a yarn better than anybody.

But Neely, her mother, believed there was truth in some of the old legends. "Be careful there, girl, and don't be so sure what your grandmother tells you is teasin'." A dazzling smile would cross her mother's lips and she would take Shelby's small hands and lead her around in a circle dance until Shelby's heart sang.

Shelby did love the old stories and she loved the idea of her Scotch-Irish heritage. Martha was the only one of the McBride clan that still lived in the county. Everybody had either moved on or died. But Grandma Mart said she would never move. She wanted to be sure the fairies would find her when it was her time. She would laugh and say, "If I was to move over to Ohio, or some other foreign place, it might get 'em real confused."

"But Grandma Mart, if you've never even been to Ireland, why would the fairies take you there when you die?"

"Shelby Jean, once Ireland has a piece of your soul, it never lets go. My body might be in Kentucky, but my spirit is in Ireland with my granny."

Shelby never did quite understand the reasoning in that, but it was just more of what made her grandmother so loveable. All those "tall tales" she told were so much fun, even if they weren't to be believed. But Shelby *had* always wondered at her own God light. She knew that in Martha's eyes she had shown more brightly than anyone.

Well, I sure as hell am not shining now. Shelby's smile disappeared as the van pulled up in front of the house. Her heart sank as it always did when she looked at the run-down place she had grown up in. The house lay in shadows, dark enough to look foreboding. No lights were on inside or out to welcome her, but the sun was breaking through heavy clouds and bringing light with the dawn. She had the driver set her bags on the front porch. She handed him an extra fifty and grinned at his surprise. "I might need you again."

The driver tipped his cap to her and smiled back. "You got it, ma'am. Anytime." He gave her his card.

Shelby watched him drive off and then she peeked in the front window. No sign of Wesley. He was most likely still sleeping. Shelby hugged her coat tightly around her and walked to the back of the house. She didn't want to go in just yet. She reached into her pocket and pulled out the pack of cigarettes she swore daily to throw out. She lit one and gazed out over her father's twenty-five acres of unfertile land lying lifeless between the false promise of protective wooded hills—green and brown bringing hope and hopelessness.

Kentucky.

Shelby sighed as the gloom that had been following her around since she had read her grandmother's letter returned. Why was it she always got immediately melancholy and overly dramatic when she had to come home?

Home or prison? She was never sure which. Today she just felt mostly sad as she stared at the dry, mangled twigs crunching underneath her feet in the early morning mist. She pulled up her collar. Even though it was early spring, a trace of winter lingered in the air like a bad child, refusing to give in or give up. A broken down tractor sat out in the middle of the lower field. Why didn't Wesley ever take care of anything? Her father had ruined everything that had ever come his way and now she was supposed to fix his broken world? Not likely. But she was here. Martha had called her and she could never refuse her grandmother anything, so she had come.

Shelby shaded her light green eyes from the unexpected sunlight now streaking through the rain-laden clouds. She took a deep breath. No, it definitely was home. It felt like home. The hills had always done that for her. They were the only things she really trusted—the soft way the world looked when the sun kissed the evergreens blanketing the rounded, rising mounds, turning them into emerald dreams.

Away from Wesley, that is.

Her father could take "home" and put his own brand of hell on it in a heartbeat. But she was determined not to let him in this time. She would try to help, but not get caught up in his twisted way of thinking.

A strand of wavy, sandy hair escaped her ponytail and she tucked it in neatly behind her ear. All the sophistication she had spent years honing left her the moment she set foot on the old man's property. She was instantly transformed into that tall, gangly kid with striking features that didn't fit her face in the right way. At least, that was the way her father saw her, but not the lady from New York who had spotted the fifteen-year-old in a farmer's market near Ashland. Shelby had been behind the tomato stand and a woman who'd looked like a leather-clad goddess had approached her.

"Dear, do you mind if we take your picture?"

Shelby had nodded mindlessly as the woman waved to a photographer who snapped several shots. Afterwards, she handed Shelby a glossy card. "Call me. You need to be seen, young lady—away from this place." She had waved her diamond-studded hand in the air and walked off.

The photographer had whispered in Shelby's ear, "You're lucky, kid. We're just here shooting a documentary, but that lady is the real deal." He winked and pointed to the goddess as she got into a silver Jaguar that might as well have been a spaceship in Shelby's inexperienced eyes.

It had taken her a year, but finally Wesley berated Shelby one too many times and she called the New York number. The woman remembered her and arranged for a meeting.

Her career had begun just like that.

The agency took her in, schooled her, gave her a fabulous place to live with other young models, and met her every need. Even Grandma Mart recognized the once-in-a-lifetime opportunity. And there was no talking her out of it. Shelby wanted it. She was more than glad to be whisked away from Greenup County. The fashion magazine loved her down-home quality and, as it turned out, her arresting facial features made her uniquely photogenic. She was successful enough to make her own way in the City.

She had never looked back.

But that was years ago. She had made some good investments and now she could easily afford to live with Caitlin Sotheby in their stylish Upper West Side apartment, only modeling when a shoot called for a more mature look. Shelby was just thirty-four, but she felt old, past it. It had surprised her when Jack called last week, but it turned out to be just a reminder of what drudgery the business had become to her. Shelby had had her fill. All the glamour of high-fashion modeling was just smoke and mirrors behind long, grueling hours in front of hot lights and unforgiving cameras. Then there were the endless invitations to amazing restaurants and parties and the push to look perfect, but never being able to enjoy the food or drink for fear of putting on that dreaded extra pound. Added to that, was the incessant physical insult of her long, slender limbs being twisted and manipulated into impossible clothes; the tedious hours in makeup; the appalling embarrassment of being at the mercy of competing hair stylists trying to break out with their own outrageous styles.

The competition and backstabbing among the models had been as draining as the long hours in front of the cameras. Everybody was gorgeous, just different versions of perfection, but the insecurities were as apparent as the beauty. It had never suited her. But she had been a real trouper. All she had to do was imagine coming home to Wesley, and it was enough to make her appreciate what she had. Early on, her friends had nicknamed her their own "Holly Golightly." You can take the girl out of Kentucky, but…

Truth was, she had done well with the fabulous apartment, the friends, and a lifestyle that most women her age only dreamed about. But now that once-heavy schedule was pretty much a thing of the past, and her days were spent exploring other aspects of life in the City.

So why was it, after just a short time back on Kentucky soil all of that disappeared as if it had been a wild dream and not her real world at all? Shelby sat down on the back steps of the house and smoked and waited for the courage to go in.

It never came.

"Shelby Jean? Girl, whatcha doin' out there? How long you been here? I didn't even knowed you was here. We gonna be late. Git your ass on in the house." Wesley Stiller's whiskey-worn voice cut through the peaceful morning like a power saw cutting through a field of tall, tender sunflowers. Shelby sighed and took a final look around before getting up the nerve to enter the two-story frame house she had been raised in.

Her father's strong voice was no proper reflection of his appearance. He had been a powerful man in his day, but now rheumatoid arthritis and emphysema had reduced him to a weak, bent version of the hulking man he had been. Even so, what he lacked in physical strength, he made up for in verbal abuse.

Nothing new there, Shelby thought, as she went through the back door into the harshly lit kitchen.

"You know, they's some ditches out in them fields that kinda sneak up on you. You best be careful out there. 'Course, a big city girl like you ain't afraid of no ditch, I don't guess." Wesley grinned, revealing yellowed teeth, as he dumped his coffee into the sink. "Git my coat, Shelby Jean. Your grandma just got here and she's waitin' on us in the truck."

She found a familiar ratty wool coat in the hall closet and couldn't help but wonder. All that money she had sent home over the years could have bought a hundred new coats. Of course, Martha had written her that her father had refused to take her "charity" and Martha had just deposited the checks.

"Grandma Mart, spend the money. That's why I'm sending it. I want you to have some nice things for the first time in your life." Shelby had pleaded with her grandmother many times, but it was always the same answer.

"Well, maybe one of these days. But, lord, hon, I don't even know what I would buy."

Shelby just continued to send the money, and she had no idea how much sat in the savings account at the local bank.

She handed the coat to her father and attempted to help him put it on, but he yanked it out of her hands. Standing back, she crossed her arms and watched as he struggled with it. He had to prop his cane against the kitchen counter and lean against the stove long enough to get his arms in the sleeves. He almost fell twice, but she never made a move to help him. He merely cussed under his breath and she waited.

Could there be a more stubborn son of a bitch on the planet?

Finally, he had the coat on. His breathing was coming hard, and he wiped at the sweat on his forehead. He really did look like shit. But she felt no pity, only resentment. Wesley Stiller had made his own bed years ago and she was quite certain he liked lying in it.

Martha Maggie McBride grinned as Shelby got into the front seat. She reached over and squeezed her granddaughter's hand and Shelby squeezed back. They hugged and kissed. "Shelby, you are a sight for these sore eyes. I think you got even more beautiful. How is that possible?" Martha wiped at her eyes, and shook her head. "I'm sorry, hon. I just can't believe you're really here." Then she revved up the engine and hollered over the radio, "You in, Wesley? Warm enough?" She twisted to see him in the backseat.

"Yeah, I'm in. You been wastin' gas again, Martha? You know it costs a fortune."

"Well, it's pretty danged chilly out here this mornin'. Don't worry none. It ain't like we have far to drive to church." She straightened herself in the driver's seat, put the Ford F-150 pickup truck into gear, and backed slowly out of the gravel drive, turning onto US 23.

Shelby looked over her shoulder at the house. For the thousandth time she couldn't believe she had ever lived there. When the van had dropped her off in the early morning hours it had still been too dark to see it clearly, but now it was painfully clear. The faded, gray two-story farmhouse was in desperate need of a new paint job. The front porch looked crooked, like it was pulling away from the house. The foundation had to be shot. She looked at the barn sitting at the end of the driveway and smiled to herself.

She had had some good times in that barn, but it looked in sad disrepair like the house. The closest neighbor lived a mile down the road.

God. And now she was going to church. Church? She hadn't been in a church since she was sixteen. And her father wasn't exactly the church-going type. She looked over at her grandmother, who, at seventy-two, was still a force of nature, and she knew Martha was the only one the old man listened to. If Martha said they were going to church, they went to church.

Martha turned up the gospel music on the local radio station and Shelby settled back and watched the familiar landscape fly by. The hilly rural area soon gave way to Main Street with its small houses and tiny lots and too many cars in the driveways. The Church of Christ sat on a hill at the north end of town. Martha drove expertly around the parking lot and managed to squeeze the truck into a pretty tight spot.

"How am I supposed to git out of this dang seat, Mart? I ain't got no room," Wesley complained from the backseat.

Martha lifted her eyebrows in humor at Shelby and turned back to answer him, "I think we can manage it, as long as you didn't eat a big breakfast this mornin'?" She grinned and he grunted. Shelby took his cane as Martha helped him wiggle out of the backseat.

"Mornin' Martha, Wesley. Is that Shelby Jean you got with you?" A gray-haired man yelled from the other side of the parking lot.

"Mornin' Joe. How you doin'?" Martha grinned and waved. "And yeah, Shelby is home for a while. We're so glad to have her."

The gentleman waved back and then Martha took Wesley by the elbow and helped guide him to the front door of the church. It seemed like it took forever for them to get up the steps, but Shelby just stayed back and watched. She wanted nothing to do with this. Others greeted them and exchanged pleasantries on the way in. Shelby tried to be polite, but her stomach was churning and she felt like grabbing her grandmother's keys and escaping.

Shake it off, Shelby, she thought, as she followed her grandmother and father into a back pew. This was her life for now, like it or not. Three middle-aged women made room for them, and reached over to shake Shelby's hand. She recognized her grandmother's closest friends, Violet, Jolene and Bella, and smiled in response to their obvious joy in seeing her. They all sat down with barely enough room to move. Heady cheap colognes mixed too strongly in the heated air.

Shelby looked around at the people crowding into the long benches. The church was packed. She was familiar with a lot of the faces but found it difficult placing their names. Too many years had passed. Everyone was dressed in their Sunday best. Shelby couldn't help but imagine that church was about the only outlet people had. There was really no industry anymore in the small town. Many of Kentucky's coal mines had been shut down, and the steel plant Wesley had worked at had gone under years ago. The only work available now was at gas stations, Family Dollar or IGA, or whatever other mom and pop stores were scattered about.

"All rise and turn to page 33," the minister's voice rang through the sanctuary as he led his congregation in the first hymn. A blue-haired woman with thick glasses pumped at the foot pedals on the three-keyboard organ. Its booming sustain propped up the voices beautifully in a full-throated version of "Bringing in the Sheaves." Shelby was impressed by the power of the singing.

"We will come rejoicing, bringing in the sheaves," Her grandmother and her friends were singing their hearts out while her father stood with his mouth in a tight grimace. Shelby waited until the third verse to take her chance to slip out of the pew. She caught Martha giving her a disapproving look, but she just couldn't sit through the service. She shrugged her shoulders, as if to say: Sorry, Grandma, I just can't help it, and then squeezed her way past the singers and back outside to the front of the church.

Shelby sat down on the lowest step and took out a cigarette. She lit it and took a deep drag as she looked out at the little town she had grown up in. Sorry's Run, Kentucky. She had always thought it was a "Sorry" place, sure enough, although its history had fascinated her. The McBride name was special in Sorry's Run, and not just because it was her grandmother's name. The town had been named after Sorina Duncan McBride, who had been an active abolitionist in a day when women weren't considered viable outside of child-rearing and homemaking. The town's name had originally been "Sori's" Run until one of its more notorious mayors had officially changed the spelling on his deathbed when a scourge of deadly fevers nearly wiped out the already small population. Ironic for sure, but the new spelling had stuck, and somehow it was more appropriate anyway.

Shelby liked the idea that her little town was the home place of such a strong, unusual woman. Grandma Mart always said Sori's blood was in the soil and the town's women drew strength from it. Shelby took that particular "tale" to heart. It gave her courage when she had none, and strength when she was too weak. It helped to make her what she was. If a pioneer woman could survive living alone in those raw times and then manage to find a way to bring freedom to enslaved people, it made anything possible. "Sori's" Run had done that for her. Kept her from being afraid. Otherwise, she could have never gone to New York when she was so young.

Shelby took another drag off her cigarette. She watched the smoke curling up lazily in front of her face, and for the thousandth time she swore to herself she was going to quit.

But not today.

She gazed up and down Main Street. The town never really changed. Maybe a little more worn, just like she was.

The depressing thought surprised her. *God, what happens to me here*?

"Shelby Jean? Shelby Jean Stiller?"

A deep voice broke through her reverie and she nearly jumped in surprise.

"Excuse me. Didn't mean to scare you." A good-looking man of about her age with a mustache, goatee and thick dark hair sat down next to her. "You know, you shouldn't smoke. It's not good for you."

"And you are?"

"Ah, Shelby, you don't remember me? Man, you break my heart. I'm Russell James. Sat behind you in geometry, remember? I liked to mess with your hair." He smiled then, revealing beautiful teeth.

She sat still for a minute and just studied him, before it came to her. "Oh, my god. Russell. Is that you? You were an awful pest in high school." She studied his brown eyes and curling dark lashes. "You look different."

"You look great." He was staring at her hair.

She felt a flush of embarrassment and tucked an unruly wavy strand behind her ear. "What are you doing here?"

"Well, I think that question would be more for you? I live here, remember? You are supposed to be in New York, and here you sit on the front steps of the hottest event in town." He nodded back to the front door of the church and asked, "Why aren't you in there, by the way?"

"Gosh, Russell, I don't know. Maybe it's just not my scene. Or maybe I knew you would show up to keep me company?" She answered, her pale green eyes flashing with humor. "But since you brought it up, why aren't *you* in there?"

"Well, maybe it's just not *my* scene." He laughed and added, "Come on, let me buy you a cup of coffee. We can be back before the service is over."

"Sure thing." She followed him down the steps and put out her half-smoked cigarette. The coffee shop was three doors down and they had it all to themselves.

"I guess you're right. The whole town must be at church."

"Yeah, pretty much. What would you like?"

"Caramel latte, please."

He grinned, looking at her slender shape. "You never had to worry about the calories, did you, Shelby? Served you well."

He brought the coffees over. "Have you been in town a while? I'm surprised I hadn't heard."

"No. Actually, I just flew into Huntington pretty much in the middle of the night and got a cab to the house early this morning. And to tell you the truth, I really don't know why I'm here. Grandma Mart swears Wesley is too much for her to take care of, but I know better. She's got more energy than I ever had on my best day. No, I think she just wanted me to visit. It's been too long since I've been back. But it was just strange the way she made it sound really urgent that I get here—like now. Like she really needed me to be here. I didn't have anything pressing, so I caught a flight."

"Well, I'm sure you have made your grandmother very happy. Nobody is gettin' any younger, after all." Russell got quiet for a moment and took a sip from his steaming cup before continuing, "Martha is such a force of good around here, Shelby. Everyone loves her, and I hear what you're saying about her energy. It seems like she's always there when anybody needs the least little thing."

The old schoolmates chatted easily for the next forty-five minutes. Shelby shared highlights about her successful career and she learned some of his story, which included a failed marriage.

"Well, it sucked, but I'm okay now. We never had kids, so that was good. Just this year I enrolled into some online college courses from a university in Huntington. I do pretty well as an insurance agent in

Ashland. I've been there long enough that I can almost make my own schedule, but I really want to get my teaching certificate. We need good teachers around here." He looked down into his cup and Shelby was struck by how sincere he seemed. He was so good-looking, he could have gone anywhere.

"I don't get it. Why didn't you leave?"

"Well, Rhonda and I fell in love and then it took some time to fall out of love. Hell, by then I was pretty well dug in. And, really, I think I wanted to stay to see if I could maybe be of some use to Sorry's Run one day, just like Martha." He grinned.

Church bells cut their conversation short and Russell escorted her back down the street.

"Thanks, Russell. It was really great running into you. I'll be here for a while. Maybe we can hook up again."

"I'll catch up with you. The Pit Stop is still open. The martinis suck but the beer is cold." He grinned and waved goodbye to her at the church steps.

CHAPTER THREE
FAERIE DOCTOR

"WHERE WERE YOU, GIRL?" Wesley growled at her once they were back in the pickup.

"Yeah, hon, I wondered, too. Folks wanted to see you."

"I'm sorry, Grandma Mart. I only meant to smoke a cigarette, but I ran into an old classmate and we had a cup of coffee. I didn't mean to be rude."

"Yeah, sounds like the same self-centered brat as always."

"Shut up, Wesley," Martha snapped and Wesley complied.

Shelby looked at her grandmother with greater respect as they drove back home. Martha asked, "I thought the Reverend was downright inspired this mornin', didn't you, Wes?"

"Humph, that old gasbag wouldn't know inspired if God came down and whispered in his ear. I can't believe one man can be that borin' and nobody has strung him up."

"Ah, Wes, he ain't always borin'. Just sometimes." Martha grinned and continued, "Although I must say, lots of times I do take issue with his interpretations of the Scriptures. I would have liked to known what you thought of Reverend Parson's sermon, Shelby Jean."

"Oh, Grandma, I'm sorry I didn't stay. I think I was too tired from the flight. Chances are I would have nodded off. But the singing *was* inspired. I was very impressed."

Martha grinned and started humming along with an old gospel tune on the radio. In just a few minutes she pulled the truck into the driveway in front of the barn. Shelby helped her get Wesley out of the backseat and into the house. She had to blink several times before she could see where she was stepping. The living room was cloaked in dreariness.

Martha immediately went about opening all the curtains and pulling up the shades. "Wesley, why in the world do you insist on keepin' it so dark in here? It's like a cave."

"Ah, hell, Mart, I can't see the TV when you do that."

"Well, you ain't gonna watch no TV right now. You're gonna have a nice lunch with me and your daughter. Now you rest for a spell and we'll put something together. Won't this be nice? Like old times." Martha raised an eyebrow.

"Humph," Wesley grunted and limped his way to his recliner.

"Shelby, I hope you like soup beans and cornbread. Lord, it's been so long since we've spent time together that I have no idea what you eat." Martha frowned as her eyes took in Shelby's slender frame. "Or I could just make a big salad?" She asked, as she went about pulling dishes out of the kitchen cupboards.

"Soup beans sounds perfect, Grandma." Shelby smiled.

Martha let out a sigh of relief, and said, "Oh, good. You stay with me and I'll have you fattened up in no time. 'Course then you'll look just like the rest of us country bumpkins with rolls of fat around our middles," she kidded, before adding in a more serious tone, "don't worry, Shelby Jean. I'm just teasin'. Ain't no way you could ever look like the rest of us." She put her hand up gently and caressed Shelby's cheek.

Shelby squeezed her grandmother's hand and was suddenly rocked with emotion. She cleared her throat and shifted gears. "Come on, Grandma Mart, let me help. My roommate is like a gourmet chef, and I am clueless in the kitchen. Teach me something."

"Well, all righty, then." Martha laughed. "Grab the ham out of the fridge."

The small family sat down together for the first time in many years and ate their lunch. Martha kept an easy conversation going and Wesley was surprisingly pleasant. Still, when he at last grabbed his cane and hobbled back to his bedroom for a nap, Shelby was relieved.

She and Martha cleaned up the kitchen, and as they stood at the sink, Shelby watched out the window while a misty rain fell like a gray blanket over the back land, covering the hills. *It looks like the whole world is crying,* she thought. She turned to face Martha. "So, what is it, Grandma? Why am I here? And really, why are you here? He's not even your son. Why do you put yourself through this?"

"Oh, hon, Wesley needs me. And I need you. That's why. Your dad is gettin' much worse and I'm gettin' too damn old. Speakin' of which, let's sit down and have our tea at the table."

Shelby took a steaming cup from Martha and pulled up a chair across from her. "Grandma, seventy-two is not old. Haven't you heard? Eighty is the new sixty."

"Well, somebody forgot to tell these old bones that juicy bit of information." She giggled before adding, "But I love Wesley. I really do. He's got nobody else. He's really not so bad as you think. Somewhere under all that fussin' is a heart. He's just got it so walled up that he can't remember it. The only place he can be properly cared for is in Ashland and he refuses to go to a facility. He really needs to be on oxygen, but he fights me at every turn." She sighed. "I wonder how your mama would have handled him."

Shelby's mother, Neely, had died when Shelby was only eleven. But sometimes Shelby could still feel her and smell her. It was uncanny the way her mother seemed to come to her in a presence that was undeniable. She had never shared that with anyone, but now she wanted to tell her grandmother.

"Grandma Mart, do you ever feel her? You know, like Mom is in the room."

"Oh, yeah, hon, you bet. Your mama was a powerful person in life and she is even stronger now."

"What do you mean?"

"Well, Shelby, you know how your father was so mean to her, always callin' her a bitch?"

"Oh, yeah. That was when he was being kind."

"Well, actually, sometimes he got it more closely correct when he called her a witch." Martha stopped purposefully and took a drink of her tea.

"Huh? What is that supposed to mean?"

"Now, don't look at me like that, Shelby Jean. It's not bad. Your mama was more like a faerie doctor than a witch."

"A faerie doctor? Grandma, you've always talked about the fairies, but a faerie doctor?"

"I never told you about faerie doctors? Well, hon, it's somebody who is like a healer, you know? My granny believed in the magic of Irish fairies. You know that I do, too, Shelby."

Here we go, Shelby thought. She was well acquainted with the folklore, but they were just fun stories told with her grandma's constant humor. Now Martha was looking way too serious.

"Really, Shelby Jean, I know you don't believe it, but it's true about the magic of the fairies. They have guided me all my life and they will take me home in the end, back to Ireland, just like they will you. Your mama believed it and she spoke to her fairy guides all the time. It wasn't nothin' bad. It just was what it was. 'Course, it like to killed your dad. Wesley thought she was just crazy and it scared him. It's why he turned so mean. He never understood Neely and she was gone before he ever could.

"And she was so beautiful, just like you, honey. Your dad was over the moon about her, but he couldn't deal with who she really was. Shelby, she was truly gifted. And she loved you so. But that's why your dad is so bad to you. You look just like her, and he doesn't understand you either. It's good that you got away. But now I think it's good that you're back. He needs you."

Shelby looked at her aging grandmother. Her hair was snow white, but it had been like that forever. She had turned prematurely gray in her forties. But now her face was deeply lined, and she walked with a stoop. Even so, there was still a vitality about her that was such a comfort. When Neely Stiller had been killed in an auto accident, Martha had remained strong and helped to pick up the pieces. But it had been a painful, hard time, and Wesley had never had a kind word to say to Shelby after that. It was as if he blamed his daughter for losing his wife.

Neely was driving to the drugstore to get a prescription filled for Shelby, so he said if she hadn't been sick, his wife would not have been at that crossroads when that semi tractor-trailer ran the stop sign.

Shelby had been too young to understand why her father would treat her so, and their relationship just got worse as the years went on. Wesley acted like he hated her. When the miraculous opportunity came for her to get away, she took it and it had given her a life for the first time. It broke Martha's heart, but she had also known it was the best thing for her special granddaughter. It was her only chance and it had been the right decision.

But a faerie healer?

Now that was a first. Shelby reached out to her grandmother and stroked her beautiful soft hair. *The Irish.* She had learned a long time ago that there was no reasoning with the old beliefs and ways. And Martha had always been a little different; forever speaking of special feelings and vibrations; always carrying those weird gem stones around.

Shelby flashed back to a time when she was ten and Grandma Mart had taken her to a house where a woman was very ill and was rumored to be more than a little crazy. The shack down by the river smelled like rotten potatoes to young Shelby, and it had frightened her when she saw the pallid face of the old woman who was lying on a bumpy, dirty mattress. Shelby remembered trying to hide behind her grandmother as they approached the sick woman, but Martha made sure she watched as she took a bundled compress out of her satchel and placed it around the wrist of the sick lady. It had smelled so much better, more like mint.

"Myrtle, how you doin' today, darlin'? Feelin' better?"

"No, I ain't, Mart. The devil is layin' up inside me. I cain't sleep, cain't eat 'til I git him out. You got to help me, Mart. I tell you, the devil is in my stomach just eatin' away at me. It's when I ate that apple with the worm crawlin' in it. That worm was the devil and he got inside me, Martha. That's why I am so sick now. You got to help me." The woman's yellow eyes bugged out of her head and she raised her skinny frame up to grab hold of Martha's arm. Shelby tried again to hide behind her grandmother, but an all-too-familiar look told her to stay put. Her knees were knocking together, but she obeyed the unspoken command.

Martha began to console her patient, "Myrtle, I know you got the devil in you. I know that. Don't you worry none. We gonna git that ole' devil worm out of you." Then she pulled out a jar from her satchel. It contained an awful-looking brown liquid with some red coloring to it. "Here, hon, you drink this carrot juice now. The devil don't like carrot juice none too much."

Myrtle propped her quivering thin arms up and took the glass of juice. She drank it down and then immediately began to retch. Martha held her head as the sick woman threw up in a pan by her bed. With one hand placed over the woman's eyes Martha took something out of her pocket and threw it into the vomit as the woman heaved. Shelby thought she would throw up, too, when she saw a small, dead garter snake lying in the putrid liquid. Martha allowed the woman to see. Myrtle started screaming hoarsely.

"No, no, Myrtle. Calm yourself now. This is good. We got him! That devil worm done growed into a snake in your belly, but we got him now. We got him."

Martha took the pan of vomit and threw it outside into the weeds and when she came back in, the relief on the woman's haggard face was apparent.

Shocked by it all, Shelby asked her grandmother on their way home what had just happened. Her grandma had smiled and said, "Just a little Irish story-tellin' sweetie. Myrtle thought that worm she ate was the devil. So rather than argue with her, it was better to let her believe that. Then we just growed him up a bit and convinced her that she vomited him away. All Myrtle ever has wrong with her is in her head." Martha had laughed joyfully.

"Grandma Mart, does carrot juice really make you throw up?"

"Nah, honey, that weren't carrot juice. That was my own concoction that made her insides jump." Martha had laughed again. "I just wanted you to see that sometimes a little story-tellin' is just the medicine that folks needs. You'll want to remember that someday."

Later they learned that Myrtle had gotten miraculously better overnight.

Shelby smiled as she came back from the memory. She stared hard into her grandmother's soft, moist eyes and asked, "Grandma Mart, are you a faerie doctor, too?"

"Yes, sweetie, I am. But I was never gifted so much as your mother." She took another drink and waited on Shelby's reaction.

Silence.

"Shelby, I need you, not only because I need help with your dad, but because I'm gettin' old. I feel different. It's time you learned more about your mother, about your ancestry. There are things that you need to know, and time is short."

Before Shelby could speak, Wesley's bent figure filled up the doorway to the kitchen.

"You still here, Martha? You better git on home now. The girl can see to things." He leaned into his cane before turning back to the living room.

The television soon blared from the front room. Martha got up from the table and started rinsing out the teapot.

"Grandma, I can do that. You probably are ready to get home. We'll talk more about this tomorrow."

"Okay, hon, that would be good. I'll be back in the mornin'. But I want you to stay with me some. I want to spend time with you." Then she added, "I love you, Shelby Jean. You are so like Neely. You were the light in her darkness and she would have known such joy to see what you became. She would have been so proud, as I am now. You have the God light so strong in you." Martha wiped a tear from her eye.

Shelby put her arms around her grandmother and hugged her long and hard. Then she walked outside with her and opened the driver's door of the truck. Martha climbed in behind the wheel. Shelby watched as she fumbled with the keys.

"Why is it I feel like I should drive you home?" Shelby questioned.

"Oh, hon, you ain't seen me in a while. I know I look older than dirt, and I get a little shaky sometimes. But don't you worry. It's only a few miles. I ain't so far gone that I can't drive myself." Martha grinned as she finally got the key in the ignition. "I'll be back first thing tomorrow. There are routines about your dad's day that you'll need my help with. We'll get it sorted out. I swear he's not so bad as he acts. He just lost his happiness all them years ago, and he ain't never found it. Maybe you can help with that?" She smiled and blew her granddaughter a kiss before driving off.

Shelby waved and shivered. It was still light, but the April air was chilly, and she was still reeling from things her grandmother had said. She turned back toward the house and a dark dread creeped over her at the thought of being alone with her father. She took slow, deliberate steps up the sidewalk.

"She gone?" Wesley was seated in his recliner with the remote in his hand. He looked up at her with red-rimmed eyes.

"Yeah, Dad, she's gone. I thought I would get settled upstairs. Do you need anything?"

"Git me a beer."

She found a Budweiser in the refrigerator next to the fruit juices that he was supposed to drink. Grandma Mart had probably even freshly squeezed the orange juice. Shelby uncapped the bottle and took it to him.

He stared at the television and drank half the bottle in one gulp. Shelby stood next to him, but he never acknowledged her. Instead, he turned the volume up. She left the living room, picked up her bags and climbed the stairs she knew too well. Overwhelming loneliness crushed her with each step. She still missed her mother in this house, even though she had lived five years in it without her. It was as though the house had died when she did. She thought of what Martha had said about Neely.

A faerie doctor?

What the hell did that mean? In New York it would be considered quirky, almost glamorous, especially if you lived in the Village. Anything to do with pagan behavior or having psychic powers was just considered fun. But in Kentucky? Moonshiners, yes. But healers?

Shelby went into her childhood room. It was across the hall from her parents' old room. Her dad stayed in the bedroom downstairs now that the arthritis in his hips and knees was so bad. She was glad for that. At least she would have the second floor to herself. There was a bathroom down the hall—far cry from her modern New York apartment. Shelby walked over to her bed and tossed one of her suitcases onto the homemade quilt. She opened it and started mindlessly putting things away in the chest of drawers she had used as a kid. She glanced over at the tall windows that faced the back of the property and remembered lying in bed every night when she was a teenager, just staring out at the dark, shadowy hills that silhouetted the sky. The hills always made her feel secure, even when her small world was torn apart. She placed all of her dreams on their solid backs, knowing they could hold whatever weight she put there. The hills were her strength.

Walking across the floor, she got close to the window pane. She put her slender hand up to the glass, tracing the rounded shape of the hills with one long, elegant finger. She wondered again at why she was here and for how long. But after talking with her grandmother she had formulated a plan. She would stay with the old man just until she could get him placed in a healthcare facility. He might not like it, but he would just have to face facts. She had a life in New York, and her grandmother needed a break. He would just have to go.

"Shelby Jean, git me another beer!" Wesley's voice carried easily through the cracked floorboards.

"Oh, yeah, old man, Ashland, here we come." Shelby grumbled under her breath as she turned to go back down the stairs.

Martha climbed the four short steps to her small deck and put the key in the door of the trailer. She fought an urge to turn around and go back to the farmhouse. Maybe she should have insisted Shelby come home with her. She had such a burning need to be with her granddaughter. It was what had driven her to beg Shelby to come to Kentucky. She knew how much the girl hated to be in that old farmhouse with her father. Why in the world had she done that to her, leaving her there. She could have gotten Bella to keep an eye on Wes for one night so she and Shelby could have spent this time together. Martha had needed that, had wanted that. But no. She was so ate up with wanting things to be different between Wesley and his daughter that she thought throwing the two of them together was a good idea.

What was I thinking?

Lord, when she thought back to the decisions she had screwed up over the years it gave her chills. She was always pushing, like the rockhead she knew herself to be. Well, she wasn't young anymore and maybe it was time she started realizing that she was pretty much off the mark when it came to making the big decisions in her life. She was comparatively good with everybody else's lives, but her own family? That was a different story. Thank God she had wonderful friends who loved her, because left to her own devices…

Martha sat her purse and keys down on the kitchen counter and opened up the refrigerator. "Ah, yes." She reached for the familiar gallon jug and poured herself a glass of Paisano. She had made a point to stop at the IGA to purchase what looked like a nice bottle of wine for Shelby. Her friend behind the register had told her Pinots were popular with the "cool" set. Well, that was fine, but she would stick with her Carlo Rossi. Martha smiled. She was so happy Shelby was here. Finally they could have the talk. It would take courage, but she was ready. It was time and Shelby just had to know.

Martha took her glass and stepped back outside onto her small deck.

She saw her pet rabbit scamper out in front of the trailer. "Hey, little Rory, how you doin'? My granddaughter is in town. You are gonna love her so much." The rabbit stopped and stood on its haunches, cocking its head slightly. Martha tipped her glass to the bunny and its whiskers quivered.

She sat down on the top step. She felt tired, really tired. *Must be all the excitement.* It was still early, but she had a big day planned tomorrow. Everything was going to be made right once and for all. Martha stared up at the shadowed hills in the distance. Were they moving against the dimming sky? They seemed to puff up and deflate like someone was letting the air out. She looked down at her drink.

Maybe I better switch to the Pinot?

She giggled to herself as she went back inside and got ready for bed. True, she was tired, but more than that, excited. So much wonderful stuff was ahead. She felt it in her bones. A good night's sleep was all she needed. Martha laid her head on her pillow and breathed deeply of the honeysuckle fragrance that permeated the sheets. Snuggling into the comforting scent, she fell asleep and slept peacefully—for a little while.

A striking woman ran her fingers through her long, pale hair while staring into a crystal clear pond. She smiled at her pleasing reflection and then at her swollen belly that was close to bursting with her first born child. She caressed her stomach and hummed an old Celtic lullaby as she stared back at the pristine water. Then, as she gazed into the still waters, her image began to change. A damp wind blew around her head and threw ripples of unrest into the water.

Now, instead of an attractive blonde woman reflected in the blue pond, she took on the features of an old hag, horrible to look upon. Fear put its hands around her withered neck and squeezed. She looked down at her stomach, all wrinkled and flat, and saw bright red blood flowing between her legs. The old woman began to scream. Her haunting wail took on the ancient echoes of Banshees from worlds far away, and her lament was gruesome and sad.

Suddenly the death fairy woman stopped her screaming, and took on the knowing. She turned from the pond and looked right into Martha's eyes before opening her mouth again. The scream was that of a ghost, caught between worlds of passion, hope and fear. It was the Banshee and it was a warning.

Startled awake, Martha wiped the cold sweat from her forehead. The dream had been real. Deep down she had known, from the way she was feeling, that the Banshee would come. She reached a shaking hand into the drawer of her bedstand. Pulling out her stationery box, she waited. Honeysuckle perfume soothed her as she breathed slowly and waited for the shaking to stop. Martha got focused then. She wrote for an hour, erasing, writing again, trying to be clear. It was so important that she be clear. And it helped her, writing it down.

She put the letter in an envelope and addressed it to Shelby Jean. Then she reached under her bed and pulled out her jewelry box. She placed the envelope in a hidden compartment underneath the bracelets. Martha sighed heavily, then, but she felt surprisingly peaceful. *Satisfied.* She was ready. She smiled and went back to sleep.

CHAPTER FOUR
ROCKS ON THE ROOF

THE NEXT MORNING A STEADY RAIN pelted against the tin roof of the farmhouse. It sounded like tiny hammers pounding above her head. *Rocks on the roof.* Shelby smiled, remembering the old legend. Had she just heard three rocks on the roof? She stretched and wondered for a moment where she was. Then she remembered.

"Shelby Jean! Git yourself down here. Right now!"

She found a robe in the closet and didn't even bother with the bathroom. He sounded in trouble. Shelby flew down the steps only to find Wesley smoking a cigarette with the back door open, watching the rain.

"What the hell? You sounded like you were dying?" She threw her hands up in the air and then asked, "Are you supposed to be smoking?"

Shelby met his silent stare for an uncomfortably long time.

Finally he answered, "Well, no, I ain't. But I ain't got no coffee. I cain't reach the coffee can. Martha always makes the coffee."

"Mornin' y'all! It's rainin' cats and dogs out there," Martha's voice heralded through the front rooms and soon she was in the kitchen, her raincoat dripping water over the tile. She was carrying a laundry bag. "You got your coffee yet, Wesley? Give me just a second. I'll get this wet coat off and put this downstairs." She pointed to the bag and disappeared down the steps to the basement.

Where does she get her energy, Shelby wondered, as she watched her grandmother disappear and then reappear in the kitchen, talking the whole time.

"Here, hon, let me git that for you. I'm sorry I'm late. The electric went off this mornin' just long enough to screw up my clock. Somebody musta hit a pole or somethin'."

"Humph. Well, I am needin' some coffee. That much is for sure. The girl here is jus' now gittin' up."

Shelby felt her cheeks flush with anger. "God, Wesley, you're not an invalid. You can't get your own coffee?"

A hush fell over the three as Shelby's harsh words echoed around their heads and the rain got louder outside the door. In the corner of the room a slow drip was leaking through the ceiling.

"Shelby, why don't you go get yourself together and I'll put some coffee on. I hope you like it strong. I hate this infernal weather. Don't you? A good cup of coffee is just the ticket." Martha turned to the cabinets and Shelby knew she had been dismissed.

She went up to her room and dressed slowly. She had no desire to go back downstairs. This was going to be harder than she thought. *Wesley acts like he is in a wheelchair or something. Oh, my god. Maybe he doesn't even take a shit by himself.*

Shelby looked at herself in the dresser mirror and brushed out her honey-colored hair. Usually her reflection lifted her spirits, but she looked so different here than she did in New York. She wasn't wearing any makeup and her usually creamy skin looked drawn and older. Her full lips needed some color. But there just didn't seem to be any reason to bother. She put down the brush and picked up her cell phone to Google nursing homes in Ashland.

A loud crash followed by a thump stopped her.

"Shelby Jean! Git down here!"

It was Wesley again. *Now what?*

Shelby didn't run this time. She took her time and walked slowly down the steps. "So what is it this time, Wesley? Can't reach your cigarettes or just…" Shelby's voice caught in her throat as she entered the kitchen. What she saw, her heart and mind wouldn't let her believe. Shock lashed out at Shelby's lithe frame and every muscle in her body tensed. Martha was sprawled out on the tile floor, her eyes rolled back in her head.

"Grandma?! Sweet Jesus, what happened!? Grandma!!" Shelby was immediately by her grandmother's side cradling her head. She stared up at her father who looked like a deer caught in headlights. The coffee pot was shattered next to Martha's hand and her body was splayed in an unnatural fashion, her right leg twisted underneath her. "Wesley, what did you do?"

"I didn't do nothin'! She jus' fell! She was a reachin' for the coffee pot and she just fell!"

Shelby laid a kitchen towel under her grandmother's head and punched in 911 on her cell phone. Martha's lips were turning blue. Shelby finished the call and dropped the phone, attempting to remember CPR. She breathed into Martha's mouth and then pressed on her chest, but she got nothing. Her grandmother lay still and Shelby looked up at the ashen face of her father. He started to cough violently and turned his back to her.

"This can't be happening. Grandma Mart, please!?" Shelby tried in vain again to get some air into her lungs, but nothing was working. Martha had no pulse. Her chest wasn't moving. Her body looked so lifeless.

Minutes later the house was filled with emergency medical personnel. They hoisted her grandmother up onto the kitchen table and tried for ten minutes to revive her, to no end. The next hour was a mind-numbing blur as Shelby signed papers and watched the EMTs cover her beloved grandmother and put her on a gurney. She rode with them to the hospital where Martha was officially declared dead.

Shelby hadn't spoken to anyone, hadn't told anyone. The world phased in and out in slow motion as she did whatever she was told. A frightened voice in her head kept telling her that now she was truly alone. Neely was gone. Martha was gone. Heartache and loss swallowed Shelby up until she couldn't feel herself.

Had she died, too?

One of the ER interns approached her, and gently pulled her aside. Shelby stared into his soft eyes. He seemed so kind.

"Are you an angel?" she asked.

He smiled and replied gently, "Ma'am, is there anyone we could call to come and get you?"

She only nodded.

"Follow me." He took her by the hand, then, and led her to a gurney. "Sara?" A nurse came over and helped Shelby climb onto the stretcher. She pulled a thin blanket over her.

"Sara, get Ms. Stiller some water. Have her take one of these and let her relax here for a time." He handed the nurse a pill and looked back to Shelby. "You just lay here for a little bit. Sara will look after you and someone will take you home after you've rested."

Shelby followed his orders numbly.

It was hours later when one of the EMTs drove her home. She was feeling better, but drained. When they pulled up in front of the farmhouse, she realized she had no idea what Wesley was doing or even where he was. In all the shock and chaos, she had completely forgotten him.

The driver handed her more paperwork with contact numbers for the funeral home. "Are you gonna be okay, ma'am?" The young man stared at her.

"I'll be okay. Thank you, though."

He flew around to the passenger side door and opened it for her, helping her out. Shelby thanked him again and walked up the sidewalk to the house alone as the ambulance drove off. She opened the front door and the hard reality of what had just happened hit her again. She fought back tears and tried to control her shaking limbs as she walked through the living room. Her father was still in the kitchen. If it hadn't been for the smoking cigarette in his fingers she would have thought he was dead, too. His face had an unnatural pallor, almost gray. He stared at the floor where just hours earlier Martha had died.

Shelby took a step toward him and he put his hand up to stop her.

"Don't come near me. I don't want you. Go away." His voice came out in a hoarse whisper, but it was the way he spoke that made her heart stop. His voice was laced with hate. Real hate.

Shelby looked at him, this crippled shell of a man. She really looked at him for the first time. His hair had always been thick and wavy, like her own, but now it was thin and there was a bald spot at the crown of his head. He wore it too long and it lay in thinning wisps around his frail shoulders. A gray, unkempt beard covered the lower half of his face and even his eyebrows were gray and growing out wild. His eyes were blood shot and watery. He was only fifty-four, but he looked years older.

Wesley stared at the floor and neither of them moved.

"Dad, don't you need…"

Now he focused his red-rimmed eyes on hers and there was nothing but pain in them. "I told you to leave me alone. I don't need you. I don't need anybody. Now git away from me," he hissed.

"Fine. Suit your own damned self." Shelby left him then and slowly climbed the stairs to her bedroom. She shivered as she undressed for bed. Chills rocked her. She wanted to sleep. She *needed* to sleep. Thank God the kind intern had given her a couple Valium. She swallowed one and stared coldly at the hills out her window. Instead of comforting her, now they almost seemed to be mocking her with their unwavering dark mystery. She cursed, "Fuck you, Kentucky hills. You are supposed to protect me. Why is this happening? Grandma Mart…"

She got into bed and buried her face in her pillow, soaking it with her tears before she fell into a troubled sleep.

Shelby Jean, you are so beautiful. Here, sweetie, let grandma brush your hair. See how it shines? Your hair is the color of ripened wheat. And look at your eyes. You will break hearts with those eyes. They are the palest green so as to allow you to see the real world. All you have to do is open them.

"Shelby, hon? Shelby Jean? I'm just awful sorry to wake you, dear, but it's gettin' late and we have to get goin'. Could you come downstairs and speak with us a couple minutes?"

Shelby blinked rapidly trying to clear her vision. The sun was shining brightly in the room and she couldn't make out the face of the woman who was standing over her bed.

"It's Bella, hon. Violet and Jolene are downstairs with your daddy. We just need to talk about a few things. Get yourself dressed now. We'll be in the kitchen waitin'."

Shelby propped herself up on her elbows and now she could see the woman letting herself out of the room. It was one of her grandmother's friends she had seen at the church. "Okay, Bella. I'll be right down." Shelby dragged herself off the bed and pulled on some jeans and a turtleneck. Why was it so cold? It was April. But even with the warming sunlight shining in, the floors were like ice. *Probably doesn't pay his heating bill.* She walked over to the dressing table and picked up a brush. The bristles pulled easily through her thick, shoulder-length hair. She tied it back with an elastic band and wiped the sleep out of her eyes. Then she remembered. She remembered the dream. God, it had been so real. It was as if her grandmother had visited her in her sleep.

Downstairs, Violet, a tall white-haired woman, and Jolene, a tiny redhead, were attending to Wesley and the kitchen. They stopped wiping the counters when she came in. She noticed the heaping bowls of covered food that had magically appeared on the table.

That was quick.

It was one of the time-honored southern traditions, bringing mountains of food to the newly bereaved. And the really strange thing was how pleasant Wesley was being with the ladies, like he was actually grateful.

"Shelby Jean, my goodness, hon, you are such a pretty thing. The spittin' image of your mama," Jolene spoke in a charming accent.

Shelby thought she saw Wesley's upper lip twitch under his beard.

Bella added, "You probably don't hardly remember us, hon, but we sure remember you. Again, I'm Bella. This here is Jolene and Violet. We are all members of your grandma's church and she was our dear friend."

"Oh, Bella, I know it's been a long time, but I remember you. I remember you three and my grandma always laughing."

Bella smiled warmly. "Oh, that's good." She reached out and squeezed Shelby's hand gently. "We're here to help you through this awful ordeal. We're just shocked with grief. Martha was such a wonderful woman," Bella choked on her words. "I guess God was bein' kind, takin' her the way he did so she never had to get sick and pitiful like so many of us." Her gaze shifted to Wesley. She pulled out a chair for Shelby and gestured for her to take a seat while Jolene got her some coffee. "Cream, honey?"

"No, thank you. Just black, please."

"Jo, get me a cup, too, will ya, hon?"

The ladies all pulled their chairs in around the table and sipped on coffee. Bella spoke again, "Shelby, I have your grandmother's Will over at my house in my safe. Whenever you are ready we can take you over to her place so you can start sortin' everythin' out. There is absolutely no rush, though. You don't have to deal with any of that yet.

"And you don't have to worry yourself about the funeral arrangements. Your grandmother had that all planned out. We know exactly what she wanted, so there's no guesswork. She wanted to be cremated. You are to spread her ashes out there in your daddy's field over at the cemetery where your mother is buried and leave her urn there. She wanted to be with Neely…" Bella's voice trailed off and she burst out bawling.

"Oh, hon, here now." Violet grabbed her hand. "Don't do that, Bella. Shoot, now you got me cryin'."

"Me, too." Jolene jumped up to get some Kleenex from the counter.

"Oh, man," Wesley moaned. "If this is gonna be a cry fest, I'm goin' to my bedroom."

"Well, damn it, Wes, we just lost our best friend. Hell, she was everybody's best friend. We are never gonna stop missin' her. And it was such a shock, her dyin' like that. Aren't you just shocked?" Bella blew her nose and stared up at Wesley through tear-filled eyes.

"Well, yeah, Bella, it was a shock. But there ain't nothin' we can do to bring her back. She's gone and that's just it. She's gone! Now you got to leave it be!" Wesley shouted and his chest started to heave with a hacking cough. He bent over and Jolene handed him a Kleenex. He put it to his mouth.

"Oh, now, see what we've done. We got poor old Wesley all shook up," Violet's voice was laced with sarcasm, but she added in a softer tone, "here, Wes, let me help you to your room. You should rest." She reached for his arm.

Wesley pushed her away and spoke hoarsely, "Leave me be, Vi. Just git me some whiskey from the shelf."

"Whiskey? It ain't even five o'clock." Jolene stopped crying and stared at him.

"Oh, for the love of god?!" Wesley barked and started coughing again. His face turned beet red.

Bella jumped up and found a bottle in the cupboard. She poured him a shot. "Here, Wes, take your medicine." She handed him the glass and he drank it back. In no time his coughing eased.

"See?" Wesley relaxed into his seat and held up the glass.

Now it was Bella's upper lip that twitched as she poured him another shot. She blew her nose again.

Shelby had watched the scene play out in an almost comic sequence and now she remembered what Bella had said. *The cemetery.* Shelby had forgotten that. There were some old headstones at the foot of the closest hill on the property. She barely remembered being there when her mother was buried, but she did remember all those cars driving back the gravel lane that ran through the tobacco plants and led to the foothills. It seemed like hundreds of cars and so many people mourned her mother's passing. And then she remembered the Wake afterwards. All the men had their hooch jugs out, and the family's fiddlers played music and danced into the early hours.

She was so young and they had put her to bed, but she had snuck to the top of the stairs one time and had seen her Uncle Sidney swaying drunkenly to a sad, lamenting tune his brother played on the fiddle. She came to learn later it was an old Hank Williams song, "I'm So Lonesome I Could Cry."

That long-ago scene flashed across her memory like it had just happened. She was dazed by its clarity. She noticed Bella's lips moving.

"Shelby Jean, hon, are you all right? Did you hear me? Lord, you must be just so shook up."

Shelby nodded to Bella and lifted the steaming mug to her mouth. The hot liquid felt good on her throat and brought her back. "Yes, please forgive me. It's just that I can't believe this. I just got here and Grandma Mart was going to show me…" She couldn't finish as tears rolled down her cheeks.

Violet spoke, "There, there, Shelby. It's all right, hon. You go ahead on and cry as much as you feel like. We are all gonna cry a lot. It don't matter what Wes says, tears are God's best remedy. And don't you worry about nothin'. We're gonna take care of things and take care of you, and Wesley." She patted Shelby's hand and then looked over at Wesley.

Bella continued, "I was just sayin' that your grandmother wants her ashes to be spread out in the cemetery by your mother. And Shelby," Bella said, "cremation usually takes some time. But I'm gonna see to it that Martha doesn't have to wait."

"Bella knows people, hon," Jolene added, nodding with an air of confidence.

CHAPTER FIVE
FAIRIES ARE CIRCLING

THE PROCESSION TO THE CEMETERY was a line of cars that stretched for three miles on US 23. Shelby wondered how they were all going to make it down the weedy lane behind the house. A car hadn't been back there probably since Neely had died. But make it, they did. One by one, the cars turned into Wesley's driveway and around behind the barn. One by one, they drove slowly; big tires rolling carefully over the unkempt property. One by one, they parked in the field in an orderly fashion. One by one, passengers got out and helped each other over the rough terrain, making their way to the tombstones. It was a country cemetery.

And it had been a country ceremony.

The Church of Christ had been filled to capacity with its members and with Martha's friends. There had been much music and much singing of the traditional hymns that her grandmother loved so much. The service had been sweet and thoughtful. When the organist broke from tradition and played "Danny Boy" there wasn't a dry eye in the church. It was obvious the minister had known Martha well and had loved her. Many tears were shed and a joyful noise had been made.

It all fell over Shelby like some faraway dream. The Valium took care of her nerves and the church ladies took care of directing her through the motions. She had worn black on black, like a good mourner should. But she could have never guessed the sophisticated picture she made in the wide brimmed hat with the sheer black veil she had found in her mother's closet. People stared at the grown woman they had known as a child. They couldn't relate little Shelby Jean to this tall, elegant creature who looked like she had landed from another world. And of course, she had.

Behind the sophisticated façade, though, little Shelby Jean was there.

For a moment, she was eleven years old again and wondering why her beautiful mother was gone. She wondered, too, why her father looked so sad when all he ever did was yell at her mother. Shelby would have thought he would be glad Neely was gone. But he hadn't been. He cried and kept a bottle close by to steady himself.

Wesley had fewer tears for Martha, but he hadn't forgotten his flask. A tall, older man in a black cowboy hat had helped Bella push him in a wheelchair for the service. Shelby couldn't believe they had talked Wesley into that. He was so stubborn and proud, but he had given in easily to the suggestion. Sitting up front in that wheelchair he looked like an old man. Shelby felt a pang of compassion watching him. Life hadn't been good to Wesley. Or maybe it was just that Wesley hadn't deserved a good life.

"All rise." The minister directed the congregation to stand as the choir sang. The procession began and it was a reverent thing to behold, as rows of people lined up to pay their respects to an enlarged photograph of a younger, smiling Martha.

Clouds gave way to surprising sunshine, as the last of the mourners pulled in behind the Stiller's farmhouse. Everyone gathered around the old tombstones in hushed honor as the minister took the urn and motioned for Shelby. Bella nudged her to follow his lead. She stepped slowly in her three-inch heels and numbly took the urn from him. It felt so heavy in her arms. Too heavy. It slipped from her grip and a collective gasp from the onlookers shocked her into recovering the urn before it dropped to the ground. Shelby opened her eyes and realized she was standing right over her mother's grave.

"Shelby Jean, your grandmother asked that you spread her ashes over the holy place where your mother lies, so that mother and daughter who were so together in this life can now be together in the afterlife."

Shelby held the urn in her hand and looked down at the old tombstone. She closed her eyes as the visions started coming. Real life visions of another time. She could smell her, smell the house, smell the time when she was little…

Princess Shelby Jean! Come dance with me.

{I don't want to, Mama.}

Why not, my princess?

{Because I might not be there when Daddy needs me.}

Daddy doesn't need you. I need you.

{But Mommy, you don't need anybody.}

That's not true, baby girl. I need you. Now dance with me.

Neely reached for Shelby and took her little girl hands. Outstretched little arms met outstretched bigger arms and they danced 'round and 'round. Shelby forgot her father in her mother's dance. She forgot everything. Only happiness. She remembered happiness. And it always came with her mother's touch.

"Shelby, hon? Are you all right?" Bella was whispering in her ear.

Shelby opened her eyes. Everyone was staring at her. Again, she almost dropped the urn and again a collective gasp escaped the tight lips of the congregated friends and relatives.

Jolene squeezed Violet's elbow and they shared a worried glance, remembering something Martha had once said—*if anyone stumbles on a grave, it's a bad omen.*

"You want me to help you with that, Shelby Jean?" The minister had a tear glistening in the corner of his eye. "I know this is hard. I know it. Let me help you."

"No, Reverend Parsons, it's okay. I'm okay. Just give me a minute." Shelby moved her hand tenderly over the urn, feeling its smoothness, its graceful bronze curves. She finally let her fingers come to rest at the top and slowly unscrewed the lid. Holding the urn up out in front of her, she did a most unexpected thing. The crowd watched as the elegant woman in the black dress and veil kicked off her stiletto heels and started to dance. She held the urn up high over her head as she dipped and swayed overtop her mother's grave. Little by little she released the ashes over the sacred, grass-covered plot. Little by little, the urn gave up its precious cargo and Shelby stopped her dancing. She looked into the empty urn, put its lid back on and casually placed it down on the ground.

Reverend Parsons took his cue, "Let us pray amongst ourselves and say our proper goodbyes to our beloved Martha Maggie McBride. May God's light shine upon her and may she rest in peace." Silence followed as heads bowed in reverence. Her father's field took on the quiet hush of barren land cradled by the hills. Shelby felt more than heard the wind slightly blowing over her lowered face. It felt like the wind of change. Her hair moved softly against her cheek. The hills seemed to close in around the people gathered and a momentary calm fell over all the troubled hearts.

Shelby added her own soft voice to the prayer, "The fairies are circling real close, Grandma Mart. Your God light is shining so bright. Go with the fairies now. Let them take you home."

Bella, Jolene and Violet shared a knowing smile just as the distant whine of a fiddle broke through the quiet reverie. It was coming from the farmhouse in single drawn out high notes; a lonesome refrain that Shelby recognized. And then what sounded like an Irish jig rang through the air.

Reverend Parsons looked up and ended the ceremony. "Amen. Folks, Shelby and Wesley would be honored if you would spend a time with them before leaving for your homes. There is food and drink, and Wesley's Cousin Theodore has some music for y'all, as you can hear." The Reverend led the way and a line formed as people chatted softly, embracing each other and holding hands as they walked back across the field to the house.

"Ma'am, uh, Ms. Shelby, my name is Lucas Chambers. I'm sure you don't remember me."

Shelby stared into tired eyes that reflected a sadness not dissimilar from her own.

"I don't mean to bother you, but I was a good friend of your grandmother's and I wanted to say how sorry I am about her passing. I can't stay, but I want you to feel free to call on me for anything at any time while you're here. I really mean that."

Shelby studied the tall gentleman in the cowboy hat and boots. His wavy dark hair was cut short and streaked with gray and his lined face was still handsome; his strong, square jaw outlined in five o'clock shadow. He stood out from everyone with his demeanor. Even in her dazed mind, she took to him. His brown eyes seemed so sorrowful and kind.

"Here, Shelby Jean, take my card and put it in your purse. Bella will keep me posted on how you're doing." He handed her a card and tipped his hat before he left, walking back through the field towards the parked cars. Shelby looked at the card.

It read:

Chief Lucas Chambers
A REALLY GOOD GUY

with his number listed below. It made Shelby smile.

Bella caught up with her and took her by the elbow. She looked at the card in Shelby's hand. "It's an accurate statement, Shelby. He is that and more. And he loved Mart more than he should have. Here, hon, better put these back on." Bella handed Shelby her high-heeled shoes. "Though how in the world you can walk?" She teased, as they followed the crowd back to the house.

Bluegrass music greeted them as friends and family gathered on the back porch and in the kitchen. Food was being served in all the rooms and soft drinks were plentiful. Hooch was mostly kept out of sight in private flasks in pockets. The ladies from the church had scrubbed the old house and it was shining more than it had in a decade. The curtains were all drawn back, allowing the sun to brighten up the faded pine floors and Early American furnishings. Cousin Theo had brought the musicians who set up amplifiers in the living room. It quickly took on the festive feeling of a celebration of life, just as Martha would have wanted. A video played continuously on the 36-inch television screen in the living room, depicting Martha in various stages of her happy life. Everyone was trying to speak to Shelby, wanting to give their condolences, but then probing about her big city life, posing the endless questions: What are your plans now that Martha has passed? Are you gonna stay and look after Wesley?

At the first chance for escape, she snuck upstairs to get away.

The hills took on a purplish gray in the afternoon light, as Shelby lay on her bed and gazed out the windows. The Bluegrass twang from below was a perfect complement to her surroundings. It really was hard to feel down with that wonderful music lifting everyone's spirits. She let her mind drift to her childhood. It had been a mixed bag, for sure, but there were many good memories as she stared at the white calla lilies bordering the soft pink wallpaper. Her mother had loved lilies. She had put them everywhere in the house; on the table, in the bathroom, on the kitchen counter. She loved the stargazers the best, but she always said the callas were the more spiritual. Shelby never understood what that meant, but she liked the flowers. Her mother's funeral had been a garden of flowers. Somebody had seen to that. *Couldn't have been Wesley.* But somebody.

Martha had just the usual assortment of bouquets at her service, nothing out of the ordinary. That reflected Martha, though. She probably never considered herself anything but ordinary. At least that was the way she appeared. But maybe appearances were deceiving. *A witch?* The thought flew across Shelby's mind and she dismissed it as readily as it had come. It was not something she could think about yet.

Her cell phone buzzed on the nightstand. She reached over and saw it was Caitlin calling from New York.

Shelby picked up. "Hi, Cait."

"Shel, are you all right? Tommy told everybody that somebody died and he didn't know who. God, he drives me crazy the way he gets shit wrong. Is it your dad?"

"No, sadly not."

There was silence on the other end.

Shelby continued, "It was Grandma Mart. She wasn't sick or anything, you know? She had a heart attack. It was such a shock. Cait, Grandma Mart is dead," Shelby's voice cracked with tears.

"Oh, my god. I can't believe it. Shelby, that's awful! I got your text to call you last night but I fell asleep. Can you forgive me? I am so, so sorry. I know how you loved her. Do you want me to come there? I will. Or are you coming home?"

"No, I have to stay for awhile yet. Grandma was Dad's caretaker, so I have to figure out what to do for him. You don't have to come here. This place is too depressing. It's bad enough one of us has to be here. Her Wake is today and then I just need to take care of business and get back to New York. Is everything all right at home? Are you watering my plants?"

"Yeah. Don't even think about this end. I've got it covered. But let me know if you want me to come there to help. I mean it. I'll ask for some time off."

"Okay. Thanks. Love you, Cait."

"Love you, Shel."

She turned her cell off and plugged it into the charger. She didn't want to talk with anyone else from New York. It was comforting to know Caitlin would keep a handle on things.

Shelby put her hands behind her head and gazed up at the ceiling. The plaster was still cracked in the exact same spot and there were still the identical water stains in the corner. Nothing had changed in this room since she was sixteen. She turned onto her side and listened to Theodore's band playing a kicked-up version of "Man Of Constant Sorrow" only to be followed by a woeful rendition of "Amazing Grace." Tears dampened Shelby's pillow as she fell asleep.

Shelby Jean, you know you are missing a party?
{Am I, Grandma? If you're not there it can't be much of a party.}
Well, don't you fret none. I'm there. You can be sure, I'm there.

Shelby was startled into waking by a sudden thump that made her heart fly into her throat. It sounded just like when her grandmother had fallen to her death.

"What the..." She flew out of bed and ran downstairs only to find a house still full of guests and two burly men romping in neck holds on the dining room floor. Everything came to a standstill when Shelby entered the room.

"Sammy, Emmett, you boys git yourselves off of that floor. Good gravy! This ain't no pool hall." Jolene braced her tiny frame and reached down, grabbing one of the men by his shirt sleeve.

Violet grabbed the other one. "Lord, Shelby Jean, we are just so sorry. Can you believe these big ole' brutes carryin' on like this. I think it's time for this party to be movin' on."

Shelby was speechless. Who were these awful people? They looked so unhealthy, so overweight, so—poor! *God.* She had forgotten what it was like. She had forgotten this place. Without Martha, how could she stand it?

"Honey, you're shakin' like a limb. Here, take a sip of this. It'll help settle your nerves." Violet handed a shot glass to Shelby.

"Just a little white lightnin', hon," Jolene spoke gently.

Shelby raised an eyebrow.

Violet added, "No, no. It ain't the real strong stuff. It won't hurt you. It'll just take the edge off."

She didn't need coaxing. She shot back the liquor and let Violet lead her into the living room.

"We're gettin' everybody out, hon. You just sit here and relax. I'll be right back."

Shelby realized she was barefoot as she sat on the sofa. *Hell, I'm starting to fit in already.* The homemade moonshine did the trick and she felt herself ease up. These were her grandmother's people, her mother's people. She was just being a stuck-up bitch categorizing them. *But it's pretty easy to do,* she thought again, as she said her goodbyes and thanks. She hoped she hadn't come off like the snob that she was. With all the Valium she could barely remember the day.

Bella approached her. "Shelby, we have everythin' under control. There's enough food here for you and Wesley to live on a whole month. I've left numbers for all of us on the fridge, and the keys to your grandma's truck are on the table. We'll wait til next week to get into her trailer. Don't worry about that now. We'll help you with that."

"Thank you so much, Bella, for everything," Shelby answered.

Bella continued, "All of Wesley's meds are in the bathroom and he knows what he's supposed to take. Don't you let him tell you any different. Martha coddled him, but he knows what he is supposed to have. Everybody is leavin' now, and we're goin', too. We just want you to know that we are all so sorry this had to happen as soon as you got here. It was not what Martha would have wanted. She wanted time with you so bad..." Bella stopped talking and brought a hankie to wipe her eye.

Violet added, "Hon, you be sure to call the minute you feel lost or lonesome, you hear?" She had tears in her eyes, too.

The women gathered around to hug Shelby and then they were gone. Shelby watched the last car pull away, adding to the stream of taillights moving down the highway, and then she turned back to the kitchen. It was impossible to believe there had been a Wake. Everything was spotless and put back in its place. And Bella was right about the food. Wrapped casseroles, salads and soups, meats and cheeses, pies and cakes packed the freezer and the refrigerator. Shelby thought of her well-trained, meager appetite and her father's slight frame and appetite for cigarettes and booze, and she sadly imagined most of the food going to waste. A fifth of Gentleman Jack sat on the counter. Shelby went right to it and poured herself a shot.

"You're like your old man in that way, I see." Wesley came up behind her and she jumped.

"Jesus, Wesley, don't scare me like that. I thought you were in bed."

"Well, I ain't. I'm thinkin' a shot would do me good, too. Mebbe help me sleep."

She reached for another glass and poured him a shot. "Ice?"

"I take it neat."

For the first time, father and daughter sat down together at the table. Wesley looked especially drawn and his breathing wasn't coming easily.

"Dad, shouldn't you be on oxygen?"

"Goddamn it, girl. Don't start in on me. Your grandma ain't been dead no time and you're takin' up her talk. Let me be. I just wanna finish my drink in peace."

Okay, jerk. Kill yourself. What the hell do I care. It had been interesting to watch Wesley all day. He had shown a polite, almost friendly side. But now the real guy was back.

Shelby finished her drink and scooted back from the table. She stood and stared at him, but he didn't even look up. She left him there.

Upstairs, she tried to sleep, but even after the long, draining day, her sleep was fitful at best. She kept seeing her grandmother and her mother, almost as if they were the same person. And in her most conscious thoughts she just couldn't believe that all the family she had left was that miserable old man downstairs in the kitchen. What was it that kept him so angry? She had seen a softer side of him all day with other people, but with her? Well, it must be true, what Grandma Mart had said. She was too much like her mother and he couldn't love her for that reason. And yet, she knew that Wesley had loved Neely. She knew he had. What had killed that love? It just didn't make sense. Shelby tried to go back in her memories, back before her mother's sudden death.

She tried to picture Wesley then. But it was always the same. He was always yelling at Neely and drinking too much. Shelby was so little, but he took advantage of her and pitted her against her mother. He would tell her, "Don't you listen to what she says, girl. She ain't right in the head. Just let her be. Stay clear. You just listen to me. You'll be all right." Shelby had been so confused because he had tender moments, too. A scene invaded her thoughts from a night when there had been so much yelling...

"Mommy, mommy, what's wrong?"

{"Nothin' to worry yourself about, princess."}

"But Mommy, Daddy is so mad. Did I do something wrong?"

{"No, sweet baby, you never do anything wrong. Daddy is just mad at his own self."}

Neely had reached out a slender arm and her golden hair fell in soft waves around her lovely face as she bent to kiss her little girl. Shelby had always thought her mother looked just like an angel with her rosebud mouth, smooth white skin and soft green eyes.

Later that night Shelby had crept down the stairs and had seen Wesley at the kitchen table, much as he had been tonight, a bottle on the table, a shot in hand. He had his head bent and he was openly weeping. She had tiptoed over to him and put her small hand on his big one. "Daddy, don't cry. Don't be mad at yourself. Mommy and me forgive you."

Wesley had looked at little Shelby with caring and compassion and lifted her up on his lap. He had held her and rocked her and cried. It was one of the last times she had ever felt loved by him.

Shelby looked through groggy eyes at the hills shadowing the dark sky and she wondered how she came to be in this family. New York had been her home for so long, that she felt no kinship with these people, only Martha. She would miss Martha forever. She stared at the moon lighting up the bushy trees on the hilltops. The tune Cousin Theodore played earlier came to her, its sad refrain echoing in her tired mind, "And as I wonder where you are, I'm so lonesome I could cry."

CHAPTER SIX
MOONDUST

"WESLEY? DAD? WAKE UP. You've been here all night." Shelby shook her father's thin shoulders. He was still sitting at the kitchen table with his head lying on his arm, drool wetting his wrist. He was snoring. She shook him again, harder, "Wesley!"

"Huh? Hey, that hurt. What? Oh, shit. Shelby, help me up. I can't move."

"Well, it's no wonder. Look at you. You nearly killed the whole bottle. Come on. Put your arm around me."

He was still drunk and somehow that made it easier. He was limp, but not so heavy that she couldn't support his weight. She pulled his arm around her shoulders and together they dragged their way into his bedroom where Shelby was able to roll him over onto the mattress. He looked up at her in surprise, and for a brief moment, he was young again as he smiled sweetly at her. "Thanks, Neely. You're my angel."

"Sweet Jesus, Dad. Get a grip." Shelby left his clothes on him and covered him up. She closed the door to his room and went back to the kitchen to make coffee. She felt a slight stirring around her head, and turned quickly only to find nothing. "Okay, Mart, was that you? Hey, I know so far I'm not doing too good at this Florence Nightingale stuff, but seriously, I don't see what's wrong with him. He's just drunk and needs to sleep it off." Just then there was a knock at the door.

"Hi, Bella."

"Hi, sweetheart. I hope I am not disturbin' you? I have more food." She looked down at the large CorningWare dish in her arms. "I think it's a broccoli casserole."

"You know, Bella, I think we have enough food."

"I know it, hon, but folks at church is just so givin.' They can't help themselves."

"Well, here then. Give it to me, and come on in. I have coffee brewing."

"If it's okay? I don't want to be a busybody, but I wanted to make sure you're all right. How is your father? Sleepin' still? Poor man is probably so exhausted after yesterday."

"Yeah, just wore him out." Shelby tried to hide the sarcasm as she poured her a cup of Folgers.

"Yoo-hoo? Shelby Jean? Are you decent?' Violet let herself in and entered the kitchen holding a disposable bowl. Her white hair gleamed in the florescent light. "I saw your car, Bella. Hope you don't mind, Shelby, but I have sweet potatoes here. They're all wrapped. All you have to do is pop 'em in the microwave. They're real good, and good for you, too. How you doin', hon? Where's Wesley? Poor soul, I bet he's just fit to be tied. Restin', is he? I hope so. Lord knows, after what he's been through, he needs it."

"Hello? Anybody home? I got food!"

"In the kitchen, Jo." Bella shrugged her shoulders and winked at Shelby as Jolene joined the party.

Shelby found she never had to say a word, and the incessant chatter just filled the small kitchen. The whole day was more of the same. The front door of the farmhouse was revolving as friends kept coming, bringing more food. Shelby noticed that nobody brought any liquor, the one thing they could have used. If she had had any notion of being too lonely she was rethinking it. She might never have a moment to herself again while she was in Kentucky. She had to admit she found the women entertaining and funny. They were good about keeping the topics light.

"Shelby Jean?!" Wesley's gruff voice cut through the chatter. The kitchen got quiet. "Shelby, come in here!" He was hollering

"Want some help, hon?" Bella asked.

"I don't think so. Let me go see what he wants."

Shelby found Wesley all tangled up in his bed sheets. He looked pitiful as he stared down at his torso wrapped in flowered linen. "I can't git out of this mess."

"You think?" She muffled a grin as she helped roll him back and forth until he was free. He took her arm and righted himself on the bed and reached for his cane. Then the wheezing started and it was another five minutes with his inhaler before his breathing came under control.

"You need oxygen."

"I need a cigarette."

"God, Wesley. You are pathetic."

"Well, you're her daughter. That makes you pretty pathetic, too, don't it."

Shelby was stunned by his comment.

"Shelby Jean, is everything all right?" Bella's voice carried from the living room.

"Yeah, we're good."

"Okay, hon, we've got your dinner in the oven. Y'all enjoy the rest of your day now. Call if you need anythin' at all."

Shelby managed a weak thank you while she hoisted her dad up from the bed and onto his feet. He grunted and waved her off as he dragged his way into his bathroom. She put his bed back together and picked up the room, wondering about the laundry. It would be like Wesley to have either broken-down machines or none so she'd have to cart dirty clothes to a Laundromat. Her phone buzzed in her pocket. "You okay in there, Wes?" she asked.

"Yeah."

Shelby left him, then, and walked back to the kitchen as she answered the phone, "Hey, Cait? Yeah, I'm hanging in there." She filled her roommate in on the day's events. "Oh, my god, there must have been fifteen women in this house today, and each one bearing gifts. What's that? Oh, yeah. Well, it's kind of a tradition. Southern hospitality sort of thing. Yeah. They are pretty wonderful. Talk too much, but super nice. I am supposed to get together with a couple of Grandma's friends later in the week, or whenever I want to, really, to go through her trailer. But I think after all that, I'll really dig into finding a place that will take Dad. Okay. Yeah, I'll let you know. I love you, too."

Shelby ended the call and put the phone back in her pocket. She decided to take a look in the basement. A door straight across from the backdoor in the kitchen opened up to steep stairs. Shelby climbed down carefully, taking one step at a time. There was still just a single light bulb illuminating the way. She walked sideways and braced herself on the cracked stone walls. *Has it always been this tight?* She stepped slowly into the musty basement and was relieved to find the machines. They were old, but apparently they worked. There was plenty of detergent, bleach, and stain remover. It made Shelby smile to see how neatly the washing area was arranged. "Thanks, Grandma," she whispered.

She turned to go back upstairs when something caught her eye in the far corner. She walked over to take a closer look. Just enough light was coming through a small window to allow her to see a painted box. It was so out of place in the leaky basement and so pretty. Shelby reached for it.

"Shelby Jean, where are you?"

"Down here."

"Shelby?"

"Down here, Dad!" She knew he didn't hear her. She returned to the steps and went back up to the kitchen.

"What is it, Wesley? Why do you have to sound so desperate all the time?"

"How do you know I'm not desperate? I don't exactly get around too good, you know, and you're always runnin' off somewheres. Your grandma didn't run off like that."

"Well, you don't have Grandma anymore. You have me. So you're going to have to learn to adjust." Shelby knew she sounded like a bitch. She didn't mean to, but something about his tone always pissed her off. She took a deep breath and tried again. "Okay. I'm sorry, Dad. I just went downstairs to see if you still had a washer and dryer." The buzzer went off on the oven. "That sounds like dinner. Let's see what the girls have cooked up for us, huh? What do you say?"

"Nah, I ain't hungry. I'll just have a cigarette."

"Come on, Wesley. Work with me. You're already weak. You need to eat something. Do it for Grandma," she pleaded as she took the meatloaf out of the oven. There were complete instructions: Microwave the mashed potatoes. Salad is in the refrigerator. Wesley likes Italian Dressing. Bread is in the box.

She ignored his grunts and set the table for the two of them. "This is nice. It really does look good."

Father and daughter sat down across from each other, but neither one had an appetite. The food was just a play thing for their forks. Finally, Wesley just pushed his plate away.

"I'm gonna smoke."

"Sure thing, Dad. That's a damn good idea. I think I'll have a drink." Shelby got up to get a beer when the doorbell rang. "Man, this really is Grand Central."

"Hey, Shelby. I hope I'm not intruding, but I just got back into town and I heard about your grandmother. I just wanted to tell you in person how very sorry I am." Russell James stood on the front porch.

He looked better than ever to Shelby as he stood there, so shy, like a high school beaux. *I wonder why we never dated?* "Thanks, Russell. That's so sweet of you. Yeah, the whole thing has kind of been dreamlike. I mean, I just got here to be with her, really, and now she's gone."

"Shelby, who is it?" Wesley yelled from the kitchen.

"Never mind, Dad."

Russell winked at her. "Here, Shelby. I won't stay. I just wanted to give you these and let you know I was thinking of you. If there's anything you need…" He handed her a bouquet of spring flowers and a bottle of Cabernet Franc.

"Bless your heart, Russell. People have brought food by all day, but you're the first person to give me what I could really use. I thank you, and, yes, I will call you after things settle down a bit." She waved goodbye to him as he stepped off the porch and got into his Lexus.

Must do all right as an insurance salesman.

"Who was that nosin' around, Shelby Jean?"

Wesley came up behind her.

"Russell James. He wanted to pass along his condolences about Grandma. And he brought this." She held up the wine and flowers.

"Looks to me like he was comin' for a date." Wesley shrugged and leaned into his cane to get him to the recliner. He got settled and looked up at her.

"I know. I'll get the beer."

Shelby thought she saw just the slightest smile cross Wesley's lips. She got him his beer and then opened the bottle of wine for herself. Pouring herself a glass, she stared out the windows above the sink at the lonesome hills shadowing the sky. She felt a crushing sadness suddenly thinking of Martha and her mother out there together in the old cemetery. The thought of them together should have been comforting, but it was just sad.

Death was just sad.

Shelby's cell phone buzzed in her pocket and she saw it was a text message from Caitlin: We're all at The Grog Shoppe toasting to you and your grandma. Miss you and love you! Be safe!

Shelby smiled and the loneliness that was gripping her heart loosened a bit. She wasn't alone in this. She would have lots of help. She just had to get Wesley to agree that the time had come to give up his independence. *Talk about sad.* It was her final thought before she took her glass and the bottle to her bedroom.

Shelby woke at 3:00. She looked over at the clock and saw the empty wine bottle on the bedside table. "Damn! Wesley?"

She got up and turned on the hall light. Downstairs, she found Wesley fast asleep in the recliner. He was snoring and the television was still on. She couldn't decide whether to wake him or not, but then he moved. He opened his eyes and looked right at her. For a moment she didn't see contempt there. He looked almost pleased. "Come on, Dad, let's get you to bed." He reached out his arms to her and she took them and helped to get him out of the chair. He almost fell reaching for his cane, but she caught him in time. Once he had the cane he was able to pull his body, leaning heavily into it. This was the first time Shelby saw real pain on her father's face. He grimaced as he moved his aching joints. His swollen and twisted knuckles turned white as they grasped the walking stick. Shelby stepped back and let him stretch himself.

For a woman who hadn't moved in slow motion in all her life, watching him painfully maneuver his body into moving mode took a patience she didn't know was humanly possible. It felt like an eternity, but then he was leaning into his cane walking and she was following him to his bedroom. Shelby was aware of a growing nervousness. She didn't know if she could really do this. She had barely kissed her father on the cheek in years, but this, this required a complete release of defenses, a giving into a humiliating sharing. *Give me strength.* She helped him get settled in bed and saw that he took his pills. He never said a word.

She went to leave. "Goodnight, Dad."

"Humph." Remarkably, he closed his eyes and was immediately snoring again.

"Love you, too." She closed his door.

Back in the kitchen, Shelby stared out through the scratched window in the backdoor. It was the middle of the night and she was wide awake. The moon was full, hovering above her beloved hills, throwing shimmers of quaking light over them. They looked to her like sleeping bears. She smiled and took a fleece-lined parka from the hook on the wall. It was a coat she had seen her grandmother wear many times and it felt so comfortable, like Mart was wrapping her arms around her granddaughter. The plastic boots sitting by the door fit her perfectly. Shelby smiled and opened the door to go outside. The early spring air hit her cheeks in crisp layers of chill, but it wasn't too cold—more like an awakening. She heard the crunch under her feet and remembered the way the grass had felt so thick in the summertime when she was little. She had never wanted to wear shoes because the grass was like dense, cool silk on her naked feet. There had always been plenty of yard to play in on the way to the tobacco plants. Tobacco. Those beautiful leafy plants that somehow turned into the choking smoke that she had come to need as an adult.

Memories flooded back into Shelby's mind as she walked slowly through the field towards the hills. She had spent hours of solitude out here and it had been a land of dreams for her. And most of her dreams had come true. The only thing missing was true love. There had been plenty of men, but not the right one. Not yet. Maybe there never would be. Her mother had sure never found him. And she had never heard Martha speak too kindly of her grandfather, who had been in a chronic bad mood most of the fifty years he had lived. Maybe it ran in the family. Strong women, loving themselves more than anyone else—like the legendary Sorina. *I like that.* Shelby heard a hoot owl high up in distant branches and she followed its call. "Whoo-Hoo, Whoo-Hoo." She stepped carefully, one slender foot in front of the other, keenly aware of the uneven ground beneath her feet. The broken land gave way to a thicker cushion and then she saw the stones straight ahead.

The cemetery.

The headstones were luminescent in the moonlight, almost sparkling. Martha's urn was there just where Shelby had placed it, at the foot of her mother's grave. Shelby bent over and dropped her hands to the ground. Warmth rushed through her limbs and in her mind's eye she could see Neely's face clearly. She was smiling, approving. An image of Martha looked on and was smiling too. They both reached out waving hands to Shelby and she thought she could hear the faintest voices in the night air. They seemed to say, "Open your eyes, Shelby Jean. Open your eyes."

"My eyes are open, Mother, Grandma Mart. And I see you. I do." Shelby sank down and stretched her long legs out next to the grassy ground that covered her mother's remains. She laid her head down barely touching the headstone and stared into the lit-up sky. She wrapped her arms tightly around herself, guarding against the night chill, and started to cry. The lonely strangeness of her short time home in Kentucky rocked her in unbridled emotion. Quiet breezes sifted through the furry tops of the hills and the country night embraced the sorrowful woman whose sadness poured out of her in needed release until she finally slept.

"Whoo-Hoo, Whoo-Hoo!" A high-pitched screech cut through the quiet. "Whoo-Hoo, Whoo-Hoo, Whoo-Hoo!" Shelby jumped and rolled into something hard and cold. She reacted by throwing her arm behind her to brace herself and hit something else hard and cold. "Damn!" The moon was directly overhead and she had no trouble seeing that she was lying on top of her mother's grave. The creepiness of the scene startled her so that she kicked her foot out too hard in an effort to stand, causing her grandmother's urn to teeter, almost falling over onto the ground. "Fuck me!" Shelby caught it just in time. She stared in shock at the vase she held in her ghostly white hands and remembered. "Well, thank heavens, you're not in there, Grandma Mart." She sat the empty urn back down at the foot of the grave site and stood to brush herself off. In another moment she stopped what she was doing and looked incredulously at the fine dust on the palm of her hands. Fresh panic blew through her mind. "Oh, my god!" She crouched down, quickly wiping her hands on Neely's plot. "I am so sorry, Grandma Mart. Forgive me?" The wind picked up and murmured overhead as it passed through the evergreens in the hills. The hoot owl joined in the night sounds and Shelby could imagine her grandmother giggling at her foolishness.

Back in the house, Wesley stood at the kitchen window staring at the distant, slender figure of his daughter out by the tombstones. Her wavy hair caught the moon's reflection and shown like yellow gold. He took a deep drag off his cigarette to calm the shiver that coursed over his spine.

CHAPTER SEVEN
SINGLE MALT, NEAT

THE TELEPHONE WOKE HER UP. Shelby looked at the clock. 11:30. "Oh, crap." She heard Wesley's muffled voice from below. She got up and took a shower in the upstairs bathroom and came down the steps combing her wet hair.

"I guess when you're a hoity-toity New Yorker you don't have to git up until noon." Wesley was glaring at her behind his cigarette smoke. He was just hanging up the phone.

"Sorry, Wesley, I couldn't sleep last night. I see you got yourself some coffee?"

"Yeah, I 'bout broke my neck, but I reached the can. No thanks to you." He tossed Martha's truck keys across the table. "That was Bella remindin' me. You hafta take me to Ashland today. I have a one o'clock appointment. I guess I shoulda made it later." He smirked at her and she felt like she wanted to smack his thin face.

She took a deep breath instead. "No problem. I'll have a cup of coffee and get dressed. Do you know where we're going?"

"I reckon. I only been there a hundred times. Same old shit. They say do this, and I tell them where to stick it."

Shelby had to grin. The old man was the real deal, a true pain in the ass. It made him less scary somehow. "Well, okay, then. This sounds like fun."

In forty-five minutes they were on US Highway 23 heading for the large medical center in Ashland. The road ran parallel to the Ohio River and it lifted her spirits to see its familiar muddy water rolling alongside them. The pickup truck was a surprisingly smooth ride over the open road. "Don't they have a nickname for this highway?"

"Yeah, they call it Country Music Highway on account of so many famous singers has traveled it and lived somewheres in Eastern Kentucky, like Loretta Lynn, Dwight Yoakam, the Judds, Billy Ray Cyrus. Tom T. Hall. Bunches of 'em."

Shelby looked across at her father who for just the briefest moment must have forgotten who he was with, and allowed himself to relax into conversation. "They's a museum over in Paintsville." The moment was short lived and he caught himself. "'Course I guess that ain't nothin' to a New Yorker, but folks 'round here like it." He shut up then and returned to his closed-off posture. He cracked his window and lit up a cigarette. Shelby looked over at him as his thin cheeks sunk in deeply when he inhaled the smoke like it was his life's breath. She thought of the cigarettes in her purse and vowed to throw them out. Wesley started hacking uncontrollably. He pulled out a handkerchief and wiped at his mouth, his chest still heaving from the coughing fit, when he took another drag.

"Yeah, that's good, Wesley. Don't want to waste any of that cig."

His returned look felt like daggers flying out of his watery gray eyes. It was enough to shut her up.

King's Daughters Medical Center was an impressive hospital and Wesley was true to his word. He knew exactly where he was going.

"So this is your famous daughter?" Dr. Simons shook Shelby's hand and welcomed her into his office. Wesley was sitting on the exam table. "You sure inherited your mother's good looks, Shelby. Lucky for you, you didn't lean toward your old man's side." He grinned and Shelby caught Wesley grinning back. She could tell they had a good relationship. The doctor made small talk as he looked over his patient. Shelby was impressed at the thoroughness of the exam, and she liked Wesley's doctor.

"Well, Wesley, we're still in that same boat. It's leaking a little more, though, I fear. Have you cut down on the smokes?" Dr. Simons asked.

Wesley looked over at his daughter before answering, "No, I ain't. The girl's grandma just passed and it ain't been a good time to give up nothin'."

"I see. Well, I am certainly sorry to hear that. But Wesley, you need to do as I say and quit. And you need to let me get you on oxygen."

As the conversation went on, Shelby could imagine it was the same as it had been for years. Like Wesley said, they told him to do this… but instead of telling Dr. Simons to stick it, he just agreed to carry out all the instructions. Shelby was surprised at the way her father handled his doctor.

"All right, then. Go get your prescriptions filled, but I'm serious about the cigarettes, Wesley. One day you will wake up and won't be able to catch your breath and this pretty daughter of yours is going to be stuck trying to pull it out of you." The doctor handed the prescriptions to Shelby and they all said their goodbyes. One stop at the hospital's pharmacy and she and Wesley were back on US 23 heading for home.

"I don't get it, Wesley. Why wouldn't you want to be on oxygen when you get so short of breath all the time. What's the reason?"

He stared out his window at the passing river. "Maybe I like being short of breath. Maybe I don't want to be an old geezer pulling around an oxygen tank. Maybe I don't care if I can't breathe." With that, he lit another cigarette and Shelby pulled her pack of Marlboro's out of her purse, tossing it into the trash bag in the front seat.

"I'll take those." Wesley reached into the bag and she smacked his hand. He looked up at her in surprise and then shrugged. "Hell, they ain't my brand anyway."

The rest of the ride home was quiet and Shelby was glad. She watched the brown river waves capping as two long barges loaded with coal passed each other on the Ohio. Seeing tugboats still pushing cargo that way was like being in a time warp. She tried to imagine the hard life of a tugboat crew. Tough bunch, no doubt. The sun suddenly broke through the clouds and cast dramatic shadows on the muddy water. It made Shelby smile. She looked over at her father and saw no appreciation there, only dead eyes staring at nothing.

The phone was ringing when they came through the door. Shelby answered, "Yeah, Bella, I got him there okay and we're fine. His doctor refilled his prescriptions. Yeah, the appointment with his rheumatologist got rescheduled for next month. Huh? Yes, the casserole will be just perfect for our dinner. Thanks for calling." Shelby tossed her purse onto the couch and helped Wesley get situated in his recliner. "You've got good friends, Wesley."

"You mean Martha had good friends. They ain't no friends of mine. They just busybodies if you ask me. Got nothin' else to do but stay in somebody else's shit." He squirmed in the chair trying to get comfortable. His breath was labored, his voice hoarse. "Git me a beer," he barked, ignoring her and turning the television on, setting the volume at an annoying level.

Shelby just shrugged in disgust and brought him the Budweiser. "I think I'll go down the road a bit. I'll be back later."

"So much for that casserole." He smirked and she felt her temper flare.

"You want that casserole, Wesley? I'll be glad to put it in the oven. Will you eat it?"

"No, I ain't gonna eat it. Just bring me another beer and git on outta here."

Shelby filled a small cooler with a six-pack and placed it on the table by his chair. She grabbed her purse and slammed the door on her way out. Jumping behind the steering wheel, she had no idea where to go or what to do. She just knew she had to get away from that awful man. It was depressing her beyond belief.

She put the truck in drive and turned up the radio. She just had to get home to New York. Another week in Kentucky and she would be climbing the walls. She drove and thought of her mother. She thought of that uninspired farmhouse with its boring furnishings sitting out in the middle of nowhere. The only thing that had been a reflection of her mother's bright spirit had been the lilies she always grew in her garden and placed around the house. It must have been the one thing Wesley had allowed. Nothing else in the house suited Neely. How did she stand it?

Shelby took her cell phone out of her purse and punched in Caitlin's number. She got her voicemail. "Hey Cait, just checking in. Call me if you feel like it. Love you." Shelby tossed the phone back into her bag and saw a familiar flashing neon sign up ahead. THE PIT STOP. She turned the steering wheel hard to the left and pulled into the parking lot of the familiar honky-tonk. She had only been inside a couple times years ago, but the bar had been a mainstay forever. Wesley had sure put his time in.

She parked, yanked the elastic band out of her hair and fluffed it up before getting out of the truck. Walking through the door, she had to blink several times before her eyes adjusted to the dim light in the bar. A jukebox in the corner was blasting "Blue Moon of Kentucky" and she rolled her eyes. *Perfect.* It was just as she remembered it. A long bar across the back, a half dozen booths to the left and a few four-tops scattered around the pool table to the right. Two guys in flannel shirts were playing pool and there were three old men sitting at the bar with cigarette smoke hanging like a blue haze over their heads. *Note to self: Never allow a cigarette to touch my lips again.*

She wasn't aware of it, but all eyes in the bar turned to watch the stunning tall woman walk across the room to take a seat at the bar. They had never seen such beauty in person, only in pictures. It made everyone a little nervous. A tension fell over the room.

"I'll have a Guinness, please?"

"I hear that, but will you settle for a PBR instead?"

She smiled. "A PBR will be just fine." She looked over again at the customers chain smoking. "People are allowed to smoke in here?"

The bartender nodded and said, "Yeah, only Louisville and Lexington have the ban so far." He poured the beer into a frosted glass. "There you are, Shelby Jean. On the house."

Shelby looked up from her glass. "Do I know you?"

"John Tyler. We went to school together."

"Of course, John. It's good to see you." She had no idea who he was.

"I'm sure sorry about your grandmother. She was one of my favorite people."

"Really? Don't tell me she was a customer?"

"No, ma'am. I don't think Martha's tastes ran to liquor. She was a healer."

Shelby stared at him. "A healer?"

"Yeah. She had the gift, just like your mother. I wonder if you don't have it, too?"

"No, John. My tastes run to liquor." She winked and smiled at him and he left to wait on another customer. *How come I don't remember him?* He was so nice. *I must have been such a self-centered brat, just like Wesley said.*

"Well, now, what's a girl like you doin' in a place like this?" A dark-haired man took the seat next to her.

"Russell James? I don't believe it. What brings you to this fine watering hole in the middle of the afternoon?"

"Had something to do with that pickup truck in the parking lot. I knew Martha wasn't its driver anymore. How are you doing, Shelby Jean?"

"Oh, I'm okay. Wesley drives me nuts and I don't understand why I'm here, but I'm okay."

"How about another drink?"

"Sure. Why not?"

"John, bring us two more beers."

The afternoon passed into evening seamlessly while the two old classmates played catch-up. "He wasn't always like this, Russell. Dad used to have a kindness about him, a gentleness. I saw a little bit of that at Grandma Mart's funeral towards others. But never towards me. You know what I'm saying? You put the two of us together in a room and he is a hateful, mean old guy. Why is that?"

Russell didn't respond. He was just staring at her mouth.

"Are you okay, Russell? You look a little dazed there." She smiled. "I'm gabbing too much and I'm boring you."

He cleared his throat and squared his shoulders. "No, no, Shelby. Not at all. I'm listening." He swallowed hard. "You were saying about your dad being so hateful."

"Yeah, he is. But I actually have memories of Dad that are so different, you know? When I was little I was crazy about him, and I really believe he was crazy for me, too, but he liked to pit me against Mom in the arguments that used to go on all the time. For a young girl it was very confusing. I loved them both. But Mom did seem like too much at times. I always wanted her to be like the other moms and just bake cookies and hang out with me all day, but she was never like that. She was always very involved in other people's lives. The doorbell would ring at the strangest hours and I would hear all these muffled voices downstairs. Then I would hear Wesley yell and Mom would be gone. Sometimes I liked it better when it was just me and Dad. It was more normal. I would fix his breakfast and he would comb my hair." Shelby stopped speaking. Russell still seemed distracted, and he was still just watching her mouth. "Hey, how about a couple Scotches? You drink Scotch, Russell?"

"Whenever I can." He grinned sheepishly.

"Good. Don't happen to have any single malts in this fine establishment, do you, John?"

"As a matter of fact!" John pulled out a bottle of Glenmorangie from behind the bar. "A friend donated this from his own stash when he gave up drinking. I've been saving it forever, just waiting for the right person to order a single malt. I think I'll join you two. Neat okay?" John poured healthy shots for each of them and they toasted to old times.

Shelby kept talking and Russell kept listening while John tended to his regulars. "Yeah, Russell, it was like my mom was all the mystery and excitement and Wesley was all the steady comfort. But everything changed the minute she was gone. Just that quick all the anger that Wesley had directed at Neely was redirected at me. I could do no right after that, and he just got angrier and angrier. If it hadn't been for Grandma Mart I would have had an awful life. Well, I kind of did, anyway." Shelby finished her drink.

"Maybe we should call it a night?"

"You're probably right." She winked and ordered them another round. He grinned and they toasted again to old times. Another hour flew by.

"Damn, Russell, I have been talking your ear off. Are you doing okay since your divorce? I did notice that fine car you're driving."

"Yeah, well, we had our share of natural disasters last year and a lot of folks got nervous and bought new policies. It translated into some sweet bonuses for me." He smiled and she was struck again by how handsome he was. Women probably clambered to get him to write their insurance policies. Shelby studied his elegant profile as he sipped on his drink. He seemed like such a nice guy. He had been so attentive the whole afternoon, like he knew she just needed to talk. Shelby was feeling a little embarrassed at how much she was telling him. *I'm gonna regret this tomorrow.* They finished another Scotch. "I think I'm gonna call New York."

"Not an ex-boyfriend, I hope. That's probably not a good idea."

Shelby laughed. "No, it's way better than that. She's my best friend in the whole world." She punched in the number and Caitlin answered on the third ring.

"Shel, I think you better get yourself home, girlfriend. I'll call you tomorrow. You don't have far to drive, right?"

"Just down the road, Cait. I can do it in my sleep."

"Well, you're getting pretty close to doing that. So say goodnight and get yourself home, okay?"

"Okay."

"Promise?"

"Promise. Love you."

"Love you, too. Be careful!"

Shelby ended the call and noticed her glass was empty. She raised an eyebrow at Russell.

He grinned, and shook his head. "No more, Ms. Shelby Jean. It's definitely time we called it a night. We have almost killed off John's precious bottle of Scotch. Want me to drive you home?"

"Nah, I'm fine. It's only a couple miles."

He looked doubtful.

"Seriously Russell, I know I don't look it, but I'm not a lightweight." She wobbled a bit when she stood up, but then she gathered herself and stood straight and steady. She kissed him on the cheek as he paid up. Out in the parking lot they said goodbye and promised to meet again soon. Russell got into his Lexus and turned towards town, honking as he drove off.

Shelby fumbled with the keys before she found the one that fit the ignition of the pickup. She smiled, remembering her grandmother doing the same thing. *Only she was sober.* The radio was tuned into a classic country station and a Hank Williams song was playing.

Shelby laughed out loud. "Hank, I think you are haunting me." She cranked up the volume before putting the truck in reverse and backing up.

As she turned the pickup around to face US 23, her cell phone slid out of her bag, landing on the floor between her feet. Shelby reached down to get it, but she lost her balance and hit her head on the steering wheel. Reacting in surprise, her foot slipped off the brake, slamming down, instead, onto the gas pedal. In a sudden rush of acceleration, the truck went flying out into the highway. Shelby turned the wheel hard and the pickup started to weave violently.

"Grandma Mart? Mom?!" She cried out as startling panic seized her.

Shelby never gained control of her grandmother's truck. All she would remember of what occurred right before the crash was a blinding light coming straight at her.

CHAPTER EIGHT
OPEN YOUR EYES, SHELBY JEAN

RUSSELL JAMES PULLED AWAY SLOWLY from the bar. He wanted to watch her leave. But what he saw he couldn't really believe, and would never, ever forget. Shelby had been backing up in the parking lot to turn her truck around, when suddenly she flew out into the middle of 23 weaving right in front of a semi tractor-trailer. Russell watched in horror in his rear-view mirror, and then he heard the crash and saw the eighteen-wheeler push the pickup truck down the highway before screeching to a halt. Russell jerked his car off to the side of the road and called 911. He watched his fingers move and heard his voice speaking instructions in a reasonable tone, but he had no idea how.

Oh, God! Shelby!?

He turned his car back south towards the bar. People were congregating outside the door of The Pit Stop. Russell swung into the parking lot and jumped out of the Lexus. He attempted to run to the road, but John was there and grabbed hold of his arm, pulling him back, yelling, "Russell, you wanna get yourself killed, man?"

"Let go, John! What if it catches fire? We've got to get her out of that truck!"

Emergency vehicles were lighting up the sky in the distance as they raced towards the scene. John assured him, "Russell, they're here. The EMTs are here."

The next hour was a surreal blur of manic activity as Russell looked on with the other patrons from the bar. John brought him hot coffee from inside. In Russell's mind he had sobered up the moment he heard the crash, but John wasn't taking any chances. Luckily, the vehicles did not catch fire and the onlookers watched in fascination as the firefighters brought out the Jaws of Life and cut Shelby out of her grandmother's truck.

The driver of the semi had miraculously gotten himself out of his cab and was even able to walk, but they put him in the ambulance with Shelby. The flashing beams sped down the road to the hospital in Ashland. Tow trucks showed up to tow the vehicles to an impound lot. Another hour passed before the highway patrolman got around to questioning anybody. He took statements and then finally everyone was instructed to leave the scene.

Russell walked into his quiet house and nearly collapsed onto his living room floor. The afternoon with Shelby had been so perfect. He had watched her talk and thought she was the prettiest woman he had ever seen, with her light green eyes, full lips and shining honey-blonde hair. But there was something more to her than her appearance. She radiated something else. He couldn't put his finger on it, but he had been mesmerized watching her speak. Even more than mesmerized, Russell was a little frightened by how she made him feel. He could imagine she had intimidated her share of guys right out of the picture. And now he pictured her truck being rammed by that semi. He broke down and cried, his body shaking uncontrollably.

Wesley had gotten the call minutes after the wreck. He had still been in the recliner when he answered the phone. "Yeah, this is Wesley Stiller. Who's this? What you say? Did what? Shelby Jean? Yeah, she's my daughter." *Silence.* Later it was the hospital calling. "Yeah, do whatever you have to."

Wesley reached for the remote and turned the TV off. How could this be happening? It was enough that the girl's grandmother had passed, but now this? Emergency surgery? They didn't even know if she would live through the night. Another semi truck? Just like all those years ago when he had gotten the call about Neely. Wesley sat in the dark the rest of the night just staring into space, his eyes wells of tears.

Too much light. Why is it so bright? Shelby waved her arms in front of her to feel her way. Where am I? What is this place? She was running and then slowed to walk towards something ahead of her. What was it? She couldn't see, but in her blindness there was a strange trust. She extended her arms out to her side and felt something spongy

and soft, organic. A living wall? She kept walking and was surprised that she wasn't frightened. Just curious and excited. The air around her buzzed with vibrant snaps of electricity and warmth and smelled of garden flowers. White lilies were everywhere she looked. They were clustered over her head, looped in silver viney ribbons, growing out of the organic walls. They caressed her face and hands and the fragrance was an intoxicating earthy smell mixed with floral sweetness, soothing and invigorating at the same time. Thick, soft petals cushioned her feet and she felt she was walking on cool clouds. Shelby smiled at the flowers surrounding her. Neely? Mother? You must be here. I feel you everywhere! She stopped walking and stood for a moment in the room of flowers. They were all around her and she gave into the urge to lie down in their soothing bed. She lay flat and smelled the lilies, letting them engulf her. One of the vines dropped down from the ceiling and she reached for it and held onto it. It pulled her up, gently at first, and then faster and soon she was floating high above, looking down below.

In that instant the whole scene changed. The room of flowers was gone. She was looking down at a body in an operating room, lying flat and exposed on a cold table. People in green scrubs and masks were attending to a woman who was hooked up to noisy machines. She could see a respirator moving up and down in time to an awful hissing sound. The woman's face was covered by a large ventilating mask and there were countless tubes attached to her. Shelby looked down in curiosity at the scene and then felt a tug. It was the vine tugging at her. Her curiosity quickly turned to fear. The vine was attached to the body underneath her. She grabbed hold of the vine and pulled back but it was too strong. The tug came again and again and Shelby felt herself being drawn back down, down, down...

"Shel, I'm here. I'm right here." Caitlin Sotheby sat next to Shelby's bed stroking her limp hand. "Come on, Shelby, it's all right. Everything is going to be all right. Just open your eyes. I want you to look at me. Please? Shelby Jean?" Caitlin's words caught in her throat. She had been repeating the same mantra for over a week, with no response.

The hospital staff hadn't known what to do with the beguiling brunette from New York who refused to leave the hospital even though she wasn't family. She had finally worn the nurses down and they agreed to let her into the ICU. They confided in her that the doctors were hopeful, although there were too many unknown factors when it came to brain injuries. Everyone agreed it had been nothing short of a miracle that Shelby had survived the wreck. What was even more remarkable was that she only had some internal bleeding that immediate surgery had fixed, and she hadn't broken any bones. Her body was a mass of contusions and abrasions, but all of that was relatively minor.

If only she would just wake up.

More nurses came into the room and Caitlin took her cue to leave the ICU for a while. She rode the elevator down to the basement cafeteria and found Russell at a corner table, a cup of coffee in his hand.

"May I?" she asked.

"I wish you would." He pointed to the empty chair across from him.

"Russell, I'm going to have to go home. My boss was cool to let me leave right away, but he's not so cool to let me stay much longer. I will be here through the weekend, but then I'll be flying back to New York. And Russell, I have to thank you again for thinking to get my number out of Shelby's cell. Otherwise, I would have never known. Wesley doesn't know anything of Shelby's life in New York. I am just so grateful you're here to look out for her. It kills me that I can't stay."

"Well, don't worry. I'll be here. So much of my work is in Ashland, and you know I'll call the minute Shelby wakes up."

"Thanks, Russell. You're being a good friend to her."

"Hell, Caitlin, that's a stretch. I should never have let her get behind the wheel." Russell's pained expression told the story. He wiped at his brow, and his hand shook as he picked up his coffee cup.

Caitlin grabbed hold of his hand and spoke firmly, "Hey, you listen to me now. I know Shelby a whole lot better than you, and believe me, there's no way she would have let you drive her home if she felt like she was okay. No way! She's her own girl and always has been. Shelby Jean Stiller might come off like a country bumpkin sometimes, but she doesn't let anybody dictate her life. I have had to learn that the hard way. They found her cell phone on the floor and I'll bet you anything that had a whole lot to do with what happened. It was an accident, Russell, plain and simple."

"Well, I appreciate that, Caitlin, but still…"

Caitlin stared at the good-looking man who looked like he wanted to cry. Shelby had never mentioned him, but he was probably the nicest guy she had ever had too many drinks with. What shit luck. But the good news was that the driver of the semi had come through the accident miraculously unharmed. He was deeply saddened by what had happened and didn't want to press charges. Russell got Bella involved and together they managed to convince the trucking company to agree to settle for repairs only. No investigation would be conducted for DUI. Cait thought that was pretty unbelievable, but when she questioned him, Russell's answer was simply, "Bella knows people." Martha's pickup truck had, of course, been totaled.

But none of that mattered if Shelby never woke up.

"Have you talked to Wesley today?" Caitlin asked.

"Yeah. The women from Martha's church are still rotating shifts looking out for him."

"For a son of a bitch, he sure seems to have an army of supporters."

"Well, that is Martha's doing. She is still calling the shots." His lips turned up in the slightest smile.

"I wish I had gotten to know her. Shelby loved her grandmother so much, though she didn't spend a lot of time with her. I think that was what this trip was really all about, was reconnecting. And nobody could have predicted what would happen. The whole thing just sucks." Caitlin dug for a fresh tissue in her purse.

"Yeah, it's about as fucked up as anything I have ever heard. And I thought I had just about heard it all. I just keep hoping there's a silver lining that will surface some day, you know?"

"Well, she's going to need a good insurance agent down here. Our guy in New York isn't going to bend over backwards."

"That's the least I can do. She won't have any worries there. You ready?"

"Yeah, let's go back up and then you can go home if you want. I'll be here until they kick me out today."

Back in ICU, the nurses were just finishing up with checking Shelby's IVs and nodded at the two gorgeous people as they entered the room. Rarely had anyone on staff seen such beautiful people in the same room.

It was all anybody could talk about in the hospital, was the unusual beauty lying in a coma and the unusual beauties tending to her. Caitlin walked over to the bedside and spoke to the nurse as she was leaving, "Any word?"

"No, hon, nothin' has changed, 'cept I think they're gonna move her into a ward room tomorrow."

"That's a good sign, right?" Caitlin's heart jumped.

"Well, mebbe, but mebbe not. It means she's stable, and that's good, of course, but it also means that she could be a long time in a bed, so they don't want to keep her here." The nurse's tone was all sympathy as she left the room. Her voice left a trail of sadness.

Russell got a phone call and stepped out into the hall, and Caitlin took her usual place by Shelby's side. She picked up her hand and studied her friend's long, slender fingers. There should have been a ring there. Shelby would be good at loving someone forever. "Shelby Jean Stiller, don't you dare fade away. You have too much life in you and the world needs you. I need you. Please, you have to wake up. Do it for your mother. Do it for Martha?" Cait was sick of hearing her own voice, but she had to keep trying. She brushed back her friend's wavy hair from her forehead. Shelby looked just like Sleeping Beauty waiting on her Prince Charming.

Everything here is so comforting. Can you smell the glorious flowers? They smell like sweet memories. Mother, Grandma, why don't you come closer? You are both so beautiful. Come and be with me. I miss you both so much.

{No, Shelby, we can't come closer. It isn't time. You have much to do.}

I don't want to do anything. I want to stay here with you and just be. Do you feel how soft everything is? Do you see the spectacular colors? The lilies sparkle like glistening gold, but they feel like velvet. How is that? Where am I? It is so peaceful.

{You are resting. But now you must wake up. You must open your eyes. Shelby Jean, you must open your eyes.}

But my eyes are open, Mother, Grandma. I can see you.

{We are in your mind's eyes. And we will always be there. You can be with us anytime you want in your mind. But now it is time for you to open your eyes to your world. Open your eyes, Shelby Jean…}

Russell came back into the room and said, "Caitlin, I have a client who has had a minor catastrophe, so I better hit it. Just call me with any news. And are you sure you're okay in the hotel? I have an extra bedroom? Or I'm sure you can stay with Bella. She has a huge house."

"Oh, that's sweet, Russell, but The Hampton is fine. Keeps me close, you know? You go on now and I'll talk to you tomorrow."

"Okay. But the offer still stands. Nite, Cait."

She waved goodbye and sat back with her magazine to get comfortable. There were still several hours in the day, but she couldn't focus on the silly articles. She was like Shelby in that she was past the fake transparency of the fashion world. She had had her fill, too. She looked over at her best friend and watched her lay in peaceful slumber. Her thick eyelashes curled up softly and smooth eyelids covered those big eyes that knocked you out with their light green intensity. Shelby had a classic straight nose and perfect pouty lips that had been all the rage when the two small-town girls had begun their careers. Caitlin remembered meeting Shelby for the first time.

They had both been recruited from their hometowns, and were as green as they came. They were so scared and excited. But it was Shelby who had held onto Caitlin's hand through the first days and gained her trust. The industry would have chewed them up, like they did most of the newcomers, except for the innate savvy that Shelby possessed. She was incessantly teased about her Kentucky accent, but people learned to respect her quick enough when she let her wit take over. She could hold her own with anybody, sophisticated or not, and people grew to like her. Shelby was just different from most of the young models in that she had such a strong sense of her own worth.

When Caitlin learned of Shelby's background it was hard to imagine where that strength came from. She had certainly taken her share of abuse. But maybe it was her grandmother and her mother who had really instilled the right stuff in Shelby. And then there was Sorina, the founder of Sorry's Run. Shelby used to talk about what an inspiration the pioneer woman was. Whatever it was, Caitlin had recognized it immediately and latched on to her Kentucky girlfriend, and had never let go.

And she sure as hell wasn't about to let go now. She just wouldn't allow herself to believe God could let this wonderful person waste away at the peak of her life. He just couldn't. Caitlin bent her head and said one of the few prayers she had ever offered.

Open your eyes, Shelby Jean…

"Whatcha doin', Caitlin Sotheby? Are you sleeping sitting up?"

Caitlin's head jerked upright and her eyes nearly popped out of her head. "Shelby? Shelby Jean?" She almost knocked over the IV stand getting her arms around her friend. Joy spilled out of her in giant tears. "Shelby? You're awake?! Are you all right? How do you feel? Oh, thank you, God! Thank you!"

Shelby looked at her friend in confusion and just smiled weakly. Then she realized where she was. "I was in an accident, wasn't I?" Her expression changed to one of fear. "Cait, did anybody—die?"

"No, hon, you were the only who came close to it. The truck driver is just fine. We just didn't know about you." Caitlin's cheeks were wet with tears and she didn't even try to control her emotions. She pressed the buzzer to alert the nurse's station. "She's awake!" The nurses came running and joy was the shared emotion. Nobody had really expected the young woman to wake up. They had seen it go the other way too many times. When the doctor came in, Caitlin left to call Russell.

CHAPTER NINE
COMING HOME

"SHE'LL BE IN THE HOSPITAL a few more days. They want to get her up walkin'," Wesley explained.

"But will she be okay, Wesley? Will she be able to do for herself?" Bella asked.

"Yeah, they say so. Now, whether she can do for me, I don't know."

"Well, now, don't you worry about that. We're gonna be here for both of you. You know that. Martha has done for all of us at one time or another and we're just happy to be able to finally return the favor." Bella was massaging Wesley's knuckles with oil and Jolene was fixing his lunch.

"Well, just praise God that she is okay. This family has had enough tragedy," Jolene added. She sat a bowl of tomato soup and a grilled cheese sandwich in front of Wesley and the women left him alone to eat while they drove to the drugstore for more of his prescriptions.

As soon as he heard the car start up he tossed the soup and sandwich down the disposal and lit up a cigarette. Wesley took a deep drag and then coughed for five minutes. He didn't care. He liked the aggravation more than the kindness. The women were getting on his nerves. But he needed them. There were things that he just couldn't do without help. He was ready for Shelby to come home. At least she got as aggravated as he did and left him alone some of the time.

He took another drag and coughed again. This time there was blood on his hankie. He had been seeing that lately. Didn't matter. Nothing mattered. Wesley forced his swollen joints to move his legs to the living room. He collapsed into the recliner and turned the television on.

"Come on, Ms. Stiller, just one more lap down the hall and we'll call it a day. You're doing just great." The young therapist studied the stunning woman for her reaction. He hadn't enjoyed his job so much in weeks. His patients didn't usually look like movie stars.

"Okay, Thomas, one more, but I think I'll start calling you my personal therapy Nazi." She smiled at the young man and he beamed at her. She felt strong, just bruised. Everything hurt, especially at her incision site. The bed felt better than anyplace, but she knew the walking was good for her. She had been told she would be discharged in a couple days with pain medicine to take until her body had more time to heal from the surgery and trauma. Shelby had refused any home healthcare. She knew she would have plenty of help.

So she would be back with Wesley. *Great.* Surprisingly, she realized that she didn't dread going back to the farmhouse as much as she would have thought. She was actually looking forward to being in her old room, her old bed, looking out at those old hills. If she just didn't have the old man to deal with. But maybe he'd surprise her, be kinder to her since she had almost died. Or maybe he would be sorry that she hadn't. *God, Shelby.* She chastised herself for such black thoughts. She reasoned with herself: It's not like he hates me. He just doesn't love me…

Whatever.

She was ready. She was ready to follow doctors' orders and rest until she was healed enough to get her father placed somewhere in a facility where he could be properly looked after. Then it was back to New York.

At least that was the plan.

Why did it always sound hollow when she spoke the words in her head? Caitlin was sure ready for her roommate to get back to her life. And Shelby missed Caitlin, too. They had been like sisters for years, and Caitlin had proved herself to be a loving friend many times over. But something about New York seemed too distant now—so other life.

Why was that?

As Shelby lay the last night in her hospital bed she was aware of an unreasonable feeling that one life had been lived and she was slipping into the next one. In a strange way, it was like she really had died, even though she hadn't. It was the most frightening, fascinating thought. The wonder of it all lulled her to sleep. And her sleep was rich and deep and full of vivid dreams. It had been like that all week as she zoned in and out of drug-induced altered consciousness. She was seeing her grandmother nonstop and it was always as if Martha was telling her something, something she just couldn't grasp. And when she would awaken she was so filled with joy and happiness that she had been with her grandmother, really *been* with her. It didn't matter what she was saying, it was just the way she looked; young, happy, infused with such life force. It gave Shelby hope and a sense that there really was something beyond this transient physical world.

Maybe there just was.

She had never really bought into the idea of reincarnation or any of the afterlife philosophies that were so popular. But now, after each intense, animated dream she noticed a shift in how she was processing her thoughts, a shift in her beliefs. She was feeling different. Was it happiness? Was it just being grateful that God had spared her, given her another chance? She wasn't sure. But she was finding herself excited about something, something she couldn't name.

"Oh, Shelby Jean, just look at you," Violet cooed. "Lord, you look so wonderful. Too skinny, but so wonderful. We are just so glad, hon. The whole town is so glad. We've been praying for you 24/7 at the church. Ah, sweetie, you're as light as a leaf. Don't worry, though, we'll get you fattened up real quick. Here, lean on us and we'll get you up the stairs. You have to take it easy for a while. Don't you worry none about Wesley. We've got that all figured out. You just rest easy now, you hear?"

"Violet, you are just runnin' at the mouth. Let the girl have a moment. She just got home, for gosh sake," Bella spoke harshly to her friend as they helped get Shelby settled in her bed upstairs. "She needs some rest and quiet."

Shelby smiled and thanked the ladies as they finally left her. She was surprised at how weak she felt and there was certainly soreness. She groaned as she lifted herself to reach for the pain pills on her bedside stand. Russell had brought her home from the hospital and the drive had just drained her energy. The doctors had probably been right that it would take time for her to fully recover, that she shouldn't push it. She felt like she could sleep forever.

Staring out her window, a rush of joy washed over her. She really did feel changed. She had always loved looking out at what she thought of as her Kentucky hills, but now it was as though her grandmother was with her, watching the hills turn misty gray in the early evening light. It was such a comfort to feel her this way, like Martha hadn't passed at all.

"Goodnight, Grandma Mart. I love you. And now you're back with your Neely." Shelby shivered with emotion. "Mom, I still love you, too." Shelby looked up at the white calla lilies bordering the pink wallpaper, remembering.

Downstairs, Russell had been speaking with Wesley while Bella and Violet helped Shelby. "Wesley, I'll be back tomorrow to check on you guys, although it looks like the ladies have you more than covered on everything you need."

"Yeah, they got us covered, all right. Don't mean I wouldn't like some male company. I could really use some smokes, you know?" Wesley leaned into his cane and whispered so Bella couldn't hear him.

Russell smiled. "Yeah, I hear that. And I'll bring you some more of that fine Kentucky elixir, too."

Wesley grinned and shook Russell's hand as he left.

Shelby heard the door slam. She knew it was Russell leaving. He had been so good to her. She was certain he was riddled with guilt; as though it was his fault she had had the accident. Of course it wasn't, but he was such a kind man. She was moved by his devotion in such a short amount of time.

And it certainly didn't hurt that he was such a handsome guy.

But for some reason whenever she thought of Russell she imagined Caitlin standing next to him, and never herself, though the chances of that were remote since her friends were each dug into separate lives in separate states. But Shelby didn't feel the desire for a relationship herself. She only wanted to get stronger and figure out her feelings—all these new feelings.

Wesley had been quiet when she got home, but he had squeezed her hand. That was different. She knew she should formulate a plan to get him out of the house and into a care facility, but her thoughts were muddled. It was as though she didn't really want that yet. Maybe it wasn't time.

Maybe there was just more important stuff between father and daughter that needed to be ironed out. Maybe that was why Martha had insisted on her coming to Kentucky.

A lot of maybe's.

And why wasn't she missing New York? Probably just because too much had happened too quickly. And Caitlin would see to things at their apartment. No worries there. Shelby smiled to herself as she let her heavy eyes shut.

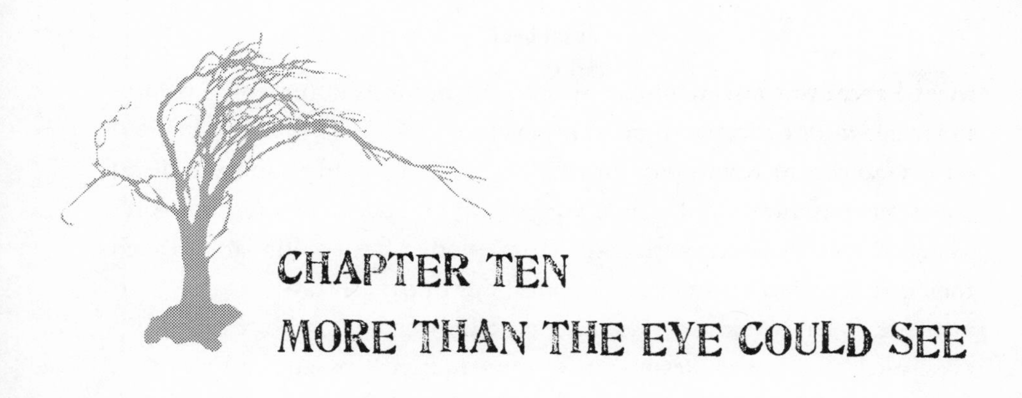

CHAPTER TEN
MORE THAN THE EYE COULD SEE

"MORNIN' SHELBY, I HOPE YOU'RE HUNGRY. I went a little overboard on the eggs." Bella sat a tray on the nightstand and went to the window. She pulled back the curtains and warming sunshine spread out into the room. Shelby squinted at the sudden brightness and then propped herself up in the bed.

"Breakfast in bed? My, my, you're going to spoil me, Bella." Shelby smiled and started to stretch her arms, but recoiled with an instant reminder that her body was still badly bruised.

"That's right, you take it easy and let us spoil you, Shelby Jean. Takin' it easy is the only way for your body to heal. Doctors' orders are bed rest for at least a week. Take care of yourself proper and soon you'll be right as rain."

"Does that mean bathroom privileges or bedpan?" Shelby grinned at her grandmother's friend who was fast becoming like family to her.

"Definitely bathroom privileges." She laughed. "Swing your legs over the side, hon."

Shelby groaned and supported her flat belly as she did just what Bella told her. Soon the two were hobbling down the hall to the bathroom. "You're pretty good at this nurse stuff, Bella." Shelby looked kindly at her grandmother's dearest friend.

"Well, hon, it's the only trainin' you get once you start gettin' old," she answered.

Downstairs, Wesley was wheezing more than usual. He put the inhaler to his lips and sucked in the medicine, but immediately after, his lungs convulsed. His chest racked with a coughing fit that was almost violent in its intensity. He nearly collapsed into the kitchen chair and wiped at his mouth, exhausted from the episode. The Kleenex in his hand was blood soaked. Wesley wiped again at his mouth, and cursed under his breath. He reached for his cigarettes and lit one up.

"Wesley Stiller, you put out that cigarette right this minute. I heard you from upstairs soundin' like you was dyin' and now you're smokin'? What the heck is wrong with you?" Bella stood in front of him and yanked the cigarette from his fingers. She put it out in the ashtray.

"Ah, Bella, you know I need my cigs. It's the only comfort I get."

"Well, that just makes no sense. You can hardly breathe the way it is. Here, take your pills." She laid out his medication and noticed the bloody Kleenex in his hand. "God, Wesley, you're coughin' up blood again. I better call Dr. Simons."

Wesley reached out and grabbed her arm. "No, Bella. I don't want you to call the doctor. It ain't nothin'. It happens sometimes when I have a specially hard coughin' fit. Now, just leave it be and get me some more coffee. How is Shelby Jean?" He changed the subject.

"She's fine. Nothin' that time won't cure. But she has to stay in bed, so don't you go hollerin' for her to do nothin', you hear me?" Bella handed him a mug of coffee and planted her feet firmly waiting on his response.

"I ain't gonna bother her, Bella. I want the girl to get better, too."

Bella sat down across from him and they had a quiet moment while they enjoyed their coffee. Outside the sky was blue and the hills were vibrant with green from the wet spring they were having.

Bella spoke, "Shelby looks so much like Neely, it's almost disturbin'."

"Yeah, I know what you mean. I have a hard time with that." Wesley's bloodshot eyes got watery and then he sat his mug down and reached for his walker. "I like my cane better than this thing."

"Well, Dr. Simons says the walker is safer. Deal with it, Wes," Bella snapped at him.

"Yes, ma'am, Bella, ma'am. Jesus. Ain't nobody got a sense of humor no more. Man, I miss Martha."

Bella rolled her eyes at him.

He took the hint. "Okay. Help me get back in the bed. I feel pretty weak myself today. Then you get yourself on home. Shelby and I will be fine. I'll call you if I need you."

"Okay. I got a pot of chili and cornbread in the fridge. All you have to do is heat it up. Vi is plannin' on stoppin' by later to check on y'all and she's got another walker she's gonna bring so Shelby can get herself to the bathroom."

"Nothin' but invalids in this house," Wesley complained.

Bella ignored the comment. "Come on. Easy does it." She helped him to his room and then she left.

Upstairs, Shelby drifted in and out of sleep. She felt as though she were seamlessly slipping from one world into the next. She was dreaming so vividly and when she would awaken, the hills out her window welcomed her back to this world before she would float off into the next. "Damn, these are some good pills." She looked at the prescribed medication and made a mental note to start easing up on the dosage.

Reaching into her nightstand, she found the old diaries she had kept as a little girl and then as a teenager. She opened to a page that was written when she was only ten years old, before her mother had died.

> Daddy is so mean to Mommy. He yells so loud at her. Mommy never yells back. She just goes away. She goes away all the time now. I think she is afraid to be here with Daddy. But I miss her. I wish she would take me with her when she goes away. I would like to go away, too.

Shelby felt her throat tighten as she read the scribblings of her own childish handwriting. It brought it all back, the pain and the loneliness. Why had her mother left so much? Was it just Wesley? Shelby had always thought it was partly her. That her mother was leaving her, too. But she would never know. Neely had been taken from life when she was so young, so vibrant and beautiful. Shelby hadn't let herself think of her mother much. It was too painful. But she always felt that Neely must have had a horrible dark side, to leave her little girl all the time with an angry man like Wesley. But Shelby knew her father never really laid a hand on her. It was always verbal abuse.

She opened another diary from years later, written when she was a teenager.

> *Sorry's Run. That's the right name for it, this dead-end, nowhere town. I hate it here. I hate this house. I hate you, Dad. I hate*

everything. I am going to get out, go away, and never come back. I swear. It's why Neely left us so much. She hated it here, too. She wanted to get out. She needed to get out. Well, I will find a way. I will do that for you, Mom. I will do that for you.

Shelby shut the diary and let it rest on her stomach. It was enough, just those passages. It was enough and too much. She had wanted out, and when that mysterious woman spotted her at the farmer's market, it was the miracle she had dreamt of. She had gotten out, and never looked back.

Until now. Now she was back and glad to be. That was the strangest feeling after all these years of hanging on to being done with Kentucky. Of course, Grandma Mart had always been important to her, but nothing else.

Until now. Now she felt like there was unfinished business that had to be dealt with. And she was ready. She wasn't an angry, scared, insecure young teenager anymore. She was a sophisticated woman and all grown up. But since the accident, something else was going on. She was softer, more open to discovery maybe? Though there didn't seem much to discover in Sorry's Run. But perhaps there was more than the eye could see.

Shelby stared out the window at her hills. She felt herself as that young girl, wanting out, away, gone. She remembered the fear and then the adventure and excitement of going to New York for the first time. That impossible Goliath of a city might as well have been another universe. She was barely able to speak at first from shyness, but then when she met Caitlin she began to adjust and soon she was speaking enough to charm everybody.

Holly Golightly. She had been the little hick beauty, and lucky enough to have never gotten too hard from city life. She smiled, thinking of Caitlin. Their friendship had been the reason for her strength. Shelby sighed. Then her thoughts jumped forward to after the accident and the powerful dreams of her grandmother. It was like she was telling her something, something that she was meant to do, to be. It was not clear. But it would come to her, she was sure. She just needed more time.

Shelby picked up the Vicodin. *I'll ease up, but not today.* Today she would sleep some more and dream some more and let her body heal itself. There were discoveries to be made, and she felt her grandmother was the guiding force.

Russell sat at The Pit Stop talking with John and sipping on a cold Budweiser. He had had an unusually hectic day and needed to unwind. He wasn't sure he could return to the "scene of the crime" in clear conscience, but decided it had been a wonderful time at the bar until the accident, and he would just focus on that. Shelby had talked on and on about her life in New York. She had spoken so much of Caitlin and how her roommate had had the nerve to quit modeling way before she did; how Caitlin had gone on to NYU and gotten a degree in horticulture and worked in a prestigious lab.

Russell had watched Shelby shine when she bragged on Caitlin's accomplishments. All he could think was he had never seen a more captivating woman in his whole life than Shelby Jean Stiller. There was something in her presence that calmed him and made him nervous all at the same time. The result was intoxicating beyond anything he could recall. To be with her felt like a drug, like he had to have more. It was a serious condition. But now that he had met Caitlin, new fantasies were beginning to surface. *I am ate up.*

"One more cold one, John, then I better hit it. This last round of tornadoes has thrown our claims office into chaos, and I will have another marathon day tomorrow."

"It seems like Mother Nature is ruling more so than usual these days, huh, Russell? I mean, in your business you must wonder about the never-ending disasters."

"Yeah, well, you'd think, but you should hear the horror stories the older guys tell. Maybe it's always been like this. Maybe we just didn't notice so much before all this information started coming at us 24/7."

"Well, mebbe you're right. But it sure seems like all hell is breaking loose somewhere every minute."

"You are right about that, my friend, and I think I better get myself down the road and prepare for the next hellfire!" He grinned and laid money down on the bar as he left. He started to turn the Lexus to the left towards his house, but in a split second he decided to turn the other direction toward Wesley's farmhouse. He had bought Wesley's favorite "hooch" in

Ashland and he figured the old guy could use it. Not withstanding, he would at least be close to her again for a second.

"How you doin', Wesley? Hanging in there, I hope?"

It had taken Wesley a while to get to the door, but when he saw who it was his scowl brightened and he moved his walker out of the way, letting Russell in. "I'm hangin' by a thread, as usual, Russell. How 'bout yourself?"

"Same old, same old. But I have a little something for you that might put a spring back into your step?" He smiled and held up the paper bag with the whiskey in it.

Wesley managed a grin and invited Russell to the kitchen to share in a drink. It was starting to rain outside. As Russell pulled a couple glasses from the cupboard, he couldn't help but notice the mist snaking through the hills. "Man, it sure is pretty around here this time of the year. Everything is gettin' so green." He poured them both a shot of the Kentucky bourbon and they sat down at the table across from each other and toasted to their health before throwing the liquor back.

Russell barely tasted the bourbon, but enjoyed its burn while simultaneously fighting the need to cough. He cleared his throat hard and his voice came out in a hoarse whisper, "So how is she doin', Wesley?'

"She's okay. Bella has been here lookin' after her and I think Violet is comin', too, later on. Them ladies don't miss a beat. I don't know how they can be tendin' to other folks all the time. Just like Martha. Damn, just like Neely..." He stopped, then, and took another drink. His lips pursed as the whiskey hit its mark.

"Well, I guess she's sleepin'?"

"Hell, I don't know. I ain't been up them stairs in two years. You can go on up, Russell, if you want to. Just be quiet and let her sleep if that's what she's doin'. Doc says that's what she needs."

Russell tiptoed up the stairs and gently cracked open her door. Shelby was laying with her eyes wide open staring out her windows. She looked up at him standing in the doorway and grinned. She patted the side of her bed. He sat next to her and took her hand.

"How you doin', Shelby Jean? Are they treating you right?"

She smiled tiredly, and said, "I have never been so cared for in my life.

I think I could get used to all this coddling. But I haven't the energy of a slug, Russell. I think the longer I stay in this bed the more tired I get. All I want to do is sleep."

"Well, that's exactly what the doctor ordered. You need to do nothing for a time, Shelby, and in a couple weeks you'll be ready to rock 'n roll. You'll see."

"Oh yeah?" She smiled again. "I don't know about that, but I'll take getting to the bathroom without any assistance. Speaking of which, could you give me a hand?"

He helped her down the hall and then back into her bed. She got herself situated and laughed weakly. "I feel like an old lady. Just a trip to the bathroom and I'm exhausted." She rested her head back on the pillow, her usually bright eyes looking dull and tired.

"I won't keep you up any longer, Shelby. I'll be in touch with you and with Caitlin."

"Thank you, Russell. That relieves my mind. I know Cait wants me to call her everyday, but I just don't feel up to it. Call her tonight, would you?"

On his drive home Russell punched in Caitlin Sotheby's number and they talked for an hour. He kept the phone to his ear as he pulled into his driveway and then let himself into his house. It was the next best thing to being with Shelby, was talking to her roommate.

Further down the road, guarded by the hush of river and forest, May apples fed off the liquid air and spread their leafy branches over the ground to welcome the sweet summer that was promised. A lone woman stared out from her screened-in porch as the day turned to night and the mist rolled deeper into distant hills off to the south. She could hear the river rushing as the rain refreshed its muddy waters. Birds whistled in the high trees and she knew her finches were once again discovering the newly-filled bird feeders, their brown feathers hinting of the yellow/gold that was coming. Cats purred and lazed about in secret shadows.

The woman breathed in the first scent of honeysuckle and loved the season that was upon her. She loved the woods. She loved the river. She loved her fragrant gardens that would be tended to soon enough. And more than anything, she loved the energy that was changing. She felt it. She didn't know where it was coming from, but it was powerful and it was good. She smiled and pulled closer to the screen to feel nature waking up.

CHAPTER ELEVEN
WHAT DID YOU DO?

DAYS PASSED IN A SLEEPY BLUR for Shelby. But one day, as if a shroud had been lifted, she really felt like getting up. She stretched her limbs in bed before rolling over onto her side, propping herself into a seated position. *Hummm, not so sore today.* Her legs swung over and dangled above the floor. She lifted her arms high over her head and let her chest expand as she breathed deeply. She felt like she was strong enough. Giving herself a push, she was standing. Wobbly, but standing. She looked at the walker Violet had brought, but she didn't reach for it. Instead, she just went slowly, gently. She took baby steps, putting one foot cautiously in front of the other. And then she was across the room looking out the windows at her beloved hills. She leaned into the glass and felt so happy, so young, like her life was just beginning. It was the most refreshing, amazing emotion.

It's like being born again. Shelby knew her Grandma Mart believed in that one big time. But it was true. She felt like herself, only expanded, greater somehow. She was ready to take on the world—but this world? This small, rural Kentucky world? Or the urban behemoth that was her home in New York City? What was she meant to do?

It doesn't matter. I will figure it out, she thought, as a pleasant shiver ran up her spine, and she walked all by herself to the bathroom.

"Oh, hon, just look at you! But how in the world?" Bella clapped her hands together as she walked into the kitchen. Shelby was sitting at the table.

"I did just as my favorite nurse told me, slow and steady. It really wasn't so bad even coming down the stairs. I feel like a new person, really, Bella. I just have to build my strength back up."

"Well, it's just remarkable. I knew it wouldn't take you long." Bella sat down across from her and reached for her hands. "Are you really better, sweetheart, really?"

Shelby stared at the woman who had been such a tremendous help to her and her family nonstop since she had been in Kentucky. Now she really studied her for the first time. Bella was attractive. She hadn't realized it until now, but she was. She had lovely skin for a woman in her late fifties, and her brown eyes were large and soft. Her graying dark hair was cut in a shag with just enough product in it to keep the shorter layers stylishly spiked. She wore long, dangly earrings. Her fingers were decked out with turquoise rings, matching the chunky bracelet she wore on her right wrist. It was sterling silver and the turquoise stone looked good against her freckled skin. *Bella is a very cool lady.* It was an interesting thought, all the more interesting because she hadn't even noticed that before.

"I am better, Bella. No small thanks to you. Speaking of which, how about you? You have been here for me all this time, and I have to make it up to you. Wesley and I both need to make it up to you. What can I do for you, Bella?"

Bella's brown eyes misted over as she squeezed the hands of the natural beauty across from her. "Oh, hon, are you kiddin' me? Just seein' you like this is enough for me. You are really kind to offer, though. Your Grandma Mart was so proud of you. And I know why." Bella let go of Shelby's hand and wiped at her eyes. "But sweetie, speaking of Martha, I know you have to get back home one of these days, God forbid," she sighed and continued, "but before you go, we really do need to go through the trailer and sift through Martha's things. Well, actually, I should say your things. Your grandmother put aside some money for Wes, but she made you the heir of everything else. Not that she had much. She only rented that trailer. She laughed when I had her fill out a Will from the Internet. She figured we should just call the "Got Junk" guys and be done with it. And there was absolutely nothing personal she wanted for Wesley. She really didn't have anything he would appreciate. But you need to see if there's anything there you want before we start tossin' stuff."

"Who is we, Bella?" Shelby hadn't thought about Grandma Mart's trailer. But now she was more than anxious to see it.

"Me, Violet and Jolene. Well, really, whoever we'd ask would be there. Your grandmother was dearly loved, Shelby. Dearly loved."

"I am so ready to see Grandma Mart's things. I haven't been in her trailer in such a long time. I think that would be wonderful. Let's keep it to just you three, okay? I'd like that."

"You got it."

"What day is today?"

"Tuesday."

"How about Sunday after church? You pick me up and take me to church and then we'll go?"

Bella smiled. "You want to go to church?"

"Don't get your hopes up, Bella, I am not looking for a soul saving. Actually, I think my soul has already been saved." Shelby loved seeing the surprised look on Bella's face. "No, I just want to go because you all have been so good to me, to Wesley and me, and I want to see everybody and thank them. Will you take me?"

"You better believe it! Service is at ten o'clock. Will we be bringing Wesley?"

"Only if he wants to come. I highly doubt it, but I will ask him. So, it's a date for Sunday. And Bella, I thank you again."

The women said their goodbyes and Shelby peeked in at Wesley, sleeping quietly for a change, before she climbed cautiously back upstairs to her room.

"Cait, I'm better, really better. My incision is healing well and I'm not that sore anymore. And the bruising is almost all gone. But Cait, I'm going to be here a while longer. Can you manage?"

"Of course, but I miss you. Maybe I'll fly back down in a week or two if you're still there. No, everything is fine here. Work is crazy, and that's good, because if I didn't come home exhausted I would be too lonely."

"Have you been going out? You need to go out." Shelby tried to sound stern.

"Oh, yeah, Tommy came and got me last night and the gang got together at the Grog Shoppe as usual. We all miss you and everyone sends their love. By the way, Shelby, Russell and I talked forever the other night. He is the greatest guy."

"I told you. And he thinks pretty highly of you, too. Yeah, I can see why you need that plane ticket."

"Oh, blow me, you Kentucky hick. I want to see *you*! If I get to see him, it's just icing on the cake."

Both women laughed. They talked, catching up, until Shelby heard her father hacking downstairs in his bedroom. "The old man is up. I think I better go make sure he's still got two lungs."

"Okay, Shel. Be a good girl and a good daughter. I think that *old man* loves you underneath all that snarling. And I for sure love you."

The friends hung up, promising to stay in touch.

"Are you all right, Wesley? Need any help?" Shelby pushed open his bedroom door and stuck her head into the dark and dreary room. It smelled of smoke and medicine.

"Shelby Jean, is that you? What are you doin' up?"

"Oh, I am much better, thank you very much. I can take care of you now, if you need me. Do you need me?"

"Come in here."

She walked timidly over to his bed. His thinning hair was lying in damp strands across his forehead. "Why don't you let me cut this, Dad?" She lifted up the hair and pushed it back.

"You think I'd be purtier?" He smiled at her and it wasn't his usual sarcastic expression. "You know, that actually wouldn't be such a bad idea. I haven't had a haircut in ten years. I guess my hippie days are over." He smiled again and she smiled back as she attempted to help him up to a seated position.

Shelby found some scissors and draped her father's shoulders in a towel as she dampened his hair and cut the long wispy strands off. He allowed her to trim his beard and mustache, and even nodded when she pointed to his wild eyebrows. When she finished grooming him, he looked ten years younger. She held up a hand mirror to his face.

"Damn!?" Wesley grinned. "I almost remember that guy!"

He laughed and started to cough deeply. It went on so long and hard, Shelby feared he would break a rib. The Kleenex she had handed him was blood soaked. She gave him a clean one. "Oh, Dad." Pity welled up in her for the first time. She sat down next to him as his whole body convulsed. "Here, Dad, lean into me. Let me hold you." He seemed so vulnerable when he was like this. *He is so sick*, she thought. She circled her arms around him, bringing him to her chest, holding him firmly. Then, without thinking, she let her hands move down his back until she felt his ribs, expanding too hard with his heaving lungs. She spread her fingers firmly on his back and pressed, holding them there perfectly still for a full minute.

Shelby felt a burning heat move from her palms, coursing into her fingertips. Bile rose in her throat and pain shot through her stomach. *Is my incision bursting,* was her immediate thought, but then she felt the heat leave her hands and go into his back. Instantly her nausea and pain eased. Wesley's muscles quivered, and he got quiet. His coughing stopped. He rested his forehead against her chest to catch his breath. She dropped her hands and he sat back against his pillows.

He stared at her. "What did you do?"

She felt her stomach, making sure there was nothing visible showing at the incision site. "What do you mean? I didn't do anything, only held you. That was a horrible spell, Wesley. It's a wonder you didn't break any ribs. Where's your inhaler?"

"No, girl, I asked you, what did you do? You did somethin'. I felt somethin'. It got hot and then I felt my insides relax. What did you do?" He was studying her now and his gaze was getting harder, more intense.

Shelby was lost for words. She knew he was right. She had felt it, too, a buzzing heat that traveled from her into him. She had felt it, too. What could she say.

"Damn it all to hell. Just like your mama. You're just like her, aren't you? I shoulda knowed. Git on outta here, Shelby Jean. Leave me be."

Shelby went back up to her room. She lay down on her bed and she noticed her whole body was shaking.

CHAPTER TWELVE
THE TRAILER

"BYE, WESLEY. I WILL BE GONE all afternoon. Just call if you need anything and Bella will bring me back. Don't bother to get up." Shelby's sarcasm cut through the dank room. She waved casually to her father, who was having his coffee in bed. He said he would probably stay put until she returned. He didn't look at her as he spoke. He hadn't directly looked at her ever since the night he had had the coughing fit.

And he hadn't coughed since.

It had been some very tense days with just the two of them cloistered together. She had told Bella that they were fine alone, but that was an exaggeration. Truth was, they just stayed away from each other, Shelby in her room and Wesley in his. They only passed coming in and out of the kitchen. But Wesley really didn't seem to need any assistance. They barely spoke the whole week.

Shelby was glad to get out of the house and she was excited about looking through her grandmother's personal things. She had dreamt of Grandma Mart the night before and she felt like her grandmother was going to go down memory lane with her.

"Is Wesley good for the day, hon?" Bella asked as she opened the passenger side door for Shelby. Bella looked like she was going to a club instead of church. Her hair was spiked and every finger donned a colorful ring. Her ruby earrings caught the sunlight as she got in behind the wheel of a white Mercedes-Benz.

"Yeah, he's good. Well, as good as he gets. I think he prefers you as his caregiver. I told him to call if he needs anything."

"You're a good daughter, Shelby Jean. You just give him time. Wesley will come around. He's just real stuck on being a hard ass."

Shelby grinned as Bella put the luxury automobile into drive. She couldn't help but show her surprise as she ran her hand over the leather interior.

"Too much?" Bella winked.

"No way. I don't think there's such a thing as too much." Shelby laughed. "I just had no idea."

"My husband did *real* good by me, may he rest in peace." Bella smiled.

The church was filled, and for Shelby it was a relief to be there just for the pleasure and not for any painful sadness. Everyone greeted her so kindly and welcomed her into the congregation. She found herself looking forward to what would happen during the service. That was a first. Shelby felt like she was having a lot of firsts. Something was surely different in her head and her heart and she opened up to the homespun people in the pews and listened intently to the sermon.

"He's got that all wrong," she leaned over and whispered in Bella's ear.

Bella responded in a soft rasp, "Hon, Reverend Parsons hasn't gotten anything right in thirty years, but he has good intentions." She smiled at Shelby and squeezed her hand.

There was exuberant singing of hymns, and the choir was actually pretty good. But Shelby found she was glad when the hour was over and Bella led her out onto the steps where people were gathering to meet and greet.

"Ms. Shelby Jean, it is so good to see you here. Your grandmother would be so proud! And how are you doin'? I heard about that awful accident. The Lord's angels must have been watchin' over you. You look fit as a fiddle!" Reverend Parsons smiled at her and she smiled back.

"I do feel good, Reverend. Thank you for asking. I am healing so quickly. And I did enjoy your sermon. There was just that one thing that you…"

Bella grabbed Shelby by the elbow and pulled her away. "We gotta run, Reverend. Shelby's gonna go through Martha's things today. Big day. Bye bye now!" Bella waved as they moved down the front steps of the church.

"Bella, what's the rush? I just wanted to point out to him that he just wasn't right in what he was sayin'."

"Girl, you never tell the minister he ain't right. Talk about sacrilege. He'll have you hung up by your toes in the town square." She grinned at Shelby and then softened her tone. "Just kiddin', hon, we ain't that barbaric. But I just think you should understand that the Reverend has been pourin' out the same dribble for a very long time, and I don't think he's gonna be too willin' to change his thinkin' at this stage of the game. He believes he's right, and I think it's best that we don't worry him none. You'll have to wait 'til he retires to get real inspiration in this church. But there's no harm done. Nobody listens to him anyway.

"Hi, John, George, Betty!" Bella changed the subject and her direction as she greeted various people standing on the church steps. Each one wanted to wish Shelby well after her accident, and shared their condolences again about her grandmother. Some of them asked about Wesley. Everyone was obviously interested in this beautiful woman who had dropped in from another world, but looked so much like her mother. The small crowd kept growing and would have held Shelby there an hour had Bella not kept moving down the steps to the sidewalk. They were finally waving goodbye and almost to their car.

"Bella? Is that Shelby Jean you have with you?" A thin woman with a deeply lined face and grayish pallor to her complexion approached them on the sidewalk.

"Hello, Rita. Yeah, this is Neely's girl. Shelby, this here is Rita Reddinger. She works at the library. She was a good friend of your grandma's."

"How do you do, Rita." Shelby put out her hand and Rita took it. Shelby jumped in reaction to what felt like a violent wave of nausea. A painful stabbing sensation rocked her abdomen and she dropped Rita's hand like it was on fire. Shelby swayed dizzily against Bella. Then she steadied herself and looked into Rita's red-rimmed eyes. She saw a shocked expression cross the older woman's gaunt face. The two women stared at each other in stunned silence until Bella jumped in.

"Well, you take care now, Rita, and we'll be seein' you." She turned to Shelby. "Come on, hon, we better get goin'. We have a lot to do." She pulled a mute Shelby toward the Mercedes and unlocked the car doors.

"Okay, what the heck was that?" Bella was driving at a snail's pace looking at Shelby who hadn't said a word.

"I don't know what the heck that was." Shelby was staring at her hand. It looked quite ordinary. Not burned, not pink, just her hand. "Bella, that woman, Rita, is she sick?"

"Yeah, hon, she's real sick. The doctors don't give her too much longer. Ovarian cancer. How did you know?"

"I think I just felt it."

Bella gaped at her passenger and then turned her attention back to the road. The two drove on in silence. Shelby tried to shake off the unnerving thoughts she was having as they passed through the small town of Sorry's Run. She couldn't help but notice the mostly empty store fronts and even some boarded-up windows. It might have been a thriving little community at one time, but now it reflected the same sad story that most of small-town America was experiencing. At least there was the coffee shop and library and a few second-hand stores. And large maple trees still lined the sidewalks, lending shaded charm to the old buildings. *Note to self: Sorry's Run could use some financial help.*

"Bella, do you know anything about bringing real estate developers into an area?"

Bella looked surprised at Shelby for changing the subject so drastically. But then she followed her gaze out the car windows.

"Well, I just might. My husband, Jared, had a few cronies with deep pockets. I just never thought about it."

"Well, maybe we should think about it. If we put our heads together maybe we could bring this little town back."

Bella smiled, and answered, "Well, maybe we just could. Your grandmother would like that."

A couple miles out of town Bella made a right turn onto a paved lane that led toward the river. A short gravel drive hooked off to the left and at the end of it sat a mobile home. They parked and Shelby stared for a moment before she got out of the car. She hadn't seen it in a long time, and she was astonished at the beauty her grandmother had created. The area around the trailer was carefully landscaped and maintained and there was a small bed of lilies to one side of a brick sidewalk that led to steps and a small deck. Shelby felt her throat tighten.

"It's so pretty, Bella. Prettier than I remembered." Then she pointed to the paved lane. "And where does that lead to? I don't remember that little road?"

"It goes on back to Sorina's." Bella saw the question about to form on Shelby's lips. "We'll get to that later, hon."

As if on cue, the door to the trailer opened. "Hey, y'all, I was beginnin' to think y'all got kidnapped or somethin' worse." Jolene was standing in the doorway dressed in jeans and a T-shirt with an apron tied around her waist. Wiping her hands on the apron, she hugged them both and waved them inside. She shut the door behind them and Shelby found herself in her grandmother's small but personally unique world.

It was so feminine. Much of the color scheme was layered in different shades of green, ranging from forest to soft limes. It made Shelby think of an indoor garden. Watercolor paintings, mostly of Irish landscapes, dominated the wall space, and crocheted lace doilies lay over two overstuffed chairs and a sofa covered in a leafy green slip cover. There was no visible television or computer and scented candles were everywhere. The kitchen was done in a soft pale yellow and the counter space was filled with every kitchen gadget imaginable. Martha had been a famous cook. Shelby smiled as she took her time and looked around, letting her hands reverently glide over her grandmother's things.

"Isn't this just the prettiest place, Shelby Jean?" Jolene smiled as she pulled chocolate chip cookies from the oven. The smell was intoxicating and added to the soothing ambiance.

"Anybody home?" Violet opened the door and peeked in.

Bella answered, "Sure, hon, we're all here. Come on in. Shelby is gettin' a look 'round. Have a cookie. Jolene has outdone herself." Bella was taking the cookies from the baking pan and piling them onto a stoneware platter. She placed the loaded plate down on the coffee table. "Who wants coffee?"

"Not me. I'll take some wine if Martha's got any?" Violet asked and raised an eyebrow. Bella and Jolene exchanged surprised glances and grinned.

"Well, alrighty then!" Bella clapped her hands together. "We'll join you. Nobody drinks alone in Martha's house." Bella opened the refrigerator and found a cold bottle of Pinot Grigio next to a gallon jug of a Carlo Rossi red. She looked up in gratitude. "Thank you, Mart." Popping the cork, she poured four glasses of the white wine. "Here, Shelby, hon, have a little grape juice."

Shelby had just come out of the bedroom. She had tears in her eyes. "Thanks. I think I could use a glass of wine."

"Come on, sweetheart, sit down." Bella patted the cushion next to her on the sofa. "We have all the time in the world and Martha would like us bein' here like this together. I never knew Martha to drink Pinot Grigio. I think this was meant for you," she said and winked. "And this is for you, too." She handed Shelby what appeared to be a legal document. "It's your grandmother's Last Will and Testament. And don't worry, hon, there's no surprises there. Just like I told you, anything you find is yours to keep."

Shelby took the Will and sat down next to Bella on the sofa. Jolene and Violet sat across from them in the chairs. Shelby stared at the papers, and stuck them in her purse without reading what was written there. Instead, she looked at the women who were her grandmother's closest friends, and asked, "Bella, propose a toast?"

"Well, sure thing!" Bella responded enthusiastically and raised her glass.

"Here's to Martha Maggie McBride. And here's to you, Shelby Jean. May you find joy in her things that you discover here, and may it keep her close to you forever. She loved you so much," Bella's voice caught in her throat.

"Here! Here!"

They all took a drink.

Bella added, "You know, Shelby, your grandmother always hoped you would spend some time with her here. I think it was in her plans when she asked you to come. She knew we could all handle Wesley, but I wonder that she didn't have a feelin' that her time was comin' and she wanted some of that precious time with you."

"Really? That would explain things, because I didn't understand why she was so insistent that I come. She just kept saying she was too old to care for him. But after I saw how you all kicked in, I knew that I was never really needed."

"Oh, hon, you was needed, all right. Just not for Wesley. Although, it's true that cantankerous man is not gettin' any better. And he won't do a darn thing to help his own self," Violet raised her voice in disgust, and then took a deep drink from her glass.

CHAPTER THIRTEEN
REMINISCING

SHELBY STUDIED THE THREE WOMEN who had come to her rescue so often in such a short period of time. She had made a point to get to know them better and they were fast becoming her friends. Her initial impressions of them had been so wrong. When she first came back to Kentucky everybody just looked like country hicks to her, but now she could see that wasn't at all true. The three women sitting around her were younger than Grandma Mart had been. Shelby guessed their ages to be either late 50s or early 60s.

Jolene had streaked reddish hair that hung in waves past her shoulders. She was very petite and had pretty features, with a rosebud mouth and laughing hazel eyes. She lived the farthest out in the country. She had a charming down-home accent and naïve mannerisms, giving her an authentic sweetness. Shelby imagined Jolene had never been too far away from the hills. Her husband was a farmer and her kids were grown. She doted on her pet beagles.

Violet had lived in Lexington for twenty years and came back home to Greenup County when her husband died. She was spunky and seemed just a bit pissed off at the world, though she laughed easily. Violet's name suited her because her eyes were an unusual shade of deep blue. She looked older than the other two, and her hair was silvery white and cropped short. She was never without her round wire-rimmed glasses and always wore flowing blouses to hide the bulges around her waist and hips.

Bella was the dominant personality with her keen wit and sassy humor, and hipper fashions. The three of them together were a perfect combination. Shelby could imagine the fun they all had had with her grandmother. Far from being *hicks,* they were funny, intelligent southern women, each with her own unique sense of style. Shelby couldn't help but notice they all wore striking jewelry.

"I have to ask. Where do you ladies get your bracelets and earrings? They look like pieces designed in some New York boutique."

Laughter filled the small living room of the trailer. Violet clapped her hands together. "Whoowee. Martha would have loved that. No, hon, our bangles and baubles are Kentucky homespun right from the boutique of Martha Maggie McBride."

"Grandma Mart?"

"Sure enough," Bella answered. "She used to rent a store front in Sorry's Run and she made jewelry for years. There's plenty of it left in her drawers. All for you, if you like it."

"Like it? I love it."

"Well, let's finish this glass of wine and then we'll dig in and see what else you'll want. Jo, why don't you go get Martha's photo album from her bedroom while we're sittin' here enjoyin' these cookies."

Jolene brought out a large book overstuffed with photographs and opened it up on the coffee table. The first picture was one of a pregnant Neely. Shelby was struck by the uncanny resemblance. It could have been her standing there in front of the farmhouse with her hands placed on her swollen belly.

"See, you do look like her." Bella winked.

The next hour passed quickly as they looked at picture after picture of a young Martha, Wesley, Neely and Shelby. Violet got out the large bottle of Carlo Rossi Paisano and it was clear no work was going to get done. It was too much fun reminiscing. All the stories were so funny, and the sadness Shelby had felt was replaced with joy, knowing her grandmother had lived such a full and happy life.

"At least until the accident." It was as if Bella was reading her mind. "Your grandmother 'bout to died when that happened to Neely. But then she showed a strength that nobody coulda known she had. She pulled herself together and poured her energies into helping you and Wesley and the church."

"And then of course, there were the healings," Violet added.

"Healings?" Shelby's interest piqued.

Jolene spoke softly in a respectful tone, her pretty mouth turning up in a soft smile, "Oh, yeah, hon, your grandma was truly gifted. Everybody knowed that. The things she done for folks in these parts is the stuff of legend. People loved her. Critters, too."

Silence followed for a moment, as though a hush was the only right response.

Shelby locked eyes with Bella, who was staring at her intently. Then Bella's serious expression was suddenly transformed into a bright smile and she started to giggle. "Y'all remember when the bunny rabbit followed Martha from the Babcock's after she took care of old man Henry that one really hot summer? That little thing jumped in her truck and became a permanent fixture around here. Never left Martha's side. She called him Rory. Like to drove her crazy!"

"The one with the screwed-up ear?" Violet smiled, remembering.

"Yeah, the one that Martha just couldn't fix. She decided her powers only worked on two-legged creatures after that. But that rabbit sure loved her. I think he still hangs around."

"Lord, there was raccoons, a fox, and then remember that baby goat?" Jolene laughed and slapped her thigh. "Good gravy! This place was a real menagerie for a time. Critters just found their way here and never left. They all loved your grandma. She would feed them and talk to them. Remember how she gave them each Irish names? She called them her little leprechauns. After a time, they would finally wander off, and Martha would be so relieved. But she missed those animals. Made for some hilarious stories."

Shelby shared in the laughter, but as soon as it died down she redirected the conversation. "What about my mother? Grandma Mart started to tell me about her before she died. Something about her being a witch?"

The women all looked at each other and then nodded to Bella to speak, "Yeah, hon, your mama had some special powers, too. Actually, Neely was more gifted than Martha in that way. Real sensitive to folks, if you get me. She could tell if somebody was ailin' miles away. It like to scared Wesley to death. I don't think he ever understood what was drivin' your mama's strange ways. He just knew she was always gone, sometimes all night. And folks started talkin'. There was a lot of bad talk. Neely was just too pretty, you know. And then, when she was rumored to be messin' in people's lives a lot of people got real nervous."

"Namely Wesley," Violet added.

Bella nodded and continued, "That's when Martha said the fights really started. I'm sure you remember that, Shelby, though you was only a little girl. Wesley acted like he hated Neely, even though we all knew he really loved her. He just hated what she was doin', and he wasn't even sure what it was. He heard the word witch one time down at The Pit Stop and when he come home he was pretty drunk and he nearly tore the house apart until he found her special herbs and potions that she used to make her medicines. Well, that threw him into a rage, and that night Neely took you and run off to stay here with Martha for a couple weeks."

"It was a terrible, frightenin' time," Jolene whispered.

Bella went on, her voice laced with anger, "Wesley came around here more than once, drunk, with a loaded pistol. He actually fired off a couple shots into the woods. That was when Martha had Chief Chambers arrest him. Do you remember Lucas?"

Shelby guessed, "The attractive older man in the cowboy hat?"

"The very same," Bella said and smiled. "Well, Lucas saw to it Wesley stayed in jail long enough to get sober and sorry. Neely didn't want to press charges, and after he begged and begged, she finally relented and the two of you went back to the farmhouse.

"But things was never right after that. Neely would get her bag of concoctions together and he would try to keep her from leaving the house. Of course, he couldn't. She would call Martha and bring you over here and she would go off. Then Martha would take you back home the next day to Wesley, and sometimes Neely would still be gone.

"That kind of thing went on more and more until she had the accident and her beautiful life was snuffed out. Her death really rocked Sorry's Run. And your daddy actually had the gall to be angry with you because she was goin' off to get you somethin' from the drugstore the night she was killed. Of course, as it turned out, she had stopped somewhere else that contributed more to her death."

Shelby sat up. What was this? She had never heard anything except her mother was going to the drugstore and never returned. She asked, "Bella, what are you talking about? She stopped somewhere else that night?"

"Yeah, hon, she went to the drugstore all right, but after that she stopped by Lester Johnson's place to see about his daughter. His girl was barely thirteen and pregnant and Lester was none too happy about that.

But then she got real sick and her feet swelled and Lester's wife, Jean, pleaded with Neely to stop by. You were kind of under the weather, too, that night, and Neely didn't want to be gone too long. But she stopped to look in on the young girl, and something she did or said really pissed Lester off. He hauled off and hit her in the face, bruised her cheekbone and blackened her eye. She was driving home half blind when she got hit by that truck."

"How do you know all this, Bella?"

"Lester's wife called Martha and me after she learned about Neely's accident. She wanted Lester locked up for assault, but Neely never came out of it long enough to press charges. Nobody even told Wesley what happened. Everybody knew Wesley woulda shot Lester. No doubt. They kept him from ever knowin' what went on that night. He was so ate up, he never suspected. Jean nor Lester neither one lived too long after that. The girl ran off somewheres. She didn't like the foster homes. But what her daddy had done pretty much ruined him in Sorry's Run. Folks might have been scared of Neely, but they loved her, too, and they really believed that Lester was the reason she wrecked."

Jolene added, "The Johnson's was just poor white trash. Lester didn't understand Neely's healin' ways any more than Wesley did, and he was just all bent out of shape about his daughter. We didn't think he really meant to do your mother any harm, and we like to think it was awful for him when she had the crash. He rarely came out of his house after that."

Bella said, "'Course, you know, we were all pretty backward in them days. There was no real investigation done at the accident scene, so it was determined that the trucker ran the stop sign and it was all put on him. But all in all, your mother's accident affected many folks. Just such a tragedy."

"So it wasn't my fault?" Shelby's voice was a whisper.

"No, hon, it was never your fault. None of it was. It was Wesley's fault for puttin' that on you. And you just a sweet child." Jolene reached out and touched Shelby's cheek in a soft caress.

Shelby shuddered as the relieving knowledge settled in. She had prided herself on putting those days of her childhood behind her, but there had always been a nagging doubt that she had had something to do with her mother's death, that she was somehow bad. When she grew old enough to understand, she knew that Wesley's anger at her was misdirected. But when she was eleven it felt like the end of the world, losing her beautiful mother, and left with her father's unbridled anger. It hurt her. She internalized all of it, and grew strong in spite of it. But now she knew that her mother's fate would have been much different had she not made that second stop.

The women watched Shelby intently. They knew what this information meant to her.

Jolene added, "We figured Martha would tell you, hon. But she didn't. She probably knew Wesley would get wind of it, and it would put y'all in danger. Then, after years passed, she felt it best to just let sleepin' dogs lie."

"She was probably right." Violet nodded. "Wesley wasn't right in his head. He was just ate up with grief for the longest time, and everybody knew then how much he had really loved Neely."

Bella took Shelby's hand and squeezed gently. "She was just too powerful a life force for this little town, Shelby. We all think that's why she was taken so soon."

"What about Grandma Mart? She had the gift, too. Why did Wesley and the town take to her so easily?"

Bella continued, "Your grandma was different. She had a way about her that was calmin' to folks and they thought of her more like a country doctor than a witch, you know? She wasn't so young and pretty, and they were all more comfortable with her. And they liked the way she used her Irish ancestry in her healings. Called herself a faerie doctor. Who could not like that? Talk about warm and fuzzy. And of course she loved the church, so that made all the difference.

"And Wesley had always liked her. Martha was funny, Shelby. She was the only one who could make that man laugh. So she put people at ease and made them feel better, body and soul. But Neely? Well, her powers were too intense and folks wondered if it wasn't the devil workin' through her. They might need her, but they were a little scared of her."

"So when Mom was killed, why didn't I come here to live with Grandma Mart?"

Bella answered, "That was Martha's decision, hon. She believed that Wesley needed you, though he seemed so hateful. But Martha never really saw him as hateful. She always had faith that Wesley could be redeemed. It was the Christian in her. And she didn't want to put him through losing you right after he had lost Neely. She hoped his love for you would soften him and ease his grief.

"So she just stayed totally involved in your lives. She was over at your house all the time, keeping a watchful eye on you. And if she couldn't be there, Lucas Chambers would drop in on Wesley for a cup of coffee. He did that for Martha, just to be sure you were safe. You should remember Luke, Shelby. He was at your house a lot."

"You know, the more I think about it, I do remember him. I was usually upstairs when he would come in, but I can recall looking down the steps and seeing these pointy cowboy boots walking into the kitchen." Shelby remembered the card the Chief had given her at Martha's funeral. A REALLY GOOD GUY. She felt ashamed that she hadn't recognized him.

Bella continued, "That's right. He always took his hat off, but never his boots." Bella giggled and then sighed. "Martha tried so hard to convince Wesley to give up his anger and be a better father. But as it turned out, his heart was just shut up tighter than a drum. It was good that you got out when you did, Shelby. Your mother should have left, too."

"And you, Shelby Jean, what about you? You think you got the knowin', too?" Jolene asked.

"The knowing?"

"Yeah, hon, passed down from your mama and grandmother. Do you think so?"

"I don't know about that, Jolene. I only know I feel different since the accident. It's hard to explain. I always loved Grandma Mart's stories about the fairies and how the magic of the Green Isle was in our blood. I loved those stories. Even when she spoke of the death fairy, the awful Banshee, I was frightened. But it fascinated me, too. I just never felt the stories, felt the truth of them. Until now."

The women exchanged discreet glances.

Violet smiled and said, "It's time for you to meet Sorina."

"Sorina?"

"A friend of Martha's who moved here some twenty years ago. She's the sweetest lady and she thinks she's a reincarnation of the woman who founded Sorry's Run. She took her name. She lives behind here. It's the most charmin' place." Violet winked.

"That's where the paved lane leads?"

Violet nodded.

"Wait a minute? Not the old cabin where Grandma Mart lived when she was little? Hell, that's just a shell. Nobody could live there." Shelby felt her breath catch in her throat.

"It's not a shell anymore," Violet responded and reached over to the magazine rack by the sofa. She pulled out a worn issue of "Better Homes & Gardens" and leafed through its pages to a dog-eared picture of a quaint Irish cottage. She showed the picture to Shelby and added, "Here's the way it looks now."

Shock pulled at Shelby's features. "No way?! You're kidding me, right? I mean, I never heard anything about Grandma Mart fixing that cabin up."

Bella answered, "I think your grandmother wanted to surprise you, Shelby. Anyway, she didn't think you'd ever move from New York back to Kentucky. Her intention was for Sorina to live there as long as she would want to." Bella smiled and added, "But hon, one day it will be yours. You'll find it spelled out there in her Will."

Shelby's head was spinning. "How in the world…" She stopped in mid sentence. The three women nodded, reading her mind.

Bella went on, explaining, "All that money you sent her over the years, that, along with some grant money, built the cottage that is there now. I had to pull a few strings to keep the county from insistin' that it be historically preserved. Otherwise, Martha would have never had her Irish cottage. But it all worked out. They settled for a plaque out front."

"And you say this Sorina that lives there now thinks she's the reincarnated abolitionist, Sorina Duncan McBride?"

Bella replied, "In this case, reincarnated is not quite accurate. Most of the time she thinks she IS Sorina Duncan McBride."

"All right. You guys are losing me now."

"Oh, good gravy, Bella. Are you gonna tell her all that? It's just too weird for words." Jolene's pretty hazel eyes were popping.

"Well, hell, it is what it is. Shelby, do you want to hear all this, or should we keep our old biddy mouths shut?" Bella asked.

"Hey, you can't leave me hanging now. All I knew was that Grandma Mart lived in the cabin for a short while when she was young. It was almost burned to the ground once, I think, wasn't it? When I was little, I used to play back there when I thought nobody knew. The only thing left of the place was a lot of rubble and a stone fireplace. I remember Wesley found me one time climbing on the bricks, and man, did I get a lashing. He said it was way too dangerous. And truly, I loved playing there because it was like a construction zone."

Bella added, "And nobody ever cleaned it up because your grandmother wouldn't let them. The county was always hasslin' her about it bein' important to the community to preserve. They were tryin' to go all "public domain" on her, and I had to pull a few *more* strings because Martha was just real clear about leavin' it alone. She always said it had another purpose that it was gonna fulfill one day."

Shelby jumped in, "Yeah, like being a part of the Underground Railroad wasn't enough? And I knew that Sorina Duncan was married to a McBride, so we're some kind of distant relations. I assumed that's why Grandma lived here. Of course, Grandma could never explain how we were related exactly. She would just laugh and say in those days there were a lot of cousins marrying cousins and it was impossible to trace the ancestry. I mean, it was like a joke, but it was fun to think we were descendants of the pioneer woman who founded Sorry's Run. I really just never asked too much and nobody ever talked about all that ancient history. But now you say this woman believes she is the pioneer woman, Sorina Duncan McBride?"

Bella picked up the story and said, "Yep. And none of us disputes it. It's too fascinatin' and it keeps this little neck of the woods all stirred up in intrigue. I don't know how much of the ancient history you know, but Sorina Duncan was rumored to be an ancestor of a Scottish woman named Gillis Duncan, who was known for her healin' abilities, but confessed, under torture, to bein' a witch.

"The story goes that Sorina came here with her Irish husband, Gerald McBride, who got himself killed in some drunken squabble, and all by her lonesome she took on helpin' slaves escape into Ohio as part of the Underground Railroad. The witch part had followed her here to Kentucky, of course, and most God-fearin' folks stayed cleared of her, makin' it possible for her to become an active abolitionist. There's mention of her in our local history books.

"Most folks in the county figure our Sorina is just a tad touched because she likes to imagine sometimes that she's channelin' the real

Sorina. She does good things for folks around here, so they let her be. She and Martha were real close. Martha fed the Irish folklore to her and it mixed in pretty perfectly with Sorina's Scottish healer notions. So whatever fantasy she wants to live with, we figure it's okay. She's a powerful person in her own right, and there's a few of us that visit with her regularly and have come to love her. You will, too."

"Where does she come from, Bella? What's her story? I don't get it."

Bella sighed. "That's the real interestin' part. Nobody knows. Martha brought her here from Ohio a long time ago, and she was a real mental case with total amnesia. You know your grandmother—always doin' good for some poor unfortunate. Well, apparently, this Sorina needed help and she was lucky enough to cross paths with Martha McBride. I helped Martha get the permits and contractors she needed and she got her dream cottage built. Sorina's been there now for years. A sweet young woman named Jessie stays with her and tends to the place. It's worked out just beautiful."

The older women's eyes locked before Violet went on to say, "Shelby, we were all just crazy with this not knowin' stuff. But Martha would not tell us. She said it was up to Sorina to tell her story if and when she remembered it. We were all instructed to let it be and not harass Sorina about her past, Jessie neither. Well, comin' from Martha, that was 'nuff said."

Bella finished, "And truly, she is the most wonderful, loveable woman. We all figure she can be whoever she wants. We're just glad to have her."

"And she stays living in the past?" Shelby couldn't imagine.

Bella smiled. "It's not as bad as all that. She knows what goes on and she is of her right mind most of the time. I think she just likes to think pioneer woman thoughts in her head. It makes her happy."

"Lord, I wish I could be somebody else most of the time. What an escape." Jolene giggled.

"Well, this Carlo Rossi is the next best thing. We thank you again, Martha." Bella laughed and lifted her glass before finishing her drink. "Okay. I think that's enough information for one afternoon. My head is startin' to hurt. I can't imagine how you feel, Shelby. Come on, hon, let's show you that boutique jewelry."

CHAPTER FOURTEEN
TREASURE CHEST

BELLA LAUGHED. "IT'S A GOOD THING I know Greenup County's finest. I doubt they'd approve," Bella was slurring her words slightly as she drove. "I can't believe we spent the whole day just gabbin' and raidin' Martha's refrigerator and cupboards. And, Shelby, I know we didn't get a darn thing done like we planned. But Violet, Jolene and I haven't spent an entire day together in so long. Just goofin' off felt so perfect. I hope us old biddies didn't bore you to death?"

"Seriously, Bella? I've got a great buzz. And nothing about the stories was boring. It's going to take me days to think about everything you guys told me. It's like a whole other world is opening up to me, you know? I don't even care that we didn't get to any packing. At least now I have an idea of things that I want to keep." Shelby hiccupped and continued, "What happens with the trailer? Will the church rent it or sell it?"

"No, sweetie, not likely. I own that trailer." Bella grinned as she steered the Mercedes back through town. "I put it there for Martha when she started work on the cottage. She had been renting an apartment above her shop, but she wanted to be closer to watch the renovation. No, you can take your good old time decidin' what things you want. I have no desire to rent it to anyone else. As far as I am concerned, it will always be Martha's place. And whatever is there, Shelby, like I said, is all yours. But hey, not to change the subject, but it's really been eatin' at me. I just gotta know. What was it about the minister's sermon this mornin' that you didn't agree with?"

"Oh, it was nothing, Bella. I shouldn't have said anything. I was just being sentimental. It was something that Grandma Mart told me. She thought Jesus was never really tested in the desert by the devil. She had this belief that he was there to reason with Satan, to try to bring him back to being an angel; that Jesus knew that through God it was always possible to turn evil into good; that we should always try. She said Jesus was clear about his mission on earth and that the devil never held any sway over him."

"Well, that sounds like Martha. She never would give into the dark side. I think it's why she tolerated Wesley like she did. She had faith that he would turn one day towards the light. But what about the forty days and forty nights? Did she not believe that Jesus really fasted for that time?"

"She did, but she thought that just proved his resolve, and that denying himself food lifted his spirit from the flesh. She would look at me and say, 'Shelby Jean, don't worry about Jesus goin' hungry. He was only dietin'." Shelby looked over at Bella and her eyes got large and then they both burst out laughing.

"God, your grandmother was a piece of work. We are gonna miss her so much. So maybe she was there in spirit with us today when the Reverend was quotin' the book of Matthew."

"I think you might be right. I mean, I have no idea why I wanted to argue the point. What I know about the Bible is next to nothing."

"But it is true that your grandmother knew hers. She loved her verses. But you know, Shelby, more than once I saw Martha reading the Good Book and just shakin' her head, like she didn't agree with what was written there. I never knew, though. We steered clear of any intellectual, theological discussions since I'm pretty much an airhead. Even so, Martha believed in her own healin' powers, and there aren't too many places for that in our church doctrine, I don't guess. And between you and me, she leaned a little too far toward the pagan ways." Bella winked.

"Well, I'm convinced Grandma Mart was speaking through me today to the pastor. She probably wanted to get the last word in," Shelby said, thinking how her comment to Reverend Parsons had felt like an idea plucked from thin air. "Yeah, I think Grandma Mart was hanging around today."

Bella dropped Shelby off, and the farmhouse was dark when she went inside. She could hear snoring coming from Wesley's bedroom. She turned on the kitchen light and poured herself another glass of wine from a box on the counter. "Not bad." She smiled after taking a sip. Box wine. She would never have gone there in New York. Oh well, *you can take the girl out of Kentucky, but you can't take Kentucky out of the girl.*

Shelby turned to go upstairs, but she noticed the door that led to the basement was ajar. She remembered the colorful box that had stood out like a shining jewel against the dull, gray walls. Flipping the switch to the light above the basement stairs, she was careful with her steps as she climbed down. She went quietly, not wanting to wake Wesley. She got downstairs and found the string to pull on the single bulb over the washer and dryer. It shed enough light to see it. The box sat on cinder blocks far enough out from the wall to protect it from leaky cracks. It was pale yellow and trimmed in green leafy vines. Red and purple flowers decorated the lid, and a gold clasp held it closed. Shelby picked it up and was surprised at its hefty weight. She shook it slightly and something rattled inside. Flipping the gold clasp back, she opened the box, bringing it over to the washer where she could see it better. She sat it down.

The box was full of jewelry, much like the bracelets and earrings Martha's friends had worn. Shelby grinned and scooped up what looked like a pirate's bounty. Her grandmother's designs dripped through her fingers and felt like real jewels. It gave Shelby such a thrill as she held the different pieces up to the light. It was all so beautiful, and much of it was crafted with onyx and turquoise and crystals and intricate etchings on brushed metals. Colorful gemstones and glass beads picked up the light. Each piece was a work of art.

Why in the world would she keep her gorgeous jewelry stuck away down here, she wondered? "Whatever, Grandma Mart. You're coming with me." She closed the lid and turned off the lights as she quietly went back upstairs.

The next morning, Shelby awoke to rumblings coming from the kitchen below. She looked at the clock. 7:30. *Wesley's up early.* She stretched and smiled when she saw her grandmother's jewelry box sitting on the stand by the bed. What a treasure chest it was. She got up and pulled on a robe before looking out her windows at the hills. Everything was so green and misty in the early morning dampness. Shelby felt excited somehow, anticipating the day, though she had nothing planned. She would have to call Caitlin and tell her about the jewelry. It would be such a splash in New York if she ever wanted to part with it. But right now that was inconceivable. She yawned and stretched again before going downstairs.

Surprisingly, the kitchen was empty. *That's strange. I could have sworn*

I just heard Wesley banging the cupboard doors. She walked over and got herself a mug and was pouring a cup of coffee when she heard him come in. He stood in the doorway of the kitchen and there was a cold, steely look in his eyes. It frightened Shelby.

"Morning, Wesley. How are you?"

But she could see for herself. It was frankly amazing. He not only looked years younger since she had given him the haircut, but he was standing straighter and wasn't using his walker. And he wasn't coughing.

"I want you outta here."

His voice was like ice, stinging her ears. She said nothing in response.

"You hear me girl? I want you outta here now!"

Russell carried Shelby's bags into the trailer and sat them down inside the door.

"Thank you, Russell. You are such a good friend to help me like this on such short notice."

"No problem at all, Shelby. I just don't understand."

"He just threw me out. Plain and simple. I think his exact words were, 'I want you outta here.' So I called Bella and she, Vi and Jo are gonna look in on him. She said I could move into Grandma Mart's and stay as long as I want to."

"But why, Shelby? I thought you two were getting along?"

"I thought so, too, so I don't know. Oh, well, fuck him. Who needs it."

"So are you flying home to New York?"

"Not yet, Russell. I want to take some time and really go through everything in the trailer. And I don't know why, but I just don't want to leave. Maybe it's because that's exactly what Wesley wants." She faked a smile as she sat down on the couch and looked around. "Does this place make you think of an indoor garden?"

"Yeah, Martha loved her green. She said it was the Irish in her. Then she would laugh and say, 'either that, or it just makes me feel like Mother Nature.'" He grinned. "It is soothing, isn't it."

"Very. I feel better already. And you know what, I think I'm going to stretch out here on the couch and nap. Suddenly I am so sleepy."

"Okay, Shelby. I'll get to work. But since you are sticking around for a while longer, you're going to need transportation. You know, of course, that Martha's pickup was totaled in your accident."

"That's true." Shelby felt a twinge of guilt.

"It's no big deal. It wasn't worth much, and it was yours anyway. But your grandmother did have a small life insurance policy that she took out years ago. You're the beneficiary. Would you like to put a down payment on a new car?"

Shelby thought for a second and then grinned at him. "I think another truck would be about right. You pick it out."

Russell smiled back at her and saluted as he opened the door to leave. "A suitable truck for the lady, it is. I'll be in touch. You call if you want or need anything. I'm here, Shelby."

She blew him a kiss and he was gone. Shelby laid her head back on the pillow of the couch and thought about what had just happened with Wesley. She stared at the jewelry box she had brought with her. "Grandma Mart, what did I do wrong?" She closed her eyes and like a clear spoken voice it came to her.

"*You cured him.*"

CHAPTER FIFTEEN
SORINA

"CAITLIN, I JUST CAN'T COME HOME yet. There is unfinished business here. It's hard to explain. Hell, I don't understand it myself."

"Then I'm coming there. Is there room for me in the trailer?"

"Sure. There's a couch, or you can always sleep with me."

"Hummm. Well, not that that doesn't sound enticing, but I might have to settle for a motel. They do have those there, don't they?" She laughed. "At any rate, I'm coming. You're starting to worry me."

"No, no, don't worry. I'm good. But yeah, I think you should come. Things are changing for me, Cait. I don't know what it means yet, but since the accident I have this feeling that I'm meant to be here, to do something. I don't know. It sounds crazy, but then I am my mother's daughter after all. But you come. I need you."

"Okay. I'll get a flight out tomorrow. My boss is out of the country and I can sneak off for a whole week. Tommy can cover for me if he has to. Maybe I'll ask Russell to pick me up. He's always in Ashland, isn't he? That's on the way to the Huntington airport, right?"

"Oh, I get it! Worried about me, my ass. You just want to see that hunky guy again! And yes, I have no doubt he would be tickled pink to pick you up. Just give him a call."

"Shelby Jean, you are one twisted chick." Caitlin laughed. "I am hanging up, but I will see you tomorrow."

"Bye Cait."

"Bye, Shel."

Shelby smiled and turned off her cell. She was glad Caitlin was coming. She did need her. Shelby rolled over onto her side and got comfortable.

Images of Wesley fell away from her conscious thoughts and a peaceful sleep overtook her once again.

Scratch, scratch, scratch, scratch. "What the..." Shelby woke to something clawing at the door. It scared her and she jumped up from the couch. *Ouch! Not quite a hundred percent yet, Shelby.* She held onto her stomach and listened. There it was again, only faster, like whatever was on the other side was getting frantic to be let in. Shelby immediately thought of the stories of the various country critters that always found their way to her grandmother's door. There was no peep hole. She pounded on the door from the inside. "Go away! Git!" She pounded again. "Go away!" The scratching stopped.

She unlocked the door and carefully opened it just a crack. There on the deck was a small brown rabbit. It saw her and she saw it as it ran down the steps and onto the ground. It stopped then and just stared up at her, like it was waiting. Shelby laughed out loud and opened the door fully, stepping outside. Other than twitching his whiskers, the rabbit didn't move. "You're a forward little guy?" The animal cocked its head as though it were listening and jumped away from the trailer. Then it stopped, stood up on its haunches and looked back at her like it was waiting.

Shelby noticed its mangled left ear. "Oh, my god, are you Grandma Mart's little bunny rabbit? Are you Rory? You want me to come? What is this, a Disney movie? *More like Brothers Grimm, probably.* Well, okay then." Shelby shut the door behind her and followed the rabbit. It kept pace with her, never running away, and always looking back to see that she was following. Shelby threw caution to the wind, and let the rabbit take the lead as it turned from the gravel drive. Instead of heading for the paved lane, it took her into the woods behind the trailer. Following Rory, Shelby had the strangest feeling of total abandon, like she was a child again. *Just like Alice going through the rabbit hole.* Her spirit soared and she sensed light-headedness akin to sheer joy as she allowed herself to be led.

Being on foot, the woods appeared thicker to Shelby, like the trees were rooted together, with a canopy of deep-green leafy tops reaching up to nestle an azure sky. It was so enticing and mysterious and quiet.

So quiet.

She found herself slowing down, almost tip-toeing at times so as not to disturb the trees. More than once she stopped to look around her, marveling at the organic feel and smell of the woods. Every time she stopped, the rabbit stopped up ahead of her. Shelby got playful, moving from side to side and watching the animal follow her with its darting eyes, only to wait patiently for her to settle down and continue on. "Okay, little guy. Lead on."

Shelby stepped over a fallen tree trunk, but then tripped over a tangled root on the other side of it that was buried underneath the leaves. She caught herself just before landing face down on the ground. Once again, she was made aware that she had had a surgery not that long ago. It was enough to pull her back from her happy place. She hadn't been paying attention and now she wasn't even sure which way they had come.

Turning around to get her bearings, Shelby suddenly felt disoriented. Everything looked the same. It occurred to her she should have left a trail to follow back. "Well, this is just stupid, but I think I could get really lost in here." She spoke the words as a chill ran over her, and her carefree feelings took a further dive. She felt for the cell phone in her pocket. *No service.* "Great. Okay. I guess I better just forget this. Sorry, little bunny, but our stroll is over. I'm going back to civilization before I get myself in real trouble. Now let's see. Come on, Shelby, think." She looked overhead at the tall birches clustered together. "I think it was this way, Rory." The rabbit didn't move. "Or maybe this way?" She did a full circle.

Just then, a surprisingly strong breeze blew through the woods, bending the birches and lower branches of the sycamores enough to reveal a small dwelling up ahead. It blended so perfectly with its surroundings that she had to squint to be sure she saw what she thought she saw. Rory looked at her and then darted off in that direction. Shelby followed, finding a worn path that led her to the most charming cottage she had ever laid eyes on.

"No way," she whispered in awe. She was looking at an exact replica of the picture Violet had shown her. It was a small, two-story stone cottage, four windows stacked in the front, with dense ivy covering most of one wall and a large stone chimney dominating the other. But it was the thatched hipped roof that took her breath. "Okay, now I know I'm losing it. This *is* a fairytale!" She half expected Hansel and Gretel to come bouncing out of the front door.

The rabbit turned and looked at her one last time before rounding the side of the cottage and disappearing from sight. Shelby moved closer to the house and observed a plaque embedded in the stone: "HOME OF SORINA DUNCAN MCBRIDE, A FRIEND TO FREEDOM." CIRCA 1848.

Sorina's house.

Shelby saw the paved drive at the side of the cottage that apparently led back to US 23 and past Martha's trailer. The rabbit had brought her through the woods as a shortcut. She knew she was being rude, coming uninvited and unannounced, but Shelby felt she had been summoned to appear. Otherwise, why had the rabbit gone to such trouble to bring her?

If I see a Cheshire cat, I'm certifiable.

She walked to the side of the cottage and around the back where again she had to catch her breath. *Talk about fantasies!* It was like a dream. Intricately landscaped gardens of wildflowers and tall grasses were laid out in geometric patterns surrounding a wooden grape arbor that sheltered two wicker rocking chairs. Farther back from the house a small, glassed-in, cedar greenhouse contained rows of early vegetable plantings. A large yellow cat was curled up, asleep on a tree stump. *Thank God he's not grinning at me.* Shelby giggled, thrilling at the lovely landscape. A goat was munching on grass next to a chicken coop populated with colorful designer hens and a fat rooster. Just beyond the sycamore trees in the back, the Ohio River could be seen shimmering through the leaves.

Two squirrels scurried in front of her, nearly causing her to stumble. This time she laughed out loud. *When did Kentucky get so beautiful*? She felt a keen sense of home.

"Howdy."

Shelby turned to see a petite woman leaning into a cane looking out from a screened-in porch. Round, amber sunglasses sat on her pert nose and a wide-brimmed hat covered her graying blonde hair that fell to her shoulders in thick, coarse waves.

"Can I be of help?" The woman opened the door and carefully plodded her way down the steps and out into the yard.

Shelby felt ashamed at her rudeness. "My goodness, I apologize. I was just taking a walk and came upon this wonderful place. Would you be Sorina, by any chance?"

"I would indeed. And you are?"

"Shelby Jean Stiller. My Grandma Mart lived in the trailer at the end of your lane."

"Martha's granddaughter? Well, my, my. Please, girl, come in and share some tea with us. We should get acquainted." Sorina turned and raised her voice, "Jessie!"

A slender, doe-eyed young woman came out from behind the trees.

"We have a visitor, hon."

Jessie pulled off her gardening gloves and joined them. She nodded to Shelby without making eye contact and then took Sorina's free hand and walked alongside her, as Sorina supported herself with the cane in her other hand. Shelby watched Sorina walk, bent just slightly into her cane. Her narrow hips seemed to be dislocated, giving her an uneven gait. Shelby followed the women back through the screened-in porch to the backdoor.

Once inside, her heart pounded as she looked about her. She was indeed in a fairytale. The cottage was decorated with charming antiques and painted rural Kentucky scenes on the walls. Hand-woven area rugs lay on gleaming hardwood floors. The rough, stuccoed walls were painted in cream and trimmed in cool shades of green. Wood and stone were prominent throughout the rustic décor.

Shelby followed Sorina and Jessie into the largest room. The ceiling was low and heavy-beamed, with a stone fireplace dominating the far wall. There was a long wooden table set out with painted coffee cups and pewter plates and flatware, as if a guest was expected. Shelby felt as though she had stepped into another century.

"Here, Shelby, sit yourself down. Jessie will bring us some tea and crackers."

Shelby did as she was told and sat across from the striking woman who had a mysterious air about her. She said nothing as they sat, only smiled and nodded. She removed her hat, but didn't remove her sunglasses. She sat her cane aside, propping it against the back of her chair. Shelby studied her hostess. She was attractive, with arched light brown eyebrows, a small nose and thin lips that curved demurely when she smiled. She appeared to be in her early 50s. Her face wasn't lined with age, and appeared stretched somehow unnaturally. *Facelifts?* No way. Didn't make sense. Still, there was something different about this Sorina, and it would take more than a chance meeting to figure it out.

"Ah, there you are. Thank you so much, Jessie."

The younger woman came back into the room carrying a tray loaded with a teapot, creamer, sugar cubes, crackers and oatmeal cookies. She placed everything on the table and started to walk away, when Sorina reached out and placed her hand on her arm. "No, hon, don't go. This here is Shelby Jean Stiller, Martha's granddaughter. You sit with us and enjoy some tea."

"Shelby, I want you to meet Jessie. She is like the daughter I never had."

Shelby noticed that Sorina never moved her head, keeping her eyes aimed squarely at her guest. It was slightly unnerving and Shelby self-consciously started fidgeting, trying to avoid her hostess' steely gaze.

"Nice to meet you, Jessie."

Jessie pulled out a chair and sat down. She barely raised her eyes, appearing painfully shy. Sorina nodded and Jessie poured them each a cup of tea, politely offering Shelby cream and sugar.

After they were served, Shelby spoke, "I think a little friend of yours brought me here today." She smiled and Sorina smiled back.

"Yes? That would have to be Martha's rabbit, Rory. He's a good friend, but a bit nosy. I think he misses Martha somethin' terrible. I hope he didn't frighten you?"

"No, not really. In fact, just the opposite. I would have never thought to impose on you this way. But the little guy was pretty enticing, insisting I follow him through the woods to your cottage." Shelby smiled and took a bite of a cracker. "I think he put a spell on me."

"Yeah, Rory has that beguilin' way about him. That's for sure. Your grandmother used to say he has the spirit of the little people. A bit of a trickster."

"That sounds like Grandma Mart, imagining a rabbit to be a leprechaun."

Sorina smiled. "Martha liked communicatin' with small animals. I overheard many conversations." Sorina leaned closer. "Shelby, I was so sorry to hear of your grandmother's passing. I couldn't even bring myself to attend her funeral. I know that was weak and wrong of me. She was such a dear friend." She took a sip of tea before continuing, "In fact, that's a most amazin' understatement. Martha was my lifeline, you might say. I have felt a visceral struggle ever since she's been gone."

Silence followed. Usually Shelby could entertain any company, but she was strangely mute in this historic Kentucky home across from the table from these Sorry's Run women. She watched as Sorina and Jessie drank their tea and ate the cookies. Still, no one spoke, and still Sorina never took her eyes off Shelby. A surreal moment passed and then another until Sorina reached out her hand, gently gesturing for Shelby to take it.

Sorina's hand felt like a delicate bundle of fragile bones covered in thin, transparent skin. Her hand was warm as Shelby held it in her own. Then it grew unbearably hot as a bolt of energy transferred from hand to hand and Shelby's mind recessed from her conscious thoughts and feelings. She was acutely aware of losing herself to another scene altogether:

The stinging branches startled her over and over as they whipped at her face in heated stripes. She fought back tears and kept her hand up in useless defense as she slowed her pace.

Samuel's breathless voice commanded, "C'mon girl, move yo legs. We ain't got that far to go."

Lizbeth kept willing her body to move, but she wanted to stop. She wanted to lie down and crawl into the ground, letting the earth suck her in. She wanted to be done with it.

This awful life.

But he kept telling her there was something else, some way to live and breathe without the masser, without the whip. That there was another life that human beings lived and endured that was not just about pain. Was it possible? Could it be real? She had never seen it. Had never even really heard of it, except for the masser's house. There they done different. But though they didn't know the whip, they didn't seem any happier neither. Maybe there was no happy life. Maybe it was only in the fairytale books that she read to Masser's children. Maybe that was all there was. But she couldn't tell him that. Samuel was convinced that there was a life that was worth gettin' to, a life away from bondage, away from the masser, away from slavery.

Freedom. That was his word for it. Freedom. It was a powerful word. Just saying it aloud seemed to change the air. And that was why she kept one foot stepping in front of the other. Maybe he was right. But if he was wrong... she couldn't let herself think on that. If he was wrong the pain would be unbearable. The pain would be—their death.

"C'mon Lizbeth, c'mon. You can do it, girl, you can." He came back for her and took her hand. He pulled her then, through the night forest, through darkness and the unknown. He pulled her like he knew; like he knew there

was hope at the end of the exhausting run. How could he know that? What kept him going? She would never understand what drove him. Freedom? Even the idea of that wasn't enough now. She was a quitter. She was ready to give in. But not him. He only got angrier and angrier.

And he was determined to take her with him.

She was blind now as he pulled her on. The only sound was them smashing through the trees and breaking the twigs and crunching the land beneath them. He used his muscular forearm to protect her from the limbs and he pulled her on and on.

The air escaped Shelby's lips in a rushed hiss as she returned from wherever Sorina had taken her. Her head reeled and then settled down to a slow spin as the women dropped their hands. Jessie watched. She hadn't gone with them on their journey.

"Did you see them?"

Shelby looked into the tinted glasses of her hostess and nodded.

"Lizbeth and Samuel, you saw them?"

"Yes, Sorina, I saw them. But what exactly did I see?"

"You saw slaves, Shelby, real live slaves runnin' for their lives, runnin' for this cottage all them many years ago to cross the mighty Ohio and find their freedom. That's what you saw."

"But how?" Shelby was aware that she was trembling.

"Because you have the seein' gift. You have it, girl, the ability to see what's not visible to other people. It's more than faith. It's a bridge between this world and another; a bridge between times. You have the gift just like your grandmother had it."

"And you have it?" Shelby already knew the answer.

"Well, I have more of a feelin' gift, I think. I'm workin' on the seein' part and sometimes I think it's comin' stronger. But it's a responsibility for sure. It's not always an easy thing to be able to see or feel things that other folks can't. You know that already, don't you, Shelby? You just came to this thing, didn't you? The accident was the gateway. You just walked through." Sorina took a sip of her tea and then reached a hand toward Jessie. Jessie took it.

"Jessie, here, she don't have it, and it's a blessin'. She is always in the here and now so's to keep me from slidin' off into the other side. Right, darlin'?"

Jessie pushed her straight bangs away from her dark eyes and she nodded at Sorina, still without speaking.

"Jessie come to live with me after her parents died, and I have been so grateful for her company." Sorina smiled lovingly at the peculiar, young woman.

Finally, Jessie spoke, and it was a sweeter, higher tone than Shelby expected. "I remember you, Shelby. You were tall for bein' so young. You always seemed so smart." Her eyes shimmered moistly as she spoke and Shelby realized how pretty she was. She had to be in her 30s, of a slender, muscular build, with olive skin. Her dark brown hair was bone straight, styled in a blunt cut framing her face at her chin. She kept pushing it behind her ears in an annoyed manner. She wore no makeup and no jewelry. Nothing about her was meant to attract, but attract she would, in the right circles. Her shyness was paramount, however, even in this easy, casual setting, and Shelby could imagine she was most content being alone with Sorina and her animals.

"Jessie is my gardener. Her gift is grounded in the earth, and she is gifted indeed."

"Oh, really?" Shelby stared at the pretty young woman. She did seem vaguely familiar, but she couldn't really be sure she remembered her. *I must have had my head up my butt in school,* she thought before adding, "My roommate in New York is a horticulturist. She is coming to stay with me for a while. You two will have to meet. She will love your gardens, Jessie." The three women finished their tea. Shelby finally found herself fully relaxing as time slipped by in a void of pleasant conversation. She was feeling nearly hypnotized by the soothing voice of her hostess.

Shelby watched Sorina as she recounted funny stories about Martha. Her pretty face never crinkled in expression, and seemed too tight somehow. Again, the word stretched came to mind. And though her long, slender fingers moved gracefully with her story telling, her gaze never shifted from straight ahead. Shelby tried not to be rude by staring, but she couldn't help herself. She looked over at Jessie who had apparently noticed Shelby's distraction. Jessie seemed to be trying to communicate something with her own eyes.

Then Shelby got it.

She stared hard into the amber lenses Sorina wore and realized a light film covered her pupils. Shelby did the unthinkable, then, and placed her hand right in front of Sorina's face and waved it suddenly. Sorina didn't flinch.

She is blind.

Shock rocked her and in the next passing moments she didn't hear a word Sorina was saying. Then Sorina stopped talking. The only sound in the room was the steady ticking of the mantle clock. Her thin lips pulled back revealing small, perfect white teeth and she said, "Yes, Shelby, I am blind."

"Sorina, I'm sorry. I didn't realize."

"Don't you worry none, Shelby. There's no need to be sorry. I been this way for more years than I can remember, and it has been a blessin' as much as a curse. I see things clearer in some ways than I could with sight."

"But how? What happened to you?"

"Well, hon, we'll save that for another time. There is only so much information that needs to be shared at a time. And time, we have lots of. You will come and visit me again?"

Shelby knew she was being dismissed, and Sorina suddenly looked tired.

"Of course. We are neighbors, after all. I'll be staying at Grandma Mart's place for a while. I'll be back many times."

"Well, that's good, because we are gonna be close, you and I. I know it. Jessie, show Shelby out, will ya, hon? I feel a terrible urge to rest a spell."

Jessie helped Sorina get comfortable on the sofa, then she led Shelby back out through the kitchen to the screened-in porch.

"Is she all right, Jessie? Did I upset her?"

"No, she's fine. You didn't upset her. She just gets tired. The seein' always does that to her. It takes her strength. She'll be fine by supper. Shelby, she's been waitin' on you."

"Waiting on me?"

"Oh, yeah, ever since Martha died. She knew you was comin'. You have made her very happy." The shy woman put out her hand and Shelby ignored it and hugged her instead. Jessie blushed in pleasant surprise. Then Shelby left the way she had come, around the front of the cottage and towards the tall trees.

"Don't you want to take the lane?" Jessie had followed her and was gesturing to the small paved road.

"No. I want to learn my way through the woods. It isn't that far, and I think I know which direction to head."

"Well, keep the river to your back and the highway to your front. You'll hear them both if you listen hard enough."

"Thanks, Jessie. I'll see you soon."

The women waved and Jessie disappeared back into the cottage, while Shelby headed deep into the woods.

It was instantly another world inside the hush of the trees. She stood still and tried to hear the river behind her and the road up ahead, but all she heard was the rustle of the leaves in the branches and the occasional dropping of berries and nuts when the wind caught the limbs just right. A low whistle echoed overhead. Shelby picked at a berry bush and stepped through the smaller pine trees crowded in between the tall sycamores and birches. Copious bushes brushed at her legs and she was glad for the jeans she wore. Nothing looked familiar, though she had just come this way an hour earlier. She strained to see the sky peeking through the high waving limbs and once again was aware of the only sound being the secret language of the woods. Birds flitted above, hovering over nests tucked away in the knotty bark.

Shelby's mind was filled with wonder. Something was pulling at her, she was certain. And Sorina seemed now to be a piece of that mysterious pulling. She thought of the slaves, Lizbeth and Samuel, and their frightening journey through unknown terrors in search of freedom. What courage that took. She could never have been as strong as Samuel. She would have been more like Lizbeth, wanting to give up, to give in. In the vision Sorina had shared, Shelby had felt those enslaved people in their flight over a century ago. She had felt them and known what was in their hearts and heads. It was a frightening realization and an exciting one.

Walking more slowly, she looked down; focusing her sight on the leafy groundcover she was stepping over. Time seemed to slow with her steps and her breaths came deeper and more satisfying. Each wildflower, each blade of grass and willowy weed took on sharper lines, brighter hues. She could see the tiniest striations in the leaves. Miniscule insects crawling over strewn bark took on a stunning clarity, as though she were looking through a high-powered camera lens at the intricate details of each spidery appendage, each bulbous eye. Shelby was too fascinated to be freaked out, though she knew something out of the ordinary was decidedly happening.

She stared at a praying mantis as it moved its spindly limbs over a green blade of grass in such detail it was like looking through a magnifying glass. Everything was focused in intense contrasting shapes and shadows. Shelby laughed out loud and her voice echoed off the tree trunks. She looked about her in mystified awe, never hearing the river or the road, only the crackling and whistling woods. She had never been so present in a moment. She had never been so here and now.

Suddenly, Shelby's breath intensified. Her heartbeat got too fast and too hard. The air around her started to heat up and the ground below her started to spin. A sharp pain stabbed at her abdomen, bringing her to knees. Nausea followed. *Oh, god, is it my incision?!*

Then the vision came.

Shelby could see the woman Bella had introduced her to at the church, the woman with cancer, Rita Reddinger. She was lying unconscious on her patio floor in a pool of her own blood. She was alive, but the blood was coming fast, spreading over the decorative designs in the stone.

The sickening feeling left Shelby and so did the vision. She took a deep breath and wiped cold sweat from her brow before reaching in her pocket. "Goddamn it, there will be service." And there was. Her cell phone responded with two bars and Shelby punched in Bella's number.

"Bella, it's Shelby. You have to get to Rita's house. She's alone and she's fallen. There's blood. Call 911."

Shelby barely got the words out before the call was dropped. But she had said it, had told Bella. Now she just had to hope that Bella believed her and would act. Shelby sat back against a tree trunk and rested. She looked down at her stomach. No redness at her incision site. She was fine. She just felt as though the wind had been knocked out of her. She was tired, as Sorina had been tired from her vision before. "This seeing gift thing is for the birds," Shelby spoke the words out loud and was immediately joined by three sparrows who lined up next to her on a tree stump. Shelby watched the birds and again thought of a Disney movie. *If they start singing to me, I'm going back to New York.* She laughed to herself as she stood and brushed off her jeans.

Now she heard the river rolling behind her and US 23 rushing in front of her, making the return through the woods easy. She opened the door to the house trailer just in time to answer the phone.

"Bella? What's that you say? Slow down. I can't understand you."

"I'm sayin' the ambulance took Rita to the hospital in Ashland. Sure enough, she had fallen outside on her patio and cracked her skull. Shelby Jean, you saved her life!"

CHAPTER SIXTEEN
WASN'T INVITED

"SHEL, THIS IS AWESOME. It's like a mobile home garden suite!"

Caitlin had come bounding in the door and hugged Shelby long and hard before taking a look around. Russell stood back by the door sheepily, watching the roommates reconnect. They were a sight for any eyes, a stunning brunette and a lovely fair-haired beauty. Shelby glanced up at him over Caitlin's hug and saw a look on his face that could only speak of a man who felt he had died and gone to heaven.

"Come on, Russell, take a load off. And thank you so much for picking my girl up!"

"Well, it was my pleasure."

"But, Shel, we drove separately." Caitlin cocked one perfect dark eyebrow and her blue eyes sparkled with delight.

"Huh?"

"Yeah, I drove the Lexus. Come on, Russell, let's show her what you drove." Caitlin took Shelby by the hand and led her back out the trailer door with Russell on her heels.

A brand new candy-apple red Ford F-150 truck sat in the driveway with dealer tags on it. Russell grinned and handed the keys to Shelby as she stared before squealing with joy. She looked from Russell to Caitlin for permission and then climbed into the driver's seat.

"Damn, it's like the cockpit of a jet airliner in here. Russell, this is a far cry from Grandma Mart's beater?"

"Well, you might say I took the liberty and made what I consider to be a pretty good deal. I hope you like it, Shelby. Your grandmother is getting you in the door, but you'll have to pay to stay there." He grinned back at her.

"That's fine by me. Thank you so much, Russell." Shelby added, "And Russell, I know what you and Bella did. Believe me. I have decided not to dwell on it for a lot of reasons, but I'm aware that things could have gone way worse for me with the wreck had you guys not jumped in. I had had too much to drink and I shouldn't have been behind the wheel."

Russell nodded and smiled shyly. "You wanna take a spin?"

"Absolutely!" Shelby laughed.

Caitlin jumped in the passenger side and Russell got in the back of the extended cab, putting Shelby in the driver's seat for the first time since her accident. The moment her hands touched the steering wheel she was zapped into vivid remembering. She experienced a sudden, painful flashback of that awful night. In a cold, cutting moment, Shelby realized she was afraid to drive. Her head dropped to her chest.

"Shel, honey, are you all right?" Caitlin put her hand out and pushed back the wavy hair from Shelby's bowed face.

Shelby took a deep breath and raised her head. She sat back in the seat. "I didn't expect to feel afraid." She looked over at Caitlin.

"Well, that's perfectly natural after what you've been through. Maybe this isn't a good idea?" Cait looked back at Russell. "Too soon?"

Shelby debated silently. Then she sat up straight and put her hands on the wheel. "No, I'm all right." She took a deep breath. "Actually, I'm better than all right. I am ready." She grinned and started the motor. It purred to life and the visual image of the accident slipped behind her thoughts and rested somewhere for another time. Shelby turned onto US 23 and accelerated in a matter of seconds to a smooth 60 miles an hour. She said, "I don't even hear the engine. I think I love this truck, Russell. Grandma Mart would be proud!"

"Check this out." Caitlin turned on the radio and cobalt blue indicator lights danced on the EQ. She turned up the volume until the state of the art stereo rocked the cab.

The women squealed as Adele's rich voice filled the interior. Russell laughed from the backseat. "I bet you two are out of control in the Big Apple. I don't know if Sorry's Run can handle it!"

"Hell, Russell, I bet you're wondering if you can handle it," Caitlin teased.

Shelby drove south, passing The Pit Stop, and then passing the farmhouse. She zipped on by, but after a few more miles did a U-turn.

Traffic was light, and on the return trip she deliberately slowed the truck to a crawl so she could look in the house windows. It was late enough that she figured Wesley would be sleeping in his recliner and wouldn't notice. The reflection of the television was easily seen, but the surprising thing was she could not see his profile in the chair. "Do you guys see him?"

Caitlin stared out the passenger side. "Nope, don't see him."

Suddenly, the living room curtain moved and there he was. Wesley stood in shadow, the light from the TV catching his silhouette. He just stood there at the window perfectly still and a cold shiver crept up Shelby's spine as she stepped on the gas.

"I need a drink."

She looked in her rear-view mirror and saw the expression of doubt followed by dread on Russell's face as she pulled into the parking lot of The Pit Stop. "It's okay, Russell. Let's go in."

"All right. But I'm driving home."

Shelby grabbed her purse and looked back at him kindly. "You betcha." She threw her new keys to him before they all got out and went through the door.

"Hi, John."

John Tyler looked up from behind the bar as Shelby Jean Stiller approached him and extended her hand. He grinned and shook it excitedly. "Well, hi yourself, Shelby Jean. What a surprise. Have a seat, y'all. Should I get out the good Scotch?" He asked, raising an eyebrow.

"That would be great," she answered, smiling easily. Shelby saw the apparent relief cross John's face. He must have wondered if she blamed him, even in some small way, for what had happened to her after she left his bar just weeks ago.

He nodded at Caitlin and Shelby introduced them.

Russell spoke up when John brought out the single-malt, "Just for the ladies, John. I'll be drinking a cold Bud, please."

"You got it, Russell. And this round is on the house."

"Ah, thank you, John." Shelby smiled, and led them to a booth where they settled in for an hour of catch-up talk. Shelby noticed that Russell seemed fine with letting the girls dominate the conversation, but she also noticed that he seemed to be staring longer and harder at Caitlin. A silent thrill passed over her.

Caitlin finished her second Scotch and massaged her temples. "Okay, guys, I need to settle in. I was up working in the lab at 7:30 this morning and then all afternoon screwing around at the airport trying to get here. I'm beat. I think it would have been easier to drive from New York."

Shelby agreed, "No doubt. Come on, Russell, drive us home."

"Shel, what exactly are you telling me?" Caitlin's blue eyes got darker in intensity as she listened to Shelby talk about her visions.

They were sitting on the couch in the trailer and had opened a bottle of red wine. Caitlin had gotten a second wind after getting comfortable in her night clothes.

"Well, I don't know exactly. I mean, I can only tell you what has happened, and these things have happened. I think I have inherited some special gifts that were completely dormant until the accident. Something happened to me in the hospital. I had such vivid dreams of Grandma Mart, and she kept telling me to open my eyes, just open my eyes, as though I hadn't really seen before. And Cait, the dreams were more like visions even then, you know? It was kind of that whole die-and-go-into-the-light thing that you read about in the tabloids. I think somehow that happened to me and I came out of the coma with my eyes open." Shelby took a deep drink of her wine and let her friend absorb what she had just said.

"And you think you are a healer now?"

Shelby heard just a bit of sarcasm in her friend's voice. "I know, Cait. I know how it sounds. Maybe we should drop it for tonight. We'll talk tomorrow. You have to meet Sorina and Jessie. You'll love Jessie's gardens."

"Okay, hon. Yeah, I'm really pushing it. I'm tired. Which side of the bed is mine?"

"Whichever side you want, Ms. Sotheby. I am just proud that you didn't get that motel room." She helped her friend up and led her to the back of the trailer to what had been her grandmother's "master" bedroom. They both laughed as Caitlin snuggled between the green sheets decorated in tiny white wildflowers. She took a deep breath. "God, it smells like honeysuckle in here."

"That's Grandma Mart. She was the fragrance queen. Nitey-nite. And Caitlin, thank you for being here. I really mean that."

Caitlin's dark hair was tousled and lay all over her pillow. Buried in the sheets she looked like a little girl to Shelby.

Cait spoke with her eyes closed, "I miss you, Shel. I can't let you stay in Kentucky. You know that."

"I know. No worries. We have plenty of time to figure things out."

Shelby turned off the light, closed the door, and went back out to the living room. She wasn't ready to sleep just yet. Too much was on her mind. She wondered again about all that had happened to her. In one single day she had had two psychic experiences. It was frightening and fascinating all at the same time. If only Grandma Mart had been around long enough to help her understand what was happening to her.

Shelby finished her glass of wine and stepped outside on the small deck. It was a beautiful warm night. She could see the outline of her beloved hills standing out in bold relief against a blue black sky. The moon was new, just a sliver, and the stars were plentiful. Sweet honeysuckle scented the air. She smiled thinking of Cait's comment about her grandma's sheets. Shelby giggled. *Damn, I feel just like a kid.* It was as though everything was fresh and new. *Just beginning.* It was a heady feeling and she wanted to walk. She took a deep breath and walked down the steps to the driveway. Her new truck caught enough starlight to reflect sparkles in the dark night, and Shelby felt a rush when she let her hand glide over the smooth rounded fender of the impressive vehicle. She smiled and kept walking in the direction of Sorina's house.

It was an easy walk down the paved lane and soon enough she could see lights from the cottage. A sudden rustling around her feet startled her and Shelby nearly tripped over a furry body. She caught herself just in time to keep from falling. "What the…?" A rabbit scurried off in front of her. "Rory, is that you?" He was more shadowed outline than real when he stopped in front of her. "What? Are you leading me again? I don't think Sorina would appreciate a late night caller." Rory sat up on his haunches in defiance and then bounded off farther down the drive ahead of her. "Okay. I'll keep coming, but we're not going to disturb Sorina." She followed him and soon enough was in sight of the cottage. It looked even more enchanting in the glow of the night sky. Soft light flickered through the windows.

To Shelby's great surprise there were several cars parked in Sorina's driveway. "She's having a party?" Shelby's curiosity was peaked enough that she tip-toed to one of the front windows and crouched down to get a look inside. Bella, Jolene and Violet were standing next to Sorina, with four or five women she recognized from Grandma Mart's funeral hovering together in close conversation. Jessie was passing around a serving tray filled with aperitif glasses and the women were helping themselves. Shelby leaned in closer to the window, trying to hear their voices when the rabbit surprised her again, jumping into the grass right next to her. Shelby lost her balance. She fell in towards the window onto her knees, stopping herself just in time before she bounced off of the glass. Sweat popped out on her forehead and she crept away from the window in embarrassment.

She stood up and brushed herself off. The rabbit was looking at her. She whispered, "Okay, Rory, I'm leaving. You brought me here again, but now I'm leaving. I wasn't invited, after all."

Wasn't invited.

She couldn't believe that Sorina was having a party and she hadn't been included. She thought she was back in the fold, but maybe not. Maybe there was still a gap that had to be bridged between the New York girl and the Kentucky girl. Maybe it would take more time for Sorry's Run to really accept her.

Shelby was surprised at how it really hurt her feelings. *What is wrong with me*? In all her years in New York, she had never felt like this, felt this kind of loneliness. In the City she had always had such determination and courage and more of a tough attitude of "I'll show them." But here, she thought all that was over, that she didn't need to show anybody anything—that she truly belonged in her home town.

So why was it that in a heartbeat she had been made to feel like an outsider? Maybe she had just been fooling herself these past few weeks, and really didn't belong in Sorry's Run after all. With Martha gone, she had no family ties anymore. Obviously, Wesley didn't want her around. He had made that clear enough. She had probably just gotten emotionally caught up in all that had happened to her and she was reading too much into it. Cait was right. She couldn't stay in Kentucky. What had she been thinking? Really, the thing to do was get back on a plane with her roommate, and back to her big city life. She had just gotten lost in all this romantic "fairytale" world of thinking she was a healer. After all, Grandma Mart had never shared any of her life involving this surreal cottage and its unusual mistress. Maybe she hadn't meant for Shelby to get involved. *But then why did she insist I come? And why would she tell me those things before she died?*

Shelby looked down at the rabbit who seemed to be reading her thoughts. "What do you think, Rory? I'm getting myself very confused here. Did you want me to see this just to break my heart or to open my eyes? Grandma Mart is always telling me to open my eyes. Is this what she meant? That I need to get back to New York? You're a leprechaun; tell me where my pot of gold is?"

The rabbit's whiskers twitched and he bounded off in front of her towards the trailer. Shelby wiped away a tear, mutely, and followed.

"Why didn't you ask Shelby to come tonight, Sorina?" Bella asked.

"I was goin' to, but her roommate from New York just flew in this afternoon. I figured they would want some time alone. They are most likely out doin' somethin' fun together. Besides, it might be better to ease Shelby Jean into these little healin' sessions of ours. Don't wanna scare her off." She smiled and added, "I really wanna have a big party for her when we can get everybody to come. Do it up right."

"She'd like that," Bella agreed. "I'll help you."

"Me, too," Violet said.

"Well, don't leave me out. I love a big party," Jolene chimed in.

"Okay, then. We'll plan on it. Maybe even surprise her." Sorina grinned and then took a deep breath, lowering her head as if in prayer. When she looked up she whispered, "Bella, it's time."

"Okay." Bella redirected her voice, speaking loudly to be heard over the ladies' conversations, "Dory, hon, are you ready?"

An obese woman with thinning hair and bloodshot eyes nodded from the kitchen.

Bella nodded back. "Dory is ready, girls."

Immediately, as if on cue, the women stopped talking and began moving in perfect synchronicity, rearranging furniture. In five minutes the large room was cleared and fold-out chairs had been set up in a circle with two chairs facing each other in the middle. Jessie helped Sorina to one and the larger woman sat across from her.

Jessie went about dimming the lights, stoking the fire and lighting candles throughout the room.

After everyone was seated, Sorina asked, "Has everyone got their drink?"

The women lifted their small crystal goblets.

"We do," Bella answered.

Sorina nodded and continued, "Let us think on the green fairy in the Absinthe as we drink. And think on Martha's wonderful energy as you take in this powerful medicinal elixir. It will help our minds to open and the energy to flow for the healin'."

The women all drank the green liquor and then sat their glasses down. Sorina lowered her head once again as if in prayer, and then looked up towards the woman sitting across from her. She held out her hands and Dory took them in her own. Sorina spoke softly, "Dory, there is love for you here in this room. Do you feel it?"

The woman nodded her head and in a hoarse, trembling voice answered, "Yes, I do, Sorina."

"Good. Now, do you believe in this love that you feel?"

"I think so."

"All the power in this world and in the next comes from love. Open your heart to that and you can be healed. We have all gathered here tonight because we love you and we want well-bein' for you. Your life can be rich with health. Wellness is your birthright and this is what we want for you. If this is what you want for yourself, open up your mind and let in the pure love that is all around you. Fill your lungs with the love and with the purified air."

The woman breathed deeply.

"Everyone breathe in the pure energy that love brings," Sorina spoke to the circle. "Jessie?"

Jessie walked into the circle carrying a glass of reddish liquid and a piece of thin rope wrapped in green leaves. She placed the rope, along with the small glass, into Sorina's hand.

"Thank you, hon."

Jessie took a seat in the circle beside the others.

"Dory, drink this." Sorina sensed the woman's hesitation. "Now don't worry none. It's just boiled-down carrot juice. Purifies the blood."

The woman trembled as she drank the thick liquid.

"Now hold out your hand, Dory." Sorina tied the thin, leafy rope around her wrist. "Mint for wardin' off disease. Now, let me feel your troubles." She let go of Dory's hands, then, and the women watching formed a closed circle with their clasped hands.

Sorina took deep breaths and then leaned in closer so she could trace Dory's body with her hands. She raised her outstretched hands around the woman's shoulders and arms and then over her head, moving slowly and purposely. Dory bent her head down at Sorina's guidance and Sorina held her hands hovering for a long minute before placing her palms on the top of her head. Dory's eyes were closed and she jumped in nervous reaction to Sorina's touch. But Sorina didn't flinch. She kept her hands steady. "I feel your troubled heart and mind, Dory. But your troubles can be lifted and scattered like so much dust into the air. Can you feel them lift? Your spirit is strong and will not give into oppression. Your troubles are weightless now, leaving your body and coming into my hands. They will float away from my hands into the pure energy that knows no doubt, knows no fear, knows no unhappiness. The life-giving energy that can save the world and can handle all your heavy thoughts and worries will carry your burdens. Our loving friend, Martha, has gone into spirit and she is a strong ally. Let us ask her to join us with her favorite chant. Repeat it with me."

She started to chant, and the women joined in:

"Bring the fairies
Circlin' 'round our head.
From the wee ancient ones
We all will be led,
To take out the demon
That lies within,
To bring peace and harmony
And health to our friend."

The women chanted over and over as Sorina pressed harder on Dory's head. Then finally, in one surprising moment and with considerable strength, Sorina pushed with her flat palms, forcing Dory's head to extend backward, causing her to nearly fell off her chair with the thrust. Tears were falling on Dory's cheeks and her round face was flushed. She was visibly shaking.

Sorina dropped her hands to her lap and then lowered her head. "Let us pray."

All heads lowered with her.

"Dear Lord, our friend, Dory, has been stricken with unhappiness that has manifested in her body. She has made herself sick with worry and grief. Take these troubles away from our sister and wrap her in your lovin' arms and help her to take the healin' that is given to her in love and full acceptance. We thank you, Lord, for the gifts you have bestowed. We are indeed blessed in our full receiving of this wonderful energy. Amen."

Sorina raised her head and reached for Dory's hands again. "Dory, you have been healed. I feel it. I know you do, too. This is God's gift through our touch and it is not to be taken lightly. You must go now with gratefulness in your heart and be kind to yourself. You must love yourself above all others and their love will come back to you. You are a powerful presence and must never forget your worthiness in this world. There is much left for you to do in this life and your body will heal itself and help you to do that which you must. Your life is a miracle, Dory. Go live it with hopeful intention and joy in your heart."

Then Sorina stopped talking and pulled Dory up. She put her small arms around the larger woman and hugged her.

Jessie brought the lights back up and everybody stood from their chairs and in turn gave Dory a hug.

CHAPTER SEVENTEEN
HEALER OR FAKE

SHELBY ROLLED OVER AND SAW the bed was empty, but a wonderful smell was coming from the cozy kitchen down the hall. She smiled and put on a robe thinking, *that is definitely not honeysuckle.* Caitlin was up fixing breakfast with the table already set and the coffee percolating.

"Man, it smells like heaven in here." Shelby realized how she had missed this. Caitlin was a good cook and loved to spoil her with great meals. It had been true suffering when Cait had given up modeling before Shelby. All those wonderful meals that she had had to pass on. But not now. Now she could eat and to hell with being rail thin.

"What time did you get up?" Shelby kissed Caitlin on the cheek and then took a seat as she was served an egg and sausage frittata with tomato slices.

Caitlin's blue eyes were bright and she had her luxurious raven hair piled on top of her head. "I've been up for a couple hours. There's something about this country air. I feel more energized than I have in weeks. I hope you don't mind, but I took the truck out for a spin and found the IGA." Cait raised an eyebrow.

"Not a problem, roomie. Mi casa and truck, su casa and truck."

"Good answer." Cait smiled and joined Shelby at the table.

Shelby reached over to her grandmother's small boom box on the counter and turned it on. It was set to a gospel station, but she kept spinning the dial until Ralph Stanley's thin, melodic voice flowed out of the speakers. "Oh, man, I love bluegrass music. Is this perfect or what?" Shelby took a bite of the eggs and then she shared what she had seen at Sorina's.

"That is weird. What do you think they were doing? Maybe it's a club, like a book club or something. Do the ladies around here even read?"

Shelby protested, "Yeah, dufus, the ladies around here read. No, I don't think it was anything like that. It looked more like a meeting than a club. Hell, I don't know. But it did make me feel a bit like the outsider that I am, I guess. Kind of did a number on me."

"Don't worry about it, Shel. You know you're doing your over-thinking bit as usual."

"Yeah?"

"Yeah. I lay you odds we'll find out soon enough what that was all about. How secret can anything be around here anyway? But for now, I think we should drive that badass truck of yours to Ashland and do some shopping. I only brought a couple pairs of jeans and a few T-shirts. And just in case we go out for a fancy dinner, I need to be prepared." She winked.

"Yeah, I hear the buffet at the Pizza Hut is the bomb."

"That's what I'm talkin' about!"

The women laughed and Shelby turned up the music.

Shelby had no trepidation this time getting behind the wheel of her new ride. She just felt excitement. "Buckle up, Caitlin Sotheby." Shelby grinned and the smooth engine whirred into life. Driving down US 23 she shared with Cait the history of the river highway so many country stars had traveled.

Cait gushed, "Wow. That is very cool. It really is different here, isn't it? I think I like it." She reached over and took Shelby's hand. "But, Shel, that doesn't change things. I'm still here to get you back home." She arched a dramatic eyebrow again and Shelby changed the subject.

"You know, it creeped me out to see Wesley standing at the farmhouse window last night. It was as if he knew we were passing by."

"Well, he probably did see you go by the first time. This red truck is kind of hard to miss." Caitlin winked. "But he looked like he was standing straight and tall. No cane."

"I know. I wonder how he's doing. I'll have to go see him eventually. Not that he wants me to. He wants me gone, Caitlin, and I am just not ready to be gone."

The friends got quiet, then, and let the highway pass easily under the large tires. The Ohio rolled alongside and Caitlin thrilled at the long barges being pushed upriver by rusty tugs; white steam curling lazily out of the stacks as the flat metal cut through the calm water.

Shelby's cell phone went off and disturbed their momentary serenity. "Hello?"

"Shelby Jean, it's Bella. Where you at, hon?"

Shelby grinned. She put the phone on speaker so Caitlin could hear. "Cait and I are on our way to Ashland to do a little shopping."

"Oh, that's perfect. Do me the biggest favor, Shelby Jean. Rita Reddinger is still at King's Daughters and she would love to see you. Could you pay her a visit while y'all are there?"

Shelby looked over at Caitlin and got an approving nod. "Sure, Bella, we'll stop by if you think we should. How is she doing?"

"She is doin' much better, but she sure wants to see you. They say she's been askin' for you even when she was under sedation. Let me know how that goes, hon. Maybe I'll stop by the trailer later."

"Okay, Bella. See you later."

"Thanks, hon."

"I wonder why Rita would be asking for me?" Shelby looked over at Caitlin and asked, "Okay if we go to the hospital first before we shop?"

Caitlin answered, "Absolutely."

Shelby drove into Ashland and turned onto Lexington Avenue. In another ten minutes they were parking in the garage at the sprawling medical center. They stopped at the information desk and got directions to Rita's room. On the elevator ride up, Shelby felt her throat tighten.

"Are you all right, Shel?" Caitlin had been watching her.

"I don't know why, but this makes me nervous."

"Yeah, I hear you. Kind of makes me nervous, too." Cait took Shelby's hand. "Don't worry, Shel, whatever it is, it's all good. Right?"

"Right," Shelby answered weakly.

Rita was in a room by herself. At first glance she looked to be at death's door, so pale and drawn. But when she looked up and saw Shelby her pained eyes brightened with life. "Oh, Shelby Jean, I'm so glad you came." Rita attempted to straighten herself in the bed, but she couldn't find the strength. She lay back down on her pillow in resignation. "Here, hon, sit by me." Rita patted the mattress. "And who do you have with you?"

"This is Cait Sotheby, Rita. She's my roommate in New York, and my best friend." Shelby smiled.

"Well, it's a pleasure to meet you, Cait. You girls are just so pretty. Just so pretty." Rita seemed to lose her breath. She put an oxygen mask up to her face and breathed in deeply before continuing, "Shelby, I know it was Bella who told you to come, but I just had to talk to you. Remember that Sunday when you took my hand. You saw somethin', I know, and so did I. Shelby, it was a connection between us and I think that's why you knew I fell. The doctors say the ambulance got to me just in time, or else..." She drifted off and tears pooled in her eyes. She wiped at them and continued, "Shelby, I want you to take my cancer away."

Shelby moved back from Rita on the bed. She felt a jolt of an emotion she couldn't even name. "What?"

"I know you can. I want you to make me well."

Shelby fell silent as her mind reeled. She realized with cold clarity that she had been having some fun with thinking she was a healer, but now this woman seriously believed she had the power to cure her of this awful disease that was wrecking her body. *No way.* Shelby fought the urge to run out of the room. What had she been thinking, playing with people's lives like this? She was no healer. *No fucking way!* Her mouth was suddenly so dry she couldn't even speak. She started to get up from the bed, but Caitlin stopped her.

"Shelby, where are you going?"

Shelby nodded toward the door and her eyes were liquid pools as she stared in surprise at her best friend.

"You can do this, Shelby. Or you can at least try." Caitlin's blue eyes locked into her friend's green eyes as the sick woman lay on the bed watching them both, her breath coming anxiously as a decision was being made.

Rita spoke softly, "Shelby Jean, Martha wanted to help me. She thought she could help me, but I didn't believe her. I just didn't believe. I should have let her. She used to come to the library every day tryin' to change my mind. But I was too scared or too stupid. And she was so dear to me. Your grandmother came to me in my dreams last night and she told me to ask you, ask you to do what it was she had wanted to do."

The last bead of energy seemed to fall from Rita's frail frame in the telling of this. Her body racked with a dry cough. She sunk back in her pillow, knowing she had done all she could to make her case and convince Shelby.

Shelby felt her whole body tremble. She had never known such raw fear in her life. She had an incredible urge to flee. "I can't, Rita. I just can't. Forgive me. But I just can't." She barely got the last words out when she got up from the bed and left the room.

Caitlin looked back at the pitiful woman, and said, "Don't give up, Rita. She's just confused. We'll be back."

Cait followed Shelby back down the elevator and to the parking garage. Neither of them said a word until they got to the truck. Shelby was still trembling.

Cait spoke, "We'll shop another day. Let's go home." Cait put her hand on her friend's arm. "Want me to drive, Shel?"

"Would you?"

The friends switched places and Shelby directed Caitlin back to 23 North. Cait just waited and after a short time Shelby let it out, "What was I thinking, Cait? God, I am so ashamed. I am no healer. Now I've got a seriously ill woman thinking I can save her life. Sweet Jesus, Cait, what have I done?"

"I think what you've done is already saved her life once. That wasn't a fluke. You said so yourself, Shelby. You saw that woman in your vision. Why are you denying this now? You have spent a fair amount of time convincing me you have this gift, and now that I'm about to believe you, you're saying you're a fake?" Caitlin's eyes flashed and her high cheekbones reddened.

Shelby looked over at her and then back at the road and said nothing. She didn't even glance toward the farmhouse on the way back to the trailer. She just wanted to forget all this and go back to New York to her normal life.

When they pulled into the drive Bella was already there sitting on the steps of the trailer. "Y'all didn't do much shoppin'? Where's your bags?"

"Didn't do any shopping, Bella." Caitlin nodded at her friend who walked right past Bella and opened up the door. The two followed her in and sat down on the couch. Shelby went to the bathroom and stayed for a long time before finally emerging, looking like she had been crying.

"Hon, what in the world? Caitlin tells me you walked out on Rita?"

Shelby threw a hard glance at her friend, but had to nod in agreement. "Yeah, I did. That's exactly what I did."

"Well, Shelby Jean, you have to go back. You have to help that woman."

"Why? Why do I have to help that woman? And what in the world makes you think I can?"

"Because you are the daughter of Neely Stiller and granddaughter of Martha Maggie McBride, that's why. It's in your blood, Shelby. You have to recognize that and you have to be respectful of it. Hon, you're gettin' yourself confused like other folks do when they get to thinkin' somethin' like this is a curse instead of a blessin'. It's not the devil workin' through you, hon, it's God. You have to believe it's God." Bella's brown eyes were round and big as she spoke.

The hospital corridor was dimly lit, except for the nurses' station. Shelby slipped by the skeleton hospital staff without being seen and silently entered Rita Reddinger's room. The gaunt woman was swimming in layers of sheets and an oversized hospital gown. Mechanical sounds surrounded her, monitoring her life force with various soft whistles; measuring her heart patterns with dancing spikes on a lighted screen; throwing stringy shadows over her face. Lengthy tubes were hydrating her with slow drips from clear plastic bags. An oxygen tank hissed at regular intervals. Rita was asleep, heavily sedated to keep her from moving her securely-wrapped head.

Shelby stared for an interminable amount of time without moving. She was hoping Rita would awaken and scream and she would have to run fleeing out of the hospital ward. But Rita slept soundly. The oxygen regulator hissed in even inhalations and exhalations.

Shelby's heart felt like it would explode with anxiety. She had never tried this intentionally. The strange things that had happened to her had been just that—strange things that happened to her. She had no idea if she could command this new "gift" into making an appearance. Her blouse was suddenly soaked in sweat. She watched the sleeping woman and then she moved the sheets aside, opening Rita's gown just slightly to place her hand over where she imagined the diseased ovaries to be. Shelby said a silent prayer. *God, if I am to do this—if it's your will—then use me.*

Then she felt it. Heat slapped at her hands and raced up her arms. It was all she could do to keep her hands in place and not wave them in the air to cool. Sharp pain cut through Shelby's stomach bringing nausea, followed by a clear vision. She saw Rita healthy and playing with her grandchildren. She saw it, and at the same time she felt another jolt of energy pass from her to the sick woman.

Then it was over. Just like the other times, the vision disappeared with the nausea and pain. Shelby placed the sheets back over Rita and left the room like she had come, silently and unseen.

CHAPTER EIGHTEEN
A TRUE HEALER

HER CELL PHONE WOKE HER. "Shelby, hon, are you awake? We're comin' over."

There was no asking; only telling. Bella was on her way. Shelby got up from the bed too quickly and her head pounded. "Damn." She put pressure on her temples and put her feet to the floor. Caitlin was already up, as usual. The kitchen smelled of cinnamon and sugar. Caitlin was pulling gooey rolls out of the oven when Shelby came out. "How in the hell do you stay so skinny, Cait? God, haven't you ever heard of low-fat yogurt?"

"Oh, shut up and sit down, you old grump. Here, have one of these fat-filled beauties I found in your grandma's fridge. You need some plumping up."

Shelby did as she was told. She licked the icing off her fingers before speaking, "Bella and the girls are on their way over."

"This early? Lord, there must be a serious book club dilemma." Caitlin smiled and got Shelby to laugh with her.

"Girls? Sweeties, are you decent?" Bella had knocked twice and then let herself in, followed by Violet and Jolene. "My goodness, it smells good in here. You got cookies in the oven?" The women found ways of getting situated in the small trailer and each helped themselves to a sweet roll and coffee. After some small talk, Bella got to the point.

"Rita Reddinger made a remarkable recovery overnight. They're callin' it a bonified miracle. Did you by any chance have anythin' to do with that, Shelby Jean?" She stared at Shelby over the rising steam of her coffee mug. The other women leaned in to hear the answer.

"I don't know what you're talking about, Bella. I told you how I felt about that. But that's great that Rita is feeling better. That's just great."

Shelby's heart was pounding. She couldn't contain her excitement. Had she really cured that woman?

"Well, I think we should go tell Sorina and Jessie," Violet spoke.

"Yes. This is the most astonishin' news! And this pretty girl needs to meet the neighbors," Jolene jumped in, turning her attention to the beautiful brunette.

"By the way, Caitlin," Bella added, "This here is Jolene and Violet. Together, we're considered the local busybodies." She grinned.

"Well, I'm certainly glad to make your acquaintance, ladies. I'm the pushy roommate." Laughter went around the small room as they finished eating before piling into Bella's car to drive the short distance to the stone cottage.

"Hey, why didn't you guys tell me Sorina was blind?" Shelby asked from the backseat of the car.

"I don't know. Why didn't we?" Violet looked at Bella.

Bella answered, "We didn't? Lord, I can't believe we left that little part out. We told you so much that day in the trailer, I guess we just forgot. Sorry, hon, didn't mean to do that to you. Didn't take you long to figure it out?"

"Not really. But it was kind of uncomfortable. And why is she blind? Didn't Grandma Mart ever try and help her?"

Bella nodded. "Oh, yeah, she did, about a million times. She just couldn't do it. She said she wasn't a powerful enough faerie healer."

Violet looked back at Shelby, adding, "But then she'd always say, too, that Sorina just wasn't ready to open her eyes."

"Open her eyes?"

Jolene added, "And none of us really knows how she lost her sight. She don't have a memory of anythin' and Martha always told us to let it be, so we just let it be."

"Did you guys always do everything Grandma Mart said to do?"

Jolene looked at Violet and Violet looked at Bella. They answered simultaneously, "Pretty much."

Caitlin and Shelby laughed as the car pulled into the driveway of the cottage.

Sorina and Jessie were sitting in the wicker rocking chairs examining the grapevines. Shelby saw the older woman smile under her hat as though she knew who it was without seeing. She said something to Jessie, and Jessie disappeared into the cottage.

"Mornin', Sorina."

The women joined Sorina in the grape arbor. They all greeted each other.

"I'm afraid the last freeze has taken its toll on our vines this year." Sorina felt the wilted leaves and sighed. "Ah, but Jessie will remedy that." She grinned, then, and looked in Shelby's direction.

"And who do you have with you, Shelby Jean? Could this be your roommate from New York?"

"It is. Sorina, I'd like you to meet Cait. Cait, this is Sorina."

Sorina extended a hand and Caitlin took it. They exchanged pleasantries and then Sorina escorted everyone into the cottage. Jessie had already set the table and a carafe of coffee sat next to sweet rolls piled high on a platter. Shelby grinned at Caitlin when she realized they were about to have their second fattening pastry of the morning. For women who had known the curse of weight gain in the fashion industry they were about to commit a mortal sin.

Soft Celtic music wafted from hidden speakers as they sat down at the table. Shelby saw the look on her roommate's face. She leaned over and whispered, "See, Cait, I told you this was an enchanted cottage."

The mantle clock chimed ten times.

"Lord, we are early this mornin', Sorina. We hope you don't mind, but we wondered if you heard the good news." Bella was already chewing on a jelly roll.

Sorina leaned her cane against the table and adjusted herself in her seat. She addressed herself to Jessie first, "Hon, sit yourself down now. We thank you for gettin' all this together. And yes, Bella, I did hear about Rita's amazin' recovery."

"How did you…"

Bella stopped in mid sentence when Sorina turned her blind gaze on her. "Well, Bella, I guess I heard it through the grapevines." She sounded so serious, but then Jolene started to giggle and the laughter traveled around the table. She continued, "Most remarkable. And the doctors have no idea, huh?"

Violet grunted, "'Course not. And Shelby, we were by Wesley's a couple times this week, and you wouldn't believe how well he's doin'. It's like he don't need us anymore. Just remarkable." Violet raised an eyebrow in Shelby's direction.

Shelby knew she wasn't fooling anyone, but she didn't respond to Violet's comment. She just nibbled on a roll until their hostess changed the subject.

"Jessie, hon, you feel like playin' this mornin'?" Sorina raised an arched golden eyebrow inquisitively.

Jessie answered with a shy smile and walked across the room to where a carved-top mandolin was propped up against built-in wooden bookshelves. She picked up the instrument and tuned it. After hitting the button on the stereo to turn off the Celtic music, she sat down in a straight back chair and began to play.

Shelby was shocked at the unexpected talent that Jessie displayed. She looked over at Caitlin and saw surprise there, too. Jessie's long, slender fingers glided over the narrow frets forming bar chords, and her long nails plucked on the taut strings bringing to life a lonesome melody Shelby was not familiar with. Then Jessie began to sing. Her clear, soprano voice carried through the room like a second perfect instrument. Shelby was reminded of Emmylou Harris and Alison Krauss combined as she shut her eyes to focus on the sweet, high voice. There was so much emotion in Jessie's delicate vibrato that it moved Shelby to tears.

Sorina leaned over to Shelby and whispered in her ear, "Would you care to accompany me down to the river, Shelby Jean, while Jessie entertains the girls?"

Shelby wiped at her eyes and nodded. She handed Sorina her cane and helped the older woman to her feet.

Out back on the far side of the gardens Sorina was the one who guided them to where a worn path followed a creek that snaked through the sycamores toward the water. She went slowly, but was amazingly surefooted for someone with no sight. It was obvious she had walked the path many times. She was quiet and Shelby felt no need to talk.

The Ohio River announced its presence through pungent smells and lapping liquid noise. The women went slowly down the path that led to a steep embankment and right to the water's edge, where several aluminum chairs were folded up and stacked against a huge piece of driftwood. The water splashed noisily, depositing woody refuse on the bank before rolling back out to join the fast-moving current. The air smelled of earthworms and dead fish.

"Shelby Jean, unfold a couple chairs, hon." Sorina panted and pointed her cane in the direction of the driftwood. Her breath was coming in hoarse rasps.

Shelby mutely did as she was told and helped Sorina get comfortable in a webbed chair. She sat next to her and stared out at the water.

"We have been so lucky this year with no floodin'. I've been able to come down to the river every day since the weather turned warm."

Shelby looked over at Sorina, really looked into her eyes through the amber sunglasses. Where her pupils should have been there was a whitish film. *Glaucoma? Cataracts? Whatever it is, it must not be curable.* Sorina didn't blink and seemed completely lost in thought.

After a time, Sorina's breath returned to normal and she spoke, "When I first come down this river with my husband I was so excited and so afraid all at the same time. But it was a new life I was wantin'. You see that clearin' over there on the Ohio side? There's nothin' but grass surrounded by big shade trees? I know it's still there. You see it?"

Shelby shielded her eyes and stared hard across the wide expanse of water. Sure enough, there was an area that was flat with no homes.

"That's where I wanted to homestead. I thought it would be perfect, close to the river and not so many trees to hide the Indians. But my husband wanted to be on the Kentucky side with his brothers. He insisted on that, and he insisted on homesteading right in the middle of the thickest part of the forest. He said the trees would protect us. Turned out he was right. We became Kentuckians right then and there. I never stopped bein' scared and excited for a long time. But I had the old ways to help me, and help me they did."

Shelby watched the lovely woman speak about a life that surely couldn't have been hers. But she was so clear in the telling of it, it was hard to imagine she wasn't actually remembering.

Sorina picked up on Shelby's thoughts. "Oh, I know, Shelby Jean, everybody thinks I'm daft 'cause I talk like this. But I do remember it like it was this lifetime. I do. And sometimes the rememberin' is almost too much to bear. Too much sufferin'." She reached her hand out and Shelby took it. Their palms got hot as the vision came …

Lizbeth watched Samuel while he slept. He wasn't sleeping peacefully. His eyes moved rapidly behind closed lids and his breathing came hard and uneven. She laid her calloused hand over his forehead and wiped at the sweat that was forming there. He didn't awaken. His dream had him gone somewhere off to where she couldn't go. Lizbeth always felt that around Samuel. He was all the time in a place she didn't understand. But she followed him, always. She would follow him to the ends of the earth and even to the hangman's noose if need me. She loved him that much. But she would never understand his drive, his anger. She was too aware of hurting all the time to be angry. Her feet felt like somebody had put a flame to them. The burning was raw and the bloody cuts were sore and aching. She rubbed her toes and winced at the pain. They had been running more than walking for hours and still there was no end to the forest, no sign of a clearing. She thought they were lost, but Samuel wouldn't admit it. He said he knew where the river was, where the white lady was that would help them cross to the Ohio land into freedom. Samuel would never say he was wrong. Never. If they were lost he would find their way again soon enough. She wouldn't say anything, just follow.

Lizbeth listened to his ragged breathing and realized that as exhausted as she was, she couldn't sleep. Her heart was beating too fast and she felt so scared. The forest frightened her so, especially when Samuel was sleeping. It was the only time he looked vulnerable. She listened to the stillness of the dense trees, and thought she heard something. Was it voices? Did she hear dogs? Oh, no, not the dogs! "Samuel, wake up! The dogs is a comin'. They all is a comin'! Samuel!"

Sorina let go of Shelby's hand and their shared vision was gone in that instant. Shelby realized she had been holding her breath and now she released it in a long, low sigh. Sorina's skin was paler, but she smiled. "I know what you're thinkin', and no, I don't know what happens to them. I am watchin' just as you are."

"So you're not sharing a memory?"

"No, I am just sharin' a vision. I don't know Lizbeth and Samuel. But I worry about them."

"You think they don't make it?" Shelby asked.

"No, I can't believe that. I think they must make it or I wouldn't have the connection. They must have found me and my cabin all those many years ago. They must have," Sorina spoke in a whisper, "but Shelby, I have never seen them like this. Not until I took your hand. For me, they have always been more like shadows, their voices distant, like way far off."

"And now?" Shelby sat up straighter.

"And now I see and hear them as you do, like a moving picture. I'm blind to the waking world but in my visions I see clearly. I see everything. It's your energy, Shelby. I felt you before I ever met you. I knew the air was different, more electric, and it was you I was feelin'. I think now that you're here I can more easily follow Lizbeth and Samuel on their journey to freedom. It's all so excitin'!" A smile transformed Sorina's delicate features into a youthful expression and she turned her head in Shelby's direction. "So, tell me now. Tell me what it is like for you."

Shelby knew what she was asking. She hesitated before speaking, chōosing her words carefully, "Well, when you and I are having the vision of Lizbeth and Samuel my palms burn at the beginning and I feel kind of a jolt, like a burst of energy, but there's nothing else physically that I experience. I just see them clearly and I watch, just like you said you do. But with Wesley and with Rita I felt this intense pain that made me sick. I closed my eyes and there was a detailed picture like they were starring in their own movie. It was that vivid. Then I laid my hands on what I sensed were their afflicted parts. When the pain and sickness were gone, the vision was gone, and I guess the healing was done. At least I think that's how it was. I'm pretty new at this game."

"Hummm. Then you take the pain onto yourself when you heal? You are able to be rid of it through the vision." Sorina relaxed her shoulders and sighed. "You are a powerful medicine woman, Shelby Jean."

"Is that what I am?"

"I think you can ask Rita's family that question and they will agree with me. And it sounds like you can ask your own daddy, too. I am considered a healer in these parts, but I mostly just get notions about things. So many folks just need to feel loved, you know? I use incantations for changin' negative energy into positive, and natural herbal medicines to make healin' potions that are better than any over-the-counter pills. But you have a true gift. A true healer. That's what you are, Shelby Jean Stiller, a true healer."

"Grandma told me she was a faerie doctor and that my mother and I were as well. Have you ever heard of that?"

Sorina smiled. "Anybody who comes from people of Scotch-Irish background knows that, especially in Appalachia country. The legends are old as the hills," she joked. "Sorina Duncan was of Scottish heritage, so that's where I draw my strength, and your grandma felt her strength came from her Irish ancestors, especially her granny. She wanted you to feel that, too." Sorina patted Shelby's hand and sat back in the chair, getting comfortable again. She looked tired.

"Do you want to go back to the cottage, Sorina?" Shelby asked, knowing how drained she felt after the vision.

"No, hon, if you don't mind I would just like to sit a spell."

Shelby sat back, too, then. The two women passed the next hour that way, listening to the big river roll.

CHAPTER NINETEEN
AN OMEN

LATER THAT AFTERNOON, Shelby woke from a short nap and found the trailer empty. "Cait?" she called out, but got no answer. She freshened up in the bathroom and walked over to the window by the table. Caitlin was sitting on the small deck, staring at the lilies in Martha's flower garden. It made Shelby so happy to see her best friend in all the world sitting on her grandmother's stoop. It was so perfect. She went into the kitchen for some glasses.

"Hey, you, it's not quite happy hour in Manhattan, but in Kentucky the moonshiners get started a little early." Shelby stood in the doorway with two wine glasses filled to the brim. She winked and asked, "Are you in?"

"You know it. Bring it on, girlfriend." Caitlin patted the spot next to her and Shelby sat down. "Your grandmother sure did a good job with her little garden, Shelby. Look at the lilies. They are glorious!"

"Lilies were my mother's favorite flower. They were everywhere when I was growing up; in the yard; in the bathroom; on the wallpaper." She smiled. "Maybe she got that from Grandma Mart." Shelby took a drink of her wine and got reflective looking at the distant hills.

Caitlin asked, "Something I never really understood, Shel, is why you rarely came here? I mean, I know you and your grandmother spoke on the phone, but why did you stay away like you did? And why didn't she ever visit us in New York? I mean, how is it I never got to meet her. You should have put her on a plane."

Shelby laughed. "There was no way that woman would get on a plane. Something about the Banshees flying outside the windows. I mean, I figured that was a joke, right? But that's what she would say. She refused to deal with a bus and I never had the time to drive her. But I really think she just had no desire to come to the City. I begged and begged because I hated coming here. I just hated it. She knew that. You can imagine what this place looked like to me, Cait. We were living this unbelievable life as models and then coming back here? Well, it was too depressing for words. And of course, Wesley always treated me like shit when I did come. Talk about not feeling welcome."

"Why didn't you stay here at the trailer with your grandmother when you visited?"

"Because Grandma Mart absolutely insisted I stay with Wesley. It was so fucked up. She always believed we could get our relationship back on track. Well, that just never happened, so I came back less and less, and we just grew apart. It all really hurt me, but I didn't allow myself to think about it much. It was just another part of this whole Sorry's Run thing that I had been born into. I just wanted not to care and I pretty much got there." Shelby took a drink of her wine. "I knew something was up when she begged me to come and stay for a while this time. She understood what it was like for me here."

Shelby got quiet, then, just thinking. She would always regret not making more time for Martha. She could never get that back. And she had so many questions that she would never have answers to now that her grandmother was gone forever.

Caitlin saw tears pool in her friend's eyes. She squeezed her hand. "Shelby, I think your grandmother lived her life just the way she wanted to. I mean, look how she got you here at the very time when you could finally appreciate it. She was a strong, wonderful woman and you have that in you, too. You know she loved you. She knew you loved her. Just remember that." Cait leaned over and kissed her best friend on the cheek. Then she moved on, saying, "Shelby, Jessie knocked me out today, first with her music and then with her incredible gardens."

Shelby took the lead gratefully, wiping her eyes. "Yeah, they are really beautiful, aren't they?"

"It's not just the beauty of the wildflowers, although that's enough, but it's the well-thought-out way in which each garden is arranged. You know what I mean? The designs are downright scientific. So I asked Jessie where she learned to garden. And you know what she says? She gets real shy and, I swear, Shelby, she looked up at me with those impossibly big dark eyes and she says—I didn't learn it. I just did it. Well, you could have knocked me over with a feather. Girl is one seriously talented gardener. And then her music? Man, Shelby, is all of Kentucky like this? Hidden talent everywhere?"

"Well, we do have our toothless wonders and three-legged dogs, too. You know, we're an all-inclusive state." She giggled. "But you are right, Cait. I am more than knocked out, too, by what I am seeing. It's why I don't want to go back to New York yet. I feel energized in a way I haven't since we were kids taking the big walk down the runway for the first time with the lights blinding us and all those people staring. Remember? God, it was the scariest, coolest thing in the world."

Cait smiled. "Yeah, and you took to it like it was why you were born. I was always so scared and I watched you looking so confident and I just tried to imitate everything you did."

"Yeah, well, it was the old baffle 'em with your bullshit. I was scared all the time. But I was thrilled, too. It's kind of like what is happening to me now. This healing thing has my stomach tied in knots and I don't understand what I'm doing, but it's also exciting beyond belief. And Cait, Sorina affects me so intensely. I just love being around her. There's something so electric, and at the same time soothing, about her presence. I think she will help me figure out what I'm doing here, you know? Today she called me a medicine woman."

"Hummm. Medicine woman, huh? Wasn't there a TV show with that title?"

Shelby jabbed Cait with her elbow and sat her glass down. She fumbled with the beaded bracelet on her arm.

"Where did you get that awesome bracelet? Did Tommy buy that for you at that hip little shop in The Village?"

"No. Believe it or not, this is a piece from Grandma Mart's collection. Apparently she designed jewelry for years."

"Get out! Okay, now I'm convinced. Sorry's Run is the unsung artistic center of the universe. I'm not leaving either."

Shelby draped her arm around Caitlin. "It's the hills, Cait. I told you the hills are magical."

"I am starting to get that, Shelby Jean Stiller—medicine woman." Cait looked boldly into Shelby's eyes and then smiled, her white teeth lighting up her face. The friends hugged.

"Is anybody invited to this party or do you have to be best friends?" Russell James jumped off a ten-speed Trek bicycle and leaned it up against a tree. He was wearing all the gear; helmet, backpack, gloves, cycling shorts and jersey. Shelby thought he looked like a poster boy for physical fitness.

Shelby ignored his question. "I didn't know you liked to ride."

"You bet. I try to get at least twenty miles in on the weekends. It's what keeps me sane. Seriously, though, am I interrupting? I was just on my way home."

Shelby laughed. "God, no. We were just about to get all goofy talkin' girl stuff anyway. You want some wine?"

"Twist my arm." He smiled and took off his gloves while Shelby went into the trailer for the bottle and another glass. When she came out Caitlin was studying the bicycle.

She looked up at Shelby and said, "I haven't been on a bike since I was a kid."

Shelby handed the glass to Russell and he took a sip before asking, "Cait, you wanna go for a little ride? There's a great trail not far from here that runs by the lake."

Shelby watched Russell drink his wine and stare at Caitlin like he was drinking her up, too.

"You know what? I would love it." Caitlin clapped her hands in excitement, and asked, "But don't I need a helmet? I mean, isn't there a law or something?"

Russell walked over to his bike and picked up his backpack, pulling out a helmet. "Just happen to have a spare."

"Smooth, Mr. James, very smooth." Shelby laughed. "Here, let me have your wine, you guys. No drinking and driving." She took their glasses as Caitlin hoisted her slender frame up onto the handlebars and they took off down the lane heading for US 23.

Shelby hollered after them, "Good thing you don't weigh anything, Caitlin Sotheby. But you're gonna need a bigger ass! Russell, can you really ride like that?"

He laughed and flashed a handsome grin as he pretended to lose control of the bike. Caitlin squealed.

Shelby laughed to see her friends riding off like a couple of teenagers on a first date. They were so cute and there was such an obvious attraction going on. *Don't have to be a "seer" to see that.* She smiled happily as she gathered up the wine with the glasses and took them back inside the trailer.

Shelby was glad to be alone. She wanted to think about the vision she had shared with Sorina earlier. It had been hauntingly real. As much as she tried to let it go, she couldn't shake the images of Lizbeth and Samuel and the horrifying sound of dogs barking in the dark forest. She had sensed Lizbeth's fear and choking panic. It was awful not knowing what happened next. Shelby wanted to think she could save them somehow, like the vision was a manifestation of Sorina's imagination and they could take the story any way they wanted it to go. But if it was real, if Lizbeth and Samuel were real and the visions were real, then they were just observers. At any rate, she planned to visit the cottage again the next day and see if Sorina would take them back in time again.

Shelby lay down on the sofa, breathing deeply, letting the cool green colors of the trailer sooth her until she got surprisingly sleepy again. She fell into a deep slumber. The dream was of green gardens and angels playing mandolins under weeping willow trees:

Heavy branches swayed gracefully and fanned the luminous seraphs as they made their celestial music. But the beauty was almost too much, too perfect. Something was false about it. Just an illusion? Shelby stared hard at the draping willow trees. She reached for the leaves but they felt flat, one dimensional. There were transparent, worn spots in the branches where she could make out something behind them.

The perfect scene was just a cover-up. It wasn't real. She was standing in the middle of a giant painting and there was a rip in the fabric that was getting larger. Her heart leapt in her chest as she realized something on the other side of the canvas was tearing at it, trying to get through. Shelby couldn't breathe as she stared in horror. Before her eyes, the willow trees were being torn apart and one by one the angels were being ripped to shreds.

Vicious dogs came tearing through the canvas running straight for her. Shelby threw her hands up to cover her face as she ran through the shredded trees, through the torn canvas. She ran as fast as she could, but the dogs were catching up to her, their teeth bared and snarling. She ran and she ran, looking over her shoulder at a terrifying darkness that was rolling up behind her. The dogs were right at her heels, lunging for her with horrible fangs. She screamed and cried out, wildly reaching for something, anything to pull herself up and away from the animals. But she was cloaked in black. Sightless. And the dogs kept coming...

Shelby's scream woke her up. She was covered in sweat and her heart was racing. She was frozen in fear. *Oh, my god.* Am I all right? She looked down at her body and felt for her stomach, her arms and legs. They were fine. She was fine. She wasn't being eaten by wild dogs. It had just been an awful dream. *A terrible nightmare.* Shelby tried to calm herself with deep breaths. She couldn't remember ever having had such a horrible dream.

Easing herself up, she sat on the couch looking around at her grandmother's sweet living room. She looked at the clock. She had been sleeping for an hour. It was getting darker outside and Caitlin and Russell weren't back yet. She was still shaking from the horrid nightmare and now an added worry rocked her as she wondered why her friends were still gone. Then she saw her cell over on the table. It was lit up with two texts. Caitlin was telling her they had found a little hamburger joint and did she want anything to go?

Thank God. Shelby texted back that she wasn't hungry and to take their time if they were having fun. She put the phone down and got herself another glass of wine from the kitchen. The dream had been seriously disturbing. Her heart was still racing. *I hope it isn't an omen.* She suddenly felt a compelling need to see Sorina, to tell her about the dream. Maybe it meant something.

Shelby changed into her jeans and a long-sleeved shirt and traded the delicate beaded bracelet for another one of Martha's designs. She ran her fingertips over the turquoise and crystal stones on the silver band as she clipped it over top of her sleeve. It comforted her to wear something of Grandma Mart's.

Shelby texted Caitlin before she left that she was going to Sorina's for a little while and would be back later. *It will give the love birds some more alone time.* She smiled and went out the door.

Shelby decided to hike through the woods instead of taking the lane back to Sorina's. Bella had told her it really was a shortcut and she was so anxious to get to the cottage. She felt a nervous urgency after the dream; more like a visceral need. The dream had been too real, too frightening. Sorina would sort it out.

Shelby went around the trailer and into the cover of the trees. She looked up at the sky through the tall sycamores. It was still light, but clouds were moving in, blocking already-diminishing sun rays. "Rory, where are you?" Shelby asked out loud. She was surprised her rabbit guide had not shown up to escort her. "Okay. I guess I'm on my own." She knew the cottage wasn't far. She just couldn't understand why it always seemed so hard to find.

Enchanted.

She walked quickly, trying to follow a rough, overgrown path. Again, she looked up at the sky. It was getting dark quicker than she anticipated, and the nightmare still lingered in her mind like a reminder of some unnamed evil lurking. *Why the hell didn't I just walk the lane?* She chastised herself. The birches looked bewitching as they moved slightly above her, and skinny shadows flitted around her feet. Shelby tried to keep her mind and her eyes on the elusive path she was following, but mostly she listened for the river. Why couldn't she hear the water? It was as if the dense woods blocked any outside interference on purpose. It was a guarded world of trees. A possessive tree world?

She repeated to herself, w*hy in hell didn't I take the easy, paved road?* It was getting dark way too fast.

She shouted, "Sorina? Help me find you!"

Shelby berated herself. If she was this "medicine woman" and gifted visionary, why couldn't she pick up on vibrations from the cottage? She felt nothing, but an inexplicable dark dread. She was starting to believe she was in real danger.

Damn nightmare.

"Well, this is just stupid," she spoke out loud. Her voice echoed in the organic denseness around her as she added, "Why are you coming unglued like this, Shelby Jean? It's not that far. There's no danger. You're just being a candyass. The last time you thought you were lost, the cottage was right there, right in front of you. It will be the same this time. Even in dusk, Sorina's lights will be on. It won't be long now. Just keep going straight. Listen for the river," she scolded herself, and the sound of her own voice steadied her.

She continued on, one hand guiding her and the other swatting at unruly branches. Her grandmother's bracelet caught on a bare branch and the clasp came loose. It fell from her wrist. Shelby stopped to look for it, but it was as though the unruly ground had swallowed it up. *Oh, no*, Shelby thought, *I couldn't have lost one of Grandma Mart's bracelets.* She stared at her feet looking for the silver braided jewelry and promised, "Don't worry, Grandma. I'll find it if I have to scour these woods for a year."

Just then something moved in the trees. She shifted her attention and looked up. A huge grin replaced the worried expression on her face.

Ah-ha!

She had been right. It wasn't that far. It was as if she just walked through a closed door. *Or the rabbit hole?* She thought of "Alice in Wonderland" again. Where are you, Rory? She suddenly heard the Ohio as it rolled, waves lapping up against the distant banks. Ahead, through the thickest part of the woods, light popped up in stages as house lamps were turned on one by one. Fireflies lit up the flowering bushes bathed in early evening shadow, and provided an illuminated ballet of tiny sparkles. Shelby saw the artificial light washing over the tall trunks and her spirits lifted. *There you are!* Sweet relief flooded her senses.

CHAPTER TWENTY
GOOD WITCH

"SHELBY, YOU HOME?" Caitlin opened the door and Russell followed her into the trailer. They were greeted with silence. "Hummm, I guess the lady of the house is still at Sorina's." Cait turned on the lamps. "Can I offer you a glass of wine, sir?" She batted her long dark lashes and smiled coyly.

"You girls and your wine. Don't you have a beer?" Russell grinned back.

Cait opened the door to the refrigerator. "Let me see. I don't think we have too many beer drinkers." She bent over, reaching to the back of the top shelf, and murmured, "Ah, here we go." She grabbed a Budweiser and just as she turned around to shut the door, he was there. Inches from her face. He put his hands on her arms and held her against the refrigerator door. Her breath quickened.

He asked, "Caitlin?"

"Yes."

He leaned full against her then and kissed her lightly at first and then deeper. She raised a leg and wrapped it around his hips and the refrigerator rocked as they found each other's rhythm. Cait dropped the beer and the can rolled away on the tile floor. She groaned as he picked her up and carried her to the bedroom.

"This room smells like honeysuckle," Russell spoke hoarsely as he held Caitlin in his arms. She was curled up against him, her head on his chest. He twisted her silken dark hair in his fingers and smelled the top of her head. "Even your head smells like honeysuckle."

She punched him lightly in the side and giggled. "Shelby says her grandma was the fragrance queen. I like it. Do you like it?" She rolled her eyes up at him.

"Oh, yeah. I like it." He smiled and kissed her head.

"Well, that's good, but you better slide out of this garden before Shelby gets home. There's only one bed in the house."

He looked over at the clock. 10:30 pm. "Yeah, I guess you're right. Shelby must be having a good time with the *good witch*."

"Good witch?"

"That's what most folks call Sorina around here. They think she's off her rocker, but they love her, too. She has done so much good for people in the strangest ways. It's always some kind of smelly concoction or funky root stuff, but man, that lady can cure the hell out of most illnesses." He pulled on his cycle shorts and added, "Good thing I'm not in health insurance or I'd be out of a job." He laughed.

"So, some kind of herbal remedies?"

"Yeah, I guess. You know, half the time she thinks she's Sorina Duncan McBride, founder of Sorry's Run. Sorina Duncan was a direct descendant of a Scottish woman who supposedly was burned as a witch."

"Ouch!" Caitlin teased. "This Sorry's Run is one wicked, surprising place. It must be the name."

"Yeah. It's all in a name all right. Hell of a thing to overcome." Russell pulled her up from the bed and took her in his arms.

"Russell, Shelby saw a gathering of women in Sorina's cottage last night. I think it bothered her that she wasn't included."

"She will be if she wants to be. Give it time. It was probably a healing. You can ask Bella. Truly, Sorina's damned lucky nobody has wanted to burn her at the stake."

Cait's horrid expression made him laugh.

"Nah, I'm just kidding. They don't take anything she does too seriously except when their eight-year-old has the croup and they can't afford the family clinic. The county is steeped in superstition anyway, mostly Scotch-Irish."

Cait responded, "How fascinating. No wonder Martha was all into fairies and Banshees. And Shelby is just taken with Sorina. I can't blame her. That woman is as charismatic as they come. And Jessie, too. Such special, unusual women living such a surreal existence in that gorgeous cottage. I think Shelby has just fallen in love with the whole romantic idea of it.

"But I will confess, Russell, I have been worried sick about my best friend. I want nothing but her happiness and I sure don't want to get in the way of that. But, my god, she comes back to Kentucky after such a long time and gets thrown into this other world so quickly. It was enough that she lost her grandmother, who she adored. I know Shelby has huge regrets that she didn't get more time with Martha. Then, on the other hand, she never cared much for her dad and now Wesley is all the family she has left. So ironic. And then after that horrible accident that nearly took her life, she miraculously comes out of it unharmed, but changed somehow. It's all very weird and confusing."

Russell nodded. "Yeah, and now Wesley apparently is doing much better and he goes and kicks her out of the house. You're right. It's a lot of strange. But you know what? I remember Shelby when we were in grade school together. Even then, she could handle strange."

"Yeah?" Caitlin watched his deep brown eyes twinkle in his remembering.

"There was this big ugly kid in Sorry's Run that everybody was scared of. His face looked like a train wreck and he was a foot taller than anybody in our class. I think they had held him back three or four grades. Big, dumb, badass kid. Hands as big as a bear's claws. We were all afraid of him. Except Shelby. She would stand in front of him when he was bullying some kid and she would point a tiny finger up at him and tell him to back off. And damn, if that kid wouldn't always back off. He didn't do that for anybody else. Something about Shelby was always powerful."

"Yeah, well, I hear that. She pointed the same finger at the entire City of New York. Nothing scared Holly Golightly." Caitlin grinned.

"Well, there you are. Whatever path she's on, I think you're just going to have to travel it with her and trust that she knows what she's doing. But if she does crash and burn, she's going to need you. She will always need you, Caitlin."

"And you, too, Russell. Now go! Before she gets home and puts a curse on us for doing the nasty in Grandma Mart's bed!" She smacked his perfect ass in the tight shorts and her heart flipped in her chest as she visualized their recent lovemaking. *Hot.*

Russell left and Cait found her cell phone. "Should I wait up for you?" She texted Shelby. There was no reply and it was answer enough for Caitlin. She was tired, but mostly she wanted to crawl back in the "honeysuckle" bed and think of the way Russell had just made love to her. She had never been with such a sexy, sensitive man. She felt like she was falling over a cliff.

What is it about Kentucky?

It was her last thought before she drifted off to sleep.

Caitlin was startled awake in the middle of a vivid dream of Shelby. Her iPhone was sliding across the nightstand chiming. Bella's name came up on the screen.

"Hi, Bella."

Sun was shining in through the windows. Caitlin looked at the empty side of the bed next to her as she held the phone to her ear. "Huh? Oh, yeah. Okay. She must have her cell turned off. Yeah, she probably crashed at Sorina's. I'll have her call you later." Caitlin punched the end button and then checked her messages. Nothing. No message from Shelby.

That's strange.

She thought of the dream she had just had. Shelby was dressed like Audrey Hepburn in "Breakfast at Tiffany's" with her hair twisted high on her head and large sunglasses sliding down her nose. Her ears and neck dripped in diamonds. But as glamorous as she was, she looked so sad. She held her gloved hand out towards Caitlin and spoke to her in a lamenting country twang, "Cait, I need you." Over and over Holly Golightly was saying, "I need you. I need you." It was disturbingly real.

Caitlin mimicked Shelby's favorite cure all, "Shake it off, Caitlin, shake it off." And she did just that, literally shaking off the worry that was mounting. She took a shower and dressed in a pair of cutoff jeans and T-shirt. Combing out her hair, she wrapped it loosely in a knot at the back of her head. She stared at her reflection in the mirror. In the florescent lights her skin looked paler than usual, but it made her big blue eyes pop. She smoothed out her eyebrows and put on some lip gloss before slipping into sandals. She checked her cell phone again. There was still no message from Shelby. A clock chimed eleven times in the kitchen and her stomach reminded her that she hadn't eaten.

Her phone rang. She didn't even look at it before answering, "Shelby?"

"No, it's Russell. Don't tell me you haven't heard from her yet?" His voice held a note of concern.

"No, and that's totally unlike her."

"Well, don't worry. Like we said, Shelby can handle herself. More than likely she and Sorina got into some 'Bubble, bubble, toil and trouble; fire burn and caldron bubble,'" he snickered.

"Shut up."

"Seriously, Cait, do you need me? I can probably rearrange some things around here."

"No, no. I'll just go to the cottage and see what's going on. I'll call you later."

"Okay. And Cait, for me, last night was off the charts."

She smiled demurely and ended the call.

CHAPTER TWENTY-ONE
DEVIL BE DAMNED

"HELLO? ANYBODY HOME?" Caitlin had walked down the lane and now she was behind the cottage staring at the breathtaking riot of flowers and tall grasses blowing in the breeze. She could smell the river, and the warm air was moist on her skin. Stepping towards the wild strawberries, she picked a couple and couldn't believe the juicy sweetness that erupted in her mouth.

"They are especially tasty this year." Sorina was standing directly behind her.

"Oh, Sorina, I didn't see you." Caitlin wiped juice from her chin.

"I was just over there with the chickens." She pointed her cane towards the coop, and added, "But I smelled the berries opening up and I knew somebody was here."

"I'm so sorry. I hope you don't mind. I just couldn't resist."

"Who, of God's creatures, could resist such a perfect gift growing wild?" She joined Caitlin in eating a berry and continued, "But I am pleasantly surprised that you are here. I thought you girls would be off doin' somethin' fun today."

"You mean Shelby isn't with you?"

"No, hon, she ain't." A cloud passed overhead, throwing Sorina into shadow. "Did you think she would be?"

"Yes. She texted me last night to say she was coming over to visit you." Caitlin felt her pulse rise and the air seemed to shift around her.

"Oh, my. Well, she never came that I know of. But maybe…Jessie?!" She yelled towards the woods and Jessie appeared holding a basket full of berries.

"What you need, Sori?"

"Jessie, honey, have you seen Shelby Jean?"

"No."

"So she never dropped by last night, maybe after I went to bed?"

"No, nobody was here last night."

Sorina turned back to Caitlin, her eyebrows raised, and asked, "And she ain't been home?"

"No. And Sorina, her truck is still in the driveway," Caitlin choked on her words.

Sorina took her hand. "Hon, have you had your breakfast?"

"No. It hadn't even crossed my mind."

"Well, then, come on. You gotta eat. We'll feed you and sort this out."

Caitlin numbly followed Sorina back through the screened-in porch to the large, low-ceilinged living room of the cottage. She was again struck by its rustic beauty, but now there was a touch of the unnatural to it all, like something was just off about the way everything looked. *Shelby, where are you?* She felt a cold shiver course over her.

Sorina led her to the long wooden table in front of the fireplace and leaned her cane up against her chair. "Here, hon, sit yourself down. You need some coffee. You want coffee? Or would you rather have tea?"

"Uh, tea would be…no, I'll take coffee. Yes, a strong cup of coffee if you have it, Sorina."

"Of course, dear. Jessie will get it for us. Jessie?"

Caitlin sat down and looked around the room. There was nothing here that looked like a witch's coven. It was just homespun Early American. Except for the fireplace. The fireplace was almost big enough to look medieval.

Cait, get a grip. It's just a quaint Kentucky cottage.

She was caught off guard for the second time when Jessie surprised her with a steaming cup of coffee. Caitlin's hand shook a little as she took it. "Thank you, Jessie. That was quick."

"Jessie almost always has a brewed pot handy. She's gonna scramble you some eggs. You do eat eggs, don't you?"

"Oh, I hate for you to go to any trouble."

"Would you mind, Jessie?" Sorina reached for Jessie's hand.

"No, 'course not."

"See, no trouble at all. You sit still, Cait. I'm gonna call Bella."

Bella argued, "Sorina, Shelby couldn't have just up and disappeared. Have you spoken to Wesley?"

"No. Caitlin just got here, but maybe you could stop by the farmhouse and see if she's there? She might be trying to mend fences."

"Yeah, you're right. Okay. Let me see what I can find out. I'll call y'all in a little bit."

"Thank you, Bella." Sorina hung up the phone and spoke confidently, "You know, that's probably where she's gone off to. Shelby feels uncomfortable about the way she left things with her daddy and she probably needed to see him."

"I don't know. I hope you're right. But I find it hard to believe since her truck is sitting in the driveway."

"Oh, hon, anybody could have picked her up."

Caitlin felt a momentary wave of relief. "I guess that's true. She did grow up here." She got quiet before asking, "But Sorina, can't you just feel her or see her somehow? I mean, Shelby says you're gifted in that way?"

"Well, hon, in some things I am. But I don't have the seein' gift like folks thinks. I am just real sensitive to feelin's. And to tell you the truth, I do find it a bit disturbin' that I am not feelin' Shelby. On some level I have been aware of her energy from the first day she came to Sorry's Run and now I don't have a sense of her at all."

"What does that mean? God, Sorina, you're not sayin'…" Caitlin sat her cup down too hard and coffee splashed onto the table.

Jessie was there in a flash wiping up the spill.

Sorina nodded her head and assured her, "No, no, no. I didn't mean to sound like I think she is gone. No. I just think she is tuned down. She could be sleepin' or just not vibratin' as strong. She wasn't feelin' sick last night, was she?"

"No, she was fine. Russell and I went for a bike ride and she texted me that she was coming to see you. That's all. But to tell you the truth, Shelby has been different ever since she got out of the hospital. I just don't understand any of it, Sorina."

Sorina looked in Caitlin's direction and held out her hand. Cait took it and placed it in her own. Sorina spoke gently, "I know, hon, and the understandin' always takes longer than the doin'. But you just listen to me now. Don't worry your pretty head 'cause it would most likely be worryin' for nothin'. Bella will call after she visits Wesley."

Jessie came out of the kitchen carrying a plate with scrambled eggs and toast. She placed the food in front of Caitlin.

"Thank you, Jessie, for the food and for cleaning up my mess." She smiled at the shy girl. A few minutes passed as Cait tried to eat.

The house phone rang shrilly, cutting through the mounting tension.

Sorina reached for the receiver. "Yes, Bella?" Sorina didn't speak for another minute and Caitlin wanted to yank the phone from her hand. "Okay, then. I think you're right. Thanks, hon. I will."

Sorina hung up and spoke calmly, "Bella went to Wesley's, but it's the strangest thing. She couldn't get in."

"Couldn't get in?" Cait put down her fork.

"No. She said she tried the front door and then knocked on the windows, hollerin' for Wesley. But she couldn't tell if anybody was home. Now, that is odd. I don't think that man has left his house 'cept for a doctor's appointment for years. Where in the world would he have gone?"

Cait asked, "Maybe I should text Russell? He might have better luck."

"There you go," Sorina agreed.

Cait punched in a message on her phone. Russell texted her back right away: I'll stop by Wesley's on my way home. I'm off early today. Don't worry. I'm sure there's a simple explanation.

Caitlin put her cell phone back in her pocket and got up from the table. "Thanks for the breakfast, Jessie, Sorina, but I just don't have an appetite. I do feel better, though, and I thank you. Please let me know if you hear anything, anything at all. Okay? Here, I'll give you my cell number." Cait wrote her number down and handed it to Jessie. "Call me the minute you hear anything. I don't care what time it is."

After a quick goodbye hug from Sorina, Jessie escorted her out to the screened-in back porch and squeezed her hand at the door. "Caitlin, I sure do hope there ain't nothin' wrong with Shelby Jean. She is so special. We all love her."

Cait looked into the doe eyes of this curious woman who sang like a bird and made magical gardens. Her voice was filled with emotion as she replied, "Thank you for saying that, Jessie. I'm sure she's fine. She has always been independent. For all I know, she's getting drunk in some bar with a handsome stranger. And believe me, if that's the case, I'm gonna kick her butt from here to high heaven." The women hugged and Cait waved goodbye.

She walked toward the lane, but then decided to take the shortcut into the woods. *Maybe Shelby came this way. Maybe she met with an accident?* Caitlin's thoughts caused a quiver in her chest. It felt like something was eating at her, nibbling away, leaving a hole in her heart. That's what it would feel like if something ever happened to Shelby. *Empty.* Cait couldn't imagine life without her best friend who was more like a sister. The two of them had come through everything together; had pretty much grown up together in the bizarre, frightening world of high-fashion modeling. Shelby was her family, her life. She couldn't imagine living without her.

Caitlin took a deep breath and tried to relax as she walked through Martha's woods for the first time. It was a heady feeling, all the trees and shrubs clustered together. *Almost claustrophobic.* Caitlin kept her head down just looking for anything out of the ordinary as she made her way back to the trailer, but there was no sign of Shelby.

The beautiful brunette was not even aware that a small rabbit followed her the whole way.

"Wes? Are you in there? Anybody home?" Russell stood on the sagging front porch of the farmhouse. No one answered his knock. Then he stared in through the living room window. There was no sign of anybody in the house. "Okay, that is different," Russell spoke under his breath. It wasn't like Wes to be anywhere but inside his house. Then he thought he heard something. A motor? Russell followed the sound around back behind the house and saw a tractor far out in the field. The man sitting on it plowing through the earth was Wesley Stiller.

He punched in Caitlin's cell number. "I'm tellin' you, Cait, Wesley is farmin' his land. That might not sound so remarkable, but believe me, it hasn't happened in twenty years. No, I won't get to talk to him. He probably can't even see me. I tried the doors, and they were locked. I'll just have to come back tomorrow to see if he has heard from Shelby Jean. Huh? Oh, sure. I'll be there in five minutes."

Russell put the phone in his pocket and climbed into his Lexus. He smiled as he started the ignition. *I got a date with a hot dame in a trailer.* As scary as this business was getting with Shelby, he couldn't help but feel excited at the thought of being with Caitlin again. He had been in love before, and he had been totally taken with Shelby, but there was something about Caitlin Sotheby that was like nothing he had ever experienced. It wasn't just that she was the most perfect woman he had ever been with; there was a warmth to her that surprised him. Usually gorgeous women put him off; made him nervous. He never trusted them, figuring every guy on the planet wanted to make time with them and they knew it. But Caitlin was different. She was breathtakingly beautiful, but she didn't flaunt it. There was a small town quality to her. As sophisticated as her life had been and was, she still seemed naïve, sweet, untouched by the harsh realities of the world. She was the most desirable woman Russell had ever been with.

He cranked up Sirius and drove the few miles down the road to Martha's trailer.

Out in the field Wesley wiped at his brow and cut the engine on his brand new John Deere. He had seen Russell nosing around. It was an aggravation. He just wanted people to stay away. He didn't need the busybodies anymore and that was a blessing. He had had to tolerate those bitches because he was so disabled. But not now. Now he felt strength returning to his limbs and his breath filled his lungs in a comfortable way for the first time in years. It might have been the devil's work that cured him, but he would take the cure and damn well do what he wanted to do. And right now he wanted to ready his fields for tobacco. It was too late in the season to do any planting, but his twenty-five acres would be ready by next spring.

He reached into his pocket and pulled out a cigarette and lit it, taking a deep drag, pain free. He grinned. He didn't care that the State didn't want anybody growing tobacco anymore; he was going to grow it. He didn't give a shit that the whole pussy-whipped world was not allowed to smoke; he was going to smoke until he dropped. He was going to start the seeds in the winter in the barn and then after the year of planting and cultivating he was going to hang those big gorgeous plants in his barn and cure them and the hell with what made sense.

Wesley loved tobacco plants. He always had. They were so hearty looking, with their broad, thick leaves that turned from lush green into such an inviting golden color. He took another drag and smiled again. He never thought he would feel this good again. Maybe he had sold his soul. Devil had come to him for sure. He must deserve it, but he would have his way. Yes, he was going to ready his fields for planting tobacco, just like his father had done and his father before him. Devil be damned.

CHAPTER TWENTY-TWO
A TAD BIT CONCERNED

RUSSELL STOOD IN THE TRAILER and held onto her for a long time. Caitlin laid her head on his chest and let herself be held as tears came.

"Don't, Cait. We'll find her. I'm sure it's just some weird kind of misunderstanding."

"I don't think so. Russell. Her truck is here. The keys are in the drawer. I have texted her and left voice messages over and over and she doesn't respond. And now her mailbox is full. Her phone is either turned off, which is totally unlike her, or she's lost it, which makes me worry even more, you know, that maybe she is lost along with it. And Russell, I walked through the woods, wondering if she had fallen or something worse, and it is larger than I thought. I think we need more people to really search. And I have to get back to New York. My plane leaves in two days." Her blue eyes filled with fresh tears that rolled down her cheeks.

He wiped them away gently with his thumb and spoke, "It's only been a day. We can't file a missin' person's report yet. But you're right about that search. If she doesn't show up, we'll have to organize one. Martha's woods can be deceiving." He hugged her and continued, "Cait, I have another bike at my house. Go ridin' with me and we'll cover the country side until it gets dark. Maybe somethin' will trigger an idea, or maybe she'll be home when we get back?"

Caitlin swallowed hard and nodded. "Okay."

"I'll go get the bikes and be right back. Wear long pants. We might be in some scratchy territory."

"Okay."

Caitlin watched him pull away and went into the bedroom to change. She was so grateful for Russell. She would be completely lost without him.

Something was terribly wrong. She could feel it. Shelby was in trouble. But Russell was right. There was nothing more to be done. Nobody had gotten into Wesley's house and Shelby could be there. It didn't make sense, but it was a possibility. She would call the police before she left for New York, and just have to pray. And she knew Bella and her friends would search nonstop.

If only Sorina could pick up on something. Cait realized in that moment that she was starting to buy into Shelby's whole psychic mumbo-jumbo. Sorina was supposed to be super sensitive. Why wasn't she getting a vibe on Shelby? Caitlin just kept imagining Shelby lying alone somewhere, her head bleeding from who knows what. She could be anywhere.

But then Caitlin remembered countless dangerous moments in New York. She thought of a time when echoing steps had followed them all the way home after a splashy party. They hadn't been able to get a cab, and they were still struggling models, so limos weren't their mode of transportation. They were just two young women dressed to the nines on New York streets. The menacing footsteps had gotten closer and closer and Caitlin remembered being so scared, thinking the worse. But Shelby had squeezed Cait's hand and suddenly started singing at the top of her lungs. She had literally pulled them to a stop, had turned toward their stalker, and had screamed the lyrics to the John Lennon song, "Give Peace A Chance." The startled loser had run like a scared rabbit, and the girls had laughed all the way home. Cait smiled at the memory. She reminded herself once again that there weren't too many ways to take down Shelby Jean Stiller. She was made from good Scotch-Irish stock.

In a half hour Russell was back; bikes loaded onto racks on the car. He pulled out two backpacks from the backseat and handed her one. It contained bottled water, a small bag of almonds and two power bars. He had the same thing in his backpack.

"Well, now I see why you're so fit, Russell. No junk food for you, huh?" She smiled as she examined the label on the energy bars.

"I try. But if you don't like that stuff, there's a KFC down the road?" He grinned.

"Not on your life. I'm doing this your way. You lead and I will follow. Where are we going, anyway?"

"I thought we could ride past Wesley's again if you want? Maybe he's in the house. There's some great side roads down that way."

Caitlin put on her helmet and got on the seat of a bike that was identical to his. "Okay, you're going to have to give me a speed course on how to operate this thing." She was staring at the gear levers on the handlebars.

"My pleasure." He grinned and instructed, "The lowest gears allow you to pedal easily and the higher gears are harder, but allow you to go faster. While we're on 23 we should both be in high gear, and when we get into some hills, we'll be in low gear. The trick is to kind of stay at the same pace, like the same cadence, and just switch gears instead of pedaling faster and slower. You see?"

She had watched him demonstrate, but she barely heard what he said. He was so close to her that she could feel the heat emanating from his cologne-scented skin. In his form-fitting bike jersey and pants he was as handsome as any of the male models she knew in New York. Her whole body shivered suddenly, as she remembered their lovemaking.

"Okay. I think I've got it. I'll follow you, but just don't go too fast?"

He jumped on his bike, and Cait followed him out of the driveway and down the lane to US 23. He used all the proper hand signals, and she mimicked him. Out on the highway, Cait felt a rush of exhilaration and fright at the same time, but it was so much better than the great worry that had been her constant companion. The ride was just what she needed. A perfect distraction. Traffic was heavier than she thought it would be and she worked hard to focus on Russell in front of her. She tried to time her pedaling to match his and soon she was right in sync with him. It was a wonderful feeling. The traffic finally lightened up and she was only aware of the soft air she was traveling through and her muscles waking up, propelling her forward.

In no time at all, they were approaching the Stiller farmhouse. Russell signaled that he was crossing to the left and Cait looked both ways and followed him across the road. He pulled up in front of the house and leaned his bike against the porch. Caitlin did the same. They walked up to the front door and knocked. Again, no answer. Cait looked inside the window and saw no one. Then they heard it. A distant motor. Going around back they saw Wesley out in the field, still churning up the long-neglected land. They stood for awhile hoping to catch his attention, but he never let on that he saw them. After trying both front and back doors, they got back on their bikes and Russell led them to a road off of US 23 that wound up into the hills.

Caitlin felt herself really letting go as she followed Russell through the windy country road. It was so quiet and her mind relaxed and took in the beauty of Kentucky. Each bend in the road brought different serene landscapes of early plantings of wheat and wild grasses. Cows grazed in fertile fields enclosed in white fences. They passed rolling hills dressed in soothing mossy groundcover, pine trees, and morning glories bursting with bright hues; purple, pink, blue. Caitlin just kept taking deep breaths, as though each would be her last. She felt she was on such a strange ride, intoxicating, really. And she kept a perfect cadence with Russell ahead of her.

He signaled to her that he was moving off to the left. She slowed and followed him to a creek bed where there was a flat area of smooth rock.

"Hungry?" he asked, as he got off his bike and laid it down against a tree stump.

"Sure." She did the same and then joined him at the bank of the creek. They sat down and dug into their backpacks for water and the power bars. The dappling water bubbled with effervescent energy.

"It's beautiful, Russell. Thank you for bringing me here."

She wasn't aware of how she looked, her blue eyes sparkling like the water and her blue-black hair gleaming in the lowering sunlight. She was only aware of how she felt—alive, young and strong, her muscles hot from the burn of the pedaling, her body on fire for the man sitting next to her. She put down the food and looked over at him. He looked back at her and she saw in his eyes the same desire she felt reflected back at her. Caitlin leaned in and put her hand up to his cheek. He took it and kissed her palm and then put his hand on the back of her head and pulled her closer. They stared into each other's eyes, blue into deeper blue. Their breath quickened. He looked down at her mouth and kissed her full lips gently over and over.

He laid her back on a bed of mossy stone and slowly undressed her, tossing her clothes over into the bushes. She was naked, then, lying on the wet flat rock. It was hard underneath her and cool. A strong breeze fanned the water that splashed up over the stones in tiny rivulets, trickling over her naked thighs in a delicious tease. The more the water licked at her, the more Russell kissed her, her mouth, her breasts. His tongue played with her as the water gurgled over her stomach, and then lower. Her heart raced and she closed her eyes, listening and feeling everything. Sensuous pulses throbbed deep inside her while the water caressed her skin, bathing her in pure physical pleasure. "Oh, my god," she barely spoke above a whisper.

When she opened her eyes he was standing tall and naked in front of her.

Her breath caught and tears welled up in her eyes. "You are so beautiful, Russell."

He lowered himself to her side and his fingers got into a rhythm with the current of the creek as he fondled her. She closed her eyes, imagining cool and hot tongues tasting her everywhere in gentle, sexy strokes. It brought her to near madness with desire.

"Russell, please?"

He rolled over onto her and cradled her head in his hands as he took her. She lifted her hips while the bubbling water splashed them. He swelled inside her, going deeper until at last they came together in hot, wet explosions of release. He collapsed onto her, then, letting the creek wash them. They lay, listening to the beating of their hearts until their breath eased.

"We have to get out of her, Cait. I want you again," Russell whispered, pushing her raven hair off her forehead.

A fluttering of wings startled them. Two black birds lighted on the stone next to them, cocking their fluffy heads. They dipped their wings into the water and shook, spraying the lovers. The birds looked at them curiously, but didn't fly off, as if nothing was out of place.

Cait laughed. "Yes, we have to go." She sat up and the birds flew off, their wet, black wings shadowing the blue sky. A shadow fell over her happiness, too, for just a flash. She found her clothes and Russell helped dry her off with a cloth napkin from his backpack. As she watched him she knew she was lost to this handsome Kentuckian. She had never made love so passionately. It was sexy beyond belief to be naked and intimate in the outdoors. She had never felt so free, so uninhibited.

"Are you all right to ride?" He asked, his eyebrows lifting in concern.

"Oh, yeah, I'm all right." She smiled and got on her bike. The warmth between her legs would only be a constant reminder of the way he had felt. She put on her helmet and followed him back towards the road as the light grew dimmer in the sky and more black birds gathered overhead.

They got back to Martha's trailer just as nighttime fell. The trailer was still empty. Caitlin looked about sadly.

"Are you coming in?" she asked.

"No, Caitlin, I better not. I have a long day tomorrow. But call Bella in the morning and have her go back out to Wesley's. Then, if there's no word, call the police."

"Okay. Will I see you tomorrow?"

"Do you want to see me tomorrow?"

"Oh, yeah."

"Then you will." He took her face in his hands and kissed her again.

Heat raced through her limbs and she felt like she would explode with longing. "Are you sure you can't stay?"

"Goodnight, Caitlin Sotheby." He smiled and turned from her, going out the door.

That night, lying beneath Martha's honeysuckle sheets she relived every moment of her time with Russell and tried to keep the impossibility of Shelby's disappearance at bay. But she felt traitorous somehow. On the one hand she was desperately worried about her best friend, but on the other hand she was falling head over hills for this guy.

She snuggled into her pillow and wanted to cry and giggle at the same time. She thought of Russell and his beautiful eyes and his beautiful hair, and the way he had looked, his hard body standing in front of her, ready for her, surrounded by nature and water.

Then she thought of Shelby.

She thought of the countless runways they had shared. Too many to count. She and Shelby had walked together, blinding lights of the paparazzi flashing all around as they put one high-heeled foot in front of the other. The hardest part had been not showing a sign of emotion. It was exciting beyond belief, but they were to appear as walking mannequins, rigid and perfect. No one was supposed to look at them, only the fashion they were displaying. It was a dehumanizing experience, and one that Shelby never really got the hang of. No matter what they said to her, how they scolded her, how they berated her, she managed to show a bit of herself in front of the ogling buyers. And it worked. She sold whatever she was wearing, and soon enough the designers became aware that Shelby Jean Stiller was a star and they wanted her to wear their clothing. Shelby strutted and winked at just the right time and the gawking VIPs thrilled to her slightest display of charm. She was a hit and Caitlin stayed glued to her side and got the good jobs along with her.

"Ah, Shelby? Where are you?" Caitlin called out her name and hugged her pillow harder. She tossed and turned. She was a wreck of tangled emotions. How could this be happening? How could Shelby have disappeared when everything was so sweet and simple in this small Kentucky town? In all of New York, nothing had ever scared her like this was scaring her. She felt powerless. Maybe Shelby was just taking a time out and not wanting to be with anybody. But Caitlin didn't believe that.

A clock chimed in the living room. It was still early, but Cait wanted to sleep. She reached over and took a pill from the bottle she always kept close. Then she took another one.

Nine hours later her cell phone buzzed on the nightstand.

"Hello?"

"Caitlin, tell me what's goin' on?"

She recognized Bella's voice. Cait looked over at the empty pillow next to her, and answered, "Shelby is still missing. I'm going to have to file a missing person's report if I don't hear something from her today. Bella, would you go out to Wesley's again and see if he knows anything?"

"I am on it! This just don't sound right. I'll call you this afternoon."

Cait thanked her and plugged her cell phone back into the charger. Bella was the perfect person to help. She would find out something at the farmhouse. Relieved, Caitlin turned over in the bed sheets and let her mind drift off to romance. She was way too groggy to do anything else.

"Wesley, you in there?" Bella was knocking at the front door. He didn't answer and she peered into the living room window. *Not in his chair.* She knocked and hollered again, and then decided to go around behind the house.

She saw him, then, out in his fields. *God, now ain't that somethin.* Bella hadn't seen Wesley Stiller on a tractor since they were young. She sat down on the back porch steps and pulled out a Coke from her purse. This time she had come prepared. If Wesley thought she was going away, he had another thing coming. She took a swig from the can and settled herself into a comfortable position.

She fell asleep.

"Ouch." Something nudged her foot and woke her. Her head felt like it was twisted the wrong way. "Goddamn it." She rubbed her neck.

"I thought you Christian ladies weren't supposed to cuss?" Wesley was grinning at her.

Bella struggled to straighten herself up.

"Well, sometimes we weaken."

He laughed and helped her up.

"How long you been out here?"

"Oh, I don't know. Long enough to take a good nap. Wesley, you look different."

He took off his ball cap and ran his hand through his new short haircut. He smiled and looked years younger. "Well, I feel different. What you want, Bella? I have work to do."

"What I want is to find out where Shelby has gone off to. Is she here?"

"No, I ain't seen her. Ain't she at Martha's trailer?"

"No. Nobody has seen her goin' on three days and we're all gittin' just a tad bit concerned."

"Oh, hell, Shelby is probably hangin' with one of her old school buddies. She was pretty popular before she took off and went to the other end of the earth."

"I don't think so. Caitlin is worried sick and I'm startin' to join her in that. But, okay. If you say you ain't seen her, I believe you." She stretched and looked out at the field where the tractor sat. "So, Wesley, you are plowin'?" Her eyebrows arched.

"Yeah, I'm gittin' her ready for plantin' next spring."

"Ain't that a new tractor?" She asked suspiciously.

"Martha left me a little nest egg from the money she got over the years from Shelby."

"Will wonders never cease." Bella grinned, though she knew full well about Martha's generosity when it came to her son-in-law. "Okay, then, you just promise me you'll call if you hear anythin' from Shelby?"

"Yeah, I will. But I highly doubt if she'll be in touch. Me and Shelby is kind of not speakin'."

"So I hear. But you never know. A girl and her daddy is a hard thing to sever. She just might come around. You be sure to let me know if she does."

He agreed and Bella left him to get back to work. She got in her car and punched in Caitlin's number. "No, hon, he doesn't have a clue. I am beginnin' to wonder, too, if she has met with some real trouble. I'm drivin' over to Sorina's. We'll decide what to do." Bella put her car in drive. She looked over her shoulder at the ramshackle farmhouse as she headed down 23. Something most assuredly wasn't right.

"Sori, how in H are we gonna form a circle with just the three of us?" Violet demanded. "And don't you think it's a might hot in here with the fire roaring? It's late May, for god's sake!"

"Well, you're in a mood." Jolene raised an eyebrow.

"That's right, I am. This don't feel right. I mean, gettin' Dory Jenkins to lose some weight is one thing, but Shelby gone missin' and us tryin' to talk to Martha is another." Violet took a drink of the absinthe.

"You wasn't supposed to drink that yet, Vi," Jolene scolded.

"I don't care. My nerves are shot."

Bella jumped in and said, "Well, Vi has a point, Sorina. What are we doin'? And where is Caitlin? Don't you think she should be in on this? She is closest to Shelby after all." Bella wiped sweat from her forehead with a hankie.

"Russell is takin' her to the airport real early in the mornin' and I think they wanted this evenin' together."

Bella shook her head. "Well, that's sweet. But don't you think this a little more important? I mean, after tomorrow she'll be gone?"

"Shelby is closed off, Bella. Her energy is quiet. So I don't think Caitlin would be of any special help. And I know Cait fears the worst." Sorina paused just long enough to allow their imaginations to run wild. Then she added, "But I don't think Shelby is gone. I really don't. I feel twinges of her. Just the slightest breeze of a Shelby feelin', like her hand just waved over my head, rustlin' the air ever so slightly. It's really hard to explain, but I don't think she is gone."

"Well, praise Jesus for that," Jolene whispered under her breath.

Sorina continued, "I only wanted you three here because you're the perfect extension of Martha's vibration. I would include Jessie in the circle, but you know how Martha loved Jessie's music. Jessie needs to play to entice Mart to help us. Maybe we can get her to come through the veil of the spirit world and give us some answers. Unless you think it's too soon? I know Shelby's only been gone a short while." Sorina waited on their reply.

Violet and Jolene looked at Bella. Bella answered on cue, "Hell, no, it ain't too soon. I say bring it. It's what Martha would do. It won't do any harm to try, right, Sorina?"

Sorina nodded, and hoped she was right. "I thought we should try some of Martha's ways from the old country, stay with her spells and try to reach her through her druid ancestors."

"Can you do that, Sorina?" Violet asked.

"I don't know. But I must try."

"Good gravy, we all must try. This is awful." Jolene wiped a tear from her cheek. "Give me some of that Absinthe, Jessie?"

"Here's to the green fairy," Bella toasted and they all drank.

"That don't sound the same as when Sorina says it." Violet's lips turned up in a smile. "Mighta lost somethin' in the translation."

Sorina got serious. "Now listen, y'all. It is important that we clear our minds except for thoughts of Martha; thoughts of lovin' her; thoughts of laughin' with her; thoughts of her strong beliefs. Her beliefs guided her in her life and must guide us now. And Vi, I apologize for it bein' too hot, but the fire will help protect us."

"It's okay, Sorina. I'm used to it. I have ten hot flashes a day."

Sorina smiled. "Now, do you think you can do this or not?"

"No, no. We're with you. We can do this. Right, girls?" Bella asked.

Violet and Jolene nodded and drained their glasses. Without anymore direction than Sorina's nod, Jessie dimmed the lights overhead and then stepped to the nearest candle and lit it. She did the same throughout the spacious room until candlelight flickered from all corners. Then Jessie picked up her mandolin that was leaning on the bookcase and began to play softly. She added her own high sweet voice that sounded more like chanting than singing. The women stood tight around Sorina and joined hands forming a small, closed circle.

Sorina's petite frame fit easily in the middle of the circle with room enough for a small triangular-shaped stand loaded with rock crystals and colorful decanters. She opened the lid to a squatty, purple jar and ran her fingers through fresh dirt she had dug up from one of the flower gardens. An earthy organic aroma rose. She bowed her head and whispered, "Bring the goddess power from Mother Earth to this circle of love that cannot be broken."

The women tightened their grips, allowing themselves to feel the energy from each other's hands as it passed between them.

Sorina continued in a hushed, reverent voice, "Martha Maggie McBride, we honor your life in this physical plane, and we honor your soul in the spirit world where you reside in peace. You were our beloved friend and guide. Please bring your wisdom to guide us now. We need your help."

Jessie stopped her melodious chanting and playing. The room was still except for the crackling coming from the fireplace.

Sorina added, "Ladies, breathe slowly and think on Martha. See Martha."

After a minute of silence Sori picked up a quartz crystal and let it roll around her palm, feeling it with her fingers. Then she placed the quartz in a square decanter filled with water from the river. She dipped her hand in it, sprinkling the quartz-infused water over her arms and around her neck.

"The water is for carrying unseen things. The fire is for strength and will protect us. The music will guide the druidess to us."

Jessie picked up the mandolin again and this time played a delicate Celtic melody.

Sorina's fingers traced each decanter until she found the one she wanted. She opened it and a glittery powder floated out. She spoke, "The fairies track the ways of the spirit." Then she chanted:

"Bring the fairies
Circlin' 'round our head.
From the wee ancient ones
We all will be led,
To keep back the evil
But bring the eye
To see the otherworld
Where our ancestors lie."

Sorina picked up more of the sparkling dust and tossed it into the air. It caught the candlelight and became effervescent in the darkened room.

"To find where the daughter lies,
Sow a seed that discovers
Her heart, her mind
Her soul that hovers
O'er her body that waits
For help from the others.

Our souls will then fly
And be bringin' us nigh
To wisdom and knowing
From the druidess on high.
Bring the fairies
Circlin' 'round our head.
From the wee ancient ones
We all will be led."

Sorina repeated the last part of the incantation three times. Then she lowered her head again. All was quiet except for the mandolin and the fire, which took on an unexpected intensity. The heat blew through the room as the women kept their heads down, their eyes closed and their hands clasped. But something else was happening. The largest candle lost its flame, and then one by one they were all extinguished as if someone was methodically snuffing them out. The air changed drastically from hot to cold. The fire continued to diminish, as an unnerving dampness drifted down through the chimney causing each woman to chill. No one opened their eyes. Jessie stopped playing the music. Everything was silent.

Too quiet.

Then a wind whistled through the fireplace. A real wind; not just a draft. It blew embers around and Jessie jumped to put them out. The women stayed still, but it got harder and harder as a sense of doom permeated their thoughts. It never felt like this in Sorina's house.

Something wasn't right.

Bella opened her eyes and just in that instant an unseen force knocked the glittery decanter onto its side, spilling its sparkling contents over everything. The decanter rolled off the small table and crashed onto the floor.

Bella's voice came out in a weak quiver, "I think Martha is sayin' no."

CHAPTER TWENTY-THREE
THE BIG APPLE

CAITLIN SAT BACK IN THE CAB and relaxed. The traffic was backed up on the Parkway. She didn't mind. She was in no hurry to get back to the City anyway without Shelby. She stared out her window, as if for the first time. New York. She had always thrilled to the massiveness of it. The giant behemoth had frightened her and excited her at the same time when she had first laid eyes on its impossible magnitude. But today she only felt a palpable loneliness looking out the window.

Caitlin was a small-town girl, the same as Shelby. She had been discovered, the same as Shelby, by a photographer who had insisted on taking her picture, and then insisted further that she allow him to submit the pictures to New York magazines. She had been tall and thin as a kid, with long luxurious shining black hair and cobalt blue eyes that bordered on violet. High cheekbones, lush lips and delicate features had given her a face that the camera loved and she loved being photographed. But everything had frightened her. She had been terribly homesick when she met Shelby Stiller, another waif from another hick town. They had bonded and been an inseparable pair ever since.

And now her soul mate was lost to her, lost to some thing or someone. Just lost. It was inconceivable that this could have happened. Not in Sorry's Run. But maybe there was something to that haunting name, maybe even prophetic. She thought of the slaves who had struggled in those long-ago, terrifying days to find refuge with a woman named Sorina. Caitlin had been captivated by the imagery of the story and she remembered Shelby telling her of the scenes that had played out in her head of Lizbeth and Samuel and their desperate flight towards freedom. Shelby said Sorina had shown her the moving pictures, and Caitlin had thought she had taken one too many Valium. But now she was hoping and praying that Sorina really did have the ability to see what was just underneath the "real" world and that she would find Shelby. And soon.

There was a feeling in Caitlin's stomach that wouldn't go away, a feeling that something more than terrible was happening to her best friend. It burned in her gut when she thought on Shelby. It bordered on nausea.

And then she forced herself to think of something else. Or someone else. And that was Russell. Out of all the strangeness with Martha's death, Shelby's accident, followed by her mysterious disappearance, there was Russell James. She had never felt this way about anybody before, and the timing seemed sordid almost. But maybe that was the way this life worked, something good always skirting something bad to keep you from going over the cliff.

But she was falling for sure, falling for him. He had been so tender with her last night in Martha's trailer. She knew Bella and her friends were going to Sorina's and Caitlin thought she should go, but she didn't want to. She wanted to be with him. And Sorina had sensed that and suggested she do just that, so she had. And she was glad. There were fresh memories now swimming in her head and her body. Memories of him and memories of how he made her feel. She was alive in an electric way. Every nerve tingling at the thought of his touch. All that mixed with her worry and fear about Shelby made for an emotional roller coaster, the likes of which she had never experienced.

She needed her best friend to ask her how to handle all these feelings.

Russell had filed the missing person's report. He was so connected in the area and he said the police would make a real effort and maybe would recruit some of the locals to help scour the woods in a few days. It was a nightmarish thought, people walking through the trees with flashlights, looking for any signs of Shelby, her clothing, her possessions, or even her body.

Caitlin's cell phone buzzed in her pocket and made her jump in surprise. She came back from her reverie and answered, "Oh, hi, Tommy. No, it's cool. I took a cab. Huh? Because I wanted to. I didn't want you to have to take off work. Yeah, I'll be back at the lab tomorrow. No, she's still missing. I know. Call me later?"

Tommy Roe was her other best friend, and thank God for him. She was going to need him. He was her perfect confidante. He loved Shelby, too, and would be of help to her in the days ahead.

Cait returned her focus to looking outside her passenger window at the passing concrete jungle that introduced the newcomer to a city that refused to be ignored. It pushed itself to the forefront of any preoccupation, any daydream, any dream of any kind. It's because the City knew it *was* the dream, everybody's dream. It was where the real world converged and all other geographical spots on the map disappeared. The Big Apple, the land of possibilities and the sinkhole of disappointments.

The quintessential New Yorker was the guy who had learned to live with the heartache and promise of what the City offered, but not relying on either one. He could roll with its temptations of excitement, heady culture, creativity, and road to riches beyond comprehension, all lined with crime, filth, noise and chaos. Somewhere in all those extremes, he found a comfort zone that only his fellow New Yorkers understood.

Cait and Shelby had not experienced much of the shady side of the City. They had been shown a shiny, ravenous Big Apple that welcomed young, naïve, pure things to its juicy inflated reality.

The cabbie parked in front of the Manhattan high-rise and pulled Caitlin's bags out of the trunk. He was from the Dominican Republic and his taxi was decorated with every imaginable island trinket from home. *Probably spent more time with strangers in his backseat than with his family.* But he had a good handle on English and that always impressed her. She often thought about how the big city had frightened her when she had first come. What must it be like for the countless immigrants who arrived daily, not speaking a word of English? She gave him a hefty tip and then carted her bags up the steps.

"Hi, Jeremiah."

"Hi yourself, Miss Caitlin. Welcome home. Here, let me help you with those bags. How was your trip? Kentucky, wasn't it?"

Jeremiah was the doorman and he was a trusted friend. Shelby and Caitlin loved him and he seemed to love them, too. He had become a father figure to them over the years. He always took a special interest in the young beauties who he said "classed up the place." He knew they were small-town girls and he was always looking out for them.

"Not so good, Jeremiah. Well, it was good, but then Shelby went missing." The words caught in her throat.

"Went missing?"

Caitlin's defenses broke down in the saying of the words and she started to cry. Jeremiah immediately sat her bags down. She was tall, but he was a head taller, and when he wrapped his long arms around her she felt like she was being wrapped by all that was safe. She allowed herself a moment to stay there.

Sorina made her way down to the river's edge the way she always did—carefully. Her cane had a knack for finding just the right nooks and crannies to guide her safely, as though the wind and water never changed the often muddy, wood-strewn bank. A warm breeze came off the river bringing with it soft scents of water and purpose.

The Ohio meant everything to her in this life and in the previous one, which were always intertwined. Sorina knew she was living in the 21st century, but this other life lived in her as well. And the two were inseparable. Truth be told, she wouldn't want them to be separate. The historic Sori had been a remarkably courageous woman, and Sorina liked feeling that way. If she wasn't Sorina Duncan McBride, she didn't know who she was.

The Scottish pioneer woman had been a talented historian and had written everything down in vivid detail and with such description that it became more than mere words on a page. Her diary was a living, breathing account of her daily life; her fears, her triumphs. Jessie had found the little Reader book hidden behind a loose stone in the fireplace. Remarkably, it was the one place in the cottage that had not been completely destroyed over time.

A hidden treasure.

Sorina had wanted it described. "Jessie, is it in long hand?"

"No, it's in scratchy print."

"So it's hard to read?"

"Yeah, kinda."

Sorina pressed, "What's the handwriting like, Jessie? Are the letters made all perfect?"

"No. It looks like it was written very fast, like there wasn't enough time to make it look pretty."

"So, it's like somebody jottin' down notes at the end of a long day?"

"Somethin' like that. But there's so much detail. It's much more than notes. But it's like she was tired, real tired when she wrote it. But it must have been so important to her to write all this down."

Sorina knew it was fate that brought the journal to her—that she was meant to read it. So read it, she did, through Jessie's narration.

Jessie was a woman of very few words, but each night when she opened Sorina's diary to read, her melodic voice took on a surprising confidence, as it did in her singing. Her Kentucky accent became peppered with inflections far different from her own, as though she were channeling the Scottish story teller. It had been captivating to listen to, and Sorina was indeed captivated. It excited her to take this personal journey into the intimate thoughts of such a unique woman. A woman who founded Sorry's Run by living life on her own terms in a wild and savage time. A woman who, through her own sheer will and determination, became a human pathway to freedom for many unknown slaves.

The nightly readings had become a necessary ritual. And though Jessie seemed to truly enjoy it, for Sorina it was life changing. Her past was a void, filled with emptiness instead of memories. She had no reference for her own personal history, so she soaked up the words Jessie read from the pages, and they became so much a part of her daily thoughts that she sometimes couldn't really distinguish the past from the present. It was disturbing, but fascinating, and it made her happy to mingle the two lives.

Sorina listened to the water as it lapped lazily against the muddy banks. The spring sunshine caressed her cheeks and she could feel herself lifting up and away with a delicious lightness. She always came to the river to imagine, to see with a clarity that nobody else could. People thought the blind were incapable of "seeing" but they had no idea how the mind provided the visual images that gave her sight when her eyes did not. She could see her alter ego. She could smell the smells and feel the pain…

Sorina Duncan heaved over the side of the ship. It was so uncharacteristic of her to be sick. She was used to caring for others, never needing to be cared for herself. But this voyage, this was something she couldn't have fathomed, even in

her own wondering mind whose imagination seemed to know no boundaries. Sailing over such churning, angry waters was too much even for her. After all, she had never spent a moment of her life away from the land, and now she was being tossed like a ragdoll over the high seas on her way to the New World.

But she was glad. Even with the horrible nausea and having to endure the sickening stuff they called food, and the rancid water she was forced to drink, she was glad. She was a Duncan and she would survive. Others on the ship had not been so fortunate. Several of the women had been stricken with sickness and had died horribly—one, whose unborn child still lay alive in her womb. Sorina had tried to help, but the crew watched her too closely. The name of Duncan still carried a badge of heresy in Scotland. A hanging would have been considered fair entertainment for the dimwitted crew.

So, though she was a natural healer, she tried to appear merely as a caring young woman, bringing the infirm some Christian relief in their last hours. It was nearly intolerable, not being able to use her skills. But she had no choice. So she did her best to administer comfort and kindness.

But now she was feeling the rage in her own intestines, too, a rage against the inhuman conditions on this godforsaken voyage. Sorina considered herself to be a modern woman, not given to the "old" ways, but when she looked out at the stormy seas she couldn't help but imagine the legendary "Kelpie" water horse out there wailing and warning of stormy waters. She retched again, though there was not much but green spittle coming up from her stomach.

She was starting to imagine she heard the Banshee over the howling wind. But who could know the difference in the horrid screaming? Now if she saw *the Banshee, then it would mean her own death. She was certain of that. Unless the fairies came and brought the light. It was all that could save you from the Banshee. The sweet fairy magic was stronger than the Banshee. But so far the dreaded death fairy hadn't made an appearance. She said many hail Marys to that, and kept her Bible close to her heart.*

The trip on the schooner lasted weeks, but at last land was sighted on the horizon and Sorina's tired heart lifted for the first time since almost the beginning of the trip. She was going to get there. She wasn't sick and she was going to get to America's shores. Her mind shifted to the man who would be meeting her. Gerald McBride, an Irishman, but well known to her clan, was her betrothed. It had all been arranged before she left Scotland. She had never met the man, but he was said to be close to her age and handsome in a rugged way. It didn't matter to her. She would be married and then she would forge her own way if the marriage did not suit her. She would be in America. America stood for freedom and that was what she sought.

But she had heard rumors on the miserable voyage. Rumors of witch hunts, just like in the old country. It was said that America had some very backward-thinking people, just like Europe. She had heard this and she believed it. She would go far away from the Massachusetts land and find her way to the west. She would convince her new husband to take her into America's wilderness where the laws and prejudices of man would leave her alone for once in her life. Her name had been a burden, but she loved it. She had revered the stories of her great-great-grandmother, who had been tortured for having healing abilities. She had been caught sneaking out at night to tend to the sick, had been accused of witchcraft and burned for her heretic sorcery—though none of it had been true.

Sorina was determined to live her life in the new world free of bondage, able to be who she was. But she knew it wouldn't be easy. Nothing in her life had been. Still, she was ready.

A tug's low whistle brought Sorina back. She imagined the coal barge gliding over the water, being pushed to whatever destination its cargo was headed for. Pittsburg maybe? A tough life for sure for its crewmen. But she had heard it repeated that once you grew accustomed to the river life, you couldn't live any other way. It made her think. Made her remember once more. Sorina lowered her chin to rest on her chest and she slipped away again…

She remembered the smell of the river from the long-ago time when she and her young husband had made the trek on a flat boat from the north to find new lives in Kentucky. She had liked him, liked Gerald McBride. He was headstrong and foolish at times when he drank, but she had found him exciting. He was a hard worker and a charismatic Irishman who people took to. Their marriage had been consummated quickly and Sorina was happy with her husband. It hadn't taken anything to convince Gerald to travel west. As it turned out, it had been his plan all along. He had two brothers who had settled in Kentucky and he intended to join them there. So as soon as the wedding was over, he took his new bride for a very long ride down the rivers of America.

Sorina knew Gerald was proud of her, proud of her strength, proud of her unusual courage and independent spirit. Most women would have wanted a gentle life in the rising cities on the east coast, but not her. Her new husband told her over and over how lucky he felt to have her for his bride. He affectionately called her Sori and told her she was beautiful. No one had ever said that to her before. And for the first time she felt beautiful.

The young couple reveled in their love of adventure. The farther west they traveled, the more their spirits soared. Sori watched the red men on the shores and felt tremendous fright and excitement at seeing their exotically painted, nearly naked bodies.

They were floating down the Ohio into another world. And it suited her. She was always afraid, but she was also deeply thrilled. It was an electrifying time and her bold ancestry served her well. Her famous name of Duncan had preceded her in the Scotch-Irish settlements, but in this new, raw world, her healing was seen for what it was, healthcare, rather than sorcery or witchcraft. There were some who whispered of her strange ways, but mostly they were glad she had the uncanny ability to heal people in the virgin frontier where doctors were scarce.

Sorina was happy.

But her happiness was not to be. Gerald McBride's life was cut short. He had just finished building the cottage before he met his fate in a senseless brawl at the local tavern. Sorina had heard three rocks on the roof the night before and she had known. She had tried to convince Gerald not to go celebrating his achievement with his brothers. But he only swept her up in his arms and kissed her with tremendous passion.

"You can't be believin' that old Irish wife's tale, now can ya, lass? Not my headstrong Sori?" He had laughed heartily and told her he would be back by the time the moon rose in the sky.

She had fallen into a restless sleep that night and was awakened by an eerie wailing that sounded neither human nor animal. The Banshee, *she thought to herself, and her heart stopped. The moon was high in the sky when the bawling young man, who had fired the rifle accidentally, carried Gerald's body by himself to Sorina's cottage to be laid out.*

The Wake lasted for days, but Sorina didn't even remember it. She was numb with loss and sorrow, and her sharp-witted mind shut down for the first time in her life. As the days passed, folks assumed Gerald's young childless wife would leave the cottage, leave the wild, untamed Kentucky land. His brothers offered to accompany her back to the east, but she wouldn't hear of it. It never even occurred to her to leave Kentucky. Sori stayed on alone. And she thrived, even through her grief.

Days melted into weeks and weeks into months and Sorina refused any help from her neighbors and her husband's brothers as she grew more and more reclusive. It wasn't long before the families in the territory came to respect Sorina's capable independence and anti-social behavior. After a time, they left her alone.

What she didn't know, was the reputation she had gained among the red men that still lived in the forests. They understood her magic. They lived their lives much like she did, all spirit ruled. What they didn't understand was the materialistic desires of most white men. But this white woman with the golden hair was different. She was more spirit than flesh. They could see that when they watched her. They called her Earth Mother around their campfires and their medicine men sought out her advice. It hadn't taken Sorina long to know she had nothing to fear from the few Indian tribes that still existed along the Ohio.

As years passed, she learned to hunt as well as any man, and she survived easily off of squirrels, rabbits and deer. She planted vegetable gardens and raised chickens. She chopped wood and stitched hides and furs together to warm herself in the cold winters. In the springs, she ran through the forest like a young gazelle, her golden hair flying and her muscular body carrying her easily through the trees. She was legendary and she lived outside of civilization. Any lingering whisperings of her witch heritage were rare indeed and never fell on her ears, as the old world slipped farther and farther from her mind.

Only the trappers crossed her threshold, and it was from them that she learned of the changing world and talk of an impending war. Many years passed before the red man disappeared from the forests altogether only to be replaced by the black man, whose life was more akin to that of a wild animal in flight than a spiritual being living off the land.

She became most interested in their plight when a crippled Negro man, covered in mud and blood, darkened her doorstep one night. She nursed him back to health and learned of his passion to be free from the shackles of the white man's plantation. He told her of his life and the lives of his family lost to slavery. It had been an eye-opening revelation for the woman who had lived apart from society for so long that she hadn't been aware of how cruel and inhumane the world had become.

She was reminded of the old stories of her great-great-grandmother who had been falsely accused of witchcraft and the atrocities and injustices that had occurred in Scotland. She had vowed then and there to help the slaves in their flight to freedom.

Sorina had learned from the trappers about a secret society so perilous that if discovered it would mean death to anyone involved. It was the Underground Railroad. She was warned of the danger but she wouldn't listen. She knew her cottage was a perfect "safe house" because of its location close to the river, affording escape by boat to the Ohio side. There was no talking her out of this dangerous decision and eventually the trappers helped her, becoming conductors of the slaves through the Kentucky woods to her cottage. They would take the rowboats loaded with frightened "cargo" under new moons in the black of night across the Ohio River and onto Ripley and New Richmond.

Gerald's brother, Eugene, helped her, too. He was madly in love with her and tried to talk her out of helping the slaves. It was no use. So he rowed the boats many times himself. Sorina cared about him, but she refused to marry him. He settled for being with her when she would allow it. At forty-one she was considered an old woman when she gave birth to their child.

It was a baby girl and the difficult delivery took Sori's life.

Sorina lifted her head and breathed deeply of the river-scented air. She thought of the last pages of the journal that Jessie read to her over and over. Jessie told her the writing was especially jerky and really hard to read. Apparently, Sori had written it in the midst of her labor with her only child. She had described the pain the child was bringing. She knew she was too old and she feared the worst. It was the only time in all the pages when Sorina Duncan McBride sounded hopeless.

But she had seen the Banshee.

The horrifying death fairy had appeared to her during her painful pushing, its haggard features barely visible behind a blood red veil. It had swept in the room and hovered over her, floating close to her face, beckoning through a chilling mist. And the sweet fairies had stayed away with their magic light that could save her. Fear was real to Sorina then. *Because she knew.* Knew she would die. Her handwriting was more like vague scribbles as the life flowed out of her with her hemorrhaging blood. Jessie said the last page of Sorina Duncan McBride's diary was stained with that blood.

That was Sorina's one life.

Her other life had begun after Martha brought her to stay in the cottage, which was built around the wreckage that had been home to the McBride clan long after Sorina Duncan had died.

The wonder of it was, Sorina couldn't remember why she was here. Why had Martha lived in a trailer and let her live in this lovely cottage? She had asked Martha over and over and Mart's answer had always been the same, "I am comfortable in that trailer. I don't need nothin' else." And she hadn't really pressed Martha for information. She was happy, and she thought there was always time. But now Martha was gone, and there were no answers.

No one knew where she had been before this special place. Martha had been so hush-hush with her friends about it all. And Sorina was glad and didn't push. A large part of her didn't want to know, or even care to know. Martha always said it would come back to her when she was ready and shouldn't be revealed before.

But sometimes it felt like insanity when her only memories were not her own. Or maybe it was a form of possession when she remembered the time she first came down the river with Gerald, when she remembered the Underground Railroad, when she remembered being a middle-aged woman in the cottage that Gerald had built. Maybe she was just sensitive and susceptible to Sorina Duncan McBride, whose spirit still lived on in the cottage? Was it spiritual possession or was she truly insane? Had the stories from the journal been so encapsulated in her mind that she would never be able to separate reality from fantasy?

She only knew it was all a blank until Martha had brought her to Sorry's Run. She had no memory of being a young girl, a young woman, where she had come from. She had no idea of any other family members or friends. She knew of nobody and nothing until this cottage. Everybody said the same thing, that it would come back to her in time and she shouldn't force it. Her amnesia was clinical and it would take as long as it would take.

And whether a blessing or a curse, she couldn't even remember not being blind. The only visualizations she had for reference were those of the pioneer woman. She could remember that world and what it looked like. It made it easier somehow. So she didn't worry about filling in the blanks. She lived out her life very happily as Sorina Duncan McBride. It kept her close to Martha, sharing her name, and that made her feel loved.

Sometimes she was surprised by brief recollections of hissing mechanical sounds that seemed familiar. But she could never put the sounds together with an experience. She simply had no memories of anything else. Only this peaceful place now, and the long-ago life she had led as a wilderness woman who had befriended the black slaves.

Sorina lifted her chin higher and took another deep breath. The river smelled heavy, weighted with debris and rotted wood. It sounded hurried, as though it rushed to empty itself into the Mississippi quickly for relief. Sorina liked to think about the water and how it must look. Her sense of smell described it for her and she felt one with it. Her senses were heightened in its presence and that's what she was hoping for today.

Maybe the rushing water could tell her where Shelby was. Martha surely hadn't. Even Bella had been unnerved when she and her friends had made a spiritual plea for help. They had chanted over and over, but had gotten nowhere with the Irish incantations—only frightened.

Sorina wrapped her arms around herself tightly. She felt fear dancing on her heart. It came with a palpable dampness that lay over her skin. The fear made her cold. She should have been warmed by the river breezes, but they only chilled her. She rarely knew fear, but she recognized it clearly.

Martha, where is Shelby?

She needed to get angry. Anger was more powerful than fear. Fear blocked her senses, dulling her vibrations. It closed her off to the other world that fed her when this one was too empty.

A wind kicked up and pebbles flew about her feet as she sat on the chair and waited. For what, she didn't know, but she felt like she should wait. Sorina closed her blind eyes and laid her chin on her chest again, and waited.

"Samuel, git up now. Them dogs is a comin'! They's a comin', I tell you. Git yoself up! Samuel!" Lizbeth pulled on the big man's shirt and he finally rolled his eyes open and the whites caught the moon's reflection. For a split second he looked at her with desire and love in his eyes. But it was quickly replaced by something else. He jumped to his feet and took her hand. They ran, ran like they had never run, but still the dogs sounded closer and closer. Samuel was half dragging Lizbeth now. She tried not to scream out in pain, but her feet felt raw and chewed up. Each step was like wedging sharp blades into her calloused soles.

Just when she was really done—when she knew she wanted to rip her hand away from Samuel so she could stop at last and just die, a miracle happened. They ran right into a dark, silent creek. They fell into it, really, not having seen it or heard it. Lizbeth's breath escaped her lungs in increments of life-giving relief as her swollen and cut feet met the cool, soothing water. Samuel picked her up, then, carrying her from where they had entered the water. He got her as far away as his waning strength would allow and then he put her down. He found two hollow reeds they could breathe through and they sunk themselves down into the water. Completely submerged, the dogs wouldn't be able to pick up their scent. She hoped Samuel had gotten them far enough away that they wouldn't be seen reflected in the light of the full moon overhead. In their watery haven muffled sounds of dogs barking and men shouting rolled over them, distant and gurgling.

Lizbeth and Samuel tried to make themselves invisible. It was an old trick the slaves used to escape the realities of the impossibly cruel life they had been born to. They would close their eyes and see themselves off somewhere, playing, singing, their bodies healthy and running free. All the darkies did it. It was the only way to live in bondage. Feel freedom. It was almost impossible, but they never stopped trying. Some of the older slaves really got there, really could do it. Become invisible. Even under the whip. Lizbeth and Samuel tried. Lizbeth could never get there. She felt herself in this real, tortured life too much. But Samuel, he could get close to disappearing. It was almost as though he stopped breathing sometimes. She would know he was becoming invisible. It scared her. She thought he might really leave and never come back.

He was doing it now. Being as still as stone in the shallow water. She tried to do the same, but she was starting to feel panic rise in her chest. The water felt smothering. She had to breathe through her nose, she had to breathe…

"Sorina, wake up. You are gaspin'." Jessie shook her small shoulders. "Come on. I got supper waitin'. It's damp out here. Sori? Are you all right? You look kinda pale?"

Sorina sat up and literally shook the sleep off her. But she couldn't shake the dream. Lizbeth and Samuel had come through loud and clear.

Sorina reached her hand out and grabbed Jessie's wrist. "She's alive, Jessie. Shelby is alive. I just saw the slaves in such vivid scenes. Shelby has to be alive."

CHAPTER TWENTY-FOUR
THE CHIEF

BELLA SAT IN THE BOOTH across from the Greenup County Sheriff. She had called him to meet her at the Portsmouth Brewing Company.

"How you doin', Bruce?"

"I been better." The handsome sheriff took a swig of his bourbon and pushed his hat back off his forehead. "I got the whole force startin' to work this missin' person's case."

"Whole force meanin' you and who else?" Bella asked as she lifted a foamy beer to her lips.

"Whole force meanin' Greenup *and* Ashland. Shelby Jean is kind of an important person, you know."

"Well, I guess I know that. And darlin', I appreciate what y'all are doin'. But that's really why I asked you here. I know you're off duty and Sheree wants you home for supper. One drink and we'll be done, I promise."

"Hell with that." The sheriff held up his empty shot glass and the waiter immediately filled it. "I guess you got an opinion about how I'm runnin' this case?" He raised a dark eyebrow.

If only I was twenty years younger, Bella thought. "Well, here's the deal. I want you to pull everybody off it. I want Lucas Chambers on it—alone." Bella took another long drink of her beer letting what she said sink in.

The sheriff just stared at her, his steely blue eyes almost cutting a hole right through her. "You're shittin' me, right?"

"Now hear me out, Bruce. We both know Lucas has done some stupid things bein' chief of police, but you also know as well as I do that nobody is better at bein' a sleuth than him. All that rhubarb he pulled in the past is just that—in the past. He hardly drinks anything but beer anymore. And here's the thing. He loved Martha more than a man has a right to.

She kept him at a distance, but that was never his doin'. It would feel like his life's purpose to find her granddaughter. I'm tellin' you I'm right about this. You gotta put him in charge."

The sheriff shot back his drink and tried to look pissed off, but it was obvious he was relieved. He held up his glass once more and again it was filled. He sipped this time and sighed heavily before saying, "All right, Bella. But this is on you now. It ain't on me. I'm gonna tell my boys that this is outta respect for Jared. A lotta the boys still hold some hard feelin's over things that Lucas did."

"But they all still respect him, don't they?"

"Oh, yeah. We'll never say it to his face, but hell, everybody knows there ain't never been a better cop."

The two friends toasted with one more drink.

Chief Chambers rode slowly past Martha's trailer and stopped short before continuing on to Sorina's. The retired cop sighed slowly, feeling his grief surfacing in a raw pain that hung in his chest and throat. Lucas Chambers had loved Martha. Really loved her. He had popped the question more than once when they were young. But though he knew in his heart Martha loved him, she would never answer in the right way. Instead she would say, "Ah, Lucas, you don't really love me. You're in love with your job. Ain't no woman ever gettin' her hooks into you." She would laugh and blow him off, as usual. Well, damn it, he had meant it. He had loved her. And now it was too late. At seventy-two, he was an old man and only on the force very part time as a token retired cop who didn't want to sit at home.

And he missed her.

Lucas powered down his window and stared out at the pretty flowers that dressed the mobile home. He and Martha had been high school sweethearts, but then he had gone off to the service and when he returned he found her married to somebody else and pregnant. Martha made a mistake marrying the man, but it was no mistake having the baby. She loved being a mom, but the marriage had been a joke. Lucas laughed aloud, reminiscing over the fun they had had playing at innocent flirtations while she was in the bad marriage. It had been enough to keep him hoping.

But the ball had remained in her court and she had never thrown him a straight pass.

God, the laughs they had had. In the later years, after the cottage was completed, he harassed her about staying in the trailer. She would quickly correct him. "Hillbillies live in trailers. The upwardly mobile live in mobile homes." Then she would wink at him and he knew the subject was closed. Well, Martha might have lived in a trailer/mobile home, but she was a classy lady as far as he was concerned. Truth was, between taking care of her family and everybody else, she had no time left for herself or for him. His chances had really ended when Neely died.

Lucas reflected on the morning glories climbing up the railing on the outside of the trailer, each bloom explosive in its lush, vibrant color. He watched a fat, pink petal float off its stem in slow motion, caught in a lilting breeze. It depressed him, seeing such promise in a flower. It was like the false promise of life that fell off the human vine just when it was at its most interesting.

And Martha had been interesting. She had been one of the funniest women he knew. He even loved her wacky obsession with her "healing" powers. She used to get out all those crazy stones and gems and try to convince him that she could feel pain in folks. Well, he believed that sure enough. Martha had unending compassion and empathy. But she lost him when she would go on about being a faerie doctor, whatever the hell that was. And she never let up about those damned *Irish fairies.* The picture that brought to his mind was plain twisted.

So he was nothing, if not relieved, when she started turning her gems into jewelry. At least that was something he had understood. And she was good at it, like she was good at taking care of sick folks. God, how they had loved her. Martha just had a way of making people feel better. If that's what she called her gift, that was okay by him. Whatever it was, there was a big gaping hole in the world left from her passing.

He sighed again and buzzed his window back up. He was getting too melancholy in his old age. It was time to start focusing on Shelby Jean. He had not really believed in the rumors that she had gone missing. After all, Shelby was a woman of the world and had only been visiting Sorry's Run to see her old man and her grandmother. More than likely, depression had gotten her, too, and she had bolted. But then as the days went on and her

New York roommate hadn't heard from her, and no one seemed to think she had wanted to leave Kentucky, well, he began to seriously wonder.

When the call came from the sheriff's department to head up the investigation he was surprised, but he was ready. He had always liked Shelby Jean. She was a good kid, and had never deserved a hard ass father like Wesley. After Neely was gone, there was nothing much good left for the little girl. Just her grandmother and now she was gone, too.

Luke pressed his foot gently on the gas and tipped his hat to the woman he would always miss. He drove on down the lane.

He found the mistress of the cottage sitting in the grape arbor. He made small talk and then got down to business, cautioning, "Now, Ms. Sorina, you be sure to tell me if you get an idea of where she might be. I know you think you can do this on your own, but we really need to get an all-out search going. An APB has been out there for some days with no word."

"Chief Chambers, if you'll just give me a few more nights, I truly believe I'll pick up on her and it won't be so complicated as all that you're plannin'," she said, lifting her chin and fixing her blind eyes on his face before adding, "and Lucas, I know she's alive."

"Now, how do you come to know that, Ms. Sorina? I been talkin' to Wesley and he ain't so certain. So how do you know?"

Luke liked this part. He liked egging her on and then watching as she puffed up her five-foot-four petite frame in defiance.

"Because I can feel her, Lucas. That's how I know it."

Her answer was always the same. Detectives had come to Sorina before, soliciting her help with unsolved cases in the county, the ones that went on and on. Sorina had put the department on the right track more than once by "feeling" her way through the course of someone's disappearance.

"Well, that's all well and good. You do what you gotta do and we'll do what we gotta do. Maybe between the two methods we'll uncover something." He tipped his hat to her, though he knew she couldn't see. But she was that kind of lady; always deserved a tip of the hat. He got back in his cruiser and rode slowly past the trailer again, tipping his hat for the third time before turning onto US 23.

Lucas Chambers had been the police chief for more years than most guys could imagine. The 20-year cops took their retirements and found other employment to supplement their pensions, but not Lucas. That was the one thing Martha had always gotten right. He was in love with his job. He never officially left the force; just kind of floated into part time when he finally relinquished the chief's job over to a younger man the Commonwealth had sent down. Luke knew his time was up and the younger guys just tolerated the "old man" and didn't figure he had much juice left in him.

But the older guys knew better.

There was nobody with a sharper nose than Lucas Chambers. He could smell a bad scene from a mile off, and nobody could pull anything over on him. He knew when people were lying. It was his curse. He could pick out a bullshitter from here to high heaven, and it hadn't always made him popular. The only thing that was stronger than his uncanny keen vibe about people was his penchant for speaking the truth. They had almost taken his badge many times for being "politically incorrect."

And he had kept his flask in his pocket nearly his whole career. There was much that escaped him from those days, and he knew he had much to atone for. But nobody ever brought the old days up, and he was just as glad to let "sleeping dogs lie."

But he had mellowed. Age had beaten him down, and by now he had come to realize there was so much bullshit in the world that you had to learn to dogpaddle for your life just not to drown in it. And it wasn't worth it. Nobody cared. All the assholes that rose to the top of the pond were just that, assholes. He wanted no part of it. So now he showed up at the station a couple times a week and worked cold cases sometimes with the detectives from the county. They liked the old guy in the cowboy hat and worn boots. They even let him keep the rusty bucket that was his cruiser back in the day when he had rolled every day through the country roads. He knew the back roads and he knew the people that lived on those back roads down in the hollows. And those people trusted him. Lucas had a way with the hill people. He never spoke down to them unless they deserved it. And they always knew when they deserved it. It was a good relationship.

It was why he respected the little blind lady. She was no bullshitter. She was the real deal, whatever that was, and he liked her. He would let Sorina keep trying to *connect* with Shelby in her own way. Maybe she could point him in the right direction. He knew she would give it all she had. Meanwhile, it was time to really comb the woods. The roommate had been through there, but a more thorough investigation was needed. Russell had helped him coordinate it and it was happening in the morning, come rain or shine.

Lucas' cell phone rang. "Chambers here."

"Chief, we're all set."

"Great. Have you heard the weather report?"

"Yeah, it's gonna suck."

"Terrific. I'm goin' back to the station to make some calls. And Russell, thanks, bud."

"No problem, Chief. See you bright and early."

Lucas ended the call and turned up the heat in the cruiser. He felt a chill just thinking about what they were in for in the morning. *It's gonna suck.*

CHAPTER TWENTY-FIVE
THE SEARCH

"RUSSELL, SAY THAT AGAIN? You're breaking up." Caitlin could only catch every other word. "Hang on. I need to go outside. This building is pretty much a dead zone."

She walked out through the front lobby of the six-story brick building that housed the horticulture laboratory where she worked. Nodding at the receptionist, she pulled her sweater tight around her neck. The air was still cool in New York.

"Okay. Try again."

"Can you hear me now?" Russell laughed on the other end, reciting the old ad.

"Yeah, I hear you now. So, please, tell me something good is happening?" Cait was in no mood for jokes.

Russell heard the near whimper in her voice. "Well, I think a couple good things *are* happening. A cop has come on the case who is a friend of mine. He really cares and has been around long enough to know his way around a missing person's case."

"Really?" Cait stood up straighter. "Who is this guy?"

"His name is Lucas Chambers and he and Martha were close friends all their lives. And he just happens to be the best cop in the county, or all of Eastern Kentucky, in my book. He's in his early 70s, though, and a lot of guys think he's past it. But I don't. And neither does the sheriff. They called him in just yesterday, and that gives me hope, Cait. I believe in this guy."

Cait felt her throat tighten. "Then I believe in him, too. What happens next?"

"We have an all-out search goin' tomorrow mornin'. Dogs and the whole nine yards. Bella and the girls and most of the church people are helpin'. We're gonna really comb the woods between Martha's trailer and Sorina's cottage."

Caitlin was silent as she pictured the scene like she was watching a movie. It gave her shivers and she pulled tighter on her sweater.

"Cait, are you there?"

"Yeah, I'm here. I just got a bad feeling. But I guess you're right. I didn't see anything in the woods when I was there, but I could have easily missed something. But Russell, I was so hoping that something else would happen. You know, like Sorina would find her by communing with Martha's spirit or something crazy like that."

"Yeah, I know. But it's good that the whole town is gettin' on board. The more people involved means somethin' is bound to turn up. Everybody is takin' Shelby's disappearance serious now, you know? Just don't worry too much. I will call you the minute I know anything. And Cait…"

"Yeah?"

"I miss you."

"I miss you, too." Her throat tightened again. "I gotta go, Russell. I'll be waiting to hear from you tomorrow, okay?"

Caitlin turned off her cell and put it in her pocket. She sat down on the steps outside the building and watched all the students walking past her to their classes, laughing and talking amongst themselves. Suddenly she felt like the oldest person on the planet. Everybody looked so carefree. Probably the worst thing on their mind was the next term paper, or maybe flunking out. What a joy that would be. Caitlin could not believe Shelby was still missing. She could not believe it. She thought she would get home and there would be a call from her best friend, apologizing, saying she had just taken a breather from the world.

She remembered a time when Shelby had done just that. It was shortly after Cait had dropped out of the modeling scene altogether to enroll in school. Shelby felt deserted in a way, and kind of lost. She took off for a long weekend and didn't tell a soul where she was going. Caitlin had been frantic by the time her friend returned saying she just had to get away and clear the cobwebs—whatever that had meant. But when she returned, Shelby had known she would stay in New York, stay in modeling and keep the money coming instead of moving on. It had been a big decision, and Cait understood Shelby's need to be alone to think it through. But it had really scared her and hurt her that she would just disappear like that without telling anybody.

The doorman had been there for Caitlin that time, too, and just yesterday he had been the one to remind her of it. "You know Shelby Jean has an independent nature. Remember how she worried you that time years ago when she just took off?" Jeremiah had put his long arms around Caitlin and hugged her gently. "She came back. Remember? She loves you. She's probably just working some things out again."

It had made her feel so much better. Jeremiah was probably right. She had forgotten about that episode. And this latest thing with healing Rita Rettinger had really unnerved Shelby. So maybe Shelby was just being Shelby and putting her loved ones through hell for no reason. *I'm going to kill her when she finally shows up.* Caitlin smiled to herself at the lame joke. *Shake it off, Caitlin, just like Shelby would do if the roles were reversed.*

She wouldn't think about all of Sorry's Run tracking through the woods looking for evidence of violence. Instead she would picture Shelby in a Kentucky lodge somewhere communing with nature and getting hammered on Scotch.

"Wesley, you are comin' tomorrow, right? Well, good. I'm countin' on you to round up your neighbors. That's right. 10:00."

Lucas Chambers propped his tired legs up on the desk. His snakeskin boots looked rough in the overhead florescent lights. He brushed them off and sighed. He took so much shit for wearing the boots. Damn younger generation. Most of the guys showed up in gym shoes when they could get away with it.

He hung up the phone and took a moment between calls. Leaning back, he rested his head in his large hands. He thought of how Wesley Stiller was like a different man all of a sudden. The guy had been racked with emphysema, COPD, you name it. Barely able to get around. And now he was out digging up his fields from morning to night? Just didn't make sense. He seemed to have gotten healthy overnight. If Martha were alive she would credit his remarkable recovery to having his daughter back with him. Lucas highly doubted that. From what he had heard, Wesley and Shelby weren't on speaking terms.

Doodling on a legal pad, he let his mind work the scenario. He drew two stick figures. Above the man figure he wrote: Strangely energetic, all fired up, staying to himself. He drew the girl with her lips curved downward in a frown. Luke wrote the word: Argument? Then he erased the girl figure and wrote: Disappears.

Stinks to high heaven.

Highly suspect. But when Lucas confronted Wesley, something didn't fit. He might have done Shelby wrong, but hurt her? Unlikely. It was more likely that he was just glad to be left alone. Still, after tomorrow's search, if they got nothing, Lucas would have to get a search warrant for Wesley's farmhouse just to cover all the bases. It would piss Stiller off, no doubt.

"Luke, you got a moment?"

Russell James was standing in his doorway looking sheepish.

"Hey, Russell. Didn't expect to see you until tomorrow. Pull up a seat there, bud. I'm just lookin' over my call list. What's up?"

"Nothin', really; I think I'm just gettin' antsy. I have confirmed with Bella that she has her group organized. They'll be at the trailer on time. Of course, I just heard the latest weather report. It's gonna rain like hell in the morning." Russell sat down in the chair across from Lucas.

"Lovely. All we need. Damn. You know, this thing is eatin' at my gut like nothin' I've felt in a long time. Part of me thinks Shelby is havin' one over on all of us and part of me thinks we're gonna find somethin' in those woods nobody is gonna want to find." Lucas turned his tired eyes toward the pictures spread out on his desk. Glossy magazine pictures of a drop-dead beautiful woman named Shelby Jean Stiller.

"Hell, I'm too old for this shit." Lucas leaned down and opened a drawer. He pulled out a bottle of Jack Daniels and a couple of paper cups. "Join me?"

"You bet."

They shot the whiskey back and Lucas refilled their cups. This time they sipped, letting the liquor take the edge off the dark dread that came with every thought.

"Folks, we sure appreciate your cooperation in this preliminary ground search," Chief Chambers addressed the fifty volunteers who stood before him in the rain in Martha's driveway. They were in raincoats, hooded parkas, and holding umbrellas that did little to keep the blowing rain from drenching them. There were old people and young people, but no kids. Bella, Violet and Jolene were in front and Wesley stood directly behind them, his face expressionless, but his mouth set in a hard line. A dozen officers stood behind Chambers with five hound dogs pulling hard on leashes, howling, chomping at the bit. The dogs had been given several articles of clothing with Shelby's scent and their noses were high in the air, sniffing hard, their furry heads shaking off the heavy raindrops.

Lucas looked out at the mixed crowd who were far from physically fit. Now they were his responsibility. He was tempted to call the whole thing off because of the awful weather. He sure didn't need anybody slipping in the mud and breaking a leg, or worse, a hip. But there was so much time and effort that went into getting all these people together and there was just no more time to wait. Rain or no, the search had to happen.

He shouted through the downpour, "Now, we all know it's a terrible mornin' out here, so you'll just have to go slowly and take your time. Be careful and watch out for each other. Travel in pairs. Don't veer off too far from your neighbors. You'll be able to hear the dogs and just keep following their barking. We don't want any accidents. We need to scour the woods behind Martha McBride's trailer before we can open up a full-scale investigation. We'll all meet up at Sorina's cottage. She will have hot beverages there for us."

He stopped talking and tried to assess the attitudes. He looked out over the old and young faces, some deeply lined and ashen from age, some pink with youth's excited flush, but all with the same determined expressions, steely, not frightened. On a clear mission. He scanned his neighbors and decided no one looked as though he didn't want to be here. Lucas knew each of them personally.

Salt of the earth.

He continued, trying to keep his voice up over the loud rainfall, "This is one hell of an unpleasant thing we're doin' here this mornin'. I don't have to tell y'all that. You know that. Because you know there's a possibility that Shelby Stiller's body will be uncovered." It seemed like a communal shiver went through the people crowded together in front of him. "That, of course, is the worst case scenario. But you must be prepared for that possibility. You will be lookin' for any clothing or personal items, anything that stands out, seems out of the ordinary, or even somethin' that looks like evidence of violence. We are lookin' for anything that would give us some clue as to what has happened to Shelby Jean. Do you have any questions?"

Rain was rolling off the lid of his black cowboy hat in thick rivulets as he stood, legs spread, trying to sound authoritative. What he was thinking he needed to keep to himself. *No way we're gonna find shit in this fucked-up weather.*

"Let's git on with it, Chief." The response came from the oldest guy in the search party—old enough to still think of Lucas Chambers as the police chief.

Lucas grinned and said, "Okay, Harmon. Let's git on with it."

Whistles blew and the rain-drenched townspeople fell into straight lines behind the officers. The dogs strained and the officers had all they could do to keep the wet leashes in their hands.

The search for Shelby Jean Stiller was under way.

The organized lines quickly fell to chaos as people struggled to not slip on wet leaves and hidden limbs and trunks. Bella, Violet and Jolene started out trudging through the wet woods with arms linked, trying to stay together, but it was apparent that stance couldn't last for long. There were too many smaller trees and too much thick brush to walk around.

"Harmon, watch yourself there." Bella reached out to keep the old man from tripping over a tree stump. "God, this is awful." Bella stared down at the ground, keeping her eyes peeled for anything out of the ordinary. At the same time, she was scared to death she would actually see something.

Wesley was next to her and she could hear him mumbling under his breath.

"What you say, Wesley? Hon, you better pull that scarf tighter around your neck. You'll catch your death of cold."

"Shut up, Bella, and keep your eyes where they should be," he barked at her.

"Well, excuse me for livin'." Bella could not get over Wesley Stiller. She had imagined him actually being happier now that he wasn't tied to breathing machines and coughing every minute of the day. But instead, he had just gotten crankier and was turning into a full-fledged hermit.

"The hell with the old coot," Bella muttered to herself. She felt hurt, though, just thinking how much they had all done for him. The least he could do was be civil. But she knew. Bella knew that Wesley had never asked for all the fuss they had made over him. He had just been stuck. But not now. Now he was like fifteen years younger and feeling his oats. He was on his tractor all day and smoking like a fiend and probably drinking whiskey every night. It's like he had challenged death and won. And it was all because of Shelby. Bella knew he had been cured by his daughter. It had really pissed him off. In his own words he, "hated that supernatural shit." He only took it from Martha because she was, well, Martha. But he had hated Neely's gifts and he sure as hell didn't want to know anything about Shelby's gifts.

Bella could just imagine his thought process—*if Shelby's so goddamned psychic, why the hell is every "sorry" fool in Sorry's Run out here lookin' for her in this miserable monsoon.*

He would have a good point.

Bella watched him discretely. He was staring straight down as he walked, focused on where he was stepping. With his hair cut short and wearing a Wildcats ball cap, Wesley was actually handsome, in a rugged, unkempt sort of way. Bella was surprised by that. He had been disabled for so long; she had forgotten how good-looking he used to be. But sure enough, when he and Neely had gotten married he had been considered a real hunk. They were the most beautiful couple in the county. *Damn men. He's actually gettin' better lookin'.*

Violet yanked on her arm and hollered, "Bella, are you payin' attention to what you're doin'? You almost stepped in that hole!"

"Oh, lordy. Thanks, Vi." Bella pulled her parka hood farther over her head and stared down at her feet.

"Ow! Help me!! Ow!!"

It was Harmon. He had tripped over a log and slipped in the mud.

Immediately rain was washing away blood that was flowing down his wrinkled cheeks from a deep gash in his forehead.

"Oh, god, Harmon. Hon, let us help you!" Bella shouted, and she, Violet and Jolene surrounded the old guy.

"Harmon, can you hear me?" Bella yelled.

The rain was relentless and the frail, elderly man looked unnaturally pale. Bella could imagine him melting away with the soaking he was getting. His eyes were closed and he wasn't responding.

"Lucas!" Bella screamed, but the rain was too loud and the woods were too dense. The dogs sounded far off. "Jolene, hon, run get him. We gotta get Harmon to the hospital, and pronto!"

Jolene tucked her wet hair behind her ear, nodded, and was gone. Bella and Violet stayed with Harmon as the search went on.

"What we got, Bella?" Lucas had come back with Jolene and knelt down by his old friend. "Harmon? Answer me, man?"

Harmon blinked when he heard Lucas Chambers roar at him. "What's wrong, Lucas? Why are you shoutin'? I feel like I'm drownin'. Gotta towel?"

Harmon tried to sit up and Bella and Lucas both stopped him. Lucas was on his radio, requesting an ambulance.

"Ambulance? I don't need no ambulance. We gotta find Shelby Jean." Harmon's red-rimmed eyes were wide with worry. He reached out to Bella. "Bella, we gotta find her."

"Don't you worry, Harmon, we're gonna find her. You just lie still now. You've got a nasty cut on your head and you need to get to where it's warm and dry and get a couple stitches."

He reached up to his forehead and winced at the pain. "Yeah, I guess I done screwed up. I better git this taken care of." He laid his hand back down and closed his eyes.

Lucas looked at Bella and they shared a moment. Harmon had been their friend forever.

"He'll be all right?" Bella asked.

"Yeah, Bella, he'll be all right. Ain't no little cut on the head gonna take out old Harmon."

Ten minutes later a wailing siren and flashing lights cut eerily through the misty downpour. It was no small task for the EMTs to get into the trees. They stared at the confused-looking people wandering about in the woods in the pouring rain.

"It's a special church meetin'." Bella winked at the young medic. He looked at her and she knew he was thinking goofy cult more likely. But he didn't reply, and instead knelt down to do a cursory examination of Harmon. The EMTs carried him out in their arms, forming a makeshift chair. Harmon put his skinny arms around the necks of the young medics and let them get him into the ambulance.

Lucas watched his old friend being attended to. "Take it easy, Harmon, and let them stitch you up. I'll be over to the hospital later to check on you."

Harmon nodded feebly, but brightened up when he saw the pretty EMT who was cleaning up his bloody head.

Lucas grinned, and turned back to join the search as his friend was transported to King's Daughters Medical Center.

He spoke out loud, "We should end this thing. This ain't no day to be out here no way. Somebody else is gonna get hurt."

"Yeah, I think you're right. We should call it off." Russell had stood back of the ambulance and he told Bella and Lucas he had seen others slipping dangerously over the muddy terrain.

"Yeah, let's call off the folks and just let the dogs and the cops do the search. Tell them all to just head for Sorina's. She is waitin' with plenty of hot soup and drinks."

"Okay. I'll take care of it." Russell brought a megaphone up to his lips and started shouting commands. Bella, Violet and Jolene were right behind him. Lucas headed toward the officers who were following blindly wherever the dogs were leading.

Bella found Reverend Parsons and more church friends and joined them as they tried to make a path through the wet brush toward Sorina's. But before she lost sight of him, she caught Lucas' dark eyes. She questioned him with a raised eyebrow.

He caught her expression and walked over to her, getting up close so he could talk right in her ear, "Yeah, you're right, Bella. Truth is, in all this rain, the dogs' scent is gonna be way off the mark, too. I'll be callin' this whole thing off in a heartbeat." Bella nodded in agreement and watched him walk off towards the barking dogs.

She joined the pack of people heading awkwardly through the dripping trees to Sorina's. Watching the ground below her feet, Bella knew anything that would have been an important clue was being drenched and battered and washed away.

The search had been useless.

CHAPTER TWENTY-SIX
LOST

"WELL, AT LEAST WE DIDN'T FIND Shelby," Violet whispered to Bella and Jolene as she handed her raincoat to Jessie.

They had been standing in line in the screened-in porch as everybody took off their soaked gear and made wet piles on the wicker table and chairs.

"I know what you mean. I couldn't breathe for fear of really seein' somethin'." Jolene handed her trench coat to Jessie and followed the gathering crowd into the welcoming cottage, away from the misery of the dripping woods and into the comfort of a roaring fire and steaming bowls.

Sorina approached them. "I know it's late in the season for a fire, but I figured y'all could use it today."

"Well, this time I'm darn grateful for it, Sorina." Violet smiled.

Bella hugged their hostess and agreed, "This is exactly what we need. Thank you so much for doin' this, Sorina. It was awful out there."

Jessie was passing by with a tray of steaming cups.

Bella reached for a cup. "And thank you, Jessie. You are an angel. Isn't that tray awful heavy, hon? You want some help?"

Jessie just smiled shyly and shook her head as she moved on through the room, getting everybody taken care of.

"That girl is just a jewel, Sorina. How would you ever live without her?"

"I couldn't bear to think of it, Bella. Now, tell me, girls. You saw nothin'? Felt nothin'?" Her eyes pleaded behind her amber glasses.

"No, hon, we didn't. You couldn't find the nose on your face in that torrential downpour. The whole thing was a waste. I just feel so bad for Lucas. Hell, I feel bad for everybody. And poor Shelby. We're still no closer to understandin' what has happened to her. God, Sorina, this is just beyond belief."

"Hi, y'all. Sorina, I think this Burgoo is the best I ever had. Thank you so much." Rita Reddinger had come up to the fireplace to join them.

"The minister's wife brought that, Rita. Said she had a gallon of it in her freezer at home. Wasn't it just so kind of her to share?"

"Good gravy, Rita, don't tell us you were out in all that rain?" Jolene asked.

"Of course, I was. You don't think I'd let y'all look for Shelby Jean and me stay at home, do you? She's the reason I'm even able to be here," Rita's voice caught in her throat.

"What was I thinkin'?" Jolene touched her arm gently.

More people kept congregating in the front room of the cottage. The large wooden table was piled with mugs and plates and pewter pitchers holding water and juice. Platters were loaded with pastries and breads. There was fresh fruit in wooden bowls and steaming stew in bowls on hot plates on the serving table. Hot coffee was brewing.

In no time the dreadful experience of the morning was replaced with a gathering of good friends in a picturesque setting, warm and cozy. It felt more like a party.

If it just wasn't for that little Shelby thing.

Sorina picked up on Bella's thoughts. "Yeah, hon, I know."

"Oh, god, Sori, it's all so beautiful. How can we be havin' such a lovely time when that girl is out there somewhere experiencin' who knows what? And nobody has the slightest clue where she could be. I know Lucas is at a loss. And that don't happen to Lucas Chambers too often." Bella took a sip of her coffee. "I think I need somethin' stronger."

Just then, lonesome mandolin music flowed through the chattering and a hush fell over the room as people gave an ear to Jessie's angelic voice. Her sad, haunting soprano reminded them of what their business was about on that wet morning. People listened to Jessie and soon after they began to pay their respects to Sorina, making their way back out to get their coats and head for home. The spontaneous gaiety had been returned to a depressing reality check. Jessie kept singing, but her voice quivered slightly with emotion.

Out in the rain, Lucas was telling the officers to call it a day. They had found nothing, and the dogs had been a howling pack of confusion. They piled the dogs back into the canine van and Lucas watched as the officers left in the cruisers. They were ordered to hit the computers again and network with all the missing person reports in Ohio, Kentucky and West Virginia.

Then, of course there was New York, which worried him the most. If Shelby had an enemy in New York who had perpetrated some kind of kidnapping, that would be a bigger nut than he had ever come up against. He would have to call her roommate again and re-cover old ground.

Lucas shook off the puddle that was making a home on his hat. He was chilled to the bone, and the bones weren't as young as they used to be. But he didn't feel like taking advantage of the comfort Sorina was offering. He wanted to stay in the woods for a while. It was quiet now and the rain was letting up, turning into a light drizzle. He felt like he could hear himself think for the first time in an hour. He went back over the same area where they had started the search and he retraced his steps, studying everything, the tall grasses, the tangled bushes, the wild weeds, the sycamores and birch trees lording over moss-covered trunks and viney growth that covered stubbly wet ground. Lucas closed his eyes and listened to the birds overhead, coming to life after the hard rain. It was so peaceful, and yet something had happened here. It must have. He reviewed what he knew.

The roommate, Caitlin Sotheby, was with Russell James having a fine old time cruising around on a bicycle. They texted that they were running late, did she want them to bring her some takeout from a hamburger joint. Shelby replies no, that she wasn't hungry and was going to visit Sorina. She would see them later. Shelby never made it to the cottage and just disappeared off the face of the earth. That was it. All he had.

Lucas thought of the roommate. Didn't make sense that she would be suspect. What could she have to gain by Shelby's disappearance? She was rich in her own right, and a well-adjusted, employed young woman, by all appearances. And she had been visibly distraught since Shelby had gone missing. There was no animosity between the two women, and Caitlin had sat by Shelby's side at the hospital for a week. No, he didn't count Caitlin Sotheby as a suspect. And Russell? He might have always had a crush on the statuesque blonde, but it seemed like his attentions had shifted to the brunette. No, he didn't suspect Russell. Russell had been instrumental in helping with the investigation so far. What would be his motive?

Wesley? He was an asshole for sure, but a kidnapper of his own child? A murderer? Lucas just couldn't believe Wesley was capable of orchestrating such a malicious thing. Still, he sure wasn't inviting anybody to his house these days, which was for all intents and purposes empty now that Wesley was no longer needing medical services. He had the time for an abduction. He had the room. He probably had the means. But did he have a motive? He and Shelby had had a falling out. Everybody knew that. She had apparently had some kind of laying on of hands and Wesley had been able to breathe ever since, according to Bella. And Wesley didn't like that kind of shit. He had never liked his wife going around the county healing folks, and he sure wouldn't want to live through that again with his daughter.

Was it enough to make him want her gone? Make him want to kill her, thinking she was evil? Could he be that eaten up with hate for his own daughter?

The devil made him do it?

God, why wasn't Martha still alive. She would have a handle on this whole thing. In fact, Lucas truly believed Shelby wouldn't have disappeared if her grandmother had been alive to keep an eye on her.

Lucas kept walking, carefully, slowly, through the overgrowth and thick brush. Something caught his eye. The sun had just broken through the sycamores and golden rays spread over the glistening leaves. Something was there. Something was shining in the sunbeam. Lucas' heart raced and he bent over to get a closer look. It was a bracelet. He recognized it. It was one of Martha's designs. Lucas picked it up and examined it. It was a silver bangle embedded with turquoise and crystal. He turned it over and sure enough it had her signature initials engraved inside the band. It was a beautiful piece.

But it didn't tell him anything. Half of the ladies in Sorry's Run owned some of Martha's jewelry. She had done very well with her shop downtown in her younger days. Still, he would take it with him. Maybe the lab would find something.

"Is Wesley here, Sorina?" Lucas walked through the door with his dripping hat in his hand. But he could see for himself that the cottage was emptied out. Only Bella, Jolene, Violet and Jessie remained. They were picking up after the guests, but stopped what they were doing when Lucas let himself in.

Sorina put her hand out to him, feeling his wet raincoat. "I bet you are soaked to the bone, Luke. Jessie, hon, could you take the Chief's coat and hat and lay them out on the porch furniture?"

Lucas felt better as soon as he stripped down to his dry shirt. He realized he had been shivering.

Sorina added, "Sit now and have some coffee and Burgoo. Reverend Parson's wife has outdone herself. There's plenty left over."

Lucas followed the pretty blind hostess and was glad to take a seat in one of the comfortable chairs pulled in close to the fire that was still glowing from dying embers. "Thank you, Ms. Sorina, don't mind if I do. But coffee will be just fine. Don't have much of an appetite."

Jessie brought him a large mug of hot coffee. "Thank you, Jessie. This is just great." He took a long, careful sip and then sat back, staring at the fireplace. "So was Wesley here at the cottage?"

"Bella?" Sorina asked.

"I don't think so. I didn't see him. Did y'all?"

Nobody had. Lucas just sighed. "Well, I think I better pay him another visit."

Bella responded, "He won't let you in. You might as well get a search warrant."

Lucas looked surprised.

Bella added, "I'm not kiddin'. He isn't seein' nobody, and nobody is seein' him. I was actually amazed that he came today. God, Luke, you don't think…"

"Well, I don't think nothin'. But I have to cover all the bases. Hey, does this bracelet belong to any of you girls? Did you lose it? Or have you ever seen it?" He pulled out a plastic baggie from his vest pocket that held the jewelry.

Everybody gathered around to take a closer look. Violet's clipped white hair gleamed in the firelight. "Luke, that's one of Martha's pieces."

"It for sure is. But it's not mine." Jolene looked down at her arm where another of Martha's bracelets was clasped around her tiny wrist.

"Mine neither," Bella added, "but I recognize this one. Remember when we first showed Shelby her grandmother's jewelry? I bet this is one of the bracelets from her bedroom dresser?"

"Well, I'm gonna take it to Ashland and have the boys in the lab take a look. Probably won't give us anything, but it's the only thing I got. I think I'll take a drive over to Wesley's farmhouse."

"Oh, dearest, today? God, you must be so tired," Sorina spoke gently.

"Well, I might be tired, but what is Shelby Jean Stiller feelin'? Huh? What is that young woman feelin'?" He looked at the concerned faces of the women he had known all his life. Martha's best friends.

Everybody was silent.

"I'm sorry, Ms. Sorina. I didn't mean to bark at you. And I am tired. Sick and tired of thinkin' harm has come to Neely's beautiful girl. But don't worry. We'll get to the bottom of this."

He got up and Jessie brought him his coat and hat, all wiped dry.

Sorina spoke, "Take some coffee with you, Luke."

"Don't mind if I do. It's mighty good, Ms. Sorina, Ms. Jessie. Thank you, ladies. I'll be in touch. I thank you for your help today. And make no mistake, we'll find her." He tipped his hat and left in his cruiser, wishing he believed what he had just said.

Out on US 23 he picked up his cell phone. "Russell, what you doin'?"

"Just lookin' through some of Shelby's hospital insurance records, trying to see if somethin' weird sticks out."

"I'll pick you up. Let's go pay Wesley Stiller a visit."

"Okay. I'll grab the whiskey."

CHAPTER TWENTY-SEVEN
BY THE BOOK

"WESLEY, YOU IN THERE? Wes?" Lucas was pounding on the front door of the farmhouse. "Where in the dickens is he?" Lucas pushed his hat back off his forehead in exasperation. "It's too damn wet for him to be in the fields." He scratched his head. "Hell, Russell, go look anyway."

Russell went around to the back of the house. There was no sign of Wesley anywhere.

Lucas was peering in through the front window. "He's in there. He's got to be. His truck is sitting right there. Wesley?!"

Nothing.

There was no sound or sight of anyone inside the house. "Damn, I guess Bella was right. I'm gonna have to do this by the book. Come on, let's go. Wanna drive to Ashland?"

The ride down US 23 was easy. Traffic was light and the river had a silver sheen to it, washed clean from the rain. A long barge floated on top of the water, its cargo hull empty. A rusty tugboat pushed it lazily, painting a perfect illusion of another era, peaceful and uncomplicated.

Russell and Lucas made small talk for a while. Finally, Lucas asked, "So, Russell, what can Caitlin tell us?"

"Nothing. She's as freaked out as anybody." Just then, as if on cue, his cell phone chimed. "Hello? Oh, Cait, your ears must be burnin'. No, I'm afraid not. The weather was terrible. It really didn't get us anywhere. But, Cait, the Chief found a bracelet. Do you remember that day, the day Shelby disappeared? Did she have on a bracelet? I can't remember one way or the other." There was silence on the other end as he waited for Cait to try and picture what Shelby had worn the last day she had seen her.

"Yeah?" Russell nodded, and then he put his hand over the receiver as he spoke to Lucas, "She remembers a bracelet, but it was beaded. Doesn't sound like the same one." He went back to Cait, adding, "I know. It could be anybody's. There were a lot of ladies out there today. You're right. Doesn't seem likely the women would be wearin' fancy jewelry. It isn't much to go on, but it's worth a try." Russell reassured Caitlin, trying to sooth her disappointment and growing fear. "I agree. We're gonna get a search warrant tomorrow first thing. Okay. I'll call you as soon as we hear anything. And Cait…" Russell lowered his voice in an embarrassed whisper, "I miss you, too." He ended the call and cleared his throat before saying, "She's thinkin' Wesley."

"Well, she might be right." Just then Lucas' cell phone rang. It was Wesley Stiller.

"Was you just here?"

"Yeah, we pounded the hell out of your door. Why didn't you let us in, Wesley?"

"Damn it, man, I was in the shower. I felt like shit after this mornin' and I just wanted to stand under the steam for a while. I saw you guys drivin' off."

Lucas looked over at Russell. "Good enough. Wesley, I'm on my way to Ashland now, but I'll be by tomorrow. You gonna be there? You gonna let me in? All right. I'll see you in the mornin'."

"I don't like it," Russell spoke. "Seems too convenient for him. Wesley likes to call the shots."

"Yeah, well, maybe we'll just surprise him later. You got that whiskey?"

Russell pointed to the pint in his pocket.

"Okay. Let's go pay Harmon a visit and then we'll get this bracelet to the lab."

Lucas drove through downtown Ashland and parked in the garage at the expansive medical complex. Harmon was still in the emergency department. He was lying on a gurney and his head was bandaged. He had a huge grin on his crinkled face.

"Drugs." Lucas smiled at Russell and then back at Harmon. "How you doin,' you old geezer? Likin' the purty nurses around here?"

"Don't call me an old geezer, you old geezer." Harmon giggled. "And yeah, they's some purty girls in here all right. I think I'll stick around."

The ER was in chaos treating multiple injuries from a four-car pileup, so it was hours before he was finally admitted for observation. "I'll be back to get you tomorrow, Harmon. You have a good night, you here?"

They left him then, in the better-than-good hands of a tall redheaded nurse who seemed to get a particular kick out of her geriatric patient.

Back in the cruiser, Lucas headed for the crime lab at the police station. He left the bracelet and was promised a call back pronto.

"So you wanna be my deputy? I think I should make you my deputy." Lucas had just pulled into Wesley's driveway. The reflection of the television was flickering against the living room curtains. "It could get weird."

"What do you mean weird?"

"I mean weird, like we could have a guy we've known forever to be just an asshole who has suddenly turned psycho. I mean weird like maybe you don't want to be here."

"Shit. I'm here, aren't I? I helped you get that bogus search together didn't I? Hell, I want to find Shelby. If Wesley turns out to be some kind of sick mother fucker who has hurt his daughter, I'm gonna turn psycho on him." Russell's jaw clinched in quick anger.

"Well, all right, then. But I don't need two crazies. If Wesley is our guy, we have to keep our heads. Otherwise, we'll screw it up. You get me?"

Russell took a deep breath and nodded.

"You just follow my lead. Raise your right hand."

"Seriously?"

"I ain't playin' around, Russell. You wanna be my deputy or what?"

Russell raised his right hand.

"Excuse me." Lucas reached over and opened the glove compartment. "Great, it's still here." He unfolded a coffee-stained sheet of paper he found buried under a pile of parking tickets.

"Chief, you don't pay those?" Russell was staring at the crammed compartment.

"Hell, no. Those boys in Ashland have it in for me."

"But, Chief?"

"Hey, I did my service for the Commonweath. The least it can do for me is let me park." He took a pair of readers out of his pocket and put them on.

"God, Lucas, you look just like my old high school chemistry teacher."

"That purdy, huh? Keep your hand up." Lucas adjusted the glasses on his nose and then cleared his throat. "Do you solemnly swear that you will support the Constitution of the United States and be faithful and true to the Commonwealth of Kentucky so long as you continue as a citizen thereof, and that you will faithfully execute to the best of your ability the office of the sheriff, according to law."

"I do."

Lucas read on slowly and Russell swore to each oath.

"And finally, do you further solemnly swear that since the adoption of the present constitution, you being a citizen of this state, have not fought a duel with deadly weapons within the state, nor out of it, nor have you sent or accepted a challenge to fight a duel with weapons, nor have you..."

"Wait a second. Hold on. Fought a duel? Are you pullin' my leg?" Russell's eyes were bugging out of his head.

"That's what it says here. Fought a duel."

"Oh, yeah, that's somethin' we do all the time in the insurance business. How else do you think we get people to sign on the dotted line? Jesus, Chief, this is gettin' a little goofy."

"Well, goofy or no, have you?"

"Have I what?"

"Fought a duel!"

"God almighty."

"Well?"

"No, I ain't fought no duel. Now can we get on with it?"

"Well, all right, then. Also, do you swear that you will do right, as well to the poor as to the rich, in all things belonging to your office as sheriff; that you will do no wrong to any one for any gift, reward or promise, nor for favor or hatred, and in all things you will faithfully and impartially execute the duties of your office according to the best of your skill and judgment, so help you God." Lucas sighed. "Damn, that's sheer poetry."

Russell just stared at him.

"Well, do you?"

"Do I what?"

"Swear to all that stuff?"

"For God's sake. Yes, I swear."

Lucas was satisfied. "Okay, you can put your hand down."

"So, I'm an officer now?"

"Well, it's not like you're gettin' a gun or anything, but I thought I better cover my ass in case things got outta hand. But yeah, Russell, you're an acting deputy for the time bein'."

"Wow."

"Now don't go all Barney Fife on me. It ain't that big a deal." He grinned and opened the door to the cruiser.

"Wesley, you there?" Lucas pounded on the door. Once again there was silence on the other side.

"Maybe he's sleepin'?" Russell asked.

"I don't care if he is sleepin'. Hell, it's early and the TV is cranked. Wesley? It's Lucas. Goddamn it, open this door."

At last, the front door lock clicked and the door slowly opened. It was dark enough that Wesley's face was in full shadow.

"Man, it's about time. You let us hang here on the porch for damned near forever!" Lucas took off his hat and walked by the man behind the door. Russell followed close behind. After they were inside, the door closed and a shadowed silhouette emerged until Wesley was standing in front of them.

"Well, what the hell you want?"

"Damn, Wes, whatever happened to, hey, guys, glad to see you. Come on in, sit a spell?"

"Give up the crap, Lucas. Or should I say Chief? Is this official business or what? I thought you was comin' tomorrow. I was just gettin' ready to watch *Swamp People,"* Wesley sneered.

Lucas glanced over to his sidekick and Russell pulled out the Jack Daniels and held it up.

"Actually, we thought we could combine a little business with a little pleasure?" Lucas asked, raising an eyebrow. "That is, unless you really just can't miss that episode of *Swamp People*."

Wesley looked at the bottle. "Oh, hell, why not. Come on out to the kitchen. I'll get some glasses."

They followed him and were amazed again at how Wesley had changed. He walked with a light step and an uncommon energy. Whatever Shelby Jean had done for him or given to him, they were both wishing it came in a pill form.

"Okay, whatcha lookin' at? Pour me a shot."

"Sure thing, Wes." Russell poured the whiskey into tall glasses from the cupboard.

Getting ice from the refrigerator, Lucas noticed it was nearly bare. "So you're feeling good, huh, buddy?" Before he could put the ice in his glass, Wesley shot his whiskey back. He slammed his glass on the table and looked at Russell, who immediately filled his glass again.

Nobody spoke.

Lucas looked around the familiar room. It was different. The kitchen had always been a place of feminine comforts, colorful dish towels and decorative placemats, country knick knacks; tacky, homey family treasures left over from Neely and Martha. Now these things were gone. Lucas noticed all the painted plates that used to line the top of the cabinets had been removed. He had always liked those plates. Neely had painted the lilies herself with water colors from a paint set Martha had bought her.

A painful moment of regret slipped over Lucas' mind. He was reminded of how Martha had loved helping her daughter fix up the old farmhouse. But Wesley had never seemed to fit the cozy décor. There was always too much edge to him. And all the softness his pretty wife and little daughter surrounded him with had only managed to sharpen his edges. Now, as Lucas looked around, he could see how this man was finally living the way he wanted to. There was nothing of the women left in his house. *It's like they never existed.* He had removed them. Now the house had a hard, almost sterile feel to it. But as Lucas watched Wesley drink his whiskey, he could see it suited the man. He was finally in his element.

"So, Wes, I am really sorry that the search this mornin' didn't help us none. But I wanted to thank you for comin' and tryin' anyway."

Wesley drank his second drink more slowly, this time dropping some ice into his glass. "Is that why you come over here tonight? To thank me for trudgin' around in the rain like an ignorant ass? Well, that's mighty fine. But what I wanna know is why *you* ignorant asses down at the station ain't doin' somethin' about findin' Shelby? I mean, what the hell did you drag all them people to them woods today for?"

"You know the answer to that as well as I do, Wes. We ain't had a single lead on Shelby's case. We needed folks to help us comb those woods between Martha's and Sorina's. Somethin' coulda showed up. It was just unfortunate that the weather didn't give us a break."

"Yeah, that was unfortunate." Wesley finished his drink. This time Russell didn't offer to fill his glass. "Okay, then, I accept your apology. Now if that's all, I'd like to get back to my show." Wes tugged at his flannel vest like he was chilled.

Lucas pushed himself away from the table. He could see that there would be no easy way to do this. "Wesley, if you don't mind, I'd like to take a look around."

"What do you mean, take a look around? Hell, you say. Ain't nobody lookin' nowheres."

"Wes, I want to see the basement." Lucas lowered his tone and stood up to his full height of 6'5". For a moment he felt like the police chief again. He noticed Wesley's cheek muscles flinching.

"No, I ain't gonna let you in the basement. What do you wanna go in the basement for anyways? You thinkin' I got Shelby tied up down there or somethin'? Is that what you're thinkin'?" Wesley's eyes flashed and he reached inside his vest pocket.

"That better not be a gun in that vest." Lucas put his hand on his own gun, and released the safety.

Wesley reached further into the vest pocket, and just as Lucas started to raise his pistol, Wesley pulled out a pack of cigarettes. He grinned, as Lucas' shoulders dropped in relief. A bead of sweat had popped out on his forehead.

"Jesus, Luke, git a grip. Didja think I was gonna shoot you? Man, you better lighten up. You know they only put your old ass on this case because they ain't got nobody else fool enough to take it on."

That was it for Lucas. "Well, that's just real good for you, ain't it, Wes, if you got your daughter tied up somewhere in this house. I guess you would be real glad it was just me and not somebody who might actually find her. Now I'm gonna go downstairs."

Lucas turned toward the door at the top of the basement steps and Russell was following closely behind. But they weren't quick enough. Wesley had swung in front of them and was blocking the door.

"Now, Wes, if you got nothin' to hide, you just move out the way. What do you think you're doin'?"

"What I'm doin' is exercisin' my constitutional rights and insistin' that you get a search warrant if you wanna go nosin' around my place. That's what I'm doin." He stood defiantly in front of them.

"You really gonna make us do this the hard way?"

"Yeah, I guess I am."

The three men stood staring at each other, waiting for one or all of them to make the first move. It was Lucas who finally gave in.

"All right. Have it your way. The judge won't blink an eye about givin' us a warrant. You're just diggin' your hole deeper, Wesley. You hear me?"

"Fuck you, Chief. You don't scare me none. I got nothin' to hide. You come back with that warrant. We're gonna do this thing right or we ain't gonna do it at all. Now go on and leave me be."

Wesley waited until he heard the cruiser back out of the driveway and head towards Sorry's Run on US 23 before he opened the basement door in the kitchen. He turned on the single light that swung over top of the stairs. He had much to do before tomorrow. *Damn Lucas and his goddamned search warrant.*

CHAPTER TWENTY-EIGHT
NO PEACE

LUCAS PULLED A BEER from the refrigerator and went out onto his deck. "Come on, boy," he spoke to the golden lab who was his constant and best companion. "Sit down, Saber. It's okay, boy. I'm home. You can relax now."

The dog sunk down by his master's feet, laying his head on his front paws as man and best friend looked out over the Ohio. Lucas never tired of the view from his rustic home built into the hill overlooking the river. It had been his dream and had taken all his life to complete, but it was done and now he should have been glad to sit and watch the river and go down to its banks and fish and basically vegetate in peaceful satisfaction. But no, it was not to be. As much as Luke had envisioned his peaceful retirement, it had brought him little peace.

It was not that he didn't love stepping out from his dining room onto the cantilevered deck overlooking the vista of Ohio and Kentucky situated on either sides of the swelling muddy river. It was not that. It was not that he didn't appreciate the quiet of the elevated home that he had built with slow deliberation. It was not that. It was not that he didn't enjoy all the modern luxuries laid out in a rustic style that gave a man the feeling of being wrapped up in raw nature but in total comfort. It wasn't that. It wasn't even that he had placed every log, anchored every beam, and laid every plank of wood floor in the hopes that Martha would share it. It wasn't even that.

It was him.

He couldn't feel peace because he wasn't a peaceful man. He only thrived on the job, on the hunt, on the mystery solving. It was what he was. He realized, now that his life was on the close side of finished, that he could have skipped the dream house. It wasn't what he needed after all. With no one to share it, it was just a relic of a man's life, thrown away in regret. He didn't need it, but it was his, and he tried to appreciate it. Saber helped.

"Saber, I guess it's just you and me, buddy." He looked down at the dog at his feet, who wagged his tail just enough to acknowledge the obvious truth of his master's statement.

Lucas took a deep drink of his beer and thought about Wesley. He had been as surprised as anything in his life when Wesley wouldn't allow him to see the basement of the farmhouse. It made Stiller look so outwardly suspicious that it just didn't make sense. Lucas had known Wesley all his life and he couldn't imagine that he would do harm to his daughter like that. Wesley had always been pissed off. That much was true. Even back when the Sorry's Run basketball team had been on its way to a record-breaking season, and Wesley had been kicked off for mouthing off to the coach. It just added to the things that had pissed him off. But he was a good-looking guy and when he landed the best-looking girl in the whole county, it only followed that he would have stopped being so pissed off.

Not the case.

Neely had been too good-looking, too smart and too gifted for Wesley. He had stayed pissed off, even when his baby girl was born. Neely had never given up herself and her own needs enough to devote her life to being a full-time mother and wife and it had only added to his anger.

But to hurt Shelby Jean in some cruel and malicious manner?

That just didn't figure into Lucas' way of thinking about the guy, pissed off or not. Still, he would get that warrant and look in that basement. What the hell was Wesley up to? He was up to something. Just what, Lucas couldn't put his finger on. And where else was he going with this case? Wesley had been right. They had probably put his old ass on the job only because they had nobody else fool enough to take it on.

Lucas took another drink and watched as a speed boat cut through the water on its way downriver to Portsmouth. He saw the young man behind the wheel of the boat with his hair whipping around his face, blocking his features. He saw the woman next to him smiling and laying her slender arm around his neck. Lucas stared until the boat's swells were all that was left.

Some people have all the fun.

Well, he didn't care. He was old now. But he had had his share of fun.

He had done it all, and had no regrets, except for Martha. She was his big regret. She never would let him get too close. It had probably been his drinking that kept her away. So much of what happened in those years he barely remembered, though he had managed to keep his job. Hell, in those days, they all drank.

So now he didn't care why they had put him on the case, he was just glad. It was a way of being close to Martha and doing something for her. God, if she knew that somebody was doing harm to Shelby, she would turn over in her grave a hundred times. Lucas winced at the thought of Martha in a grave. He was glad she had been cremated. He knew he was coming up right behind her and the whole buried-in-a-pine-box thing…a shiver coursed over him, and the water took on a more deeply shadowed tint for a moment. He usually didn't let himself give into melancholy, but today he was lonely. Really lonely. And he felt old.

Lucas finished his beer and nodded at his dog. Saber trotted over to a cooler on the deck and pawed at its lid until it popped open. He stuck his head in and clinched a can in his jaws and brought it back, wagging his tail.

"Good boy! I shoulda got you an audition for Letterman's stupid dog tricks!" Lucas smiled and opened the can. He took a drink and tried to line his thoughts up. Who would want to hurt Shelby Jean? She had been gone from Sorry's Run all of her adult life. She hadn't had time to make enemies. Why would anyone want to harm her? Had it been random? One of those in-the-wrong-place-at-the-wrong-time scenarios? He didn't think so. It was too coincidental. Shelby's return to help out with her family, her grandmother's death, the car accident, and then Shelby's disappearance? Nothing seemed random about any of it, but he was damned if he could find a connection.

"Yoo-hoo? Anybody home?"

"Out here on the deck, Bella. Join me for a beer." He turned his head and called out to her.

"Hey, there. Whatcha up to, Lucas? Hi Saber. God, it's so beautiful after all that rain." Bella took the beer that Saber offered up in his legendary fashion. She bent over and patted him on his head and thanked him and he returned to his spot by his master's feet. Bella stood against the deck railing and admired the view.

"Do you know how lucky you are to live here, Luke? This is breathtaking.

And this house. I never get used to it. You are such a catch for some lucky 18-year-old girl!" She grinned at him and drank her beer.

"Take a load off, Bella." He patted the cushion on the seat next to him. "Yeah, the 18-year-olds are lining up to get in here. A real nuisance."

They both laughed.

"So, what's up, Bella? You don't usually pay me unannounced visits."

"It's Shelby, Lucas. What else? What the hell. Have you got any leads at all? Sorina hasn't picked up on nothin'. She's startin' to get real sad and I don't think I've ever seen her this way. We gotta do somethin'."

Lucas looked at the bangles on Bella's wrist. He knew they were Martha's creations. He reached out and gently touched the gem in the copper bracelet. "I love this stuff. I took the jewelry I found in the woods to the lab in Ashland."

"Yeah?" Her brown eyes widened.

"Yeah. But I don't expect it'll help us any, especially after it bein' buried in all that mud and rain. I'll drive down tomorrow and see what they found. And I'm gettin' a warrant for Wesley's place."

Bella's eyebrows arched as she asked, "Oh, Luke, you don't really believe…"

"No, I don't." He finished her thought. "But he's actin' mighty suspicious and he wouldn't let Russell and me into the basement tonight, like he's hidin' somethin'. It just don't feel right, you know? Especially with the way he's gettin' around like he's twenty years younger. I swear it's like the man made a deal with the devil."

Bella sighed in agreement and leaned back into the rattan chair. "Get me another beer, Saber." The lab wagged his tail and jumped up, heading for the cooler, as the two friends passed the next hour easily, watching the mighty Ohio run its course.

From an aluminum chair on the banks of the river Sorina watched the Ohio, too. Even In her blindness she could see it, see the hidden, rushing currents pushing the water on, forcing it to just keep rolling. She could see it in her mind's eye. And she could feel it. Her senses seemed even more heightened than usual. Sorina felt herself drift off…

Lizbeth had to breathe. She wanted to die but she couldn't not live. If only her body would allow her to just die. She knew all she had to do was take away the hollow reed and breathe deeply under the water. She'd heard talk about it, about how drownin' was as easy as breathin'. So many slaves prayed for drownin' to be released from this livin'. But she couldn't do it. She felt Samuel beside her in the water, still as death. But she knew he wasn't dead. He was making himself invisible. She listened in the stillness of the creek, straining to hear the dogs, but they sounded far away, more distant each moment. Were they really safe? Lizbeth took too deep a breath on the willow reed and sucked in water. She gagged and it forced her to come up for air. Samuel stirred beside her and yanked her back under the water. But she had lost the reed and now she had to hold her breath. But she couldn't. She felt panicky and had to get out of the water. She threw his hands off her and came up for blessed air, muffling her coughing with the back of her hand. Once her convulsing chest relaxed she listened hard. She heard only the gurgle of the stream and far off hounds. She pulled on Samuel and his dark head popped up beside her. The wretched lovers remained quiet, listening. Lizbeth had learned to be quiet for Samuel, when really she just wanted to scream nonstop. But she had learned to be quiet.

When Samuel was satisfied that they were safe, he raised her up and they climbed out of the water. He didn't let her rest though. He took her hand and pulled her back into the cover of the trees. They were soaking wet and chilled with the night air, but they kept going.

How does he know where he's going? The trees blurred into giant woody creatures, at once comforting in their protection and frightening in their gnarly immensity. Lizbeth felt herself fading as her tired, ravaged legs tried to keep up with him. Not fading as in weary, but fading as in vanishing! Maybe she had learned to disappear. She no longer was aware of her own labored breath, her pain. She only felt the connection with his hand. Her lifeline. Her life. Lizbeth blindly followed her man through the woods and onward into the night until at last he dropped beside a tree and brought her with him, holding onto her too tightly, squeezing her while they both gasped for air. How long he held her like that she could never say, but she wanted it to never end. They were safe for another night. Another moment. They were safe.

Sorina opened her eyes. The vision had been more vivid than ever. She saw them so clearly, the slaves. She didn't just see them; she heard them, felt them. It was disturbingly real and now she was all the more convinced that Shelby Jean was feeding her the psychic connection. It just had to be. Sorina didn't have that kind of special sight on her own.

Shelby, where are you?

CHAPTER TWENTY-NINE
LOOK THE OTHER WAY

"OFFICER CHAMBERS?" THE LAB TECH handed him the bracelet in a plastic bag. "I wish we had something more useful. Prints were minimal, but comparing with our records, Shelby Jean Stiller definitely had this jewelry on her arm. There were four small scratches near the clasp that could be indicative of the bracelet being forcibly unhooked, but whoever else might have had their hands on it was wearing gloves. Gave us nothin'."

Lucas took the bag with the bracelet and thanked the tech, who looked to him to be all of twenty years old. He picked up the one-page report from the front desk and joined Russell in the cruiser.

"Nothin', just like I figured." He took the bracelet out of the bag and examined it more closely. It was a silver braided band with a turquoise and crystal stone set in a leafy design. *Beautiful.* He thought of Martha and how she rarely wore jewelry. He used to stop in her store in Sorry's Run. She was quite successful in her small, intimate shop. She had a knack for displaying her jewelry in the best light. She created enticing scenes utilizing her pieces arranged in artistic groupings; silver laid on brass, beads on gold.

"Babe, I get what you're doin' here. I just don't get why you don't wear it yourself?" He had asked Martha many times. She always had the same answer. "I don't feel like my body needs elaboration." She'd smile and he would melt.

"Chief?" Russell repeated, "Chief?"

Lucas came back from memory lane and grunted at the interruption.

"So what now?" Russell asked.

"Now we visit the judge."

The courthouse was quiet with an empty docket. The clerk took them back to the judge's chambers.

"Howdy, Lucas. Long time no see." Willard Thompson was a visiting judge from Ashland. He shook Lucas' hand and waved to Russell, gesturing for them to sit in his chamber chairs.

"You haven't been before me in too many years, Lucas. How is your house? And how is that talented dog of yours?"

They made small talk for a while. He and Lucas had been fishing buddies in their earlier years, back when Will was an ambitious Commonwealth Attorney before putting himself on the ballot for judge.

Finally, they got down to business.

"So, what have you got?"

"Judge, I have been assigned to a missin' person's case. Ms. Shelby Jean Stiller has been gone well over a week now, and we don't have any leads. I need a search warrant to get into the basement of Wesley Stiller's house."

"Her father?" Judge Thompson asked.

"It's a long story, Your Honor, but we have reason to suspect kidnappin'."

An hour later Russell and Lucas were back in the cruiser heading for the farmhouse, warrant in hand. They didn't have to knock long this time. Wesley opened the door looking a little too cheery. Lucas didn't like it.

"Well, come on in, boys. Glad to see you. Want some coffee? Or maybe a little hair of the dog?" He almost winked at Lucas and it made the hair on his arms stand up.

"Wesley, what the hell. We ain't here for chit-chat. I got the warrant. Now let me into the basement."

"Hell, then, all right. I was just tryin' to be friendly. I'm gonna git myself a cup of joe."

They followed him back to the kitchen. Wesley went over to the cupboard to choose a mug from the shelf while Lucas and Russell went to the door that led down into the belly of the house. Luke nodded to Russell to stay at the top of the stairs while he slowly descended the steep steps.

The basement had the typical dank smell of an unfinished basement that had known its share of water seeping in through cracks in the foundation. Lucas flipped the switch to illuminate the single light bulb hanging from the ceiling above the steps and stepped carefully down the narrow stairway. He was far too big a man for the space he was in. His corduroy jacket rubbed up against the crumbly walls and tiny flakes of paint and stone littered the steps. He was careful not to bang his head against the low ceilings as he walked into the empty rooms. He noticed the washer and dryer were gone. *Now why would he get rid of those machines?*

And it was darker than he remembered.

Luke pulled a flashlight from his coat pocket and shined the bright beam in front of him. He aimed the light up to the small windows. Dark curtains were hung, blocking any light from coming in. There were just two rooms; one larger space where the washer and dryer had been, and another smaller room that had probably served as a fruit cellar. There had always been cinder blocks stacked in the corners and several cardboard boxes sitting on top of a long bench that were filled with useless junk that Martha bragged were her family heirlooms.

But now the boxes were gone, along with the bench and the cinder blocks. The smaller room was empty and swept clean. This room, too, had a high window that was blocked with a dense material. Wesley had apparently wanted the basement sealed off for some reason. Either to keep anybody from looking in—*or to keep anybody in from looking out.* Just then the dampness penetrated his jacket and a chill coursed over his arms.

Lucas directed the light around the corners of the floor and around the low ceiling. There was no sign of anything or anybody. In fact, it was remarkable how empty the rooms were and how neatly swept. Didn't figure. He let the wide beam trace the cracks in the foundation and followed it around to see if maybe there was another room. A room not really noticeable. After all, he had been in the basement maybe all of two times to talk to Martha when she was doing laundry. He hadn't remembered there being anymore to it than what you saw easily, but he had never really asked or looked. Hadn't mattered. *I bet there's more to this basement…*

Lucas stepped slowly and carefully, trying to quiet his own breath to hear more clearly. If Shelby was locked away in another room down here, surely he would hear something.

Crash!

"What the…?!" He nearly dropped his flashlight. One resounding crash was followed by several loud clattering bangs and rolling sounds of metal on metal. It was all coming from above the stairway. Luke put the flashlight back in his pocket and took two steps at a time running back upstairs. "Russell, man? Are you all…?" Luke stopped dead in his tracks as he saw Russell and Wesley down on all fours picking up pots and pans.

"What the hell are you guys doin'? You scared the piss out of me."

"Oh, sorry, Luke. I was standing over there by the door and Wesley says he was just puttin' a skillet away when he lost his balance. He went to catch himself and knocked all this shit out of the cabinets."

"He says? Weren't you watching?"

Russell stammered, "Well, I was just lookin' out at the hills. Shit, Lucas, Wesley wasn't doin' nothin' but drinkin' coffee."

Lucas shook his head and mumbled, "Some deputy." Then he asked, "Wes, what did you do with the washer and dryer?"

Wesley was wiping off his knees and putting the pans back in the cabinets. "Oh, those machines was toast. I gave 'em to Goodwill. I'm gonna buy new."

Luke stared at Wesley and decided to accept that. "Are there anymore rooms down in that basement besides the two main ones?"

"Ah, uh, no, they ain't."

Luke decided not to accept that. "Russell, do you think you can keep an eye on him while I go take another look around. I mean, you think you can handle that without doin' any daydreamin' about those hills and a brunette?"

"Hey, cut it out, Luke. It ain't like I don't have other things I could be doin'. I'm here to help, damn it." He stood taller. "I've got this situation under control, Chief. You finish your search." Russell widened his stance in a determined pose and crossed his arms, staring at Wesley. Wesley sat back down at the table.

"All right, then. Give me another minute. Unless there's somethin' you wanna tell me, Wes, and save us a lot of trouble?"

Wesley picked up his steaming mug and looked down at the coffee. He took a leisurely sip before answering, "I ain't got nothin' to say."

Lucas grunted and turned back to the steps. He walked downstairs sideways this time to avoid hitting the walls, and made his way back to the bottom. He pulled out the flashlight again. This time his focus was sharp. He had a vibe about something—something not right.

He walked more slowly around the parameters of the two small rooms, letting the beam of the light roll over the gray walls slowly. He looked up again at the high windows and saw nothing around them to insinuate struggle. No broken glass, no scratches on the walls. He scanned the seams along the ceiling that led to the farthest corner of the big room and let the flashlight come down the wall slowly, looking for anything out of the ordinary. There was nothing. The walls were just old basement walls with the occasional damp leakage seeping through some tiny cracks and some not-so-tiny cracks.

And he heard nothing.

Lucas was just about to give it up when something caught his eye. Just the slightest silver glimmer told him he was looking at fresh paint. Fresh gray paint over the back wall. Now that he paid attention he recognized a whiff of fresh paint over the dank atmosphere. Now why would Wesley be painting his basement? *Why now?* Lucas followed the line of paint with the flashlight and there it was, an apparent seam underneath the heavy sealant. Lucas took his finger and traced the line that was just underneath. He pressed hard and broke through the sealant. Sure enough, the line was deep and ran all the way down the wall. On closer look, it was obvious that it was a door. The paint sealant had been applied to hide a door.

Lucas' heart took on a faster pace. He put his hand over his gun and unlocked the safety. Then he took a Swiss Army knife from his pocket and ran it down the length of the painted seam until he had the outline of the door revealed. There was no doorknob, so he had to use the pocket knife to jimmy the frame until he could get his fingers around it far enough to get leverage to pull it open. It creaked as it strained against the paint, but then it cracked open. Lucas felt his breath tighten in his chest as he got both hands around the door now and yanked as hard as he could.

The door stood open now. He couldn't see inside, but a pungent, organic smell hit his nostrils. He shown the flashlight into the interior and his tightened breath left him in total surprise. The room was filled with plants. Marijuana plants. There were three benches filled with tall leafy potted plants. There was a whole system of ultra light panels stacked up against the walls. Spray cans of pesticides and fertilizers were piled high against the walls.

"Jesus Christ." Lucas whistled softly. "So this is what the old coot has been up to."

Lucas felt his whole body relax and his lips turned up in a smile.

"So that's what you been doin' out in the fields? Cultivatin' weed?"

Lucas and Russell were sitting at the table with Wesley and now they were all sharing a cup of coffee.

"Well, why the hell not? I'm still gonna plant tobacco, but I'm investigatin' hemp. Hell, it's the way of the future. Ain't gonna be no time before marijuana is legal. I just thought I'd git a jump on it. And I was doin' fine experimentin', tryin' to figure it all out until you had to come nosin' around. What you gonna do, Luke? What you gonna do about my plants?" Wesley looked like a kid who had gotten caught with his hand in the cookie jar.

"Hell, I ain't gonna do nothin'. I don't give a shit about your plants. That's not my bailiwick. I was hired on for one thing and one thing only and that was to investigate the disappearance of Shelby Jean Stiller, and to put all my experience and knowledge to bear in findin' her. And that's all I aim to do. Now, if Russell here feels the moral and ethical obligation to report your sorry ass, that's his affair. He is a sworn deputy, after all." Lucas put the coffee to his lips and watched Russell squirm.

After an uncomfortable silence, it became apparent that Russell had made a decision. His mouth set in a firm expression and he puffed up with confidence and authority, "You know, Wesley, growin' marijuana is still a felony in the Commonwealth. Things might be changin', but they ain't changin' that quick. Now, how many people know about this?"

"Ain't nobody knows about this. I ain't let nobody in this house hardly since I kicked Shelby out."

"Well, then, I didn't actually see it myself, so that means I'm just goin' off hearsay..." He looked at Lucas and grinned. "And I didn't *hear* Luke *say* anything."

Visible relief swept over Wesley, and his shoulders relaxed. Then he turned to Lucas and asked, "You didn't really think I had Shelby tied up in that basement, did you, Luke? I mean, Jesus, she might be a pain in my ass, but she's still my kid."

"No, Wes, I didn't really think you had Shelby tied up in that basement. Now, how about some of that hair of the dog you offered up earlier?" Lucas grinned.

CHAPTER THIRTY
POOR RUSSELL

"WANNA STOP FOR A COLD ONE?" Lucas asked. They were just passing The Pit Stop.

"Sure, why not. I could use another drink."

"Yeah, Wes is a little stingy with his hooch."

Lucas pulled the cruiser into the parking lot and they went inside.

"You're not plannin' on drinkin' and drivin', are you, Chief?" John Tyler grinned at them from behind the bar.

"Well, yeah, I was plannin' on doin' just that. You gonna bust me, John?" Lucas took off his hat and pulled out a bar stool.

"Well, if I busted you, I'd have to bust the judge, too. He just left."

The men laughed and shook hands. It was a moment that Lucas felt keenly, another last remnant of the "good-ole-boys-club" days. At one time they had all been members, skirting the law and many times their ethics to get to the bottom of a case. And they had all watched out for each other's backs.

But not anymore.

Too many greedy assholes had screwed up the system by taking advantage, and after the lawyers got involved, there were very few rules that could be broken without risk. But Lucas was too old to change and he still liked breaking the rules. It wasn't like they could fire him. Hell, he was barely hired. But still, he found he was more diligent about the way he did things. He didn't need to spend his final days in a jail cell, after all.

"Nah, John, just give me a beer. One beer. That'll keep me under the limit."

"What'll it be?"

"PBR of course."

John smiled and turned to Russell.

"Oh, no PBR for me, thanks. I'll have a Scotch."

"I still have a couple shots of the Glenmorangie left," John said.

"Thanks, John, but just give me a Dewar's." The memory of sharing the rare single malt with Shelby still burned in his mind, and he couldn't go there.

Lucas noticed the pain cross Russell's expression.

"That must have been a hell of a thing on the night of Shelby's accident. Hell of a thing." Lucas threw back the cold beer.

"Oh, yeah, I've relived it a million times trying to recreate it, you know, tryin' to make it turn out different. But then the ironic thing—she survives that horrific night just to get well, get all happy and settled and then she disappears? I mean, who could believe such a thing would happen to her."

"I know. And that's what keeps eatin' at my gut. It just doesn't seem like a random kidnapping. It seems more like someone or some thing in Sorry's Run has it in for her. That's what boggles me. Because how could she have enemies?"

"Unless it's not an enemy of Shelby's? Maybe it's an enemy of someone close to Shelby?"

"Like who?" The men sat and ran over the list of acquaintances, people Shelby had reconnected with since her return to Kentucky. None of them seemed suspicious or even remotely capable of pulling off such a horrendous deed.

"Well, nothin' makes sense when you logically figure on it. We gotta start thinkin' outside the box." Lucas sighed.

Just then Russell's cell phone lit up and starting scooting across the bar as it buzzed. He picked it up and saw Caitlin Sotheby's name there. "Excuse me for a minute, Chief."

Lucas watched Russell talk into his phone at the far end of the bar. He had all the signs and symptoms of a man in love. It was written all over him. Too bad the girl was a New Yorker. But man, what a looker.

A New Yorker.

Something about that thought resonated with him. He hadn't really believed he would have to investigate New York, but maybe there was no getting around it. Shelby had this whole other life in New York that nobody but her roommate knew anything about. Maybe they were all barking up the wrong tree by confining this thing to somebody in Greenup County. Maybe there was somebody wantin' things to go wrong for Ms. Stiller from her "other" life. Maybe her coming back to Kentucky had been just the opportunity they had been looking for. *Hummm.* A lot of maybes. Lucas finished his beer and laid money on the bar.

"Caitlin is comin'." Russell was beaming, even in the muted light. "The reception is bad in here and she was breakin' up. I have to call her back, but I think she said she's comin' in day after tomorrow."

"Well, all right, then. That's a good thing. Let's get on out of here and I'll get you to your car so you can make that call."

"Russell, yes, I'm flying back to Kentucky. My boss has given me a leave of absence. I'm staying until we find her," Caitlin's voice broke as emotion rocked her. "I've spoken with Bella and she says I can stay in Martha's trailer as long as I like. I've booked a flight and will land in Huntington day after tomorrow at 6:30. Can you pick me up?"

"Of course I'll be there. And Cait, I'm glad you're comin.' Really glad." Russell ended the call and breathed a sigh of relief. He had been missing the fetching brunette more than he cared to admit. He had it bad. He closed his own brown eyes and all he saw were her striking blue ones. And he could feel her hair and her skin every moment as though she were next to him. He hadn't had it this bad for a long time. He knew it was impossible. She was a New Yorker all the way, and, well, he wasn't. It couldn't go anywhere, but for the time being they would both be stronger just being together through this ordeal. Of that much, he was certain. He needed her. He was pretty sure she needed him.

Russell's cell phone chimed again, and this time it was Lucas. "Hey deputy, am I gonna have your services for a while longer or are you off the force since your girl is comin'?"

Russell heard the sarcasm in his gravelly voice on the other end of the phone.

"No way. You're not gettin' rid of me that easy. I might not be as clever as Barney Fife, but I'm loyal. And besides, I've taken time off work. I was lettin' all my cases slide anyway. Not good. The area supervisor has been very understandin'."

"Well, that's great because I'm gonna need you. Andy couldn't get through the day without Barney. Now get your head back on the case before that pretty girl steals away what little brains you got left."

On his way home, Lucas couldn't stop thinking about the budding romance between his partner and the enticing New Yorker. *Caitlin Sotheby.* She could be the key to a door that he hadn't wanted to unlock. It would be very helpful to have Russell close to Shelby's roommate. It would be helpful, but it could also turn out to be hurtful.

Poor Russell.

Lucas pulled into his driveway and shut the engine off. He sat behind the wheel for a minute before slowly easing his tired body out of the car. Muscles ached in the strangest places for no apparent reason. *It's hell getting old,* he thought for the millionth time. When he opened up his front door there was a shaggy blonde head greeting him happily. "Hey, Saber, where's my beer, man?"

Later that night, Lucas turned off the flat screen and looked out his bedroom window. He wanted quiet for a few minutes before he nodded off. It had been an interesting day. He had felt almost like his old self in that dank basement. It had scared him to death, but it had felt good to feel scared. Hell, it had felt good just to *feel.* And there was a moment there when he had really and truly expected the worst. He had expected to see Shelby Jean's body exposed or lying under a heap of who knows what. But man, had he been glad to know he was so off base. *Marijuana, for god's sak*e. That sure explained a lot of Wesley's behavior.

And thank God, it hadn't turned out to be him who was his daughter's abductor. That would have shook the community up too much. People who lived in Sorry's Run had their place. Everybody had known each other for most of their lives, and they were comfortable with the predictability of things. The fact that there might be a kidnapper, or worse, a killer among them, was just too much for a small community like his Kentucky town. Folks would have a hell of a time recovering. They all knew Wesley Stiller and his shortcomings, but they sure as hell didn't think him capable of real evil. So, thank God.

As good as all that was, it left him with a blank sheet still on Shelby's disappearance. Another day and nothing. But now his mind was shifting to Shelby's New York life. *Poor Russell.*

"Sorina, do you wanna hold onto this?" Luke pulled out the bracelet he had found in the woods.

They were drinking tea at the wooden table in front of a fire that Jessie had just stoked. Sorina took the jewelry and held it in her palm, feeling its shape with her fingers. "I can tell it's beautiful. I thank you, Lucas. Are you sure it isn't evidence?"

"Nah, it doesn't tell us anything more than Shelby had worn it at some time."

Sorina ran her hand over the metal hoping to get a Shelby vibration. *Nothing.* Her dismay was increasing hourly since Shelby's disappearance.

Jessie poured more tea into their cups.

"Thank you, Jessie." Sorina smiled sweetly at the quiet girl before adding, "It just makes me so sad. I haven't been this devoid of intuition in, I don't know how long. It's like Martha left and took my second sight with her. I am so sorry, Luke. I really did expect to be of some help to you in findin' Shelby. I really did."

"It's okay, Sorina. You'll get your juice back. You're just traumatized like everybody else. Give it some time. And you be sure to let me know as soon as Martha has anything to tell us. Uh, and by the way, if you do speak with her, tell her I miss her." Luke looked sheepishly down at his lap and Sorina reached across and found his hand.

"Now that is mighty sweet comin' from you, Lucas Chambers, seein' as how I know you don't believe a word of all the mumbo-jumbo I spew. But don't you worry none, Martha knows you miss her. She knows. And I don't know why she's bein' so damned quiet on the other side. It just isn't like her. I'm startin to get really mad!"

Lucas looked up and grinned at the pretty woman who he could never understand. She did look angry, and that beat the socks off of the sad look she had had when he got there. "Well, that's good, Ms. Sori. Anger is good. We need a little of that. We gotta get good and pissed off and just maybe that will get Martha's attention."

Sorina added, "Yeah, knowin' Martha, she's probably floatin' on some cloud somewheres gabbin' with other angels and makin' her jewelry and just havin' a good old time." Sorina pointed to the ceiling. "That's it! She is just not payin' attention!"

They both broke out in laughter, and Lucas added, "You know, you might be onto something there, Sori."

"I think I better change my tactics." Sorina giggled and took his arm as he led her back through the rooms and out to his car.

When Luke left the cottage he felt uplifted somehow. Sorina always did that for him. People thought she was certifiable but they liked her, and he understood why. She was a beautiful soul. She would keep the bracelet and honor it. He knew that. It's what Martha would have wanted. He turned up the radio in the cruiser on his way to pick up Russell. It was time to search the Internet for anything about Shelby Jean Stiller, the model.

Sorina waited until she heard the car drive off and then she went back into the cottage. She walked through the rustic rooms holding her cane in her hand lightly. She didn't need it to guide her to the living room. She had every inch of the cottage memorized. She and Jessie had arranged it with the clear intention of never changing anything in the rooms. Not even something as insignificant as a pillow ever moved from its usual spot on the sofa and chairs. When they needed to replace something or add something to the furnishings they took special care to make sure Sorina knew exactly where the change had taken place. So after all these years of consistency, Sorina could easily maneuver through the rooms without assistance.

She pulled her feet up and stretched out on the leather sofa in front of the fireplace. She wondered again why she had insisted on a fire on such a mellow day. The weather had been wet, but not cold. They were into late spring, after all. But she couldn't seem to stay warm. She wore sweaters and wrapped herself in caftans, but for the past forty-eight hours she had just had a non-stop chill in her bones.

"Should I get you to the doctor?" Jessie had felt her head.

"No, hon. I'll be all right. This chill I'm feelin' has nothin' to do with an infection. I am sick in my soul at the moment and ain't no antibiotic gonna cure that."

Jessie had seemed to understand and left her alone. She went over to her mandolin case and took the instrument out. Soon a melancholy melody lifted up from its taut strings and filled the room.

"God, hon, that is so sad it's makin' my heart hurt. Don't you have somethin' else to play today that could cheer us up?"

Sorina got no response, but the music stopped immediately and she heard Jessie latch her instrument case. She instantly regretted her words. "Aw, sweetie, I didn't mean to be so insensitive. What you was playin' was beautiful. I just hate feelin' like cryin' is all. I'm sorry. Forgive me?" She heard gentle footsteps and knew that Jessie had moved to the sofa and was looking down at her. Sorina waited.

Finally the willowy, shy woman spoke, "I know, Sori. I feel the same way. I just don't have anythin' cheerful in me right now. I think I'm gonna go lay down for a while. Will you be all right? I'll put more wood on the fire, if you want."

"No, that's all right, Jessie. I'm bein' foolish heatin' up the house like this. I'll just throw this blanket over me and take a little nap, too. I'll be fine. You go ahead on. Maybe if we rest for a spell we'll feel better?"

Jessie leaned over and kissed her on the forehead. "I love you, Sorina."

"I know, hon. I love you, too. Don't you worry now. I promise everythin' will be okay." She patted Jessie's hand and focused on her graceful footsteps walking away from her.

Sorina pulled the knitted throw over her legs and listened to the fire. It was the thing she appreciated about being blind; the hearing. The hearing was sensational, along with her other heightened senses. The fireplace was noisy, popping and hissing with its ever-changing form. She tried to imagine what it looked like as the firewood expanded with energy and then collapsed into ashy piles of what was, just moments earlier, a formidable log.

Sorina was sad. She couldn't remember ever having been so sad. Her strange life had never been boring, never been predictable, and certainly had never been sad. But all that had changed when she lost Martha. And now Shelby was gone. But Sorina knew that Martha's grandchild wasn't really gone. She knew that Shelby breathed somewhere. Their connection with the slaves was too strong. But why Martha wasn't helping her find Shelby was beyond understanding. The missing person's investigation wouldn't go on much longer. Shelby's disappearance would be shelved eventually as another "cold case" that would remain a mystery. That is, unless Sorina could get herself in a more receptive vibe where she could pick up something from Shelby or her grandmother from the other side.

Sorina sighed as she listened to the fire lose its fury and settle down to a crackle. She pulled the cover up tighter and tried to stop her mind from its usual ramblings. If she could quiet herself, meditate for a while maybe she could tap into the other side. Maybe she could. She slowed her breath to a deeper inhalation and listened to the room.

As what usually happened to Sorina when she quieted her thoughts, her psyche drifted to another life—not Shelby's, not Martha's, not even her own. But another life. Sorina Duncan McBride's long-ago life. The images of a fantastic past life became real to her, real in smell, in sight, in feelings—real in thoughts...

CHAPTER THIRTY-ONE
DRUIDESS (A LONG-AGO LIFE)

THE REFLECTION OF A YOUNG sunburned woman with wide blue eyes and wild, wheat-colored hair stared back at her from the still creek water. She splashed her face and the cold water startled her fully back from the dull sleepiness she had felt just moments before. She dipped her calloused hands into the creek again and stirred her watery image until it disappeared in the ripples, blending with the blue, cloudless sky above her head. The young woman stood up and wiped her palms on her long skirt and yanked her unruly locks away from her face, tying them back with a leather strap. The day was crisp and she breathed deeply of the invigorating Kentucky air.

Sorina was alone now. Her husband was gone. He had acted foolishly, losing his life in the local tavern where other foolish young men gathered to dull their senses. It had been Gerald's weakness and it had killed him. She had loved him dearly, but she would never marry again. She knew she should allow his brothers to take her back across the Ohio and then back to their New England people, far away from this primitive land, but she didn't want to go.

She wanted to stay.

Of course, it was unheard of, a white woman alone in such a cruel, untamed land of harsh winters and devils behind every tree. She knew that. And it was true, the winters were harsh and the two-legged and four-legged devils did lurk. But when the winters gave way to the caresses of warm spring breezes, all the harshness was quickly forgotten with the first morning scent of honeysuckle and rosemary growing unchecked in the tangled, sprouting greenery that exploded in fragrant aromatic blasts. It was Kentucky and she felt it was hers now.

She had worked hard, she and her young, hot-headed husband. They had built a sturdy cabin and he had put in a good stone fireplace, carrying flat rocks up from the creek. The lay of the land gave them the creek to bathe in, which trickled down to the wide river to fish in. There was natural protection in the forest that helped guard them from high winds, and kept them hidden from strangers. But the devils knew they were there, the red devils, Gerald McBride had called them. But they had managed to bond with these red devils and so far they had stayed away.

She didn't know if that would still be the case or if, without the man, the white woman alone would be hunted and taken. She didn't know. But she didn't think so. Sorina believed in herself. She was independent in a time when women were not expected to be. She had found her true, authentic self in the forests of Kentucky and she wasn't going back to the civilization she had come from. Sorina didn't feel civilized any longer. She felt more a child of nature, one with the trees and the river and the animals. She would stay because she belonged. There was enough strength born in her from her Scottish ancestors to fortify her and she believed the Indians would respect that and continue to let her alone.

She was partially wrong.

A year had passed since Gerald's death. Sorina was out gathering wood when she came home to find visitors outside the cabin door. She recognized the tall, painted medicine man who had come to her one other time with his hand badly burned when Gerald was still alive. The language they communicated in had been that of common healers. She soon came to understand that this proud man had come to her humbly because he could not heal himself and wanted no one in his tribe to know his shame. He felt it weakened him in stature and in respect. She learned all this from his eyes and his gestures and his silence. The two healers had bonded then, as she smoothed a honey compress gently on his hand and used cooling herbs to take the sting out of his palm. She had come to learn his name was Shaya.

Now he had returned with a young boy of about eleven years. The boy wore feathers in a band around his head and his brown body was naked except for a wide swatch of leather covering his narrow hips. He had tears in his dark eyes and his lips were trembling in pain. He stared from the medicine man back to her. Shaya put his fist in the small of the boy's back and nudged him toward her. He stumbled but recovered his composure quick enough. Sorina looked at Shaya's face and he nodded to her and then nodded toward the boy's back. She could see that the boy had boils on his back, festering and puss filled.

The medicine man looked at her and shrugged his shoulders as if to say—he wasn't sure.

She motioned for them both to come into the cabin. Smiling kindly, she took the boy's hand and led him gently to her bed. She lay him down on his stomach and brought a lantern close to better see the ugly carbuncle that had erupted on his skin between his shoulder blades. It was oozing and raw. She went to a shelf over her pot-bellied stove and pulled down several jars full of dark herbs. Each jar was labeled, but she handled the glass containers as though from memory, barely glancing at the printed description of what was inside: dogwood root, sassafras, tobacco. She spread the roots over the bottom of a small bowl and broke them down until the leaves were finely crumbled. She stirred in some white vinegar and whiskey and mixed the potion. She took boiling water from her tea kettle and poured it over a cloth.

When it had cooled somewhat, she placed it on the boy's back gently. His back muscles flexed in pain but he didn't cry out. She looked up at Shaya before giving the boy a small glass of the whiskey to drink. Shaya nodded his approval. The boy winced as much from the strong drink as he did from the sores on his back. Sorina and Shaya smiled. Then she took the poultice and spread it on the cloth and laid it over the puss-filled abscesses, gently massaging the sores. The boy was so brave. He only whimpered, never screaming. And she knew it hurt—bad.

Then she started the incantation. It was one her mother's mother had taught her and it worked to silence the mind enough to allow the body to begin healing with no fearful thoughts to inhibit the process. She massaged and she sang the words at first in the old Gaelic and then in English:

"Bring the fairies
Circlin' 'round our head.
From the wee ancient ones
We all will be led.

Our souls will then fly,
And be bringin' us nigh
To wisdom and knowing
From the druidess on high."

Then she lowered her voice and in deliberate intensity continued:

"Fire on the skin
Comes from deep within.
Cool the burning heart
And let the healing start."

For hours Sorina dressed the wounds on the boy's back and sang different incantations. Slowly, the pus drained and the abscesses diminished. By morning there were only red blotches where the angry adhesions had been. All through the night the medicine man, Shaya, had watched the white woman make her medicine magic and he had been transformed as he saw her become more spirit than flesh. He knew that she walked the line between worlds and he trusted her as he never believed he could trust a white person.

From that time on, the Indians protected Sorina from any thing and anybody who might have wished to harm her. She had her small band of body guards who let her alone to be the free spirit that she was, but came to her when they needed what they thought was her sage advice and healing prowess. She became a white shaman to them, and she was dearly loved.

Sorina lived very well and very peacefully in the woods for many years until the few small tribes eventually either died off or left Kentucky for farther Western regions, and soon there were none left. It was these years that saw the most change in her wilderness life. She missed Shaya a great deal. He had come to be a true friend to her and she had been with him when he died.

The world was changing and Sorina had been isolated for so long that it took much convincing for her to believe that the southern white man was holding, as his own property, black men and women who had been bought and sold in foreign markets. It had finally become a reality to her when a crippled Negro man found his way to her doorstep one wet, stormy night. He looked near death and she had let him in and nursed him until his strength returned. He shared his whole struggling life story with her then and she came to realize a compassion for a people she had never known. It was then that Sorina's life path changed. She changed from being the isolationist, living safely and quietly outside of society, to becoming an active abolitionist, living on the edge of social mores in a very dangerous time.

That was then and this is now, Sorina thought, as she heard what she knew must be the final embers popping in the fireplace. She really did know the difference between the long-ago life that wasn't hers and the now life that was. Sori's journal that Jessie had found had been the gateway to that long-ago life. It had been an amazing discovery of historical significance, but she and Jessie hadn't shared it with anyone. They kept the treasure to themselves, this living record of a pioneer woman's life. Sorina Duncan McBride's life, abolitionist, healer…*witch*? No. Spiritual being more than anything. She had been enlightened and open to receiving gifts that were hers alone. It was the sharing of those gifts in helping others that really captured her essence. What bravery it had taken to have lived such an honest life against all odds.

The modern Sorina wondered if she had ever been brave in her enigmatic life. How could she know? On rare occasions something would trigger a flash of a sound or sensation that held a glimmer of familiarity, but it was always accompanied with an undefined, shadowy horror. So, as quickly as a shade of her past would try to resurface, she pushed it back and would not let it come. Martha had made weak attempts at revealing things to her, but she didn't want to hear it, wasn't ready to hear it. Something in her psyche had shut all that down and she wanted to stay in the present, in her good place. Martha had seemed to understand that and had never pushed.

But now even her good place was disappearing. She felt tired and empty because without Martha she wasn't sure what her own life meant. Had she lived honestly? She put on quite a show. She knew that. And no one could have guessed at the mass of insecurities that Sorina felt on her own. She wanted to think she was a portal to the spiritual world, but she was never certain that she wasn't just playacting. All her friends, even her community, believed in her. And she had believed in herself, too, whenever she felt a chilling ripple in her vibration that led to a healing. Martha had fed all that in her; had been the catalyst for her psychic abilities.

Martha had shared her Irish superstitions enough that Sorina had been convinced it was all real. The fairies were real. At least she wanted to believe they were real. It gave her life such purpose. Martha called herself a faerie doctor and she was convinced Sorina had the same gifts. The tone of her voice would grow uncharacteristically serious sometimes when she'd say, "Sorina, you have the knowledge from the otherworld in you. I can see that. The fairies track your deeds in this world and they tell me you're a natural druidess." Sorina heard those words from her dearest friend and mentor and she believed them. *A druidess.* She liked the sound of it. It had a nicer ring to it than *witch.* But everything that Martha said had a nicer ring to it.

But now Martha was gone.

And then Shelby had arrived and her amazing energy brought the imagery of Samuel and Lizbeth to life in a way Sorina had never dreamed possible. It was as though Martha lived on through Shelby.

But now Shelby was gone, too.

Sorina turned on her side on the sofa and warm tears leaked from her sightless eyes onto the pillow. It all felt so hopeless. But she couldn't have seen Lizbeth and Samuel like she did without Shelby's energy feeding into her own, could she? No. The answer was no. *Shelby couldn't be gone.*

CHAPTER THIRTY-TWO
CARNY

"YES, SIR, THIS IS OFFICER LUCAS CHAMBERS calling from Greenup County, Kentucky. Am I speaking with Jeremiah?"

"You are."

"Sir, I got your number from Caitlin Sotheby. How are you this mornin'?"

"I am fine, and I can guess what this is about. Oh, hold on just one second there, Officer."

Lucas sat his phone down and put it on speaker. City noises blared in the background. *This might take a while.* He heard the doorman speak, "Ms. Finklestein, ma'am, let me get that door for you. You are looking brighter than sunshine today. What's that? Yes, ma'am, I sure will. You bet. Don't worry and have a good day."

Luke heard a car door close before it drove off. He turned up his phone.

"Sorry, Officer…is it Chambers? Are you still there? What did you say your name was?"

"Lucas Chambers, Greenup County, Kentucky."

"Ah, Kentucky. Yes, sir. You hafta be calling about Shelby."

"That's right. Yes, Shelby Jean Stiller. Would you happen to have any knowledge of her whereabouts?"

"No, I haven't seen Shelby since she went to stay with her father. I know she planned on caring for him for a while and visiting with her grandmother. Caitlin has filled me in pretty much."

"Well, then, I guess you know we have a missing person's file out on her and are doing a full investigation into her disappearance. We are lookin' for any information that anybody has to help point us in the right direction. Can you think of anybody that stands out over the past couple years that might be suspect in your mind?"

"Hummm. Let me think about that." Then he raised his voice, "Oh, and the same to you, Mr. Saelinger. Here, let me help you with that bag." A trunk slammed shut and a high-powered engine revved up and then grew faint. Jeremiah came back. "Sorry, Officer, it's been a busy morning at the high-rise. Okay. Let me think. You know, there have always been lots of people coming and going. Shelby and Caitlin are pretty popular. They're gorgeous women and single, if you get my meaning. But those two never really did go in for the wild party scene. And God knows they could have, with their looks. But they always kind of kept to themselves, really. Nobody sticks out in my mind as being a weirdo type.

"They do have one close friend who might be able to help you. His name is Tommy, but I don't know his last name. I think Cait works with him at the University. He is always here. Maybe you should give him a call. I'll keep thinking about it, though. If I come up with anything, I'll let you know."

"Well, we sure do appreciate it. You can imagine how much folks are startin' to worry around here. This thing is goin' on too long."

"I hear that. And Caitlin tells me she is going to be returning to Kentucky until they find Shelby, one way or the other."

"Yep. That's the word we got. Well, sir, I won't take up any more of your time, but we sure thank you for any help you can give us. You think on it. You know, has there been anybody that just doesn't fit the profile? Anybody hangin' around, maybe watchin' the girls? Anything at all comes to mind; you give me a call."

"Will do, Officer. But one thing I should say, Shelby has always been an independent girl. There was a time once before where she just kinda took off. Scared everybody. Then she came back with her head screwed on straight. It made Caitlin crazy. So there is that possibility. Kentucky women seem to have a mind of their own."

"Well, ain't that the truth. Okay. Got it. Appreciate it. Maybe we'll all get lucky and Shelby will just return from Mexico or someplace with a nice tan and a big 'ole grin on her face."

"Yeah, maybe, just maybe. Good luck, Officer."

"Thank you, sir."

Lucas hung the phone up and looked over at Russell. "I guess you heard some of that. Doorman Jeremiah says Shelby has took off before without tellin' anybody. Maybe it's just that simple?"

"Well, wouldn't that be great. Of course, once Cait found out she wasn't dead from some psycho she'd want to kill her for scarin' her to death."

Lucas chuckled. "God, wouldn't that scenario be a relief. We could all have a beer together down at The Pit Stop after the hissy fit ended. Hey, call Cait up and ask for this guy Tommy's info. Doorman says he's their best friend. He might know somethin'."

"Yeah, Cait has mentioned him. He's a gay guy they've known forever." Russell placed the call with no luck. "Got her voice mail."

Lucas shrugged, and looked closely at their surroundings. He had to smile. It was all so familiar. This drab room with its plain book shelves that hadn't seen a coat of paint in fifty years, loaded with outdated government regulations and legal books, a pea green tall file cabinet holdin' who knows how many cold cases in over-used folders. The long, chipped wooden table was flanked by mismatched chairs ranging in style from kitchen to outdoor furniture. Two large desktop computers and even an antiquated rolodex sat next to a rotary phone. The sheriff's department had rooms packed with state-of-the-art gear, but not here. This was where they stuck the has-beens and the wannabe's. If you could find out anything in this ghost of a research room, you were one hell of a detective.

"This is bullshit. What is this, dial-up, for god's sake?" Russell had broken out his personal laptop, but the Internet was moving slow as molasses.

"It's this room. I think it's steel coated to keep out the cyber world. The rest of the department works just fine. You just happen to be the deputized flunky of an out-dated older flunky. Sorry about your luck, Russell."

"Hell with that. I know when I'm in the presence of greatness, even if the rest of these yeehaws don't know it. And besides, I got the info without having to bug Caitlin."

Russell handed a slip of paper to Lucas. He punched in the number on his cell phone.

"Horticulture, Tommy speaking, may I help you?"

"Tommy Roe?"

"Speaking."

"Mr. Roe, this is Officer Lucas Chambers calling from Greenup County, Kentucky. Do you have a minute to speak with me?"

"Sure. Give me a second. I'll put you on hold, but I'll be right back."

Lucas rolled his eyes at the garbled, distorted music in the background. "Why can't anybody tell these corporations that their background music is crap? No wonder people are pissed off all the time."

Russell smiled and nodded as Lucas tapped his fingers on the table and put the cell phone on speaker so they both could listen.

"Hello? I'm back. Officer Chambers, is it?"

He doesn't sound gay, Lucas thought, before answering, "Yes, sir. I'm the investigating officer in a missin' person's case and I wondered if I could ask you some questions?"

"It's about Shelby, isn't it? Oh, my god. Caitlin keeps me informed and I am just sick about it."

Okay, now he sounds gay. "Yes, sir, it is about Shelby Jean Stiller. We are talking to anybody who might have any information. Just trying to cover all her tracks."

"What do you mean? What kind of information?"

"Mostly anybody who might want to do her harm or who perhaps has threatened her in some way? Anybody who seems out of the norm in Shelby's life. We are talking to people in her home town in Kentucky, but she's been a New Yorker all her adult life. So anything you can think of would be helpful."

"Hummm. Let me think. Can I call you back?"

"Absolutely." Lucas gave Tommy his cell phone number and ended the call.

"Sounds like a brick wall." Russell was staring at his computer screen.

"Hey, he's gonna think about it."

"Uh-huh."

Just then Lucas' phone chimed. "See? I had a feelin' about this kid." He hit the speaker again. "Officer Chambers here."

"Lucas, are you and Russell hungry?"

"Huh?"

"It's Bella. I've got fried chicken and potato salad from KFC. I'm comin' over."

"Bella, what the…" She had already hung up. In the next second Lucas noticed his stomach was growling. *God, that woman has uncanny timing.*

In five minutes Bella was standing in the doorway with a picnic basket. "Come on, you two. I know how y'all are. You gotta eat."

Bella found a spot on the table and started emptying the contents of the basket. True to her word, there were several large pieces of fried chicken, a plastic bowl of potato salad, green beans and biscuits. She sat out paper plates and forks and spoons before glancing around at their surroundings. "Man, do they even have water in this dump?"

Lucas stood up, left the room and walked down the hall. He returned with bottles of water. "Bessie said we can have as many as we like." He tossed a bottle to Russell.

"Well, thank God for Bessie bein' on dispatch today. Why do they have y'all back in this depressin' place?"

"Ah, it ain't so bad. It's far enough from the action to be good and quiet. Just what we need. Right, Russell?"

Russell was already chewing on a chicken leg. He wiped his chin and spoke, "Right, boss."

Bella laughed. "Hell of a pair." She served up the side dishes and then sat down to watch them eat. "Do you think it's right that it's just you two workin' on Shelby's disappearance? It must piss you off, like they don't think she's important enough."

"Nah, it's not that. They know they got the best guys on the case." Russell looked up at her and grinned.

Bella had thought about her conversation with the sheriff many times. She had been so sure about having Bruce pull off his men. *I hope like hell my gut instinct was right.*

Just then Lucas' cell phone rang again. "Officer Chambers here."

"Officer, this is Tommy Roe. I was thinking about what you asked and somebody does come to mind. It's been some time ago and I have no idea if it's important or not, but you said..."

"No, you're exactly right, Tommy," Lucas interrupted, "no lead is too small. You never know where it might take us. What you got?"

"Well, back before Cait quit the business full time there was this really weird guy that was kind of stalking a lot of the models on the Upper West Side. He was just creepy, you know? He would stand outside the photographer's studio and not say anything, just hand each of the girls a carnation as they came outside. At first they all thought it was sweet.

But then it went on for weeks. And nobody ever knew where he got all those carnations. But he had them every day. He never missed giving each of the girls a flower. It was like he was some rich eccentric. But this guy couldn't have been rich. I mean, the way he dressed! God. And dirty!! Just disgusting. Well, everybody thought he was pretty harmless. They called him Carny. Then he took a special liking to Shelby. He seemed to enjoy her Kentucky accent. Back then everybody liked to call her Holly Golightly because of it.

"Well, this Carny person started following her home. At first Shelby thought it was kind of funny and she tried talking to him. But he would never say a word. Then she started getting freaked out. She and Caitlin would call me up when they were getting ready to leave the studio and I would walk with them. Like I could have done anything if he had pulled a gun or something, you know? I was scared of him, too. We always tried talking to him, but he would just kind of grin a little bit and stare. He always wore a ripped hoodie and nobody could really see his face very well. Only his mouth. And that was disturbing. When he did smile one of his front teeth was missing and the rest were so gray." Tommy got quiet for a moment, before continuing, "Sorry, Officer, but it gives me the shivers just thinking about it. Anyway, finally, one of the photographers had had enough and called the police on Carny. It was just too weird, you know? Nobody wanted him hurt. It wasn't like he did anything wrong, but the girls had gotten to where they were really afraid of this guy.

"After the police were involved they followed him down into the boroughs and caught him stealing carnations and magazines from a little Russian lady's sidewalk stand down on 169th. Even though they clearly had him, he resisted arrest when they tried to take him in. He actually socked one of the officers in the jaw. Well, that was the end of Carny. We heard they took him downtown and threw the book at him. Of course, he was deranged, so he was admitted to Bellevue Psychiatric, and nobody ever saw him again. No more carnations for the girls, but it was a relief for Shelby.

"I don't know what made me think of him, but really, through all the years, he's the only person that sticks out as being strange. Of course, that was a long time ago, so it makes no sense that he could have anything to do with her disappearance now. But still..."

"Hummm, yeah, don't seem to follow that there could be a connection.

But you never know. Bellevue, huh? Thanks, Tommy. We'll check it out. And keep our number."

Lucas ended the call and looked at Russell, who was already Googling Bellevue. "Here you go, Chief."

"Damn, Deputy, you are good." After only two rings someone picked up. Lucas gave a thumbs up and spoke, "This is Officer Lucas Chambers of the Greenup County, Kentucky Sheriff's Department. We are doin' an investigation in a missin' person's case and wondered if you could give us some information."

Even with the little information he had, the person on the other end of the line seemed to know exactly who he was talking about.

"Sure, I can hang on." Lucas reached for some chicken. "They got me on hold. Gonna get a nurse. Hello? Yes, that's right. Anything you can tell me. Sure. I see. Really? What did she look like? Hummm? Is that right? Well, thank you. You've been very helpful."

Lucas hung up and put a chicken leg to his lips.

"Dang it, Lucas, what did they say?"

Ignoring Bella, he chewed slowly on the dark meat. "I thought you wanted me to eat?" He teased. "Sure enough, this Carny fellow was a ward of the state for several years. The nurse said he was a very strange character. Never said nothin'. But he had pictures of the same girl from different magazines cut out and plastered all over his wall and bedside stand and even stuffed under his mattress."

"Shelby?" Bella's eyebrows rose in surprise.

"Shelby. Nurse said he never got any better. Just stayed quiet and to his self. Never hurt nobody. And when the City lost some funding for mental cases, he was released."

Bella stared at Lucas and Lucas stared at Russell.

"I guess you better git yourself on up to the Big Apple there, Deputy."

"Me?" Russell stopped the spoonful of green beans just short of his mouth. "Why me?"

"Well, hell, you're the one with the New York girlfriend. Just call her up and tell her to delay her flight until you get up there and check this fella out. Then the two of you can come back home together."

"But Lucas, I ain't no real..."

"Russell, I highly doubt that some wacko who had a hard-on for

Shelby ten years ago has got her hid somewheres. We just can't ignore any potential leads at this point. You git me?"

"I git you. But I think you should go, too. You're the one with the badge. Hell, I wouldn't know a perpetrator from a percolator."

Bella busted out laughing. "And you two are supposed to be our finest. God help Shelby. I think I better get back to Sorina's. The way this investigation is going, if we don't get help from the *other side*, there ain't gonna be no help."

Lucas ignored her and ate his food. He wiped his mouth and asked, "Bella, the sheriff will pay for this?" He raised an eyebrow. "I mean, the Commonwealth should have enough in the slush fund for a couple airline tickets, right?"

Bella nodded and picked up her cell phone. She punched in a number. "Hey, Bruce."

CHAPTER THIRTY-THREE
AN OLD MAVERICK

THE LANDING GEAR ON THE American Eagle flight slammed into the runway hard, and the airplane rocked with hitting too much resistance too fast.

"Welcome to New York's JFK International. This is the final stop for Flight 1708. Be sure to check the overhead compartments and under the seat in front of you before departing the aircraft. Have a good day." The flight attendant looked a little green around the gills.

"Well, that was just about the worst flight I've had in twenty years. I think that pilot musta been dippin' into some moonshine before he left Kentucky." Russell pushed his damp, dark hair back off his forehead.

Lucas looked too pale.

"You all right, Chief?"

"I'll be all right when I'm back home. I got a bad feelin' about this trip." Lucas reached for their carry-on bags and then got in line to disembark the plane. His lips pursed tightly.

Russell nodded in agreement. "I hope Caitlin has some whiskey at her place. We both could sure use a stiff drink." Russell led the way through the airline train system and then to the baggage checkout where he was hoping, but not expecting. But then…

Caitlin Sotheby looked like a movie star. Her long hair shimmered blue black under the florescent lights. Her cobalt eyes sparkled with happiness. She ran to Russell and jumped into his arms, wrapping her long, slender legs around his waist. Onlookers smiled at the two beautiful people intertwined in an embrace there in the crowded airport.

The tall, older man with the cowboy hat stood off to the side and gathered his own looks and stares.

"This way, gents." Caitlin led them through the terminal and out to the parking garage where her car was parked on the second level. The men piled their bags into the trunk and Cait got behind the wheel for the drive to Manhattan.

"This just ain't normal." Lucas stared out the window as they drove over miles of concrete ribbon winding through residential and commercial real estate. "It's like we flew less than two hours and dropped onto another planet. I mean, what the hell is all this?"

"All this is urban America, Luke." Caitlin grinned at her passenger in the backseat. She had borrowed Tommy's car to pick them up and maneuvered the congested lanes expertly.

"I think you could handle the Indianapolis 500, Cait." Russell added her driving ability to the list of things this woman could do better than almost anyone.

She laughed. "Well, you have to grow some balls to be a real New Yorker. Believe me, I didn't always drive this way." She laughed and cut off a minibus full of obvious out-of-towners.

Russell looked nervously over his shoulder. He caught Cait's satisfied grin as she glanced in her rear-view mirror.

"Why, Ms. Sotheby, I believe you might have a bit of a bitchy side?"

She smiled at him and winked. "Just a bit."

Soon they were pulling up in front of the elegant high-rise Caitlin and Shelby called home. A tall, middle-aged man dressed in a navy blue uniform was quick to open up her door.

"Hi, Jeremiah!"

He tipped his hat. "Hi yourself, Ms. Cait. I take it these are the folks from Kentucky?"

"The very same. Meet Chief Lucas Chambers and his deputy, Russell James. Gentlemen, I believe you all have talked?"

Lucas and Russell were standing on the sidewalk and nodded, acknowledging the doorman. Jeremiah handed them their bags and greeted them. "Welcome to New York, officers. I sure hope The Big Apple brings you some luck in finding Shelby." He tipped his hat again and took the car keys from Caitlin.

"Just park it in my old space. Tommy's cool with leaving it for a couple days."

"Sure thing, Ms. Cait. Let me know if I can do anything for you while your guests are here."

Cait smiled and kissed the tall man on the cheek. He sunk in behind the steering wheel and drove the BMW around the corner.

"Come on, guys. This way."

The Kentuckians followed Caitlin to an elevator on the far side of a plush lobby that was reminiscent of a bygone era. Despite several people mulling around, a hushed ambience embraced the visitors. Thick Persian carpets covered most of the polished mahogany floors. Fat Boston ferns burst out of heavy ornamental pots surrounding brocaded settees. Classical music was piped in through recessed speakers hidden in the gilded ceiling. The building had the obvious atmosphere of old and rich. Lucas and Russell just gawked.

The bell to the elevator clanged and the three friends rode up to the 14th floor.

"Follow me," Cait said and sashayed ahead of them. She put her key into the fifth door down the hall from the elevator. The door opened up to what was yet another world. This one was hip and modern. No hint of the stately world they had entered from the street. Here it was all color and youthful flamboyance.

"IKEA, right?" Russell smiled.

"How did you know? Don't you love it? We ordered everything online and then made poor Jeremiah assemble it all." Caitlin laughed. "There are three bedrooms down the hall. Mine is at the end. You pick the one you want."

Russell grinned and said, "I'll take the one at the end."

Cait jabbed him in the ribs. Then she asked, "Are you guys hungry? There's a great little Italian place down the street."

"You two go ahead." Lucas could see the sexual attraction circling the two young people like electric lassos. "I need to talk with somebody from the 44th Precinct. See if we can get a handle on where to find this Carny guy."

Russell looked from his boss to his dream girl. "Are you sure you don't need me, Chief?"

Lucas smiled. "I think I can probably handle a couple phone calls by myself. Besides, after that not-so-restful flight, I could use a nap. You go on."

Russell and Caitlin almost ran out the door.

Luke punched in the number on his cell. "Hello? Yes, this is Lucas Chambers with the Greenup County Sheriff's Department. I spoke with Detective Armstrong yesterday?" He was put on hold. Tapping his thumbs on the plastic table that sat next to a plastic chair, he thought, *what the hell kind of décor is this?* He knew IKEA was Swedish, so that explained a lot. He had to laugh. Young women living the life. That is, until somebody or some thing was trying to change all that. Beautiful single girls were easy victims. He had given a lot of thought to what Tommy said about this Carny. It was a long shot for sure, but it was worth looking into. Damn sicko, probably. "Yes, sir, I'm still here. Okay. Give him this number. I'll be waitin' to hear from him before I proceed."

Lucas put his cell phone back in his pocket and walked down a long hallway where breathtaking photographs of Caitlin and Shelby hung on either side. It really brought to life who and what these girls were. High fashion models at the top of the world in their day. He chose the room on the left. It was spacious and sparsely furnished. He liked it. Then he caught his own image in the mirror.

Damn, I look just like an old Maverick.

And he felt old as dirt. Sometimes he doubted his own sanity. Why wasn't he sitting at home, relaxing and letting Saber bring him cold beers. Instead he was in this strange place that might as well have been a foreign country. Definitely not his turf. *Who am I kidding?* He had had a feeling about this since they landed at the airport. They were chasing a goose. He knew it, but here he was.

"Martha, what the hell am I doin'?"

He pulled off his snakeskin boots, put his black cowboy hat on the dresser and unbuttoned his top buttons. He climbed onto the king-size bed and fell asleep as soon as his head hit the pillow.

"God, I have missed you." Russell covered Cait's slender hand with his own. They had ordered a bottle of wine and some steamed calamari. The restaurant was nearly empty. Russell looked around at the checkered table cloths and could picture a scene from "The Godfather."

"I have missed you, too, Russell. I think I dream about you every night."

"Really? What am I doing?"

"Everything right." She smiled and took a seductive sip of her wine.

The waiter brought some bread with their appetizers and took their dinner order. The atmosphere between the two young people turned serious.

"Have you gotten any leads, Russell? Anything at all? I mean, I can't believe Carny could have anything to do with Shelby's disappearance. That was such a long time ago?"

"I know. And we highly doubt it, too, but stranger things have happened. The Chief just thought we shouldn't blow it off. Might lead to somethin' else, you know?"

"Yeah, I guess. At any rate, it got you here. I love that. Now you can see where and how I live. I'll take you down to the lab and introduce you to Tommy. He has heard all about you. He'll be thrilled. But tonight you're all mine." She squeezed his hand and slowly chewed the steamed squid.

Outside, New York was coming to life in urban riotous interruptions, but Caitlin and Russell didn't hear it. They heard cellos and violins and the beating of their own hearts. Their Italian meal had been more an aphrodisiac than filling. Instead of taking in the sights, the only sights they needed were looking in each other's eyes. They could hardly get back to the apartment fast enough to crawl into bed and feed their desire.

Russell woke first and gently rolled onto his side to watch her sleeping next to him. To him, Caitlin Sotheby was more heavenly creature than earthly woman. Her dark hair lay in shining waves around her creamy shoulders. Her full lips were parted slightly as she breathed. Dark lashes fringed her closed eyelids.

She is an angel.

Then she moved abruptly and slung her slender arm over her forehead, nearly punching him in the nose. He got out of her way as she flung her hand across the pillow. Then she opened her perfect mouth and snored so loudly it woke her. "Huh? What? Oh, god, Russell. I just had the weirdest dream."

"Oh, yeah?" He grinned as he brushed the hair out of her eyes. He sat up next to her. Now she really was perfect. His angel snored. Relief rolled over him and he laughed out loud.

"What?" She punched his arm. "It wasn't a funny dream."

"No, no. I was just thinkin'…never mind. So what was your dream?"

"It was about Shelby. She was running in the dark, trying so hard to get to the sunlight, to break free. But she couldn't get there, Russell. She was so scared and she just kept running and running…" Caitlin flailed her arms. "It was horrible. But yet, she wouldn't give up. She wasn't ready to give up. Oh, Russell. What does it mean? It means she's alive, doesn't it? It has to. Shelby has got to be alive?"

Caitlin sat up in bed and buried her face in his chest. He put his arms around her and held her. "That's right, Cait. She is alive. You must believe that." He tipped her chin up with his fingers and kissed her tremulous lips. She leaned into him and kissed him back. Her tearful mouth tasted salty. Russell felt his hunger for her return in hot spasms. He covered her full lips with his own and she put her hand behind his head, pulling him into her. Their bodies pressed against each other and he lay her back down on the bed so he could feel the length of her, her long legs, her slender torso, her firm breasts. He would never tire of looking at her. But now he wanted to feel her again as he had just moments before. He took her slowly at first and then with total abandon as she arched her back and opened to him softly, fully, demanding...

His cell phone vibrated next to the bed. It skipped across the nightstand bringing their passion to a sudden halt. Caitlin reached out a hand and looked. She handed it to Russell who was bearing down on top of her. He saw Lucas' name on the screen.

"Hey, Chief." He tried to control his panting breath, but it was no good.

"Well, I am sorry about the timin' there, brother. But it happens when you've been deputized. At least I didn't barge in."

Russell could hear the muffled chuckle on the other end. "This better be good." He wiped his eyes, slowing his breathing as he put the phone closer to his ear.

"I heard from Detective Armstrong down at the 44th and he wants to meet with us. Think you can pull yourself away from your other duties for a short minute?"

"You bet. I'll be right out."

"Don't forget to pull your britches on first."

Russell rolled off of Caitlin and onto his side of the bed. He took one last long look at the bombshell lying next to him. He smoothed the hair away from her face and kissed her gently. "You make it pretty impossible to remember there's a world of trouble out there beyond these closed doors, Caitlin Sotheby. I could get really lost in here with you in my arms."

"I think getting lost once in a while is a beautiful thing." She smiled at him and returned his kiss. "You go find my best friend. I'll be here waiting."

He smiled as he stood and pulled his jeans up. "Get some sleep and see if you can get a clearer picture in your dreams. Maybe Shelby is trying to tell you something." He bent down and kissed her on the forehead and went out into the hall.

Lucas was waiting for him in the living room, twirling his cowboy hat with his right hand. He looked at Russell who was looking at the hat.

"Too much for New Yorkers?"

"Hell no. You look just like Maverick," Russell said, and smiled as the two Kentuckians found their way back to the elevator and out to the street.

"Jeremiah, can you get us a cab? We need to get to the 44th Precinct pronto."

"Sure thing, Chief." Jeremiah only needed to raise his hand and a yellow cab magically appeared. He opened the back door for Russell and Lucas and gave instructions to the black man driving. In less than a minute they were rushing past more affluent neighborhoods and then the scene began to change outside the cab window as they entered the Bronx.

On the street, an old man dressed in a tattered wool coat leaned his head into the wind. He watched his feet in the holey Converse shoes step one after the other. He wasn't sure how they knew to do that. His feet always knew where to go more than his head did. They always ended up in the same place, and that was good because Carny didn't really remember where that was anymore. One time on television he had seen horses heading for their barn with blinders on. He was the same as those horses, just moving forward without seeing anything. He was sure that's how he got home. At least in his clearer moments he was sure. But most of his awake time he wasn't sure about anything. He knew his heart was still beating. He could feel that sometimes too hard. He knew he felt the cold and the hot and the wet. He knew that because he stayed in the street most of the time even though he had a room to live in. He liked it outside in the noise. The noise was like his head. Constant clatter and annoyances. It felt more comfortable than quiet. Quiet allowed him to feel too confused. He needed the noise to distract him.

Carny's name was William. At least that's what he thought. Nobody had called him that in so long he wondered if he had imagined it. When the pretty girls nicknamed him Carny it made him smile because he loved carnations. He thought the flowers were pretty like the faces on the girls. So he would have told anybody who asked that his name was Carny. But nobody ever asked. He didn't talk to anybody.

Carny never said a word.

Not since his father had killed his mother in front of him when he was just a little boy. One minute she had been frying bacon. The next minute she was being stabbed over and over. The blood went everywhere, squirting out in crimson streams on the kitchen table, the kitchen walls, the kitchen tile. Bright red blood on dirty white counter tops. Carny screamed and screamed at the sight of his mother's slumped and bloody body on the floor. Then his drunken father had turned his blind rage on his young son. He had aimed the butcher knife at the little boy's chest and shouted in a slurred roar, "Shut the fuck up! My old lady used to love me good until you come. You retarded brat. You fucked up everything!" He raised the knife and meant to slam it into the child, but in his recklessness, he fell against the stove. The frying pan was filled with bacon grease. It spilled all over his arm, splashing hot dollops of oil rolling in thick layers over his skin. The little boy stared in abject terror as his father dropped the knife and tried to stop the burning grease. Slapping hard at his arm, he turned in a panic, laying his skin directly in the flame on the burner. His whole arm caught fire. He screamed in surprised horror as he flailed out of control, unable to put out the fire. Grease spilled onto his legs and he batted at the hot liquid with his flaming arm until he was a human torch.

Little William had stopped talking then, and had not talked since.

And sometimes when he smelled bacon frying he could still smell his father's burning flesh.

Carny passed the stand on the corner with all the magazines. He stopped long enough to look, but she was never there. The Kentucky girl was never in the pictures. He was sorry that she wasn't there. But he still had most of his old copies of pictures, even though they were getting faded and crinkled from his holding them too much.

The dark skinned man yelled at him in a funny language and told him to move on. He always yelled at him. All Carny ever did was look for the Kentucky girl, but the man didn't want him even doing just that. He always yelled at him.

And Carny never said a word.

His room was located in a shabby building in the South Bronx. A lady came and gave him a check each month and he signed an X on the back of it and the black man down the hall cashed it for him. Nobody bothered him and he slept there most nights, except when it was warm. Then he slept on a park bench. It smelled better to be outside.

CHAPTER THIRTY-FOUR WOUNDED ANIMAL

LUCAS STARED OUT THE BACKSEAT window and remembered why he loved Kentucky. The immensity of New York was mind boggling to him. How did people live like this, all crushed up against each other in endless row houses and no yards. Life in "the hood" seemed like another world for a guy who thought the noisiest thing in life was a speed boat on the Ohio River.

The only thing he knew about The Bronx was Yankee Stadium and the Bronx Zoo and all the bad guy movies that depicted edgy street kids in gangs with bad news on their minds. As the cab passed and slowed for traffic he saw that most of the people hanging out were Latino or black.

The cabbie had noticed the out-of-towners gawking at the sights and it was his cue to educate. "You fellows ain't from around here, right?"

Lucas touched his hat and grunted, "You got that right."

"Thought so. You kinda stick out. The Bronx is a pretty awesome place. You got time to see some sights while you're here?"

"Nope. Here strictly on business. Once we wrap that up we're gone." Lucas sank back into his seat. He was hoping the cabbie wouldn't get too chatty. He had his mind on what he was going to say to the New York cop. He felt like they were on a wild goose chase anyway, and he was fearful that he and Russell would look like the hick fools they were.

The cabbie got chatty. "Well, that's a damn shame, because, like I said, the Bronx is an awesome place. We got baseball. We got culture. We got world class rappers. You guys like rap? You know, hip hop?"

Lucas and the cabbie locked eyes in the rear-view mirror. *Don't give a shit* came across loud and clear. The driver went back to driving.

They pulled up to the 44th District and Lucas paid the cabbie.

The cop behind the desk didn't even notice the Kentuckians. The cramped space was buzzing with a strange energy and plenty of local characters demanding attention. Russell and Lucas stepped back to make way for three women, or at least that was what they appeared to be at first glance. Lucas stared and Russell stared and the ladies stared back. Then a dangerously seductive tall blonde with perfect everything got too close to Lucas and he could make out the faintest five o'clock shadow poking through the pancake makeup. Lucas felt his cheeks burn from embarrassment.

Russell whispered, "Dude looks like a lady."

Lucas tried backing off, but the transvestite kept in step with him and got way too close for comfort, and then spoke in a husky voice, "Are you a real cowboy?"

"Chief Chambers?" Another deep voice bellowed from behind them. "Move it, ladies, the desk sergeant has a few words for you."

Their immediate area cleared in a heartbeat and the only person left standing in front of them was a burly-looking officer with Armstrong on his name tag. He wore a dingy shirt that had been white at one time, but now was an off-color gray. *Definitely not married*. Lucas took in the wide, colorful tie that hung halfway down his chest and looked out of place on the drab shirt. His khakis were belted low underneath a prominent beer belly. He reached out a hairy arm with rolled-up sleeves and Lucas shook it. The two men stood eye to eye. Assessments went to instant respect. Then the officer checked out Russell.

"My deputy, Russell James."

Detective Armstrong shook Russell's hand and then led them back through a chaotic hallway, finally bringing them to his office. He shut the door behind them and gestured to a couple chairs. "Coffee?"

The burned coffee permeated the small space. Lucas figured it was about eight hours old by now.

"I'll pass."

"Me too."

"Suit yourselves. So you flew here from Kentucky on good intel about this guy, I hope?" The detective raised a thick eyebrow as he filled his stained cup.

"Well, no, we can't exactly call it intel. More like a couple blind hound dogs sniffin' after a three-legged rabbit."

Armstrong just stared at the old guy in the cowboy hat. "I take it that means no?"

Lucas relayed what Tommy Roe had told him about Carny and his obsessive stalking. "Seems he had a special thing for Shelby Jean."

"You say they had him in the nut ward at Bellevue and then he got released?"

"Yeah. Apparently back out on the streets free as a bird, but definitely a few floors short of the top, if you git me. It's a damned long shot, but at this point we got nothin' else. Kentucky is comin' up dry, so we figured this sounded just weird enough that it was worth checkin' out. Shelby might have come back to New York without tellin' anybody. She's been goin' through a lot of shit lately. So here we are."

Russell pulled out a photograph and handed it over to the officer, but he waved it off. "No need. I got her right here." He was looking at his computer screen. "There's no shortage of photos on these girls. We ran a search on the arrest of this Carny guy and Social Services is running his current position. He supposedly has a case worker, but these people are so overworked there ain't no way they can crawl after every one of these slimy vermin that slide and hide under the rocks of the City."

Russell and Lucas shared an uncomfortable reaction to the harsh analogy, but it appeared the detective took no notice.

"Sit tight and I'll find out if we have anything."

Detective Armstrong went back out into the hall, letting in the loud chaos caused by the "ladies" being escorted back to their cells. The tall blonde locked eyes with Lucas as he passed, and stopped.

"Hey cowboy, I bet you got a big ole horse between your legs?"

Lucas lunged at the door, but Russell caught him and held him back.

"Oooh, you are a cowboy." The transvestite grinned and walked on down the hall.

"Come on, Chief. You never lose your cool."

Lucas backed up and sat down in the chair. "I'm sorry, Russell." He felt his blood pressure popping through his head. "This just ain't my turf."

Just then Armstrong reappeared in the doorway. "We got an address and I spoke with his case worker." He wiped his head with a worn handkerchief. "She says he keeps to himself. Never says a word and manages to pay for the room where he stays in the South Bronx. She couldn't find anything unusual going on with him. He's not in the greatest health. Something about weak bones. Anyway, she doesn't see him ever turning into a contributing citizen, but she doesn't think he's dangerous either. She takes him a small disability check every month. You guys still want to bother this old misfit dude?"

Russell looked over at Lucas and they both stood at the same time. Lucas took a deep breath and spoke, "We're here. No sense in not takin' a look-see."

They followed the detective back out into the hall to the front desk area and out the door. Lucas sat in the front with Armstrong, and Russell settled in the back of the cruiser. Armstrong flipped a couple switches and the siren blared and the bar lights threw blue rays over the parking lot as he pulled out into the stream of cars.

"Now, I can't see gittin' our shorts in an uproar. You think you need to announce our arrival?"

"You ever been to the South Bronx?" Detective Armstrong looked over at Lucas as he expertly maneuvered the police car through the congestion of the afternoon traffic.

"Well, no, I ain't."

Armstrong just grunted in response and made no attempt to shut down the emergency calling card.

Lucas stared out the passenger side window at the blur of cars and buildings until he saw the sign announcing their entrance to the poorest borough in the City. He understood why Armstrong needed to enter in an official capacity. Lucas felt a shiver snake up his spine as they passed the decaying urban sprawl.

Armstrong pulled in front of a five-story tenement building that sat behind rusted metal and wire fencing. Across the street more rusted metal enclosed a city dump. Everywhere they looked, graffiti covered brick walls and broken concrete in lime green and purple colors. Spray-painted faces with anguished expressions seemed to stare at the strangers as they cautiously exited the vehicle.

Lucas and Russell followed the detective as he walked up to the building. The door was half off of its hinges and inside the pungent smell of stale urine assaulted the police officers. Loud muffled music and voices could be heard high over their heads. Armstrong looked at the mailboxes on the wall and found what he was looking for.

"Let's see if Mr. Carny is receiving visitors."

The elevator looked like it probably hadn't been in operation for twenty years so they took the steps, being sure to avoid any vermin that were scattering ahead of them. Lucas couldn't believe his eyes. *Hell, this makes rural Appalachia seem like a paradise.*

They found the door they were looking for and Armstrong placed one hand on his holstered gun and one hand on the door. He knocked loudly. They stood and waited for what, they had no idea.

Lucas was aware of his heart beating too hard and he was reminded once again that he just might be too old for this job.

After a time, Detective Armstrong announced their presence and called out Carny's name. Still nothing from the other side of the gray, metal door.

"Well, shit. I think we need an invitation." Armstrong positioned himself to kick his way in when, losing his balance, he nearly fell through the doorway. The door hadn't even been securely closed.

Suddenly the officers found themselves inside Carny's room. Dim light bled through the dirty windows enough to see Shelby Jean Stiller's radiant young face looking at them from fashion photographs wallpapered over every conceivable space on the peeling paint.

"There must be a hundred pictures here," Russell spoke under his breath.

Lucas whistled and nodded in agreement. A lot of the pictures were tattered and faded, but it was Shelby all right. Looking young, innocent and spectacularly beautiful. It shook Lucas to his core and he could see his partners felt the same way. A creepy uneasiness permeated the fetid air. Where was this strange man who obviously was still obsessing on a young beauty from years ago?

Luke carefully moved his body around in a circle, staring at the plastered photos, but also at any dark corners where their suspect could be hiding himself. The three men remained quiet as Armstrong and Russell followed Lucas' lead and stepped gently over the strewn litter and torn cushions that peppered the worn carpet. The apartment smelled of stale urine and something else.

Lucas reached for his gun and unhooked it from his belt. He held it high with both hands as he backed around in circles, his eyes scanning every inch of the room. Something clicked in him and he didn't feel his age. He only felt keenly aware of his surroundings. Every muscle taut and ready to spring into action. Every nerve ending on edge. Every thought focused on the possible threat.

He didn't feel past it. He was the Chief again.

The smell got more potent as he followed the scent to a closed door that most likely led to a small closet. He nodded to his partners as he crept towards it, one booted foot slowly landing in front of the other. Armstrong and Russell flanked him on either side. Lucas reached out a hand and slowly turned the knob, all the while keeping his gun aimed at the ceiling.

The door creaked as it opened and the smell was too much. The men reacted by trying to cover their noses as Lucas opened the door wider to allow light to enter the closet. One last pull on the door and the large rotting body of a yellow cat was clearly visible lying on the closet floor. Lucas jumped back instinctively, and revulsion rushed over his limbs.

"God! Lucas, what the hell. Shut the door!" Russell looked like he was going to vomit.

Lucas stepped over the cat and peered into the corners of the closet. A threadbare coat hung on a hook and two pairs of holey shoes were all that he could see. He stepped back and bumped into the cat. His stomach lurched as he slammed the closet door.

At that moment, the apartment door slowly opened wider. An old man walked in, his spine dramatically curved, his gray head hanging down. He hadn't seemed to take notice of his open door. He made no sound as he headed toward the one piece of furniture. An old chair sat in front of a wall where the largest pictures of Shelby were taped up in an overlapping montage. The bent figure collapsed heavily into the chair and rested his head against the back and stared at the wall in front of him.

The officers stood quietly. Carny hadn't seemed to notice them. Lucas put his finger up to his lips and they remained still, just watching the strange little man.

Lucas' heart raced but his mind remained clear and focused. He watched Carny's head sway gently from side to side in a rocking motion. A faint murmur could be heard, as though he were humming to himself. Watching from behind, Lucas could see enough of his profile to tell he was smiling.

Carny was enjoying himself.

Lucas had a bad feeling about this. "This is the police. Put your hands up."

Carny jumped in shocked surprise and fell out of the chair, tumbling onto the ground. He started crying and put his hands over his head. Armstrong got down beside him and helped him to his feet. Carny didn't put up a fight.

"Drop the weapon, Chief. You don't have a warrant and this ain't an arrest."

Lucas lowered his gun. Armstrong directed his next words to Carny. "You had your door open because you was wanting visitors, right, William? Right?"

The old man nodded in assent, never saying a word. But tears were streaming down his lined face, wetting his scraggly beard.

"You wanna come down to the station with us for a little while? We'll give you donuts and coffee? Whadaya say?"

Carny nodded dumbly, hung his head again, and let Armstrong take him by the arm. "Chambers, give the place a once over again to be sure there ain't no more dead felines in here. Come on, Deputy. We'll get Mr. Carny in the squad car before he changes his mind about the donuts."

"I'll be right behind you." Lucas checked the corners of the room and looked under the sink, but found nothing. He couldn't believe anyone could possibly live in the place. Filth covered every conceivable space and there was no food that wasn't moldy and half eaten by insects and rodents. *Inhuman.* That was the word that kept coming to Lucas' mind. It's inhuman for a body to live like this. Then he turned back to look at the walls again. He ran his hand over the faded magazine photographs to be sure they weren't covering up anything that would be a clue to foul play. He felt nothing and really saw nothing in the shoddy apartment that would lead them to Shelby. Carny didn't look capable of kidnapping someone even if he wanted to. He had no weapons and appeared weak and disabled. Lucas knew they had been on a goose chase. The demented guy might be infatuated with the Kentucky beauty, but that was all it was. He was sure.

"Poor sod has to have somethin', I guess," Lucas spoke out loud. He couldn't wait to be done with this nasty business and get back to Greenup County. They were wasting precious time.

The ride to the station was uncomfortable at best. Carny emitted an unbearable odor. Lucas put the window down to keep from breathing what smelled like the inside of a garbage dumpster mixed with stale urine and caked feces. It felt like an eternity, but they finally pulled up in front of the 44th District. Carny had not stopped crying but he hadn't moved. Armstrong parked and came around to get the old guy out of the seat. It wasn't easy. Carny acted as though his bones would break with too much movement. Nobody had the patience to be too kind with their suspect and the detective pulled too hard on his arm. Carny let out a moan and pulled back from Armstrong. The Bronx cop yanked this time on the old guy's arm and all three of the officers heard a horrible cracking sound come from underneath his tattered sleeve. Carny's features crunched in a wretched, pained expression and his hoarse scream sounded more like a wounded animal than a man.

"Oh, fuck." Armstrong whistled in stunned disbelief.

CHAPTER THIRTY-FIVE
HOME TO THE HILLS

"SO, LET ME SEE IF I GOT THIS RIGHT. You went to New York. You got together with some big-city, tough cop. You all broke into an unlocked apartment, harassed a poor unfortunate, ignorant soul for likin' to look at old pictures of Shelby Jean. Then you hauled his old behind down to the police station and broke his arm gettin' him out of the cruiser, puttin' him in the hospital? Now, Lucas, did I leave anythin' out?" Bella sat her empty beer can down. "Saber, hon, git me a fresh one?" She petted the golden lab on the head and the dog trotted happily to the cooler. He brought the beer back to Bella, wagging his tail. "Thank you, sweetheart." She gave him a treat.

"Yeah, Bella, you about got it right. Makes me feel like a million pieces of crap. We never shoulda bothered that old guy. Hell, I didn't feel right about that New York trip from the git-go."

"But Lucas. You broke his arm?"

"Well, technically, I didn't. It was the New York cop who pulled too hard. Apparently, from what the ER doc said, Carny has some kind of rare degenerative disease that makes his bones break like toothpicks. Truth is, Bella, he's better off in the hospital than in that pigsty of an apartment. I swear it wasn't fit for humans to live in."

Bella patted his arm. "Well, maybe. But I think you all better rethink how to treat a suspect from now on. Point is, of course, I guess you got nowheres?"

"Yeah, I guess you could say we got nowheres," Lucas agreed, and smiled at her Kentucky vernacular. "I gotta tell you, I never thought I'd say I was glad to get on a plane, but I wanted out of that city worse than a starvin' hound wants out of a pad-locked cage."

"And you left Russell there?" Bella took a long drink of the cold beer.

"Yeah, he decided to stay a couple more days so he could fly back to Kentucky with Caitlin. Those two are hot and heavy for sure. I think they needed some time away from this whole mess, you know?"

"Yeah, I can imagine. Ah, to be young and in love. Remember what that felt like, Lucas?" Bella batted her eyes in a flirtatious mood.

Lucas laughed and nodded. "Yeah, Bella. I might be old but I ain't dead."

"You got that right. Here's to still kickin'!"

They toasted their beers and got quiet watching the river off of Lucas' deck.

Bella was the first to break the silence. "So what now?"

"Tomorrow I'm goin' back to square one and look through all those files at the station. There has to be somebody with connections to Shelby that we're missin'. I don't guess Sorina has come up with anything?"

"Lord, Sorina has been depressed like I have never seen her. She swears she can feel Shelby; that she is alive. But she can't get a picture of her at all, and that's just not what Sorina is used to. It has got her all tied up in knots. She says that's why she can't pick up on nothin'. Somethin' about her energy bein' too fuzzy or somethin'. Anyway, we've all been stayin' away hopin' some time to herself would clear things up. So far nothin', though. Now that your New York trip was a flop we need to get back over there and see if we can't help her raise her vibrations."

Lucas watched Bella talk about vibrations and energy, and he didn't understand a bit of it, but he sure liked watching her talk. She was an attractive woman. Her brown eyes were so warm, and he liked the way she always wore Martha's jewelry. It made Martha seem alive somehow. And it was good to have someone on his deck. He hadn't shared his spectacular view of the river with anyone in a good while. Saber got him another beer and he sank lower into his chair.

"It sure is good to be home, Bella. I missed the river."

She smiled and clicked her can against his and leaned back into the soft cushion on the wicker chair.

"Yeah, you can't beat it."

The sun was setting on the muddy water and throwing the distant ripples into shadow. A barge moved lazily, like a slow metal serpent.

While Lucas and Bella enjoyed their respite from stress, very close by a younger woman breathed in and out and tried to keep calm. She thought of the slaves, Lizbeth and Samuel, who were her constant mental companions. She kept imagining them in their perilous flight and she knew their fear now. Knew their terror. She remembered Lizbeth's thoughts as though they were her own. She remembered that Samuel knew the trick of disappearing, of becoming invisible to escape the reality of his impossible life. He knew the trick of disappearing into another one, if even for short moments at a time. Samuel could do it. Lizbeth could not. It took great will and intense focus to do it.

Shelby could do it.

She could put herself in her New York apartment with the IKEA furniture and the flat screen television and the excitement of the high fashion world. She could put herself in the clubs with her best friend, surrounded by photographers and fun-loving people, glamorous like herself. She could put herself on her Grandma Mart's lap when she was small and remember how it felt like everything that was good. She could see the lilies her mother planted in the backyard and wallpapered in the bedroom. She could smell her mother's flowery perfume. She could put herself at the farmhouse before Neely's death. She could put herself back to happiness, before Wesley became bitter and so hurtful. She could put herself at Sorina's and into the vision of the slaves and the Underground Railroad. Shelby could smell the Ohio River and feel the comfort of the Kentucky hills she loved so much.

Shelby could do it. She could make herself invisible—watched over by Grandma Mart's Irish fairies. The fairies were always circling, bringing their magic. It was keeping her sane. At least for a while longer…

"Yeah, that's what I said. A high school yearbook. You must have one somewhere in the house from Shelby's class?" Lucas chugged back his fourth mug of coffee and waited on Wesley to reply.

"Well, I'll go look after a bit. Probably in the girl's closet upstairs in a trunk or sompin'. Give me some time. I got field work to do."

"Yeah, well, that particular field work can wait, if you get my drift? I think you better go look for that yearbook first."

Wesley grunted on the other end and hung up.

Lucas smiled. This could work out. He figured he could keep Wesley in line the rest of his days with what he knew. *Nothing sweeter than a little blackmail, so long as it worked in your favor.* Lucas smiled again and finished off his coffee.

"You need some more, hon?" The elderly dispatcher stood at the door with a steaming pot.

"No, thanks, Bessie. I'm gettin' the jitters."

"I hear that. All righty then. You just holler if you need anythin'."

Lucas smiled again. Only in Greenup County would the female help still offer to bring you coffee. Thank God. Sometimes it was good to be in a place that was always backing up. *Except when it came to police work.* That was most assuredly the wrong kind of backing up. He pushed a button on the phone. "Bessie, get me Russell on the line?"

Bessie was not only courteous; she was the most efficient employee in the station after forty-three years of continuous on-the-job training. Everybody relied on Bessie. She had Russell on the phone immediately.

"Got him for you, Chief."

"Thank you, Bessie. Remind me to remind these knuckleheads around here to give you a raise." He heard her chuckle before she disconnected.

He picked up the phone on his desk and hit the blinking red button. "Russell, when is your flight?"

"It's early, eight o'clock in the morning."

"Can you change it to later, or even the next day? I want Caitlin to take you down to the modeling agency and ask around one more time. I've been on the phone with different women down there, but I don't think they took me serious. Thought I was some yeehaw. But you take Cait with you and see if you have better luck."

"Sure thing. What exactly are we lookin' for?"

"Deputy, use your nose. Feel around the place. See if anybody has kept in touch with Shelby. You know the drill. Caitlin will be a big help. I just don't want to leave that end with anything overlooked."

"Okay, Chief. You got it. What are you gonna be doin'?"

"Same thing. I'm gonna concentrate on Shelby's friends and possible enemies from here. With her looks, she coulda made a lot of the young girls jealous. Hell, I don't know, Russell. I'm grabbin' at straws, but we can't give up yet."

"I hear that. Okay. I'll keep you posted."

Lucas hung up and dialed Wesley again. The phone rang and rang. "Goddamn it, Wes, I ask you to do one thing," Lucas cussed under his breath.

"Would this be the one thing, Chief?" Wesley was standing in the doorway holding up a high school annual. He had a big grin on his face.

"That would be it! Appreciate it. Give it over, Wesley."

"Now, do you need me, or can I get to my plants?"

"Christ, Wesley, don't you give a damn about finding your daughter?"

"Ah, Chief, now that ain't fair. I know me and Shelby was fightin' all the time, and that I probably did real wrong by her, kickin' her out the way I did. That eats at me mornin', noon and night. I got a knot in my gut that won't go away. The only thing that calms me down is farmin'. That's why I got to get to it."

Lucas studied Wesley's face. He looked sincere enough. But it was still disturbing the way he seemed fifteen years younger. "All right. Go ahead. I got this. That is, unless you can think of anyone in her class who would maybe be suspect?"

"Shit, I don't remember none of them kids. Shelby was a popular girl, though. That is, until she run off."

"Did it piss some kids off, her takin' off that way?"

"Hell if I know. I was a little pissed my own self."

"All right, then. You can get on with your day. But if anybody comes to mind you call me? And Wes, don't be tellin' me what you're farmin'. I'm still an officer of the law."

"Yes, sir, Chief. I'll be seein' you then. And if I think of anybody, I'll call you." Wesley almost dashed out of the office with relief written all over his face.

"Yep, this could most certainly work out." Lucas laughed to himself and opened up the yearbook from Shelby Jean's high school. His mind clouded over when he saw all the young faces. They all looked so innocent.

He flipped through the pages of pictures of her classmates, and murmured, "Everybody is so cute when they're just pups." He pulled the book closer when he recognized a girl who was now working at The Dollar General. *Jesus, Cheryl Ann, what the hell happened to you?* He got to the Z's in the photographs and started to put the book down, when he saw a list of names at the bottom of the last page. It was titled: Classmates not depicted in the photographs.

One name caught his attention.

Lucas turned off of US 23 and onto the lane that ran past Martha's trailer. He stopped the cruiser and put it in park. The trailer looked neglected. Good thing Caitlin was coming back. It made him sad to see weeds growing in the flower beds. Martha didn't take to weeds. Lucas sighed and put the car in drive. In another minute he was pulling up in front of Sorina's house.

The cottage looked neglected, too. What the hell was going on? This thing with Shelby was tearing everybody up. It was unusual to pull up to Sorina's and not have her greet you at the screened-in porch. She always knew when a car was coming. But today nobody was there. Just the cats lazing around the flower beds and vegetable gardens. Even they seemed too sad to greet their visitor.

Lucas rang the dinner bell that hung on a pole next to the screen door. The loud clanging cut through the quiet in an annoying manner, but it was the only bell Sorina ever used. Jessie came to the back porch and opened the door.

"Hello."

Now this is weird. Jessie never came to the door. "Uh, mornin', Ms. Jessie. I hope I'm not disturbin' you ladies. I know I shoulda called, but I got a hankerin' for one of those blueberry muffins you always have around and just thought I'd take a chance."

Jessie's lips curled up slightly when she answered, "Well, that's sweet, but I haven't been bakin' lately. Sorina ain't been feelin' too good."

"That's what I hear. And I am sure sorry to know that. Would it be possible to come in and sit with her a spell?"

"I think maybe you shouldn't. She just laid down on the couch. She was so tired. I hate to keep her from her sleep."

"I understand. All right. I'll make it another time. You tell her I stopped by and that I sure hope she gets to feelin' better, you hear?"

"Sure will."

He tipped his hat and started walking toward the cruiser. Then he stopped and turned back around. She was still standing at the door.

"You know, Jessie, now that I'm here, I would actually like to talk with you for a minute. Do you mind?"

"Well, no, I guess not."

Jessie joined him outside and led the way to the wicker chairs. They sat down in the grape arbor. Lucas was again surprised that she didn't offer any refreshments. Everything just felt out of whack.

"Are you all right, Jessie? I know everybody is really upset over Shelby's disappearance."

"I know. I hate what it's doin' to Sorina."

"Jessie, I was just curious. Did you and Shelby know each other when you were both young girls? I mean, before she left for New York?"

"Yeah, I knowed her a little bit. She probably wouldn't remember me. Everybody knew her. She was so pretty. And then, when she got to be a model it was just the most amazin' thing. Yeah, I thought about her a lot."

"Jessie!?" Sorina's voice was barely audible from inside the cottage, but Jessie heard it and jumped up. With no thought of Lucas, she ran back inside.

Lucas followed.

Sorina was sitting up on the sofa and a crystal goblet lay in broken chunks on the floor. "I'm so sorry, hon. Forgive me. I was havin' the awfullest dream. I think I just swung my arm out and knocked the glass over. Is someone with you?"

Jessie looked surprised to see Lucas standing right behind her.

"It's me, Ms. Sorina, Lucas Chambers."

"Oh, Luke, I am so glad. I have been wantin' to talk with you."

Jessie started picking up the glass.

"Jessie, honey, why don't you leave that mess alone. It's only water. I promise I won't step in it."

"Sori, you can't see. I have to clean it up!" Jessie raised her voice.

Somethin' is definitely out of whack. Lucas had never heard the meek girl speak loudly.

"Here, Jessie, let me help you. We'll get this picked up in a heartbeat." Lucas got down on the floor and helped clean up the broken glass.

"Thank you both so much. Jessie, I want to speak with Lucas now."

Lucas thought he noticed a hurt look cross Jessie's features, but she quietly left the room.

"Sit down, Lucas. I'm sorry about that. I think I have Jessie upset. I know she's worried about me. But tell me now. What is happenin'? Bella told me a little bit about New York and it didn't sound good. But I need to know. Are you gettin' any leads at all?"

Lucas watched as the blind woman talked. She didn't look the same. Her color wasn't right. "Well, I'm sorry to say that Bella is correct. It wasn't good in New York. We followed a long shot and it came up real short. But Russell and Caitlin are still there and gonna take another stab at Shelby's old modelin' agency to see if anything comes up. And I am workin' possible leads from folks she knows here in Sorry's Run. Don't you worry, Ms. Sori. I am still hopeful. But you don't look well, ma'am. Maybe you should let the girls take you to get checked out?"

"Oh, there ain't nothin' wrong with me that a little good news wouldn't cure. I am just tired all the time, you know? Like there's a sadness in my soul."

"Yoo-hoo? Sorina? Lucas?"

Bella came into the room followed by Jolene and Violet. The three women crowded around the sofa.

"Lucas, what are you doin' here? You're supposed to be out findin' Shelby Jean."

"Well, maybe I'm doin' just that, Bella. We all have our particular methods, you know."

"Humph. Sori, hon, how are you? You look so pale." Bella nudged Lucas off the couch and scooted next to Sorina. She took her hand. "Seriously, dear. Let us take you to the outpatient clinic. That's not as bad as the hospital. You might really have somethin' goin' on here."

"Well, you're probably right, Bella. Give me one more day and tomorrow if I don't feel any different you girls take me."

"It's a deal."

Jolene asked, "Sweetie, are you hungry? Where's Jessie at? Can we get you somethin'?"

"A little tea would be good. Jessie is in her room. I'm afraid I hurt her feelin's. But let's not disturb her right now. Lucas was just tellin' me about the investigation."

"Oh, yeah. Some investigation." The sarcasm was apparent in Violet's voice.

"Well, I think I'll just be goin' now." Lucas sensed the conversation stacking against him.

"No, no, Lucas. Stay a spell. You and Jessie were talkin', weren't you?" Sorina asked.

"Well, I was just askin' Jessie about her relationship with Shelby back when they were young girls. I saw her name listed in Shelby's yearbook."

Bella raised an eyebrow. "Really? I find it hard to believe Jessie was even in her yearbook. Her daddy, Lester, kept her out of school most of the time. Rumor was he worked her to death."

Lucas said, "Well, she was just listed in the afterthought section. Didn't even have her photo. But she musta made it to school enough to be impressed with Shelby. Said she thought about her a lot."

Bella said, "That does surprise me. I didn't realize she knew Shelby Jean. 'Course, the school wasn't very big. I guess everybody knew everybody."

Jolene came out of the kitchen with a loaded tray of tea and sugar cookies. She passed out cups and added, "And a thing like that, a young girl becomin' a high-fashion model in New York? Can you imagine? Good gravy, that's just about the biggest thing that ever happened in Greenup County."

"Yeah, it don't get any bigger than that around here, unless you're a serial killer or somethin'," Violet mumbled.

Bella poked her in the ribs.

"What?" Violet took a cookie. "It's the dang truth."

Lucas continued, "That's why I'm tryin' to find out if Shelby had any close friends. Her goin' off to be a star while her classmates were stuck here in Kentucky doin' chores coulda been a pretty hard pill to swallow." Lucas took a cup from Jolene. "Thank you, Jo."

Sorina sipped on the herbal tea. "Ummm. That's good. Tastes real good. Just what I needed. Thank you, Jolene. Well, it sure ain't hard to imagine how some of the kids mighta felt. I never heard Martha say if Shelby had any really close friends in school."

Bella nodded in agreement and said, "I'm not sure either, come to think of it. She was a different child. Kinda did her own thing, you know. Of course, I think Neely was her best friend in the whole world. That girl doted on her mother somethin' fierce. When she died I think Shelby probably pulled away from relationships."

"Did Jessie say if she was close to Shelby Jean, Lucas?" Sorina asked.

"Didn't sound that way, Sori. But maybe you could ask her later? Let me know if she can think of anyone who might have held a grudge about Shelby's success."

Bella sighed. "Well, Lucas, this is just silly. All that is such old news. Anybody who woulda been jealous of her in high school would have long since gotten over that. You know what I'm sayin'? Just don't make sense."

"I know it, but no stone left unturned. And I wanna do another search. Not a big production like the last time. Just me. I'm gonna really comb the woods tomorrow. We all know she was headed here and never got this far."

"Well, count me in." Bella raised her hand in a high five.

Lucas looked at Bella's painted fingernails and watched her dangling earrings swing.

"I think I can handle it, Bella." He grinned.

"Just sayin'…"

Sorina had been aware for some time that she was really sick. She hadn't felt right for days. Her energy was waning more and more. Her stomach felt like it was on fire and she had lost her appetite. Her arms and legs were weak, and to get her limbs to move took incredible effort. She was living with horrific headaches and it was getting harder to breathe. Sometimes it felt like her heart was going to jump out of her chest and she sensed frightening anxiety. She was having hallucinations, and this terrified her the most. She had always been open to receiving healing visions, visions that she saw clearly with her mind's eye. But what she was seeing in these spells was fragmented and confusing. Her imagination would take her to an uncomfortable-feeling place that was unfamiliar. Then, when she would come out of it, she would be in a different part of the house, not remembering how she got there. Her heart would be pounding and she would struggle with trying to catch her breath.

Thankfully, Jessie never seemed to be around when this happened. Or at least she never let on. Sorina was most surprised that she couldn't heal herself. She prided herself on being in tune with her own body and her physical needs. But ironically, she had never been able to cure her own blindness and now she wasn't able to cure this, whatever *this* was. She needed help.

CHAPTER THIRTY-SIX
MARTHA'S GARDEN

"YOU KNOW YOU CAN STAY with me, Cait. My place isn't a palace, but it's homey enough. I think you'd be comfortable there."

"Oh, Russell, I know I would be. But I feel that I need to stay in Martha's trailer. It feels closer to Shelby somehow. You know what I mean?" Caitlin raised her moistened blue eyes at him and wiggled in the cramped airplane seats. "God, could they make these damn flights anymore uncomfortable? And to think I used to like flying."

"Yeah, me, too. Not anymore. I think it's easier to drive."

The couple sat back and tried to get situated as the small aircraft coasted down the runway before making its groaning ascent into the cloudless sky. They were heading back to Kentucky and the flight would take less than two hours.

Once the captain instructed his passengers they could unfasten their seatbelts, Cait stretched and sighed deeply. "Jack is such a great guy. It was good to see him. He was always everybody's first pick for photographers. He used to take such good care of us in the day. We were all a little in love with him, but figured he was gay. That is, until Tommy set us straight on that score." Cait laughed. "He was just one of those cool guys who kept his private life completely separate from his professional life. I knew he'd remember Carny, though, since he was the one who finally called the police about him. I could tell he's truly worried about Shelby, couldn't you? They just did a shoot together this year. First one she had done in forever. But man, do you believe how young those models at the agency were? Could I have ever looked that green?"

Russell tried to picture her at sixteen. Took his breath.

She continued, "But I was really sorry to hear that Shelby's old agent, the one who discovered her, had passed away from cancer. I didn't know that. I am sure Shelby didn't even know. They never really kept in touch. It's no wonder no one there has ever heard of Shelby Jean. What a cutthroat, here-today-gone-tomorrow business that is. It's the kind of thing that you have to make as much money as you can and get the hell out. I can't believe Shelby stuck with it as long as she did. I was sick of it after my first day on the job. If it hadn't been for Shelby I would have gone back to my hometown, and probably worked at the post office or something."

"With your looks? No way. You were destined to be photographed."

"Well, maybe. The pay was sure better. But I am happy to be out of it. I think I like plants better than I do people. Present company excepted of course."

"Well, that's good, because I am not goin' anywhere." He squeezed her hand. "But it is awful that we got nowhere on this trip. The whole thing was a waste of time, and we're not one step closer to findin' Shelby."

"Yeah, and poor Carny. He was so *not* a viable suspect."

"Well, I understand why the Chief tried, though. At this point, we have to grab at any straws we can find."

"Well, at least you got to see our apartment and meet Tommy. You liked him, right?"

"Oh, yeah, Tommy is good people, even if he butters his bread on the wrong side."

Caitlin gave Russell a quick jab in the ribs.

He laughed. "I'm just kiddin', Cait. Tommy is a friend of yours and that makes him a friend of mine."

"Well, I know he felt just sick about getting you and Lucas into this wild goose chase."

"Well, he shouldn't feel like that. We asked for anything unusual, and Carny definitely fit that description. It was worth a shot."

The plane dipped dramatically and then leveled back out.

Caitlin looked over at the handsome man she had truly come to care for. "I think I'm going to try to get some sleep if this crate will stay up in the air like it's supposed to."

He smiled at her and touched the end of her nose. "No worries. We'll be home in a flash and soon you'll be in the comfort of Martha's garden again."

Caitlin smiled. But instead of heeding his "no worries" advice, she was aware of a darker worry suddenly invading her thoughts. New York hadn't helped. There were no leads in Kentucky. Caitlin leaned her head back and shut her tired eyes. But instead of peaceful dark, right there under her eyelids were Shelby's green eyes. Caitlin could feel the warmth of her best friend, her sweet energy. She could feel her. But Shelby was still gone. Maybe they really weren't going to find her anywhere. It just seemed impossible, but too much time was passing. Something had to give, and it had to give soon.

"Hey y'all, over here!" Bella hollered at them from across the terminal at Huntington's Tri-State Airport.

Cait and Bella hugged while Russell pulled Cait's bags off the conveyor belt.

Back in the cruiser, the conversation was subdued. Lucas finally asked, "So you got nothin'?"

Russell answered from the back seat, "Not a damned thing, Chief. We spoke with Jack, the photographer who had reported Carny to the police, and he sure remembered the old dude. Said he was weird but he thought he was more annoying than dangerous. Even so, he hadn't seen or heard another thing abut him through the years. Just pretty much disappeared off the grid, and never bothered the models any more. And the girls at her agency now are too young. Not too many old-timers, you know?"

"Sorry about their luck," Lucas grunted in response and the car got quiet.

Caitlin stared out the windows at the darkening sky casting gray shadows on the brown Ohio River. "It always seems so peaceful here. Like the rest of the world never touches this place."

"Well, hon, it rarely does. Only in a bad way, like what's happening with Shelby. Lord almighty, if we don't do somethin' and do it quick there's no tellin' what will happen. We may never find her." Bella turned back to facing the front in the passenger seat and the conversation stopped until they got to Martha's trailer.

"How is Sorina?" Cait asked as Lucas pulled into the gravel driveway.

Bella answered, "Well, now, that's another can of worms. Sorina ain't doin' so good. She swears it's just worry over Shelby, but we're startin' to think somethin' else entirely is goin' on. She has finally agreed to let us take her to the clinic, so maybe we'll get some answers. We don't need to lose Sorina, too. It would just be too much, after Martha's death and Shelby's disappearance. Just too much."

Lucas looked over at her and reached for her hand. "We ain't gonna lose Sorina. Just get that out of your head. And we're gonna find Shelby. One way or the other, we're gonna find her." He set his thin lips in a firm line and nobody responded. "Are you stayin' here tonight, Russell?"

"Yeah. I don't think Cait should be alone. Pick me up tomorrow?"

"You bet. I have a couple ideas that I'd like to run by you." Lucas got their bags out of the trunk. "But you two relax for the evening. We'll all be fresher in the mornin'."

Bella and Lucas drove off and Russell unlocked the trailer door. Even though no one had been inside for a while, the rooms smelled faintly fragrant, like Martha was still there.

"Martha's garden." Cait smiled again at all the green in the décor. It really was a welcoming place and she was glad to be back. Kentucky was beginning to feel more like home than New York. "Russell, I want to walk down the lane and say hi to Sorina before it gets too late. Why don't you take Shelby's truck and get us some wine?" She threw the keys at him from the counter.

"Anything else, ma'am?"

"Maybe some cheese and crackers? Or better yet, maybe a pizza?" She smiled.

"How in the hell do you stay so thin?" He grinned at her. "I'll text you when I get back. Don't go anywhere other than Sorina's, right? And don't go in the woods." He raised an eyebrow.

"Absolutely. I'll just stay a few minutes. I want to let her know I'm here."

He backed out of the drive and headed south on US 23 as Cait turned in the direction of the cottage. *Enchanted cottage?* Maybe it was bewitched and had swallowed Shelby up into a mystical NeverNeverLand. The lights were already lit in the windows and the storybook cottage looked like the safest place in the world. A little girl's dream and a grown woman's refuge.

Or maybe all that was an illusion—its captivating beauty only smoke and mirrors hiding something dark and treacherous behind its fairytale walls.

Oh, knock it off, Cait. You're starting to think like Shelby in her fantasy Irish world of fairies and Banshees. Shelby had loved sharing things her Grandma Mart had told her of the old country. Caitlin was always giving her shit about it. "God, Shelby. It's not like your grandmother wasn't Kentucky born and raised." Shelby would look at her and reply, "You don't have to be living in the Green Isle for the fairies to find you. Grandma Mart always said they were circlin' her even though she had never set foot in Ireland. It was what made her light shine."

Cait always made fun, but she loved those stories, and they had a good time thinking they might be true somehow. And now she wondered if the fairies were circling Shelby right now, wherever she was.

"Hello? Sorina, Jessie? It's Caitlin." She knocked at the screened-in back porch door and waited for what seemed to be a long time. It gave her a moment to look around at the stunning property. Once again she marveled at the unique landscaping. Jessie was a talented girl, for sure. She could learn some things about how to grow a garden from her. Cait watched in fascination as a young goat chewed peacefully on the grass just beyond the grape arbor. The chickens were quietly tucked away in their coops. Two fat yellow cats lazed about and just watched her in silence while the river rolled off in the dim distance.

"Hello? Anybody home?" Caitlin tried again.

This time a willowy shadow moved the air behind the door, causing Caitlin to jump in surprise. She hadn't heard the quiet girl come out to the screened-in porch. She was barely visible.

"Oh, hi, Jessie. You scared me. It's Cait. Caitlin Sotheby? Shelby's roommate?"

There was an awkward silence.

"I hope I'm not disturbing you?" Cait was once again struck by the doe-eyed beauty's demeanor. So shy. So retiring. Like she was afraid to look into anyone's eyes.

Finally Jessie opened the door. "Come on in. I just made some tea."

Cait followed her to the front of the cottage where Sorina lounged, her legs stretched out on the sofa in front of the fireplace. She was sipping from a porcelain cup and Cait noticed her delicate hands were shaking.

When she got closer she was taken aback at the sight of her. It hadn't been that long since they had seen each other, but Cait was shocked at how thin Sorina was. Her pale skin was stretched tightly over her high cheek bones, giving her a gaunt look, and even with the amber glasses she wore it was obvious there were dark shadows under her eyes.

"Sorina, it's Caitlin. I hope I'm not disturbing you?"

"Of course you're not disturbin' me."

"I just wanted to let you know I was back from New York."

Sorina sat her cup down and moved her legs out of the way, gesturing for Cait to sit next to her. "I'm so glad. We need you. Jessie, pour Cait a cup of tea, will you hon?"

The timid girl obeyed.

"So I hear you had no luck in New York findin' any clues about where Shelby might have gone to?"

"You're right. We had no luck. Russell and Lucas followed the only lead they had and came up empty handed. The answer has to be here in Sorry's Run, Sorina. It just has to be. But how are you? You look so thin to me."

"Well, I ain't doin' so good, truth be told. I haven't felt well for so long, that I'm startin' to get used to it." She laughed through a hoarse cough that escaped her pretty lips. "And the strangest thing is, I have no idea what is wrong with me. That's a first. I have always known how to cure my ailments. Between me and Martha there wasn't nothin' we couldn't fix that was broke on the human body—except for this little blindness of mine." She laughed hoarsely again. "But this time none of the herbs are workin' and I just keep gettin' weaker. And where is Martha in all this? She should be communicatin' with me. She is quiet as a mouse. Just not like her."

Jessie came back from the kitchen with another dainty cup brimming with steaming tea. Cait took a sip and felt herself relax into the sofa beside Sorina. "Well, Bella says you're going to a clinic tomorrow, and I think that's a good idea. Maybe this is one of those ailments that needs some real modern medicine?" She raised an eyebrow over her cup.

Sorina nodded and answered, "I think you might be right. I will let the girls take me tomorrow if I don't have a miracle in the night. But how about you, hon? Are you gonna stay for a while, or are you about to give up?" Sorina's glasses fell a bit on her nose as she asked the question that she had been afraid to ask.

"No, Sori, I am not going to give up. I am here until we find Shelby. I have made up my mind to that. I still believe we will find her, Sori. I believe Shelby is alive. Don't you?"

"Yes, darlin', I do believe that. Even though our heads tell us different at this point, I do believe we'll find her. I just have to get my energy back up to where I can be of some help." Just as Sorina spoke, her eyelids drooped heavily. She looked as though she would fall asleep right then and there.

"Okay, then, Sorina. We will keep hope alive. I am going to scour Martha's trailer for anything that might trigger a clue, and Lucas is picking Russell up to keep working in the morning. We're not nearly done yet. But I will check on you after you get back from the doctor tomorrow."

She got up and kissed Sorina's head and waved to Jessie who was standing in the doorway to the kitchen. "Thanks for the tea, Jessie. I'll let myself out. You two have a restful evening and I'll talk to you tomorrow."

Caitlin got back to the trailer and lit every candle she could find. Russell came in with two bottles of Cabernet and a hot pizza. After getting out the plates they sat themselves down at the kitchen table and ate and drank slowly, watching the flickering candlelight bring the leafy patterns in the wallpaper to life. Soon their gazes switched and they watched only each other's eyes.

Their lovemaking that night was more passionate than usual, needy, like wartime lovers the night before they faced being parted forever. Caitlin was conscious of a nagging fear, fear of the unknown, fear of an unhappy ending. Russell was fearful, too, as he stared at the raven beauty in his arms. Would she stay if they never found Shelby? Would she stay if they did? He lifted her chin then and kissed her deeply again. Their fear melted away at last behind a physical coupling that brought them to pure release. They slept finally in each other's arms, aware only of the moment and the comfort they brought each other. Acutely aware that in such a precarious world this moment might be all they had.

Farther down US 23, south of Sorry's Run and back a long, tree-lined lane, Bella paced back and forth in her large living room. She poured herself another vodka and stared at Martha's picture. "We've got us a fine mess here, Mart. Are you gonna help out or what? Where the hell is Shelby? And what is happenin' with Sorina? It's all gettin' too strange and you are bein' too quiet." Bella stumbled drunkenly on her low-heeled shoes and tossed them off.

"Damn it."

She was irritated and lonely. And that didn't happen to Bella often. Irritated, yes. But lonely, no. She missed Martha too much. The two of them had been thick as thieves and had several skeletons buried in closets that they alone shared. But now Martha was gone and it left only her. That was disturbing. Bella didn't like facing her demons on her own. She had always had Martha.

"God, girl, the laughs we had." Bella toasted Martha's photograph.

And all that crazy healin' stuff had been so much fun. Of course, Bella had become a true believer. Martha had convinced her finally of her "gift." And all that talk about her Irish ancestry and the superstitions that she lived and breathed—well, it certainly had its fascinations.

Jared, of course, had just laughed it all off. Bella looked over at her deceased husband's photograph. She toasted him as well. But she didn't miss him. "I put you through so much shit, didn't I, Jared?" She looked at his face. Not a handsome face. Not even an interesting face. But he had been a damned good provider. And she had been a handful, but he had put up with her. And sometimes she sensed that her all-powerful husband was a little afraid of what went on in that humble cottage and behind the doors of the county's poorest folks. He was a surgeon, after all, and only believed in the magic of modern medicine. But he kept hearing rumors of healings going on outside of his hospital and it was starting to get his attention. When Sorina began making her own brand of magic on those special evenings at the cottage, Bella had been a very willing participant. Jared knew that. And he didn't like it.

Bella had loved Jared once, but he was just too closed off. And he was no fun. Their marriage had been a struggle from the beginning. As the years passed, their sex life became pretty nonexistent and they grew farther and farther apart. Jared was all about work, ambition and social climbing. But even as controlling as he was, she knew Jared was always a little frightened of her. He told her many times that she intimidated the hell out of him, the way she seemed to get exactly what she wanted. And she had to admit that even in his death, she got happier. And she had more money than she could ever need.

She looked around the enormous rooms of her house that Jared had built for her when they pretty much owned their world. It was a spectacular house and she loved it. No, she had never been lonely in it, though she was alone most of the time. Alone, but not lonely. There was a huge difference. Only now, she was feeling lonely. It was all so depressing, everything that was happening. Thank God she still had Jolene and Violet. They were her dear friends, too. They weren't Martha, but they were still here. And then there was Lucas…

She poured herself a final nightcap. "Okay, Mart, I'm givin' up for the night. But if you want to visit me in my dreams?" She toasted the photograph of her smiling, happy friend. Bella had taken the picture and it was a good memory. A tear rolled down her cheek. She wiped it off harshly and sat her glass down.

"Come on, Precious. Keep me company." She picked up her Persian cat and stumbled down the hall to her king-size bed.

CHAPTER THIRTY-SEVEN HIDING SOMETHING

LUCAS STRETCHED HIS STIFF BACK on his deck and gazed out over his favorite sight, the Ohio rolling along like nothing ever changed; like the cares of the world meant nothing. *"Old Man River."*

"Mornin', Saber. How are you, boy?" The golden lab nuzzled his master's hand and wagged his tail happily.

"Come on, boy. Let's have some breakfast."

The dog followed Lucas through the sliding door and back into the kitchen where bacon and eggs were shared by man and his best friend. "I don't know, Saber. Somethin' don't smell right. It just don't add up at Sorina's. I hope those girls take her to the doc today because she sure as hell ain't right. And that Jessie. She has somethin' hidden way deep. Still waters, you know?"

Saber cocked his head and panted in total agreement.

"Well, that would be a bitch, wouldn't it? Them ladies been together a long time. I hope this old nose of mine is dead wrong. But somethin' just don't add up," he repeated as he pulled his boots on and groaned with the effort. "Gettin' old is hell, Saber. Don't do it. Go out of this life huntin' rabbits." He patted his dog on the head and left his dream house for another day of goose chasing.

As soon as he stepped outside Lucas placed a call. "Russell, what you got for me?"

There was hesitation on the other end of the line. "Hell, Chief, it ain't even eight o'clock."

Lucas loved these conversations. "You ain't an insurance agent right now, Mister. You're a deputy. Unwrap yourself from that girl and I'll pick you up in five." But just before he pushed the end button, he reconsidered.

"On second thought. I won't pick you up. You and Cait stay with Sorina today. Make sure Bella gets her over to the clinic no matter what she says. And Russell, keep an eye on Jessie."

"Where will you be, Chief?"

"I'll be close. I'm gonna scour those woods where Shelby must have walked on the night she disappeared. We have to have missed something."

"Are you sure you don't want me to come with you?"

"No, I need you to see to it that Sorina gets medical attention. I will stay in touch."

"Roger that, Chief."

Roger that? Lucas grinned and ended the call. He got behind the wheel and pulled the cruiser out onto 23 heading for Martha's. He had chastised himself more than once, wondering at his lack of judgment when he hadn't immediately organized another town search. But it was that "nose" thing. Somehow he felt he was better to go at it alone. He found himself shopping at the IGA in the late evenings just to avoid the questions. Was it wisdom or plain old guilt?

At the Speedway he bought a large black coffee to go.

"How's the search for Shelby Jean goin', Chief?" The clerk handed him his change.

"Slow and steady, Asa, slow and steady."

"Well, you'll git her figured out. You always had the nose, Chief. You always had the nose."

Lucas grinned and tipped his hat before getting back in his cruiser. So somebody still believed in him. He planned on taking his time in the woods.

And it wasn't raining.

Twigs and leaves crunched under Lucas' boots as he entered the woods between Martha's trailer and Sorina's cottage. He took a deep swallow of the hot coffee and waited until it hit his stomach before moving. He wanted to feel the woods as much as see the woods. If Shelby was here he would find her today.

He took a step and stared at the trunks all around him. Looking up to where the sun was blinking through the limbs, he pulled out his prescription sunglasses and put them on. The tall sycamores and birches caught the light in their highest branches and a breeze caused the thinnest limbs to sway. He could smell the river. Lucas felt a shiver move over his spine. Usually this kind of scene brought him peace, but not today. Today it felt off, like all the beauty was staged, concealing something. Mother Nature was the truest bitch, subject to moods. And today she was playacting at being a perfect distraction. *Hiding something.*

"Okay, Mother. What you got? Bring it," he spoke and watched the trees and then put his eyes to the ground. Placing one booted foot in front of the other, he stepped carefully between the thick brush, examining every bush, every squatty tree. He pulled back the thickest ferns and looked into the wild strawberries. His trained eyes took in the ground around the roots of the foliage, looking for areas that were matted, changed, redirected, where maybe a body had lain, or had been dragged? He blocked out all the nature chatter around him and went into a zone where he had lived most of his professional life. It was a place of detail and minute spaces where the tiniest clues lived and no one else could see. It was his gift.

But as he stared into the leaves and twigs and looked at the blanket of pine needles, watching for discolorations and footprints dug into the earth, he began to wonder if he wasn't past it. Everything looked the same to him. There were no surprises, no ah-hahs! where it became clear that the ground was showing him who had tread over it, misplacing the natural lay of the trees and shrubs. Today there was nothing like that.

It's been too long.

Lucas knew he was going for the long shot, but what else was there? Something had to give. Would Shelby Jean Stiller just become one of the hundreds of "cold" cases lost forever in the dusty files at the station house after all the energy to solve them had finally dissipated? Was that beautiful girl's legacy going to be one of those sad, unsolved mysteries? He couldn't allow himself to think so. This was too close. Martha would never forgive him if he gave up. So he wouldn't give up. But in order for him to not give up, something just had to give!

He kept stepping through the trees, careful not to catch a sharp twig or whipping limb in the face as he stared down more than up. But it wore on him, the vigilant staring. He felt a headache coming on. After two hours of combing every inch of every root and ground cover, he stopped at the trunk of a large sycamore tree and sank down beside it. He leaned back against the bark, stretched his long legs out in front of him, and pulled his cowboy hat over his eyes. *Just a little rest.* Sleep fell over him quickly like a cool shade.

Caitlin knocked on the screened door gently at first and then with more force. “Hello? Sorina? Jessie? Hello? It’s Cait and Russell. Have you have had your lunch yet?”

Russell looked at her, eyebrows raised. “Lunch?”

“What?”

“We’re invitin’ ourselves to lunch?” he whispered.

“Well?” She shrugged and whispered back, “It just came out. I’m nervous.” When Russell told her what Lucas had said earlier she found it disturbing, but Russell hadn’t thought it sounded so urgent. He had caressed her and spoken into her ear seductively, “I bet Bella is on her way to the cottage right now to take Sorina to the clinic. And Chief is close, too, goin’ through the woods. He’ll keep us posted. We have a little time?” She had given in too easily and now she regretted it.

Russell still didn’t seem worried. He looked around at the quiet backyard. “See, the ladies have probably already picked her up.”

“But what about Jessie?”

Their eyes locked. “Damn! Chief said to keep an eye on her.” Russell reached for the doorknob, but Jessie was there, appearing out of nowhere suddenly behind the screen. Her eyes looked even larger than usual and were darting about nervously. She pulled hastily at her tangled straight hair.

Cait said, “Hi, Jessie. We hope we’re not botherin’ you? We just wanted to see how Sorina was doin’.”

Jessie stared at the couple and when she spoke her voice came out in a monotone, lacking in emotion, “Sorina is feelin’ real poorly today. Bella is comin’ in an hour to take her to the doctor.”

Cait asked, “Can we come in and sit with her until Bella gets here?”

“I really don’t think you should. She needs to rest.”

Russell pressed. “Jessie, I think we should come in. We will be very quiet.” Russell moved defiantly in front of Cait. He cleared his throat and waited.

"Well, all right then. Come on."

They walked in behind the willowy girl who was standing taller, walking stiffer. Her controlled poise made her look unusually confident. She led them to Sorina's bedroom where the little woman was smothered in too many comforters. Cait took one bold look at her.

"Russell, call 911."

Scratch! Scratch! Scratch!

"What the…?" Lucas jumped up and something scurried away from him in a dusty leaf cloud. He stretched his arms and legs before struggling with standing up. The air felt warmer and the sun was rising higher in the sky. *How damn long have I been asleep?* Only a couple hours of investigating and he had fallen asleep on the job? *Christ!* He would have to take this embarrassment to his grave. He would never live it down with the young officers who already had him so far over the hill he could never climb up.

Well, if the shoe fits…

Lucas got to his feet and dusted off his pants with his cowboy hat before putting it back on his head. He felt a disgust rising in him like a bad taste from a wild night out. He was ashamed of himself. Maybe Shelby did need a real detective. Not some old fart who couldn't even get a whiff in a case anymore and didn't have the energy or the drive to see it through.

Goddamn it!

Lucas almost tripped over a branch and then something scurried behind him again.

Scratch! Scratch! Scratch!

This time he turned and saw what had awakened him. It was a little rabbit. A very familiar rabbit. "Rory? Is that you?" The animal stared back at him with his dark eyes and crinkled ear and Lucas knew he was looking down at Martha's pet rabbit. "What's up, little guy?"

The animal jumped ahead of him and stood, staring until Lucas decided he would follow. It was just like an animated film. The rabbit would take a few steps and then stop to be sure the man was following. If Lucas wasn't feeling the worst form of humiliation already he would have thought it was funnier than hell. But he followed Rory through the brush as they made their way carefully back towards Sorina's cottage. At last he could make out the cottage through the trees and the river was louder and more present in the air.

It was then that Rory took a different turn. He led Lucas away from the cottage and into a part of Sorina's property he had never seen before. At first glance it was just another walled-off garden area like the other designer flower arrangements Jessie had set out. But it was far away from the others, completely apart from the rest of the house; a small container garden not mingling with any of the other flowing perennials and annuals that surrounded the cottage. This was an isolated garden of intense beauty bordered by a square of short pines. Blue, yellow and white blooms faced just the right direction to catch the sun in its most opportune moments.

The small rabbit placed himself in the middle of this little garden. He stopped then and stared up at the man.

"So what, Rory? Is this your favorite play place? A secret garden of your very own, where the goats and chickens and cats never come to?" Lucas started to step through the triangular-shaped short evergreens to get to where the rabbit was, but his leg got caught on barbed wire. *Shit!* It felt like the sharp jab might have broken his skin. He put pressure on his smarting knee and noticed how nearly invisible barbed wire snaked through and between the evergreens. Anyone or any thing trying to enter the flower bed would be shocked into stopping. It was strategically placed to keep animals and people out. How weird. Why would anybody go to such lengths to seal off a pretty little garden?

"How did you get in here, Rory?" Lucas watched, amazed, as the rabbit showed him where he had burrowed a ditch underneath the wire. "I see. So there really is no keepin' any of you determined critters from comin' into the garden, is there?" The rabbit stared. "But then again, why would you even want to? There's nothing to eat. No reason to invade the space. So why did you show me this place, Rory?"

Lucas was beginning to feel his humiliation turn into something even more ridiculous. He spoke out loud, "Martha, would you please tell me what the hell I'm doin'?" Lucas looked up to the sky as if she would write an answer there. Then he looked back down toward his boots and realized what he was being shown.

The flowers weren't just your regular wild flowers, or pretty perennials.

These flowers were of a definite type. He whistled to himself and pushed his hat back off his forehead. "No wonder there's barbed wire all around." Lucas released his breath slowly as he stared at the ground. He was looking at a poisonous garden of wolfs bane and hemlock!

Just then he heard a blaring siren tearing through the air.

Buzzzzz!

Lucas' cell phone vibrated in his pocket. "Russell, what you got?"

"We had to call an ambulance for Sorina! We're riding with her to the hospital in Ashland. Chief, the medics think she's been poisoned!"

CHAPTER THIRTY-EIGHT
GARDEN OF POISON

"IS JESSIE WITH YOU?"

"No, Chief. She's comin' later with Bella."

Lucas stepped back out of the garden of poison and yelled at Russell, "I told you to stay with her."

"Damn, Chief, we were going to, but it didn't seem necessary. Jessie started bawling when the EMTs arrived. Totally upset, you know? Cait tried to stay with her, but she wouldn't let her. She wanted Bella to take her to the hospital. She said she wanted to put some things together in a suitcase to bring to Sorina. Chief, she called Bella right in front of us and asked her to come pick her up."

"Damn." Lucas hung up his call and punched in Bella's number as he hurried over to Sorina's cottage.

Bella answered on the second ring, "Hey, Luke."

"Bella, are you on your way to Sorina's?"

"Yeah, in a little bit. I was kind of waitin' for her to call."

The hair on Lucas' neck stood up. "Bella, Jessie didn't call you just a few minutes ago?"

"No, I haven't heard from Jessie. Why, Lucas? You're scarin' me now. Is Sorina worse?"

He stood at the door to the screened-in porch of the cottage and filled her in.

"Oh, God. I'm comin' over."

Lucas hung up and shouted through the screen, "Jessie, it's Chief Chambers. Are you in there, Jessie?" There was no reply. He knocked over and over and she never came. Turning the knob, he found the door to be unlocked. He opened it. "Jessie? Are you home, Jessie? It's Lucas."

Still no reply. He entered the cottage, walking carefully through each of the low-ceilinged rooms. No one was home. Where was she? Where was Jessie? He went back into Sorina's bedroom and found a half-empty cup of tea sitting on her bedside table. He picked it up and smelled it. Smelled like tea. Looked like tea. In the kitchen he found a plastic go cup and poured the tea into it. Then he noticed the front door was slightly ajar. Stepping outside he could tell someone had recently gone through the vine-covered yard. He examined the fresh footprints that led towards the woods in the direction of Martha's trailer. There was no use in trying to follow her. He wouldn't be able to move as fast as Jessie. From the look of her footsteps she was running.

Just then he heard Bella's car barreling down the lane. He went back inside, grabbed the go cup, and met her at the back of the cottage. "Drive to Martha's."

He just barely got in the car when Bella slammed the gear shift into reverse.

"Damn, woman, you're gonna give me whiplash."

Bella didn't even blink an eye, but gunned the accelerator the short distance back to the trailer. Lucas used the key he still kept to the trailer's front door and let them both in. No sign of Jessie. No sign she had been there. There were no muddy prints on the mat outside the door. No indication someone had just entered. He combed the ground around the trailer and saw nothing there either. It was a dead end.

"Come on, Bella, we need to get to the hospital." He pulled out a red flashing light from the backseat and stuck it on the roof of the cruiser. Bella locked up her car and they raced down the highway heading for Ashland.

Bella's brown eyes were popping as she watched him drive. "Are you tellin' me you think Jessie has been poisonin' Sorina? I mean, God, Lucas. Why in the world would she do that? She loves that woman. They're like mother and daughter."

"I sure as hell don't know. But who else would have planted a garden of lethal flowers and kept it damn well hidden from everybody?"

"I can't imagine. But it sure would explain why Sorina has been gettin' worse and worse. We all just figured she was worried about Shelby Jean, and it was breakin' her spirit and her body. It was understandable, you know?" Bella watched a rusty tugboat push its cargo down the river slowly, leaving a wake of white caps behind it. She wiped a tear out of her eye. "God, Luke, we can't lose Sorina. Why is all this happenin'?"

Lucas reached out and put his arm around her, pulling her close to him. She rested her head on his shoulder all the way to the hospital ER entrance.

Russell and Caitlin were in the waiting room.

"Where is she?" Lucas asked.

Caitlin pointed to where Sorina was being attended to behind a closed curtain. Lucas walked over to a nurse standing behind the reception desk. He handed her the go cup and whispered something to her. She took the cup and disappeared behind the curtain. In a brief moment, she returned and was seen taking the cup to the elevator.

A doctor came out to the waiting room. He addressed the tall man in the cowboy hat and boots. "Chief Chambers?"

"Yes, sir. I'm Lucas Chambers."

"You brought the tea?"

Lucas told him about the flowers and finding the cup by Sorina's bed.

"Well, that tea will no doubt confirm what we already know. She has certainly been poisoned. We are treating her with atropine and hopefully that will be enough of an antidote. The lab will tell us if there's anything in the tea. But the poisonous flowers you've described, if ingested, would result in her symptoms exactly."

"Will she make it, doctor?" Bella looked close to tears.

"Yes, ma'am, I think she will. But she's very weak and we're going to have to admit her to get fluids into her and get some IV nutrition going. She'll be a sick lady for a while, but given some time she should recover." He looked intensely over his reader glasses and added, "Another day, though, and it might have been too late." Then he directed his gaze to Lucas. "I will have to report this, Officer Chambers. It's hospital protocol. Do y'all have an idea of anyone who might want to do your friend harm?"

"We might. But we're far from bein' sure."

"Doctor, is it okay if Caitlin and I stay with her?" Bella asked.

"Sure. The staff will need your help with the paperwork before they can get her admitted. So if you don't mind? Janice?"

A young nurse came over and Bella and Cait followed her back to the front desk to get the admission started. Lucas and Russell left.

"So you really think it's Jessie?" Russell found it hard to believe.

"Well, I don't know who else could have laid out that garden? Certainly Sorina couldn't do it. I just can't figure on the motive. Russell, we have to get some more information on Jessie's past. We just don't know enough about her. Hell, I just found out she went to school with Shelby. I'm beginnin' to think Shelby's disappearance and the attempted murder of Sorina are somehow tied together. I just don't know why or how."

The two men drove in silence all the way back to Sorry's Run. When they reached Sorina's they looked through the cottage again for any clues of Jessie's whereabouts. Nothing was out of place. It didn't appear as though Jessie had intended on going anywhere. But she wasn't there. And she wasn't at Martha's trailer. Lucas dropped Russell off at his house so he could get cleaned up and pick up his laptop. Luke drove on back to the police station to use their computer to start another search; this time for any clues about the talented and enigmatic Jessie Johnson.

Shelby blinked rapidly at the light. It was always so dark, so very dark. And now there was a light. It wasn't bright, but it nearly blinded her. She knew she had been in the dark for a very long time. Somebody had been there with her off and on, but she could never make out who it was or even if it was a man or woman. Whoever it was never spoke and never touched her. There was a scent sometimes. Shelby thought she could detect a faint smell of jasmine, but even that, she wasn't sure of. It made her think her captor was a woman. Whoever it was came and went and left her food and water and emptied the bedpan. There were wipes put out for her to use and a waste basket to dispose of them, but these things were found out by her slowly. She had no idea how long she had been captive.

She knew she had been hit in the back of the head in the woods. She remembered the searing pain of that on the night she was going to visit Sorina. She had been out for some time, but it was impossible to know how long. She knew her first conscious thought was of a severe, sickening headache. She had thrown up and someone had cleaned it up and given her a pill to take with her water. She had taken it and she had been sleeping nearly all the time.

In her sleep she would take on the personalities of Lizbeth and Samuel, the two slaves she and Sorina had seen in their visions. She was running through the woods from dogs and from the elements and fear was the only thing she knew. Her fear was all encompassing. Every nerve was taut with blind fear. She slept. She ate and drank to keep herself alive. She relieved her bladder and her bowels somehow. She wasn't sure how. Sometimes she thought she was lying in her own excrement, but then she would pass out again and when she awoke she would be clean. She knew these things, but nothing else. She couldn't get her thoughts in any meaningful order. She felt like an animal. A physical being with no mind, only images of thoughts.

But she saw Lizbeth and Samuel. She saw them and she had become one with them in their terrifying flight from slavery. She was searching for Sorina's cottage. She was on Sori's Run. She knew that. She was on Sori's Run for freedom. But she never got there. Freedom escaped Lizbeth and Samuel as it was escaping her. She wasn't sure who she was anymore. She had no idea where she was and if she would live to ever find out.

Sometimes in her drugged state she thought she saw the fairies. Grandma Mart's fairies. She thought she saw them circling real close. It meant if she died the fairies would take her God light back to the Ireland of her ancestors. That soothed her somewhat. But she was so frightened of the Banshee. Her grandmother had spoken of the old hag in black with blood red eyes that was a horror to look upon, and only appeared when death was close. Sometimes the sweet fairies would take on the horrible wailing of the death fairy. Shelby would wake screaming into pitch black with no one hearing. But she never saw the Banshee, nor heard the *rocks on the roof* that meant certain death. So she still lived, in a sense…

Her hallucinations and dreams were her reality. And in rare moments when she was coherent she would practice Samuel's gift of disappearing behind another life. She would take herself back to New York and back to her younger years before she had returned to Kentucky. She would disappear behind her memories of herself and then she would sleep again.

It was that way for a long while.

Then she started hiding the pills she was given by her unknown captor. Her head had stopped its incessant pounding and her mind started to return in fragments and then in longer moments of clarity and she was becoming Shelby Jean Stiller again. But this was much worse because there was the cold, clear fear that was her constant companion. The cold fear of the complete unknown, the lonely, horrifying unknown. She had had no communication with another human being for longer than she cared to know.

Why had someone done this to her? Why? And who? And what was their intention? Why didn't they just kill her? Why were they letting her just lay, attending to her physical needs. Why?

And now there was a light. Someone had switched on a light and for the first time her whereabouts were revealed to her.

She blinked rapidly, waiting on her tiny pupils to adjust to the dim light that exposed a narrow, low-ceilinged shed. It wasn't a tool shed. There were no tools, no oily machine smells, no manly smells at all. Only a trace of jasmine from time to time, mixed in with her own dirty smells. Wooden shelves lined the walls, but there was nothing on them. They were completely empty. Whatever had been stored there had been disposed of, leaving just a long open space with a single light bulb hanging in the middle. There was a door to the left, a small window in the back and then her area of confinement in the front. The walls were painted dark and there was black paint on the high window, blocking any light.

The light bulb hung from a single wire and caught movement in the air. It swung just slightly, casting bulbous patterns on the walls. In the gloomy light Shelby thought she could make out someone there. A shadow of a figure. Her heart and breath stopped. The elusive dark figure didn't move, didn't speak, just stood there in the shadowy end of the shed.

Shelby looked down at herself, seeing her body for the first time since she had been kidnapped. She had a gown on, an old-fashioned lacy gown with long, ruffled sleeves. A gown she had never owned. It was clean, white, pressed. She had socks on her feet. Her ankles and wrists were loosely shackled. She pulled up and found she had much play in her motion before the chains held her. Just enough that she could move freely in her bed, wipe herself. But she couldn't get up. She had not even known she was chained. Her wrists and ankles were wrapped in a soft cloth that felt like part of her gown. She had never felt fully restrained, just too weak to even try to rise. Now she tried and couldn't. A fresh fear shot over her body. Now she was looking at her captor who was looking at her.

Was this the end? Was she wrapped in this ridiculous white gown because she was to be buried in it?

"My mama died in that gown," the voice came from the figure at the far end of the shed.

Shelby opened her mouth and screamed!

The figure moved, advancing quickly across the floor to the bed. Shelby was screaming, thrashing her whole body and head violently, her eyes closed in horror and denial.

"Shelby Jean, quiet now. You'll just get yourself all worked up. Quiet now." The figure came closer and Shelby opened her eyes.

"Jessie? Jessie, is that you? Oh, thank God. Jessie, undo me. Get me out of this place. What is this place? Jessie, what is happening? Where is Sorina? Is she okay?"

"Shhhhhh now, hush. I will tell you everything, but you have to calm down. You hear me?"

Jessie's lovely voice had a soothing effect and Shelby let herself be lulled by it. But her heart was beating rapidly, and she felt she would explode with this new mystery.

"Jessie. Tell me?"

"I will tell you when I feel like tellin' you, Shelby Jean. Christ, you always were so demandin', like you owned the world. Like you were more deservin' of everything than the rest of us."

"What?" Shelby watched as Jessie left her side and spoke in a much harsher tone than she had ever heard her utter. The waif-like girl picked up a broom and began sweeping the already clean, soft pine floor.

"You know what I'm sayin'? Shelby is so smart! Shelby is so pretty! Shelby is so funny! Shelby this, Shelby that. The whole time we was growin' up, we all had to listen to that and take a backseat to Ms. Shelby Jean Stiller."

Shelby stared at the graceful woman sweeping the floor and speaking like she was talking to herself. Shelby tried to understand. Jealousy? Could she be here because Jessie was jealous of her? *But how could that be?* Shelby couldn't even remember having known Jessie when they were kids. Had she really been that self-centered? Shelby racked her brain trying to remember anything that might have happened between them.

She played the only card she could think of. "Jessie, I don't know why you would say that? My dad was always so mean to me, and my mother died when I was just a kid. Hell, I never felt superior to anyone. How could I? I thought God hated me and punished me at every turn."

"Oh, yeah. You say that, but it's not the way you acted. You always had your nose in the air. Always. I liked you, though, even so, Shelby. I always liked you. But that night when your mama come to my house to see why my feet was so swelled…well, you probably don't know much about that night. How could you? She stopped to see me because I was pregnant and holdin' too much water. That was the night my daddy took a switch to me in all the wrong places and then I wasn't pregnant no more."

Shelby kept blinking her eyes, trying to keep her mind and sight clear. What was this that she was being told?

Jessie continued sweeping and talking, "Yeah, your mama spoke with mine and said she had to go out to get you some medicine and she would stop and see about me. Well, she shouldn't have done that, Shelby. It made Daddy real mad. Me and my mama both suffered that night. He killed my baby and it wasn't too many weeks after that my mama died. Everybody said it was fever that took her. It wasn't no fever took her. She died right here. Right on that cot you layin' on, wearin' that nightgown you have on. She died right here and it was my daddy who killed her."

Silence gathered in the shed and Shelby realized she was holding her breath.

Jessie continued to sweep and to talk, her head down, straight brown hair swinging, "I tried to keep her alive, but he poisoned her. Then he come after me again. It was always like that. He would beat on her and then love on me. It was his baby that he killed that night, Shelby. It was my daddy's baby in my belly."

CHAPTER THIRTY-NINE
UNRAVELING

LUCAS STARED AT THE YEARBOOK AGAIN. He had found Jessie in a group picture taken in a classroom. Apparently, she was a couple years older than Shelby. Last name Johnson. Why didn't he remember her? He had never put together that she was a Greenup County kid. Without looking up he hollered, "Bessie, bring me some more of this wicked brew, will ya?"

The older woman was standing in his doorway with a steaming pot of coffee in an instant.

"How in hell do you do that, Bessie? I barely got the words out."

"Oh, Chief, I was on my way. I figured your cup would be gettin' empty about now."

He smiled. "Tell me, does the name Johnson ring a bell with you? I keep thinkin' there's somethin' about that, somethin' from a long time ago?"

Bessie poured the coffee into his cup and got thoughtful for a moment. "Johnsons. Now there was a sorry lot, if ever there was one. Father no good, the mother useless, and the daughter just a victim. Real shame."

"Why? I can't put it together. What was their story?"

"Lester and Jean Johnson both died within weeks of each other, and their girl, Jessie, was left to be thrown into different foster homes in the area. She run off somewheres over in Ohio not long after her parents died. Martha found her and brought her back to take care of Sorina."

"Martha found Jessie?"

"Yeah, up in Columbus somewheres. You know how Martha was, always lookin' out for the unfortunates. And Jessie was a sweet girl, but kinda pitiful. Never said much."

"Here I thought Jessie and Sorina had just always been together.

Martha was so tightlipped about how the two of them come to the cottage. I never knew Jessie was from around here."

"Well, Martha was very protective of Jessie and Sorina both. She knew Jessie had come through somethin' pretty bad when she was no more than a kid. Everybody just let it alone. So strange. It was like nobody knowed that family had ever existed after they were gone, and nobody wanted to know. They had always kept to themselves. Total hermits. Don't you remember when Jean died, Chief? I think you was on that run."

"I was? I sure as hell don't remember. How can I not remember that?"

"Well, it wasn't too long after Neely died. Martha was tore up, and I think your head and heart was all tied up in knots over all that. The Johnsons were not too important to the folks around here."

"That ain't no excuse. But between you and me, Bessie, I was hittin' the bottle pretty hard back then. I was young enough I could still drink and keep it together most times, but sometimes…"

"I know, hon. I remember." She smiled. "But what made you ask about the Johnsons?"

"Oh, just a hunch. We're diggin' for anything that could lead us to Shelby, you know? And now there's Sorina's poisoning to unravel."

"Well, I believe you will figure it all out, Lucas. You always have. Just a matter of time."

Luke smiled at the woman who had been a mainstay around the station house longer than anybody. It was comfortable just knowing she was still there. "Thanks, Bessie, and thanks for the great cup of joe. It's always best when you make it."

"Only the best for you, Chief." She blushed behind her pink rouge and left him alone with his thoughts.

So Martha had had a hand in bringing Jessie back to the county and then moving her in with Sorina. He should have known that, but it was as Bessie said, nobody cared enough to ask. Martha probably just wanted the young girl to have a chance. *Wonder how much of the "pretty bad" had she come through?*

Sorina smiled at the aide who helped her back into bed. She was walking some in the hospital and she was feeling her strength return little by little. She was still getting IV fluids and the poison was leaving her system slowly but surely. *Poison?* Sorina kept trying to replay the past few days in her head. How had she gotten poisoned? In her blindness maybe she had grabbed the wrong jar of herbs in the kitchen. But Jessie was meticulous about her placement of everything so Sorina could find things. They had worked out a system years ago that worked beautifully. Sorina felt totally comfortable moving about in the cottage, familiar with where everything was.

But somehow she had gotten poison into her system, slowly, continuously. Surely she couldn't have made a mistake like that over and over. *Unless?* Unless Jessie had moved things in the kitchen on purpose to confuse her. But why would she do that? Why would Jessie do anything that would harm her? No, it just didn't make sense. But the doctor said the poison came from a plant. A plant from one of Jessie's gardens. Just didn't make sense. Nothing made sense anymore.

Sorina closed her eyes and tried to focus. There was something that was gnawing at her, something from long ago. But she couldn't put her finger on it. It felt like unraveling, like something bound up was letting loose. She was beginning to remember something else, somebody else… Sorina fell asleep wondering who or what it was.

Lizbeth and Samuel lingered as long as they could under the tree before they knew they had to move on. The light of the day was gone and they were cloaked in darkness. They still didn't hear any dogs. Maybe they had eluded their captors at last. Lizbeth let Samuel pull her to her swollen and cut feet, but she no longer felt any pain. They were just numb. She wobbled and then found a way to straighten her spine and stand tall. Samuel wrapped his muscular arms around her and she felt tears of joy spring up inside her. Maybe they would live through this all the way to the other side?

The other side of the river? The other side of this life?

Could that be possible? He kissed her forehead and then took her by the hand and they were walking again.

"Samuel, how do you know where we's sposed to go? How can you know?"

He smiled down on her and stopped walking. He turned to her and spoke softly, "I has studied on what has been tole me, Lizbeth. 'Member when they brung Solomon back after he run oft? That was when I started to thinkin' I wanted to try. He tole me he nearly made it and then he took a cut on his leg real bad and he couldn't go no further. The dogs run him down. But before dat, he say he was real close, real close to the lady's house. He tole me of a way to follow the sky. He say the black men from the Africa land used the sky to do mos everything. To hunt and find food, to find shelter and protect they selves from the storms. He say they could always find they way home by lookin' at the sky above." Samuel pointed to the sky filled with incandescent starlight.

Lizbeth followed his gaze as he traced a pattern with his finger around the North Star. With Samuel's face turned toward the blue black sky, his dark head outlined in the star shine, he looked godlike to Lizbeth. I bet he's disappearin', she thought to herself. He was so quiet, so still. So elsewhere.

But then he dropped his hand and looked back down at her. "I has got turnt around some, tho. I knowed I took us in the wrong direction for a little while, but now I really think we is right agin. I really think so." He grabbed her hand. "Is you ready, Lizbeth? We's gittin' close. I can feel it."

She nodded numbly and again followed him through the trees. She followed him through shades of all things frightening and unknown. She followed him through the startling whisk of branches and leaves smacking them as they trod through their tangled limbs. She followed him through open patches of uneven ground, threatening to bring their twisted ankles to the dark earth. She followed him through eerie, exotic sounds of the forest, daring the lovers to give into unbridled fear.

She followed him

They went on and on and Lizbeth never let go of Samuel's hand and Samuel never quit looking up to the sky every few feet. He was sure footed as he had never been and she believed he would lead them through the danger, through the impossible journey that would bring them to safety.

She believed and she followed…

"Lucas, it's Bella. I have some things to tell you. Now that we think it's Jessie who might have a hand in all this, there are things you should know."

Lucas hung up, and picked up his gun belt. He put it on and walked out into the hallway of the station, passing through the front desk area to the door. "Bessie, I'm goin' over to Bella's. Russell is on his way over here. Tell him where I'm at. I shouldn't be long."

"Will do, Officer Chambers. Tell Bella I said hey."

"Sure thing." Luke tipped his hat to Bessie on his way out of the door. He got into the patrol car and put it in gear. *Now what in the world did Bella have to say that he didn't already know?* In ten minutes he was turning into her long driveway. Her property never ceased to amaze him. She was such a down-home woman; it was hard to imagine that she was so well off. Her husband, Jared, had seen to that. He had been a preeminent surgeon before arthritis forced him to give up his practice, which led to his becoming hospital administrator. He remained in that powerful position in Ashland until his heart attacked him suddenly, leaving Bella a widow nearly ten years ago.

As Lucas approached her doorstep he once again wondered why Bella had remained in such an enormous home that bordered on being an estate. There had to be a lot of hard memories still. Jared had been a real piece of work, with an ego that had no end. Bella was the only one who could control him, and control him she did, as much as anybody could have. Luke knew she had cared for her husband, but he also believed that she had been somewhat relieved when he had left this life and left her alone to do and be as she wanted. She seemed to relax the moment they put him in the ground.

Lucas knocked on the brass knocker and waited until Bella opened the door and waved him in. He smiled at her and took off his cowboy hat. "Where's the maid, Bella? I always think there should be a maid opening the door?"

"You can leave your hat on, Lucas. For god's sake, I ain't makin' you take your boots off, am I? And quit fantasizing about a French maid. Sally comes when I need her, but I don't always need her." Bella winked.

He put his hat back on with a short bow and followed her into a room off the hall where two snifter glasses sat abreast a bottle of cognac. "Wanna snort?" She asked as she lifted the bottle.

"Does a bear shit in the woods?" He smiled at her and took the crystal glass she handed him. He sat down in a soft leather chair and enjoyed the smell of the French brandy and the feel of the luxurious furniture before he took a sip. It burned in his chest deliciously. "Damn, Bella, I still can't believe you live this way. Don't you ever get tired of rattling around in this big old house all by yourself?"

"Well, I do have my amusements, Lucas. It's not like I'm all that lonely. Besides, I like this big old house. And until somebody comes along offerin' me somethin' better, I'm content." She winked again and sat down in a chair across from him.

Is she flirting with me? Lucas took another drink and looked at the woman who had been a friend to him and Martha for more years than he cared to remember. She was as vital and full of energy as she had been years ago when she had to practically run to keep up with her busy job being Jared's wife. And she didn't look worn for the wear either. She really was an attractive woman. She had been childless and the way he remembered it, it was by choice. "Bella, it still surprises me that you didn't want a brood of your own to inhabit these big rooms."

"Sometimes that surprises me, too. But Jared didn't have time for it and I didn't really want to raise up somebody who was never gonna go away." She laughed and Lucas noticed how her earrings sparkled when she moved her head. She took another drink. "I don't think I woulda been much good at it anyway, so I think God just made that decision for me. Here, hon, let me fill your glass again. You're gonna need it."

Lucas let her pour him another drink, but he knew he was going to sip this one slowly. "Why am I gettin' nervous, Bella? Time is wastin'. Spill it."

She put down her glass. Her brown eyes looked almost black in the dim light of the spacious room. She took a deep breath like she was steadying herself. Then she spoke, "You remember all those years ago when Neely was in that awful wreck out on 23?"

He nodded. "Sure. Everybody remembers that."

"Well, what you might not remember is that Neely had stopped over to the Johnson's house before that wreck ever happened. She was over there because Jean Johnson had called and asked her to check on Jessie. She was worried about her girl because she was pregnant and havin' some problems."

"Jessie was pregnant?"

"God, you really *were* drinkin' too much in them days, Lucas. A girl who is just barely old enough to have her period, and then gets pregnant is somethin' most folks pays attention to. Of course, the Johnsons weren't anybody's favorite neighbors. They was kinda the keep-to-yourself type, if you get me? Real loners. Neely was the only one they would allow on their property. And when I say they, I really mean Jean, and only when Lester was gone all day out in the fields.

"Martha hated Neely goin' over there, but she couldn't stop her. There was stuff goin' on with that family that Neely just couldn't ignore." Bella sipped thoughtfully on the cognac.

"So Jessie was a pregnant teenager and her folks didn't like that much, I guess? Not such an unusual story." Lucas couldn't see what the big deal was.

"Well, it wasn't so much that she was pregnant at such a young age—it was more who got her that way." Bella took another sip.

"Bella?" Lucas was losing his patience.

"It was Lester that got her that way, Luke. Her own daddy raped her and got her pregnant. Apparently, he had been forcin' himself on her for years before that."

"Good God." Lucas pictured the doe-like pretty face of that shy girl. What kind of hell had she lived through?

Bella nodded and said, "Martha always had a soft spot for the girl. And after her parents both died and Jessie run off, Martha kept an eye out and finally found her up in Columbus. That's when she brought her home and let her move in the cottage to help with Sorina. Martha asked that we never bring up the past and we always honored her wishes. After all, Jessie was such a sweet thing, so quiet, and she seemed to love Sorina. So we all just left things be. Martha really saved that girl's life."

"Well, that sounds like Martha all right. Always pullin' somebody out of a sinkin' boat. But, Bella, none of that explains why Jessie would want to harm Sorina, or Shelby for that matter?"

"I'm bettin' it's just the old green-eyed monster. Jessie was torn up when Martha died. I mean, Martha was her protector in this world. Her safe place, you know? So with Shelby's return and Sorina dotin' over her a little too much, it probably scared Jessie into thinkin' her safe world was gonna disappear. There's just no tellin' what was goin' on in her mind."

CHAPTER FORTY
HOPE

SHELBY STIRRED AND LAY with her eyes closed in the comfort of her sleepiness. A thrill ran through her as she tried to bring the vision back. She had seen them again. She had seen Lizbeth and Samuel with such clarity. She had seen as Lizbeth watched Samuel explain how the stars guided him. She had felt the hope in Lizbeth's heart. Hope. There was hope. Shelby smiled to herself and then opened her eyes and remembered. She started to sit up and realized she was tethered with chains to the bed. She wanted to scream. But she didn't. And she didn't struggle. She just lay back down and looked at her captor. Jessie was sitting in a chair just watching her.

"Hello, Jessie."

"Hello, Shelby Jean."

Neither woman said another word for five full minutes. Jessie just sat and stared and Shelby tried to meet her gaze without looking terrified. Then Jessie finally got up and stepped across the room to where a teapot sat on a hot plate. Steam rolled out into the room. She poured the hot liquid into a cup and added leafy herbs. Then she stirred it and walked back towards Shelby's bed.

"Would you like some of my organic tea?"

Shelby looked at the steaming cup and wondered about what organic poison it contained. Sweat broke out on her forehead and she thought she might throw up.

Jessie got closer, but Shelby didn't move from her supine position on the bed. She lay perfectly still and found herself pursing her lips.

"Don't you want the tea, Shelby? It's not fattenin'." Jessie didn't smile, didn't have any expression at all. She just kept coming closer with the cup.

Shelby turned her head hard to the left to get her lips farther away. She knew Jessie was going to force the fluid into her. She felt panic rise in her chest and again she fought back the bile filling her throat. Her heart took her panic to a new level as Jessie got closer and closer with the cup. Shelby's cheek flushed from the steam. Jessie's words came back to her. *She died right here. Right on that cot you layin' on, wearin' that nightgown you have on. She died right here and it was my daddy who killed her. He poisoned her.*

"Get that away from me, Jessie!" She swung her tethered arm as far as she could. It was far enough. She knocked the fragile cup out of Jessie's hand. The porcelain hit the floor and broke into a hundred pieces and the hot liquid ran into the cracks, sinking into the wood.

Jessie stared at her empty hand and at the broken glass. She watched the tea roll away and disappear. She looked back at Shelby who had turned toward her. Jessie opened her mouth and groaned angrily as she pulled her hand back and slapped Shelby full in the face. The hard smack stung Shelby's cheek and brought tears to her eyes.

"Now, why did you go and break my cup, Shelby Jean? I thought you might want some tea. Ain't you thirsty?" Jessie's doe eyes had taken on the look of a mad woman. Her brown, straight hair was tangled and her whole body was shaking.

"Jessie, why are you doing this? Why are you trying to kill me? Why?" Now Shelby was shaking and crying.

Jessie brought her own face within inches of Shelby's. Close enough that Shelby could smell her acrid breath. Jessie spit on her. Spittle ran down Shelby's chin and her tears mixed with the fluid. She wailed loudly and Jessie pulled back. She turned from her and walked away. Shelby squeezed her eyes shut from fear of what would happen next, but she heard the door open and close. She was gone. Blessedly, Jessie was gone.

Caitlin held the bracelets in her hand and examined them closer. They were beautifully hand crafted and the gems glistened in the soft light of the trailer. *Martha's jewelry.* Shelby had talked about how unique it was. She thought in another place and time it could have made her grandmother famous. Cait had to agree with her, looking at the interesting designs etched into the metal. But fame was not to be. Probably something Martha would never have wanted, even if the opportunity had presented itself. So the jewelry remained in Sorry's Run and almost everyone in town had been gifted at one time or another with the spoils of Martha's "hobby."

These are all such talented people, these Kentuckians.

Cait smiled. And then she thought of Jessie, and the remarkable musician and singer she was. A cold shiver ran over her spine. *Still waters run deep?* What an understatement if all they were suspecting was true.

She had been nosying around the trailer in an attempt to find something that could be a clue to Shelby's disappearance. All she had found was more and more evidence that Martha McBride had led a wonderful life. There were countless cards and letters from people thanking her for helping little Johnnie with his ear infection, for taking care of Henry's busted ankle, for bringing hope to a whole family who had lost everything in a storm. They went on and on. Dedications to a woman who had given so much of herself. And yet, Shelby had rarely been a part of her life.

Cait found a photo album that looked to be as old as the hills that surrounded them. An 8 by 10 photograph of Wesley, Neely and a very young Shelby was the only picture of Martha's immediate family. They were so beautiful. Even Wesley looked handsome and happy.

She and Russell had stopped over at the farmhouse earlier in the day to visit with Wesley and see how he was doing, hoping maybe he had come up with something that could lead them to Shelby. As much as he was visibly shaken by Shelby's ongoing disappearance, he looked strong and healthy. Whatever his daughter had done for him or to him was a miracle. But he looked like he wasn't sleeping much. He had dark circles under his eyes.

And he was stoned.

Russell had commented later to Cait, "His *crop* is probably keeping him together. Better than whiskey for keeping his nerves intact, you know?"

They hadn't stayed long and Wesley promised to call if he thought of anything.

Caitlin stared again at the family portrait. They all looked so happy. Had they ever been? Once upon a time maybe? Neely was long gone and Wesley had spent the bulk of his life pissed off. If only Shelby could return, maybe things could really be different for father and daughter.

Cait sighed and flipped through the remaining pages of the album.

It got really interesting with old black and white photos of people who appeared to be Martha's Irish ancestors. Even older sepia photographs portrayed the McBride clan with serious faces and stiff bodies. There were countless postcards of Ireland.

As far as Cait knew, Martha had never actually made it to the "Green Isle" itself, so the postcards were probably as close as she could come to knowing the lay of the land. As she leafed through the large book she found funny plastic trinkets glued to pages. Twenty-five cent replicas of Saint this and Saint that, a leprechaun, several four-leaf clovers, shamrocks, harps. Newer pictures were labeled with names: Joel, Sandra, Sean. They were standing outside a rustic cabin. There was a blown-up, faded picture of an old lady in a gingham dress and a toothless grin. "Granny" was written boldly under it.

Two pages contained glued cutouts from magazines; mythical fairies bathed in yellow so they looked all lit up. Another photograph of a young Shelby standing with her pretty mother, Neely, was situated with fairies framing their heads like impish protectors.

And then there was a postcard of a freakish old hag with frightening, blood-red eyes and a devilish grin. It was labeled "Banshee." Next to that picture were three stones taped onto the page. "Rocks on the Roof," it said. Caitlin remembered Shelby telling her about that one. If you heard rocks on the roof when someone was ill it meant death was coming, and the Banshee was the calling card. But if your soul was true and good, the fairies would find you and take your God light back to Ireland. All Irish folklore. Shelby had joked about it, but Cait knew there was a part of her that bought into all of it. Especially the older she got and the older Martha got.

It was her heritage after all.

"Shelby, wherever you are, I hope you haven't heard any rocks on the roof," she whispered and closed the album.

Her cell phone rang. Bella's name appeared in the display.

"Cait, hon, it's Bella. I have Lucas with me. Is Russell there with you?"

"He's on his way."

"Good. We're comin' to pick you up. You guys sit tight. Cait, we think we know where Shelby is."

CHAPTER FORTY-ONE
CHASING ANOTHER GOOSE

CAIT AND RUSSELL JUMPED in the back seat when the cruiser pulled up. Caitlin was flushed with excitement. "Where is she, Bella? Where are we going?"

Bella explained they had plugged Jessie Johnson's old home place address into the GPS and it was some ten miles off of 23.

"We can't be sure, but from what Bella has told me about Jessie's family history, it's a good lead."

"Have you been out there, Lucas?" Russell asked.

"Apparently I was on the police run when we got the call about Jean Johnson's death, but I'll be damned if I remember. Hell, it was most likely Jessie who made that call. Here, all this time I thought she was from Columbus." Lucas frowned.

"What is Jessie's history, Bella?"

"Oh, hon, now is not a good time. I'll tell you later over a giant bottle of wine."

"Let's just say that this mess keeps gettin' messier," Lucas added.

The foursome got quiet then. Each one imagining what they might find at the Johnson's.

Finally Caitlin spoke, "I think I see what they mean by a country mile. Are we getting close, Lucas?"

"Yeah, we're close. In fact, we're here." Lucas made a hard left onto a weedy gravel driveway that wound through high shrubs and an overgrown field. The property lay down in a hollow, completely secluded by tree-clad hills. There wasn't another house in sight. Lucas started to put his bubble on the roof to announce their presence, but thought better of it. He didn't have a warrant. It was best to keep it at "just visiting" the abandoned place.

He drove the cruiser all the way up to the house, and there was no sign of another vehicle. An old rusty tractor sat between the house and a small barn.

Russell was staring out the car window at the two-story deserted farmhouse. He spoke under his breath, "Makes Wesley's place look like a palace." He whistled and then directed his question to Lucas, "You think it was wise to have brought the girls, Chief?" Russell's voice shook just slightly.

Lucas nodded and looked at the women, "Hell no, but you try tellin' them that."

"Good point. But are we gonna have backup?"

"Well, Deputy, we are not exactly on official business here. I didn't even take the time to get a warrant. So we're just kind of pokin' around." He spoke to Bella, "You girls are here, but you're damned straight not comin' in the house. I want you to stay put. If too much time passes or you hear or see anything that scares you, call 911. You hear me, Bella? Cait?"

The women nodded in assent and Lucas got out of the cruiser. Russell followed him towards the front door of the faded, brown clapboard house. The porch was covered in leaves and debris blown in from years of neglect. Two rusted metal chairs creaked as the men stepped onto the uneven wood surface. Russell's boot heel caught on a roping vine and he nearly tripped.

"Whoa, there, partner. You okay?" Lucas helped steady his deputy.

"Yeah, Chief. I'm all right, but there's no tellin' if this porch is full of holes."

Lucas nodded and opened the torn screened door, giving two loud knocks on the front door. A cat scrambled from behind one of the chairs and ran through their feet, nearly knocking them over.

"Jesus. Where did that come from?" Russell whispered.

"Well, I guess it's his house, not ours." Lucas knocked again and waited for what he thought was an appropriate time and then tried the doorknob.

Locked.

"Come on. Let's go around back."

On the side of the house Lucas and Russell passed steps that led to the cellar. One of the glass panels in the door was busted out. They looked at each other and nodded, knowing that was their way in, but Lucas kept walking around to the back of the house. He knocked on the back door and they waited. Russell peered through the dirty windows into the kitchen. Nothing looked disturbed. The counters and sink were clear of any dishes. The kitchen table still had salt and pepper shakers sitting at its center. An uncanny silence lay over the hollow, making it feel as though nobody had stepped foot on the property since the Johnson's had all gone.

The back door, too, was locked, so they went back to the side steps leading to the cellar. Lucas used his covered elbow to knock out the rest of the glass on the broken panel of the door and he reached inside and turned the lock to let them in. It took some pushing to open the door over the shifted and cracked concrete floor. Another cat ran through Russell's legs, bolting through the open door to the outside.

"Goddamn!"

Lucas ignored his partner and went on in to the main room of the basement. The whole placed reeked of cat piss. They both covered their noses and walked through the empty gray rooms slowly. It was cold and damp in the basement. There was enough light coming through the high windows and the door to allow visibility without a flashlight. There was no sign of anybody.

Lucas found the steps leading upstairs and Russell followed him up to the first floor. Again, there was no sign of anybody, but another cat jumped off a moth-eaten chair in the corner of the small living room. Lucas grinned at the increasing disgust on Russell's face. The ceilings were low and angled. The dirt-covered windows afforded only dim lighting into the house. Lucas walked to the front window, standing where Cait and Bella could see him. He indicated all was okay, but he could see they weren't buying it.

"I think the girls are havin' a hissy fit."

Russell joined him at the window and gave the okay sign, too, but he, too, could see Caitlin's face puckered up, like she was ready to cry. His heart swelled and he fought the urge to unlock the front door and go comfort her.

Lucas nodded at him and they kept moving through the house. Each room was small, minimally furnished and deserted. They opened every door and found some threadbare clothes still hanging in the closets. The second floor was more of the same; only the bare necessities left by people who hadn't lived a happy life. Nothing in the sparse furnishings suggested joy or comfort, only a cold life devoid of human happiness. The room that must have been Jessie's was the most depressing. It was apparent a young girl had lived there by the weak attempts at some kind of feminine identity. A few pictures from magazines were pasted onto the drab green walls. They were photographs of country music legends, Patsy Cline, Loretta Lynn, Emmylou Harris. And there were other magazine pages thrown under the bed, pictures of movie stars and big beautiful houses and cars. It was the stuff of dreams and this was the one place in the house where the dreaming most likely happened.

"Poor kid." Lucas was looking at a holey rag doll that was the only thing in the room suggestive of a play thing.

Russell had the door open to the closet. He had moved some of the hanging clothes enough to see a large shoebox sitting on the floor next to a pair of dirty tennis shoes. He picked up the box and brought it out, placing it on the bed. Inside the box were more pages torn from magazines. "Chief, take a look at this."

Each glossy page contained pictures of Shelby Jean Stiller.

Shelby on a flashy runway in a New York fashion show. Shelby wearing the latest line of designer dresses. Shelby's lovely face promising that with the right shade of lipstick you too could look like her. Shelby everywhere. Young, beautiful, glamorous.

Russell and Lucas split up the pile. Lucas took the bottom half and began leafing through each picture. "Here we go." Lucas pointed to the first of many photographs where someone had taken a black magic marker to the page. One had a bold line drawn right through Shelby's face. Another had a giant X crossing over her elegantly-clad figure. And then finally Shelby's images depicted on the photos were completely blacked out with the marker.

Lucas and Russell stared at the mutilated photographs and then back at each other.

"At least Carny enjoyed his pictures. This sure says somethin'," Russell spoke.

"Yeah, like a thousand words. Let's go check the barn."

They left the house the same way they came in, locking the basement door again. Russell followed him back around to the front of the house. When they passed the cruiser, Cait opened her door and started to get out. Lucas threw his hand up and gave her a look. She shut the door and stayed put.

They walked over to the barn and went in. Lucas remarked, "I would say this is where the man of the house spent most of his time." He picked up one of the many rifles that were hung on a far wall above a ratty couch in the corner of the barn. It wasn't loaded, but there were bullets on the arm of the couch. A small television sat on a stand next to a coffee table and a refrigerator was next to it. Luke opened the fridge and found two bottles of Budweiser and a moldy chunk of cheese. The ice box reeked from nonuse. The rest of the barn was filled with farm equipment and tools; everything needed to manage a few acres of tobacco. The barn had a small hay loft. Once again, they found no sign of anybody having been there for years. More cats nestled in the corners. These cats didn't even bother to move as the intruders roamed about looking in every nook and cranny.

After a time, they gave up and went back to the cruiser.

"Nothing?" Caitlin's nerves had gotten the best of her. She was crying. Russell put his arm around her in the back seat.

"Didn't find anythin', but we just might have a motive," Lucas explained what they found in the shoebox.

"So, the old green-eyed monster?" Bella asked as Lucas drove back down the drive.

"Yeah, I'd say your gut instinct was right on, Bella. It ain't too hard to figure. A young girl like that, pretty, talented, and not able to have a life. No chance for nothin'. Just not fair." Lucas was trying to imagine what a lonely and horrifying existence Jessie must have had in that barren place with those parents. At least from what Bella had told her, Jean tried to do right. But she was a victim, too, and the old man had the women completely under his wrap.

Bella added, "Martha always did say Lester was no good. Real white trash, fightin' all the time, dropping out of school in the eighth grade. He stayed ignorant and never did give a shit about anybody. Wouldn't have nothin' to do with nobody. This was his parents' place, and from what she said, the Johnson's was not the type who should have begot."

"God, what a horrible way for a young girl to live. But what has she done? Where has she got Shelby?" Caitlin had stopped crying, but her shoulders still quivered.

Lucas answered, "I don't know. I thought sure we would find her out here. But I'd say with the pictures we discovered, combined with the poison garden and an attempt on Sorina's life, we have enough to put out a warrant for her arrest."

He punched in the number to the station on his cell. "Bessie, this is Chief Chambers. I want an APB put out on Jessie Johnson for kidnappin' and attempted murder."

"I'm on it, Chief."

Wesley poured himself a shot of bourbon. He sat down at his kitchen table and took a deep drag off the joint. He knew this was a dream come true. Just being alone to do whatever the hell he wanted. He had never been good at the father thing, the husband thing, and now he was rid of those burdens.

So why do I feel like a piece of shit?

He knew the answer. It was clear. When Shelby did the "healing" he wanted her gone. It was like in one moment she had become her mother. Hell, she even looked like her mother, only prettier, if that was possible. And when she pulled that witch stunt on him it brought him right back to those years of Neely running off to who knew where doing who knew what, supposedly curing people of their ailments. He wanted no part of it. It scared him. She scared him. Then, when he would hear the scuttlebutt about her being a witch, it unnerved him in a violent way. He just wanted the woman to be regular, to stay at home and cook the meals and clean the house and raise the kid. He didn't take to her running off every night like she did. And he knew she wasn't whoring around. That wasn't it. It wasn't Neely's style. No. He knew she believed herself to be some kind of witch doctor.

She had tried to explain it to him, the healing "gift" that she had inherited. She called herself a "faerie doctor." That had sounded like some kind of liberal shit that he didn't even want to think about, but she had just laughed and said, "It's not what you're thinkin', Wes. I'm speakin' of Irish fairies comin' from ancient druid's blood; the little ones that protect our light in this world and track our ways. The fairies that stay with me all the time and help me to help others. That's what I mean."

He knew she got all of the Irish bullshit from Martha. But with Martha it was different. She was funny and harmless. But his woman? His Neely? She was something else altogether. He wanted her for himself. But she gave more to the lowlifes in the county than she ever did to him and her own daughter.

And now Shelby had come down with the same "sickness." The healing sickness, he called it. None of this made-up faerie doctor crap. And as if to prove him right, in no time at all it had put Shelby in harm's way. But the part that really stuck in his crawl was that he felt wrong.

And Wesley had never felt wrong. The whole world could be wrong, but not him. He was the king of his kingdom and the hell with everybody else. But not now. Now he felt like he had made a terrible mistake kicking Shelby out of the house. He could have kept her safe had she stayed, especially once she made him well. They could have been father and daughter again. Now he felt young again, felt strong.

Felt empty.

He kept remembering Shelby as a little girl. It was like he had Neely the way he wanted her, innocent and crazy about him, hanging onto his every word. The little girl was everything he wanted his wife to be. But the more she grew up, the more she grew to be like her mother, and he couldn't keep her down. Nothing could keep Shelby Jean down. She had her mother's gifts and her father's stubbornness. It's why she left when she did. And why she never came back. He had lost her all those years ago when she was a teenager. And now, just when he had a chance to make things right, his own foolish temper had chased her off again.

He took a deep drink of the whiskey, and wiped away a tear from his cheek. What was this he was feeling? It felt foreign, like he had taken a drug. *Maybe it's all the weed making me soft.* But he knew it was simple enough. He missed her. He missed his daughter. And it was killing him to think someone would want to harm her.

And who? They were thinking it was the shy, pretty girl who took care of the crazy Sorina. Jessie? It was a real stretch to think that girl could harbor the kind of hate necessary to pull off a murder or kidnapping. But apparently she had grown the poisonous plants that had almost killed Sorina. That much was real. And he knew there was something about her family. He remembered Lester. A real son of a bitch. He thought back to an encounter with Lester a few weeks before Neely had been killed in the wreck.

Wesley had been at The Pit Stop throwing back a few beers when Lester came in blind drunk. He almost fell into the bar, and demanded a PBR. John Tyler was behind the bar as usual and told Lester he had some coffee he'd give him, but no beer. Lester went off on him and tried to crawl over the bar after John. His foot got twisted on a bar stool and he fell to the floor. But as drunk as he was, he jumped up with amazing speed. He was shouting something. His words ran together and he just kept yelling and talking gibberish. He was a scary man. Real bad scary. He even scared Wesley, and that wasn't easily done.

John was on the phone calling the police, and Lester was taking another swing at John, who kept ducking just in time. Three good old boys who worked the barges, and together must have weighed upwards of 800 pounds, came up behind him and got him in an arm lock. Even totally restrained, Lester never shut up. His eyes rolled back in his head and then focused on something or someone who wasn't there. Wesley knew that look. He had been behind drunken, glazed eyes like that. Lester was gone. His red eyes rolled from side to side, not seeing anybody or anything and he shouted, his bloated chest all puffed in pride, "I gotter in the shed! I got the bitch. I fucked her raw!" His mouth curled in a demonic smile. That's when the barge boys took him down.

CHAPTER FORTY-TWO
SINKING, SINKING...

SWEET MANDOLIN MUSIC WAFTED over her head as Shelby opened her eyes. She felt light as a feather. Looking down, she giggled to see her naked toes dancing delicately over tall grass rolling over a velvety ground. High, round hills above her shimmered in emerald green. Deep green moss lay over black tree trunks. Sparkles decorated the sky like effervescent fireflies lighting up all the dark places in silver gleams. It was a magical place, this place of legend. It made her think of Kentucky. Her beloved hills in Kentucky were like this, but there was no dirt here, no mud here, no brown here. Only the greenest green. She watched, mesmerized, as the fireflies floated down from the sky. They weren't fireflies at all. They flitted and dangled in the air all around her, as if on sparkling webs. Their tiny wings were all glittery and moved the air around her head in a sweet breeze, fragrant, delicious. She took a deep breath and looked up at the hills.

There she was. Grandma Mart. Way up high on one of the hills. Her white hair gleamed as bright as the fairies all around her. "Grandma Mart, come down from there. Why are you so far away?" Martha waved a pale arm and Shelby could tell she was smiling. "I miss you, Grandma. I need you. But where is mother? Neely should be with you in my dreams. Why isn't she here?"

Martha's white head nodded slowly and then turned to look elsewhere. Her smiling expression changed. A darkness was coming. The sparkling fairies converged to keep the light around Shelby. There was so much light she was nearly blinded. But the green around her was fading, growing dull as deep shade moved over everything. Her grandmother was trying to tell her something, but she couldn't hear.

The fairies were too loud. Thousands of tiny wings flapping made the wind whistle with their frantic movement. Then she saw it. The Banshee was there on the hill next to Martha. The Banshee waved, too, to Shelby. Its red eyes flashed out of the frightening visage of an old hag. It laughed a cruel laugh. The Banshee wore a long black cape that blew around it in dark foreboding waves. It beckoned its long dark arm to her to follow. All the while her grandmother was shouting to her.

"What is it, Grandma Mart? What are you trying to tell me? I see her. I see the Banshee, but I don't think she has come for me. The fairies are protecting me. Come closer. Come away from the Banshee. Come down off the hill. The sweet fairies will keep your light safe, too. Come."

But her grandmother couldn't hear her and she couldn't hear her grandmother. All she could hear was the high cackle reverberating through the trees on the hills all around. It drowned out everything. The darkness overtook the emerald green and the fairies started to fade. She wished her mother would come. She couldn't see her grandmother anymore. The Banshee had disappeared, too.

But now the hills, her beloved hills, were covered in mud and dirt. She looked down and her feet were buried in mud. She was sinking in it. She cried to the fairies, "The Banshee wasn't for me. I haven't heard the rocks on the roof. I haven't heard them. It's not my time. I haven't heard them!"

The mandolin grew louder and found a high note and sustained it as she felt herself sinking, sinking…

"Shelby Jean. You wake up now. You've made a mess. We have to clean you up."

Shelby shook herself awake from what had turned into a horrifyingly real nightmare. But even awake, the nightmare continued. Jessie was standing over her. She had a mandolin in one hand and a pistol in the other.

Shelby gasped in fear and Jessie looked down at the gun. She smiled. "Oh, no. I'm not gonna shoot you, Shelby. You and I are not done yet. No. But we do have to clean you up. Just look at yourself."

Shelby started to cry as Jessie handed her disposable wipes. Jessie just watched in silence as Shelby stretched her tethered hands enough to wipe between her legs. The humiliation was almost more than the fear.

When she had wiped herself clean, Jessie handed her a trash can. Then she gave her a glass of water with a straw and let her drink. After setting the water glass down, Jessie stared at the pistol in her hand. She seemed to be lost in thought. Shelby held her breath. Then, without saying a word, Jessie put the gun down and brought the mandolin up and began to play, as though it was possible to forget that she had a woman held prisoner right in front of her. Jessie's pure, high voice picked up the lonesome melody and she sang. The beauty of her voice was so contrary to the horror of the situation, Shelby thought she would scream.

She sings like an angel. How can she be evil?

Shelby's confusion was growing more intense with each passing hour of her strange captivity. She knew if she didn't get some answers soon she would die anyway.

She shut her eyes tight and listened. She tried to let the beautiful music transport her away. She tried Samuel's slave trick of disappearing. But she couldn't do it. She didn't know how much longer her conscious mind would allow this insanity to go on. She kept squeezing her eyes and took deep breaths. If only she could lay hands on Jessie she felt she could sooth her hurt, her anger. She needed to lay healing hands on her. But she was tied. She was powerless.

Jessie played for a long time. And then suddenly, not even at a logical end, she quit. The music just stopped. Shelby was more afraid now than she had ever been. She was afraid to open her eyes, but she could feel Jessie's presence very close to her.

Finally, she looked.

Jessie's pretty face was right above hers. Her large doe eyes were staring right into Shelby's pale green eyes. "You like my music?" She asked.

Shelby managed a nod of her head.

"Sorina always did, too. She said I coulda been a recordin' star. I coulda taken the Music Highway and gone right on down to Nashville and they woulda signed me up. I coulda done that, Shelby Jean. But I didn't. I stayed with Sorina. I stayed because Martha brung me to stay."

She backed away from Shelby and laid the mandolin down on the chair. She walked over to the side of the narrow shed and picked up a broom. She started sweeping and she kept talking, as if to herself, "I could play any instrument I ever touched. They found that out when I was little at the school. I had a gift, they said. Well, my daddy didn't want me to have no gift. He took a switch to me the first time when I come home from school and said I was gonna take lessons. Yeah, he put a stop to that real quick. It weren't long before I couldn't even go to the school. Sometimes I snuck out, but he always caught me and I would be sorry I did. Sometimes a lady would come here and say I had to go to school, but he run her off, too. Everybody was scared of Lester. He was a scary, mean man, Shelby. My mama mostly was scared of him. He used to bring her here when I was little and he let me watch them two. And then he would strap her down and beat on her and she would cry just like you just done. And then he would beat her again. He always made sure I watched.

"I was glad when he killed her. She needed killin'.

"And I was glad when I killed him. He needed killin.'

"Now, I wonder if mebbe it's time you need killin', Shelby Jean. You and Sorina both," she added and smiled wickedly.

Shelby fought back the sob that was choking her. "Why, Jessie? Why?"

"Why? Don't you know, girl? Martha took care of me better than anybody in my life. She give me this mandolin. She give me everything. And I took care of Sorina real good like Martha wanted me to. Martha brung me to take care of Sorina. I fed her and bathed her and we worked things out. We was happy. Then I started readin' to her from that pioneer woman's diary and I even made some of it up as I read. I got lost in the story, too. Me and Sorina was happy thinkin' on that Sori woman from long ago, that strong lady who lived on her own and then helped the Negroes. Them was good stories and Sorina took them as her own. That was okay with me. Because I had a home. I was somebody for the first time in my life.

"And then you come. I knew you lived in New York. Martha always told me one day you would come. But I thought you wouldn't stay. Then, after you had that wreck and you got the healin' gift that was your mama's and your grandma's, I knew different. I could see you changin' towards things. I could see Sorina changin'. She wanted you with her. I could see that.

"I wasn't gonna kill you, Shelby, when I hit you from behind. It was just accidental that I seen you walkin' through the woods to Sorina's. I had my wheelbarrow with me, you know, so I just done it. You never heard me comin' up on you. I knocked you out cold. I was glad I took you. It was my chance to see how Sorina would do with you gone. I wanted to see if she would come back to me and it would be like it was.

"Well, she didn't. She got so lonesome and unhappy that I knew how it was gonna be. I was gonna be out and you was gonna be in. That's when I decided to kill her and you both. I went back and made sure I covered all my tracks from the wheelbarrow. I knew I would use my plants to kill you like my daddy had taught me. I would stay on at the cottage with my music and my animals and my gardens and nobody could hurt me no more.

"That's what I wanted. It was hard, though, Shelby. I always liked you. I did. I didn't really want to harm you. But it just had to be this way. You see? Once Martha was gone, nobody was gonna look after me."

Shelby pleaded, "But that's not true, Jessie. Sorina loves you. She would never let you go. And you and I could be friends."

Jessie stopped and stared at Shelby. "You don't even know."

"What don't I know, Jessie? Tell me."

"You don't even know why Sorina wouldn't want me no more once you come."

Shelby was struggling through tears for Jessie to finish what she had to say. She could almost feel the gun exploding into her brain. Terror shook her whole body.

"You don't even know who she is. You think your mama died in that wreck all them years ago."

Shelby's breath stopped in her chest.

"She didn't die. Neely is alive."

CHAPTER FORTY-THREE
TO OUR GRAVES

BELLA AND LUCAS SAT ON HIS DECK and shared a beer that Saber had just retrieved from the cooler.

"That is a good dog, Lucas."

"Man's best friend."

"Man's only friend, I'm thinkin'. Does anybody come here besides me?" Bella admired the masculine surroundings. The house suited the man.

"Oh, once in a while, but mostly no. After Martha passed I didn't see no reason for socializin'. But Bella, you have to tell me everything. Maybe there's something else that we aren't pickin' up on. I thought sure Jessie would have Shelby at the old place. It made total sense."

"I know. Just makes me sick. But yeah, let me revisit this whole thing one more time. Maybe it will trigger somethin'. So where did I leave off?"

"Your green-eyed monster theory."

"Oh, yeah, that's right. Well, Lucas, there's more. But I gotta back up. It's hard to keep my thoughts in order if I don't run that entire night in my head. You got enough beer?" Bella asked.

"Yeah, dammit, I got enough beer."

"Alrighty then. Here goes. The night that Neely went to the Johnson's house to check on Jessie's condition, she and Lester really got into it. I know this because I spoke with Jean after Neely's wreck and she told me. She said that Neely knew Lester was beatin' on his wife and rapin' his daughter and she was gonna put an end to it. She was goin' to the authorities. I guess it was a pretty bad fight. She went to leave and that's when Lester hauled off and hit her hard up the side of the head, bloodyin' her face. She barely escaped the Johnson's that night with her life, Lucas. Then she gets down the road and doesn't see that semi comin' at her because she was blinded on that side from her bleedin' eye. You didn't work that wreck because that young sheriff over in Fleming County had called you to help out with a homicide. You remember that?"

"Yeah, a homicide that turned out to be a suicide."

"Well, no matter, because I kinda think it was the tides of fortune that had you gone. Otherwise, I don't think things woulda happened the way they did. Anyway, it was amazin' that the accident didn't kill Neely. It was bad. She was transported to the ER and then ICU where they kept her alive. But she was a mess, Lucas. That beautiful young woman was a mess. Her face was torn up completely, and much of her body was broken and shattered. It was awful. I was with Martha at the hospital, and she asked me to go to Wesley's and see that he was okay. That's when I spoke with Jean Johnson. She was callin' to warn Wesley, but I got the phone call instead and I never did tell Wesley.

"Before I go on, Lucas, you have to understand that Martha and I both knew that even if she lived, Neely Stiller was never gonna to be the woman she was. The doctors didn't really expect her to pull through, but they said if she did, chances were she wouldn't be able to function as a normal human bein'. She never recovered consciousness that night in the hospital."

Lucas interrupted, "What was the phone call, Bella? What did Jean Johnson tell you?"

"She told me the whole story about Lester's abuse. She knew he would kill her if he found her talkin' to anybody, but she said that Lester was on a rampage. They had learned of Neely's wreck and how bad off she was on the TV. Jean said Lester was like a mad man. He wanted Neely dead because he knew she was gonna report him and they would blame him for her accident. He knew he would go to jail. So he was on a mission to kill Neely if she didn't die on her own."

"Lester was out to kill Neely?"

"Oh, yeah. If you would have heard Jean's hysterical voice that night you wouldn't have doubted it. Jean said Lester was comin' to the hospital to finish Neely off. He would see to it she wouldn't live through the night. Jean was hysterical. I believed her. And I sure as hell knew better than to tell Wesley.

"So I left Wesley's without tellin' him anything. Lord knows what Wes woulda done with that information. His heart was so black in them days.

But he loved Neely. As bad as he was to her, he loved her. He woulda killed Lester for sure. I figured there was gonna be murders all over the county. So I got in my car and headed back to the hospital in Ashland. By the time I pulled into the parking garage I had a plan."

"Oh, God."

"Oh, yeah. I got back to the hospital and told Martha what Lester was threatenin'. Well, Neely might have been on her death bed anyway, but there was no way her mother was gonna let her baby be killed by that lowlife. So Martha and I, we followed my plan.

"You remember of course that Jared was the big dog at the hospital. Nobody outranked my husband. Except for me. It was his misfortune that I was his only boss in this life." She smiled and took a drink of her beer.

Bella, you are one impressive lady. Lucas was enjoying watching her tell the story.

She continued, "So we finagled a kinda kidnappin'. That night Jared arranged for Neely to be transported by ambulance to OSU's Medical Center Emergency Department. Martha rode with her in the ambulance."

Lucas lowered his beer and nearly missed the table setting it down. He never took his eyes off Bella.

"It's okay, Luke." She patted his hand. "I know this is a lot to take in. Take another drink, hon."

Luke did as Bella suggested. He took a deep drink, followed by a deeper breath. Saber moved in close to his master and laid his head on Lucas' lap. Luke petted the dog. "Go on, Bella."

"You sure?"

He nodded.

"Well, Martha wasn't satisfied with just gettin' her out of Ashland. She had a vibe on Lester that she wouldn't back off of. I will never forget this as long as I live. She looked at me, grabbed my arms, and said, 'We have to make him think she didn't survive the wreck. Bella, we have to fake her death.'

"Well, at first I thought she had truly lost her mind. You know, with the shock and grief of the situation and all. But, as you know, Martha was a very persuadin' person. Soon enough she convinced me that that dirty dog of a man would hunt her little girl down forever until she was dead. I begun to see the truth in that.

"So here was where I really pulled rank on my poor husband. I coerced him to get the house physician to sign a death certificate. Damn, if he didn't do it. And Lucas, there is a statute of limitations, right? I mean, Martha and I was supposed to take this one to our graves?"

Lucas just nodded again, too stunned to speak.

"Well, sure enough, we got the whole staff to think she had died and been taken down to the morgue. I must say I was never in better form than that night. I pulled the whole thing off while Martha and Neely was ridin' down 23 in that ambulance.

"It wasn't hard. The awful way Neely looked after the wreck; there was nobody that questioned that she had died. Martha talked to the police on the phone and said she wouldn't be pressin' any charges against the poor trucker who rammed into Neely. I've often thought about that poor soul, us leavin' him to think he killed somebody. Lord, Lucas, I guess I gotta make that right. I'm gonna burn in hell." Bella thought about that for a moment before continuing, "Anyway, all I had to do was a little bribin' with the coroner, and it was a done deal. Martha and I kept in touch and I put together the funeral and everythin'.

"Lucas, I'm sure you remember how the whole darn county came out to that little affair. And poor Wes. Can you imagine? But me and Martha, we figured somehow we'd make it all right after old Lester could be dealt with, you know? We just acted that night on pure instinct. We just acted and I think we saved her. I really do."

Lucas whistled, letting air out slowly. "Okay. I get that part. But I don't get the rest. If she ain't dead, where is she?"

"I'm gettin' to that," she answered, "but this here part is where it gets pretty weird." Bella raised an eyebrow.

"Oh, yeah, like it's not been weird so far?"

"Well, Martha is in the ambulance flyin' down 23 with her beautiful Neely who is literally hangin' on by a thread. She really didn't know if her baby girl would make it through the night, regardless of what we had done. But she had to come up with a name to give Admissions at the hospital. Martha had always liked the story of the abolitionist woman, so she just blurted out *Sorina Duncan* when they asked for a name. It was in that moment Neely became Sorina."

"Neely became Sorina," Lucas repeated, thinking out loud. He let the words sink in. Then he let out a low whistle, and repeated once more, "Neely became Sorina? Wait. Are you tellin' me that pretty blind woman is Martha's daughter and Shelby's mother?"

"Yes."

"But Bella, none of us recognized her?"

"Well, I'm gettin' to that," she repeated.

Luke's voice rose, "Why in hell wouldn't Martha have told anybody that?"

"Hold on, Lucas. Neely's medical course was horrible. She never even came to for weeks. It was two months before Neely opened her eyes. Those were horrendous days for Martha. You remember how she made up that story about a distant relative in Columbus who she was carin' for and she would spend three to four days there every week. Nobody really questioned her because they figured it was what was keepin' her goin' after Neely's death. Carin' for somebody was always what Martha was doin'. And I was keepin' an eye on Wesley and Shelby for her and makin' all kinds of excuses to anybody who asked. She rented a room in Columbus near the hospital so she could spend nights there, and came home often enough to keep the gossips satisfied.

"The OSU medical staff all believed "Sorina" would never awaken from her coma. And if she did, that her brain function would be minimal. Lucas, they ran every conceivable test to determine all that. It was pretty damned hopeless. Neely should have been brain dead. But Martha wasn't givin' up. No way.

"It ain't hard to imagine that in the end Martha believed she was the one who brought her daughter back from that dark place she was livin' in. She said she brought her back with her healin'. She said it was them Irish fairies that kept Neely's light goin'. Well, don't ask me, but I sure as hell wasn't gonna argue with her. Neely came back all right, with a mind intact, but a memory completely gone. She remembered nothin' of her previous life and they couldn't save her eyesight. She went blind.

"All this time, Martha intended to tell Shelby and Wesley the truth, but the truth was so damned hard she just kept puttin' it off. Besides, after Neely came to, there were countless surgeries she had to endure to fix her body and to fix her face. And they fixed her face, but it was never the same face. You can well imagine how hard a pill that was to swallow. And

Lucas, this went on for years. I got Jared to waive the medical costs with his surgeon cronies in Columbus. Lord, he even picked up the tab for Martha's boardin' room. I'm pretty near positive that Jared went to his deathbed thinking I would blackmail him about what all we did. Bless his heart. But it kept him wrapped good and tight. Got Martha what she needed.

"But poor Martha was leadin' a total double life. Not even Vi and Jolene knew what she was really doin' in those days. 'Course Violet was living in Lexington durin' that time and Jolene was homeschoolin' her kids in the country. It wasn't hard when Martha swore me to secrecy. Neely mostly lived in a rehab center at OSU and was transported back and forth to the hospital every time there was a surgery. I can't tell you how many times, I thought that poor girl would have been better off dead. And every day I expected to hear that she had indeed died. I even started prayin' for it so my best friend could stop what she was doin' and get on with her own life. Thank God my prayers weren't answered."

"Saber, you better bring us more beer," Lucas spoke gently and rubbed his temples.

Bella continued, "Well, life went on, and by this time Shelby Jean had moved to New York where she was a successful model. She started sendin' Martha tons of money. So Martha got another plan goin' in her mind. She got the county's permission to build the cottage around the ruins of the historic McBride cabin. They were tickled pink to let her do it. The only caveat was that she had to preserve the grounds and the stone fireplace. They would let her build, but a plaque had to be placed in front of the property for posterity. Of course, you know that Jared helped us with that little political chore, too. So, Martha took Shelby's money and fixed up the cottage for Neely to come to when she was ready. It was always Martha's plan to tell Shelby then that her mother was alive."

"Well, then, why didn't she?"

"I gotta tell you, it was killin' Martha, but things got so complicated. Even after years passed, Neely never remembered who she was. And her blindness didn't help. As close as she and Martha were, Sorina never did know who Martha was. She thought she had been assigned to her because of her disability. Martha made up some stuff there. She was pretty good at that."

Lucas rolled his eyes. That was an understatement. He remembered all the excuses she had given him over the years to keep him from gettin' too close.

"And Lucas, Neely was happy in her ignorance, you know? I do believe that was the crux of what drove Martha to secrecy. Martha seen her little girl finally comin' through all those horrible years when findin' happiness again had seemed impossible. She didn't have the heart to take that away from her, you know? Let sleepin' dogs lie."

Lucas nodded.

"But in the meantime, of course, the Johnson's were gone, except for their girl, Jessie, who was a runaway. Well, for some strange reason Martha took it upon herself to find Jessie. That was just like Martha. She would take the girl in whose father was the whole reason for the nightmare to begin with." Bella shook her head.

"So Jessie came?" Lucas asked

"Jessie came. And that never was a problem either, because she had grown up real pretty. Nobody even knew who she was. Again, Vi and Jo had never even seen Jessie as a young girl, so they didn't put two and two together. No reason to, you know?

"It all just kinda worked out. And as soon as Neely learned she was livin' in the cottage of Sorina Duncan McBride, and heard the history, she just took on that persona. And that's the woman we all have come to know and love. It's like Neely died and another woman took over her body. In so many ways, that is really what happened."

Lucas let out another slow whistle and said, "And I completely bought into that story that Sorina was a distant relation of Martha's that she took under her wing to fill the void after she lost Neely."

"That's what everybody thought. We made it so, and we kept it so. But Martha was eaten up with her neglect of Shelby, and she wanted more than anything to make it right. She wanted Shelby to know she had a mother, even if they never told Sorina. That was why Martha insisted on Shelby comin' when she did. Wesley was pretty bad off, and truth be told, I think Martha was thinkin' her time was comin'. She wanted Shelby to know before it was too late. And then, damn it, if it wasn't too late." Bella sighed and finished her beer.

"Who all knows this story, Bella?"

"Only me, and now you, Lucas. And of course, Jessie."

"Jessie knows who Sorina really is?"

"Yes. So that's why I think jealousy is the real motive. Once Shelby came back, Jessie knew things would never be the same. Of course, you know we must be dealin' with a sick mind there anyway. So damn sad."

Bella got quiet and Lucas just tried to let it all sink in. It was a hell of a story. But things were starting to make more sense.

His cell phone rang and he saw Wesley's name there. "Yeah, Wes. No. Man, I'm sorry. We didn't find anything. We looked all over that house and basement and the barn. There was no sign of nobody. Huh? What's that you say about a shed way up in the hillside? Wes, we didn't see a shed."

He hung up and called Russell. "I'll pick you up. We need to get a search warrant. And Russell, this time we better have some backup."

Sorina woke up to annoying hospital sounds; whooshing of machines and constant bells and whistles. Then there were the nurses and aides and maintenance people that passed through the rooms and the outside hall on a nonstop basis.

How in the world can a body rest in a place like this? But something about it seemed so familiar. Like she had spent a lot of time in just such a place.

Sorina's thoughts turned to the slave vision. She had seen them again, Lizbeth and Samuel. It was the first time their flight had felt hopeful, like they would make it to freedom. Sori felt a thrill as she realized once again that Shelby had to be alive. She had never seen the vision so clearly until Shelby had come into her life, had joined her in clairvoyance. It had to be so. She just had to be alive. She just had to be.

Even in Sorina's weakened state she felt excited. She wanted to get well, to get out of the hospital and back to her cottage. With her strength slowly returning she felt it was possible that she would feel Shelby more strongly and maybe even find her. She just had to get home.

Her thoughts traveled back to Jessie. She cared for Jessie, but had never understood her completely. The girl had been at her beck and call for more years than she could remember. And yet, she knew so little of her. Jessie never would speak of her past or her family. Of course, it had been the same with Sorina since she had no memory of a life before the cottage. So the two women had a special bond. They literally started with clean slates and methodically created the lives they wanted.

But Sorina knew Jessie *had* memories. They had to be painful ones. Sometimes Sorina would hear her crying late into the night. But Jessie seemed content to live her life with Sorina, to care for her, to plant gardens and make her music. Jessie and Sorina had been happy.

Or had they?

If that was true, why would Jessie try to poison the one person she cared for the most? Why? When she thought back, Sorina should have noticed a change in Jessie when those remarkable women came walking into what had been a very closed world. Jessie's world. And Sorina probably doted on the New Yorkers more than anybody. Caitlin and Shelby were shining stars. It had all been so exciting. Especially when she became aware that Shelby had opened up a fount after her car accident and was allowing psychic sensitivities to develop. It had been amazing when she and Shelby had shared in the vision of the runaway slaves.

Maybe it had all been too much for Jessie, especially when Martha died so unexpectedly. Her sudden passing left a hole in Sorina's heart. Maybe there was a hole in Jessie, too, and maybe she no longer felt safe.

No answers. Only questions. The most hopeful thing Sorina could hang onto was the idea of Lizbeth and Samuel and their run to freedom. Sori's Run. It was where her focus had to remain until these other mysteries could be revealed and life could go on the way it had been. Although she knew better.

It would never be the same.

CHAPTER FORTY-FOUR
MOMENT OF TRUTH

"WHAT DO YOU MEAN, Neely is alive? My mother is alive? Jessie, what are you tellin' me?" Shelby's whole body began shaking uncontrollably. She thrashed about on the cot, pulling on her chained restraints over and over. She screamed in rage, "Damn you! Let me out of here. You have to let me go! Jessie, please?"

Jessie just stood quietly watching as her captive finally and completely lost control. She was screaming and crying and seemed strong enough to maybe break free. Jessie picked up the gun, just in case.

Fascinating, she thought. Shelby had been her prisoner for a couple weeks and this was the first time she had seen her really lose it. At first it had been understandable. Jessie kept her sedated and then gradually gave her some of her own medicinal hallucinogens to keep her confused and disoriented. It was a perfect arrangement. Jessie kept her clean and fed and Shelby was as docile as a kitten. At times Shelby seemed to come around and then right before Jessie's eyes she seemed to disappear behind her own thoughts. Neat trick. And it had kept her a patient victim. But the sedation wasn't working any longer and her patience had run out. This last piece of information she had shared gave Jessie the best thrill because it seemed to put Shelby over the edge.

Jessie's thoughts were rational for someone who hadn't lived in a rational world. Her father had seen to that when she was little. She had been molested and abused all her life until Martha came along. But it was in her: The hatred, the anger, the hurt, the envy, the self-loathing. It was all there. She wanted back the life she could have had, should have had, had she only been born to people other than Jean and Lester Johnson. White trash Johnsons. She wanted that normal life that others had. She wanted back that baby that was torn from her, though it was *his*. And how she hated him. Maybe she would have hated his baby, but she would have liked to have had the chance to know. And Lester had made sure she wouldn't get another chance. There would be no more babies.

She knew she wasn't right in the head. Jessie knew that. She wasn't stupid.

But she had believed Sorina really loved her. Until Shelby came. Then she could tell she had just been a replacement for the real thing. It didn't matter what she had done or how much she had cared for her, it was that blood-is-thicker-than-water thing.

And neither of them even knew. That was the irony. They didn't even know they were mother and daughter. Even so, they had that damned undeniable connection, that special *seeing*. Jessie knew she would never be so important to Sorina again.

Still, Jessie was proud of how well she had kept that giant secret. Martha had sworn her to it, and Martha was worth keeping a good secret for. If Martha had lived, it wouldn't have been so bad, Shelby coming back into Sorina's life. Martha would have looked out for Jessie, cared for her. But Martha was gone. It was never going to be right.

Jessie watched Shelby finally courting madness and she smiled contentedly. *It gives me such pleasure. That probably isn't a good thing.*

She chuckled.

Shelby heard the chuckle, saw the pleasure cross her tormentor's face. She stopped thrashing. She stopped and stared at the pretty woman who must truly be a psychopath. Jessie was enjoying this. All this time, Shelby had harbored pity for Jessie, but that changed in the instant she saw the satisfaction she was getting from seeing Shelby suffer. All pity was gone. Even her fear was diminishing behind the hate that was building.

"You bitch," she whispered hoarsely.

"Oh, Shelby, now why do you call me that? You were always so sweet to me. Haven't I been good to you here in daddy's shack? Don't you like your accommodations? Would you like for me to take your picture? I bet your model friends would love to see what happens when you don't care for yourself properly. This would be good on the Internet, don't you think?"

Jessie came closer and pulled out a cell phone.

Shelby was shocked. She had never seen Jessie or Sorina go near modern technology.

"Didn't think us country hicks could use a cell phone, huh?" Jessie brought the phone close up to take a picture.

In a quick rage, Shelby sat up as far and fast as she could and used all her strength to spit on the phone.

"What the... you stinkin' whore!" Jessie swung her hand back and smacked Shelby hard with the cell phone on the side of her face.

Blood oozed out of Shelby's forehead and cheek before she passed out.

Screaming permeated every bit of air space around her head. High-pitched wailing and lamenting such as surely could only be heard in Hades; an eternal shattering soundtrack of lost, frightened, regretful souls screaming for release. Any kind of release. The voices narrowed, then, to a single lost soul.

The Banshee shrieked.

Shelby saw her. The fairy woman's pale hair lay in sticky wisps around her misshapen ugly head. The hag looked down at her own withered body where the red blood had clotted and dried between her legs. Shelby watched the horror manifest on the ghost's expression, as if she were surprised. Then a sudden knowing changed her expression again and the visage pulled herself up. She floated to the ceiling of the shed.

Shelby watched in terrible fascination as the Banshee looked down at her from above. Then she drifted lower, hovering right over her. Shelby was aware of a crushing weight on her chest. She couldn't breathe. And as panic started to choke her finally, the ghostly apparition pulled itself up once more and turned away from Shelby. It pointed a crooked finger at Jessie and opened its watery mouth wide.

Shelby's own hoarse screaming woke her. She was thrashing about on her cot, gasping, and soaked in her own sweat. But she was alone. She strained to see in the dim light, but Jessie wasn't there. The Banshee had pointed to her, pointed at Jessie. Or had she? What had it meant? Shelby tried to calm herself, tried to slow her ragged breath. Her heart was pounding too hard. She expected to see it explode right out of her chest. She took a breath, then another deeper one.

Shelby gained control of her senses.

It had just been another dream, a horrible, vivid dream, but she was all right. She looked down at her body and there was no blood between her legs. But she tasted blood dripping from her cheek to her lips. That much had been real.

The dream was a warning. Someone was about to die. A shudder ran over Shelby's thin body and she started to cry wearily. Sadness and regret filled her mind like a storm cloud, swelling until it finally blocked out any light, leaving only darkness in her soul. Shelby Jean Stiller cried and cried at the thought of her own death until she passed out again.

"Bessie, this is Chief Chambers. We need a warrant. Can you bother the judge?'

"Ah, he's in court, Lucas. I think they're gonna be tied up for a while. You in a hurry?"

"I am. We think we have a line on where Jessie Johnson might be keepin' Shelby Jean Stiller."

"You just hold on, Chief."

Lucas smiled over at Russell. "You got to know the right people."

In just a few minutes she was back on the phone. "It's in the system, Chief. You get yourselves over there. We have you covered on this end. And backup is standin' by. You boys just give me the word."

"Remind me to get down on my knees next time I see you, Ms. Bessie."

"Ah, you hush now. Just go bring that girl back to Wesley, Lucas. And be safe!"

This time the bubble went on top of the cruiser and he and Russell left a cloud of dust in the trailer's driveway where Bella and Caitlin waved goodbye.

They made better time being real cops. Traffic moved out of the way and in half the time they were close to the Johnson farm.

"Do you think we should announce ourselves?"

"Nope." Lucas reached out his window and disengaged the bubble.

They turned into Johnson's drive in silence. Lucas slowed way down and this time he had all pistons working. His eyes were not going to miss a thing. He parked the cruiser in front of the house as he had before and turned off the ignition. He reached over and pulled a pistol out of the glove compartment.

"Do you know how to shoot?"

Russell looked at the gun. "No."

"Don't matter. Take it anyway." Russell got a quick lesson on handling the trigger before they got out of the cruiser. "Now just keep your hands straight up like you've seen on TV."

Russell tried to recall every cop film he had ever seen. His hands started shaking.

"Do you wanna wait in the cruiser, Russell? Seriously? I think this time it's no goose we're chasin'. So if you ain't up to it..."

"I'm up to it, Chief. Lead the way." Russell took a huge breath and straightened himself.

"Good man."

Lucas drew his gun and Russell backed him up as they approached the house for a second time. Again, they found its rooms empty. Same with all the areas they had visited, but Wesley had remembered Lester talking about a shed maybe up in the hills.

They went around the back of the house and looked on all sides. No sign of another outbuilding. Then Lucas did what he did best. He studied his surroundings with pinpoint detail. He saw it, then. Evidence of someone walking over the ground. It was subtle, but it was there. Someone who wasn't too heavy, someone with a light step. Jessie. He followed the footsteps through a copse of tall brush and pine trees. His breath came hard and he was aware of a pounding in his chest as he followed the steps up a sharp incline. Lucas stopped and bent over, catching his ragged breath.

"Are you all right, Chief? Maybe I should go it alone."

Lucas was still bent over, but pulled his head up and glared into Russell's face.

"Yeah, well, maybe that's not such a good idea. What was I thinkin'? Here, Chief, breathe into this." Russell handed him a handkerchief.

"Christ Almighty, what's that supposed to do?" Lucas stared at the hankie and then at his deputy.

"Well, damnit, I don't have a paper bag."

Lucas stood upright and faced Russell. "Just back me up."

"Right, Chief. I got your back."

Lucas shook his head and took a deep breath. He felt his strength return and his lungs stopped burning. He adjusted his hat and led Russell up the hillside through more wild overgrowth. A narrow dirt path, barely visible, wound through tangled wild ferns and squatty pines that completely obscured a small gray shed. It blended into the hill like a natural part of the landscape.

Lucas and Russell looked at each other and had the same thought. *Moment of truth.* Russell stared into Lucas' eyes boldly. He wasn't shaking. Lucas nodded and the partners approached the shed cautiously. There were no windows in the rough door. They couldn't see in. But all was quiet when they listened. The men stood still, every muscle taut, every nerve ending on edge. Lucas felt his heart popping. He reached up and knocked three times.

Shelby heard it. There it was finally, the dreaded *rocks on the roof...*

Jessie jumped up from the chair where she had fallen asleep.

Shelby screamed.

Lucas put a large booted foot into the shabby door and it flew open, slamming against the wall. Jessie was standing there with a gun aimed right him.

Russell was behind him and they both saw her, saw Shelby Jean lying there. She was bleeding, but she was alive.

"Russell?" Her voice was as weak as a kitten.

"It's okay, Shelby. It's gonna be okay. We got you now. You're gonna be fine." Then he looked back to Jessie who stood still as a statue with the gun aimed at Lucas' head.

"Jessie, give me the gun." Lucas held out his free hand.

She stood taller.

"Jessie, you don't wanna do this. You kill me and Russell will kill you. That's how it's gonna work. Nobody wins."

"Who? Him? He is gonna kill me?" She grinned at Russell. His arm was aimed at her, but he was visibly shaking again.

"Nah, Chief, he ain't gonna kill me."

Then she looked over at Shelby, her gun still pointed steadily at Lucas. "You take care of my gardens, my animals. You hear? You take care of your mama."

"Jessie, don't."

"It's okay, Shelby."

Jessie turned the gun towards herself.

"I think it's me now that needs killin'."

The pretty woman put the barrel in her mouth, and just as Shelby screamed, she pulled the trigger.

CHAPTER FORTY-FIVE
GUNSMOKE

LIZBETH THOUGHT SHE COULDN'T HOLD ON a moment longer. Samuel had been like a man possessed. As exhausted as they were, as much as their bodies cried out for rest, he didn't give into it. He pulled her, and when he couldn't pull her, he lifted her up in his large, muscular arms and carried her like a baby. She would cry with relief, but then feel so guilty that she would insist he let her down. Then she would hold back the scream that wanted to come when her bleeding feet hit the mean ground. She bit her tongue hard to keep herself quiet. The new pain helped her forget her feet and she was able to keep going. If he could keep going, how could she not.

Lizbeth had it now, that life thing that Samuel had. He had given her hope and now she knew she wanted to live. She didn't want to lie down and die in this unforgiving forest. She didn't want to die here. She wanted to live and she wanted to be free. If she couldn't have that, then she would die from the slavers' guns. If they captured them and tried to take them back she would find a way to get them to kill her. She wanted to live, but not as a slave.

Not ever again.

"Samuel, you know where we are? Do you know, Samuel? Is we right?" She spoke through wheezes as they kept running. Her chest burned from the exertion. He didn't answer her, but tightened his grip on her hand.

Then he squeezed.

Something was coming. They didn't hear any dogs, but something was coming fast behind them as they ran. Samuel looked over his shoulder and tried to zigzag through the trees to throw off whatever it was that was so close.

Lizbeth felt terror coming back strong. She could hear branches and bushes snapping and crushing behind her, sounding as though some mammoth creature was tearing through the woods chasing them. No matter what direction Samuel took them in, it followed easily. The faster they ran, the faster it ran.

"Samuel, what is it?" She hollered hoarsely through her ragged breath.

"I don't know!?" Samuel sounded scared, really scared.

Lizbeth remembered the slave, Solomon, who had gotten so close to tasting freedom, only to end up injuring himself. He was a slave still. She knew from Samuel's voice that he was more afraid now than he had been because they, also, were so close. He believed they were close to making it to safety, and now a wild animal would take them?

Was that what God had planned? After all their human suffering, that they would die a horrible death in the jaws of a ravenous animal? If God had that planned, then she knew God was a slaver, too. She would fight against this new, terrifying injustice with every breath she had left. She would fight.

Something popped in Lizbeth, then, like a new life force, and she felt strength returning to her weary limbs, to her beaten body. It was as though her mind was floating above her body and energy was being fed to her from all of the untamed nature surrounding her—like the woods was carrying her along.

She was disappearing.

She knew it. It was a survival instinct that she was really knowing for the first time. She saw the surprised look on Samuel's face as he looked back at her. He tightened his grip on her hand and they ran. They ran and ran.

But their chaser ran, too.

Hope began to wane as it went on. Lizbeth shouted raspily, "What is it, Samuel? What is this thing?"

"I don't know, Lizbeth. But it ain't gonna stop."

His answer was so final and she knew the truth in it. This was a real predator on their trail and it would not give up. It would never give up. And it was gaining speed as they were weakening. It was coming closer. She thought she could feel heat from the jaws of the creature. It was so close she could feel its hot breath.

Lizbeth closed her eyes. She couldn't watch what would happen next. She squeezed Samuel's sweaty hand hard and shouted, "I love you, Samuel. I has always loved you. I will see you in the afterworld!"

Then, from somewhere just east of them a shot rang out. Lizbeth heard the high whistle of a bullet go right by her ear. She threw her free hand to her head to block the noise as the shot rang through the trees. To her it sounded as though hell opened up and squeezed out a scream that pierced her ears and her heart. She and Samuel fell to the ground.

Had they been shot? She didn't feel any pain? She looked at Samuel who had collapsed in front of her. Oh, please, God, not my Samuel! Another deafening shot rang out over their heads.

Then she felt the earth quake behind them. She turned back to see a large gray wolf. Its head was inches from her face. It lay on the ground, blood spurting out from its heavy coat. She looked into its dead eyes.

Samuel sprung up from the ground, grabbed her hand again, and again they ran. All the while she kept hearing the blast from the gun shots playing over and over in her head. Where had they come from? Who had saved them? The forest flew by in a blurred mossy green as they ran. Now it was like angels from on high carried them on and on.

And then, as if in a dream, a dim light appeared up ahead. It flickered and played with their senses. They slowed their pace as they got closer to the light until they could make out where it was coming from. The flickering wasn't a trick their eyes were playing on them. It was candlelight. It illuminated the most magical, warm sight. In all her life of bondage, she had never witnessed such a welcoming haven. It was indeed a cabin in the middle of the woods, just as Samuel had promised. After nothing but the dense forest for days on end, it was the most remarkable vision. Lamplight shimmered from inside its windows and smoke curled out of its huge chimney.

Samuel stopped then, and held onto her. Their hearts beat wildly as one. She felt like he would squeeze her to death, but she remained silent as she watched him watch it, this vision. She knew his complete fear then. Was this real? Or was it a trap? He stood until his breathing calmed and then he released her.

He looked down at her. "Lizbeth, this here is what we been prayin' for, what we been tryin' to git to. This is the house of the woman who gonna help us git to the other side of the river. She gonna be our savior. Now, you let me do the talkin'."

She nodded at him, as she tried to catch her breath. She followed mutely behind as he held onto her hand. He approached the door and knocked timidly at first, and then with more force.

The door cracked just slightly, and a woman's voice asked, "Samuel, is that you?"

"Yesum, it be me and my woman, Lizbeth. Is it okay?"

The door opened wide and a pioneer woman stood with a smoking rifle at her side, wild, golden hair streaked with gray flowing down her shoulders and back.

"Yes. It's okay. You come on in now. You are safe."

Shelby felt relief wash over her just knowing the slaves were safe. Lizbeth and Samuel were safe! And then she realized their journey had correlated almost exactly with her own. She was safe, too. She heard the hospital sounds before she opened her eyes. She had been admitted for observation, but she'd been dehydrated enough to need IV fluids. Things were still fuzzy, but she was remembering. She remembered that Jessie had shot herself and then Lucas had taken care of everything.

Shelby saw a clock on her bedside stand. Obtrusive LED lights announced 3:00 a.m. Caitlin was asleep in a chair next to her. Shelby did the unthinkable and got out of bed. She stood up and waited for the light-headedness to stop. She was careful not to yank out her IV as she threw a robe around her shoulders, quietly, so as not to waken Cait. She put on the hospital slippers and left her room slowly, pulling the IV pole beside her. Cait had told her where Sorina was. She had to see her. The vision was so real; she needed to know if Sorina had seen it, too.

She snuck out into the dimly-lit hallway and saw a nurse with her head bent down over paperwork behind the nurse's station. Shelby was able to go the opposite direction down the hall without being spotted. Sorina was on the same floor, but a different wing. Shelby realized just how weak she was as she labored to put one slippered foot in front of the other.

But she had to see her. Had to see her mother.

Sorina was lying on the bed hooked up to various machines. Her eyes were wide open. She heard footsteps approaching.

"Nurse, is that you? I'll probably need somethin' else for sleep."

Shelby got close to the side of the bed before she spoke, "Sorina, it's me. It's Shelby Jean." Shelby felt instant tears wanting to fall, but she swallowed hard and waited.

Sorina's eyes grew wider and she smiled. "Shelby Jean? Is that really you? Oh, Shelby, hon, your voice is the sweetest sound I ever heard. Thank God, you're safe. I heard you were here in the hospital. Are you all right?" She waved her hand in the air looking for Shelby to connect and soon they were holding hands.

"Yes, I'm all right, Sorina. But I'm afraid Jessie..."

The smile left Sorina's face. "Oh, I know, hon. I know. It's too much to think about and I just can't believe it. So, for now I'm only gonna concentrate on you and you gettin' home where you should be. I want you with me, Shelby. Will you move in with me?" Tears rolled down her cheeks.

Shelby had already made that decision. "Yes, Sorina. I'm gonna stay with you from now on if you'll have me?"

"Oh, hon, you know the answer to that. Shelby, did you see them? Did you see the slaves, Lizbeth and Samuel?"

"Yes, I did. And they made it safely, too. Isn't it a miracle? It's like their journey corresponded with my own. How is that possible?"

"I don't know, hon, but it's true. You were both on Sori's Run to freedom. And I am so happy! So happy!"

Just then a nurse came into the room. "Shelby Jean Stiller?"

Shelby nodded.

"Sweetie, they just called from A Wing. We woke your friend up and she knew exactly where we'd find you. But hon, you ain't supposed to be out of bed. Come on, now. I'll help you back."

Shelby left easily with the nurse and told her that Sorina needed a sleep aid.

But Shelby didn't.

For the first time in forever she slept naturally and deeply, without any dreams.

CHAPTER FORTY-SIX
DELICIOUS FEELING

"SO, I THINK MY POLICIN' DAYS are behind me, Bella." Lucas sighed.

"Oh, yeah? Well, never say never, Chief. Bessie will probably call you tomorrow and ask you to get yourself down to the station to help out with some cold case or somethin'."

"I don't think so. I didn't do so good with Shelby. Here Jessie was, right under my nose all the time."

"Hey, don't be so hard on yourself, Lucas. She was under all our noses. Especially mine. With everythin' I knew about her, I shoulda seen that comin' from a mile off. It was clear as a bell, and I didn't see it. But you, my friend, were able to find that shed after all, and you handled it as only you coulda done. Shelby was lucky to have you and Russell on the case."

Saber brought her a beer from the cooler and wagged his tail as he went back for another round for his master.

"Shelby has asked us all to be at the cottage tonight. Something special. Can't imagine."

"Don't know what's up? Now, that would be a first." Lucas grinned as he took the cold beer from his best friend's jaw and petted him on the head. "Thank you, Saber. Good boy." The lab wagged his tail happily.

"Damn it, now, Lucas. You're thinkin' about the old days when me and Martha was on top of things. I'm no spring chicken, you know. I must be slippin'. I have no idea what Shelby has up her sleeve."

Lucas looked over at the woman who had quickly become very important to him. He was beginning to think he wanted her on his deck every night. *Wonder what she would say to that?*

"Cat got your tongue, Lucas Chambers? You looked pretty smirky there." She smiled back at him, and thought, *I love this deck. I wish I could be here every night. Wonder what he would say to that?*

Lucas answered, "I was just thinkin' that I'm glad you're not a spring chicken. I like a woman with some mileage. Keeps me goin'." He smiled again and they tipped their beer cans to each other. "But I am surprised you don't know what Shelby is cookin' up. Things have gone well since she moved into Sorina's, right?"

"Oh, yeah. They are doin' just wonderful. And Caitlin bein' in Martha's trailer and keepin' up with the gardenin' is workin' out just great, too."

"Yeah, but I can't see Caitlin Sotheby livin' in that trailer too long. Can you?"

"No. And I doubt she will. Russell's house is a far cry from Martha's humble abode." She smiled and they toasted again.

"All right, then. The New Yorkers are becomin' Kentucky residents. Now, ain't that somethin'? I wonder how Wesley is takin' to all this?"

"Well, since nobody is gonna tell Sorina who she is, nobody sure as hell is gonna tell Wesley. So he just seems real happy to have Shelby back. She's been visitin' the farmhouse and they are gettin' along this time. Apparently, he finally decided to forgive her."

"Yeah, Shelby needs forgivin' all right. All she did was give him twenty more years and great health. Yeah, that's a real shame."

"Yeah, and all she had to do was share a joint with him," Bella snickered. "Too bad they couldn't have figured that little trick out a decade ago."

If anyone had been watching, they would have seen a man and a woman lookin' like they were an old married couple, totally at ease in each other's company. And had they looked closer, they would have seen a spark of attraction there, too. The couple kept their eyes on the Ohio River below the cantilevered house. It was a beautiful afternoon and the rolling water was soothing. Bella and Lucas felt peace, where for so long there had been none.

It felt delicious.

Lucas reached over and took Bella's hand and she was glad he did.

Shelby had the box sitting on her lap. She ran her hand over the smooth, lacquered finish in pale yellow. Purple and red flowers were painted on the lid and it was all trimmed in a leafy green. So pretty. It was just like Grandma Mart to put her jewelry in such a unique treasure chest. Shelby pulled at the gold clasp and opened the box again. She had found the letter when she dumped out the bracelets onto her bed to pick out one to wear. A lid in the bottom of the box flipped open revealing an envelope. It was addressed to Shelby Jean and was in her grandmother's handwriting. She picked it up again, reading the letter for the third time:

Dearest Shelby Jean,

If you're readin this, it means I am gone and all things about our family will have been revealed to you. Bella was the keeper of the secrets, and nobody was ever better at keepin secrets than Bella. So now there are no more secrets. Only regrets that I take with me. Regrets that I didn't keep you closer to me, regrets that you and your father never could find happiness together. Regrets that you lost all those years with your mother.

Shelby, I might have made all the wrong choices, but I was only tryin to protect Neely and protect you. I truly believe that had Bella and I not acted on the night of Neely's wreck, that she would have met a violent death at the hand of Lester Johnson. Maybe I was wrong, but that was what drove me to do what I did. It was fear, Shelby, plain and simple. By the time the fear was gone, I had made the bed that your mother and I had to lie in for a very long time.

Those were the hardest years of my life, burnin up US 23 between Sorry's Run and Columbus, goin back and forth to hospitals and rehabs and livin a lie. It was exhaustin, lonely and frightenin. And lord knows, I doubted myself more than once for what I had done, but I was too bullheaded not to stick with the plan, so I did.

Again, I think I was just too afraid, afraid of what would happen if I told the truth, afraid of what would happen if I didn't.

It paralyzed me. I hope you never have to make such a life-changin decision from a fearful stance. It is the wrong vibration for sure. If I hadn't had Bella to help me in all things, I would have never pulled it off. I loved her for that, but maybe she was wrong, too. Maybe she should have told me to stop the lie. Oh, hell, I'm sure she did tell me that. I just wouldn't listen.

I was a coward.

Neely really did lose her mind in all the pain she endured. God's most sensitive creatures aren't built for tortuous existences. They can only escape, which is what she did. They told me after too many tests over too many years that she was like a clean slate. She blocked out the accident and the horrible surgeries and years of rehabilitation like they had never happened. And in doin so, she blocked out all the good things that had been in her past as well. You, me, Wesley, her healin work. For that I was so sorry. Some of the doctors thought it was likely she would regain her memories, but mostly, nobody could be certain. And when the damage to her brain caused her eyesight to fail, I knew that my dream of a reunion between you two was growin dimmer along with her vision.

But Shelby, your mother never felt sorry for herself when she went blind because, along with everythin else, she never really remembered bein able to see. In fact, I think it heightened her sensibilities in all ways. I was so surprised and grateful for that unexpected blessin.

Neely is a sensitive intuitive and healer. She is very talented in that way, and I know that's why she took to bein Sorina like she did. That strong pioneer woman was somebody she could latch onto and build a life upon. She thrived like I didn't think was possible. It gave her an identity and a strength and it was just what she needed.

And she found happiness!

I couldn't let anybody destroy that after what she had been through just to stay alive.

Maybe I was wrong. Maybe I should have confronted her with who she was, but I didn't have the strength, as it turns out.

I thought it would hurt her, and she had been hurt too much. So I didn't tell her.

And I didn't tell you.

I know that was wrong. It is why I begged you to come to Kentucky this time. I knew it was now or never. You still have time to know your mother, and Neely still has time to know you. I have no idea if that is possible, but I came to realize I had to try. I needed to tell you and let you make the decision of whether to tell Neely.

What an awful position to put you in. I hope you can forgive me for that, Shelby Jean. If you have questions about those terrible days ask Bella. She was there with me and knows it all. She will tell you anything you want to know.

As for me, I managed to live a happy life. My friends and my church sustained me, even though my family had been torn apart. I loved you with all my heart and have always been proud of you. I knew you had a better life away from Sorry's Run and I wanted that for you. But I used to dream that someday you would want to return for good and live in the cottage with Neely and Jessie and make a home for yourself there. It was my dream. And I can't thank you enough for providin me with the means to make at least a part of that dream come true. I hope you love the cottage as I do. It is yours. I hope you will allow your mother to live there until she is gone. It is a happy place, built on dreams and Irish fantasy.

If my heart is true, I'll be in Ireland when I'm gone, in that place of magic and mystery my granny used to speak of. How I loved thinkin the fairies would watch out over my soul. It has been my lifeline and I am hopin one day you'll believe it, too. But I have seen her, Shelby, in my dreams. The Banshee is tellin me my time is comin, even though my sweet fairies keep drivin her away. But I'm not gone yet. You are here and I started to tell you things today. I probably scared you a little. I didn't mean to. I hope I get the chance to explain in person.

And in case I don't get around to it, tell Lucas I always thought he was a hottie! But Bella needs a good man and that house of hers is too dang big. I know Lucas thought he had a thing for me, but that was just somethin to have some fun with. It was never meant to be.

And, Shelby Jean, in case you're wonderin, your God light has always been shinin. You might have turned it down or even turned it off from time to time, but it's always been there ready to light your way.

You just have to open your eyes.

I heard the rocks on the roof tonight. The fairies are circlin.

I love you...

Shelby folded the letter back up and placed it in its hidden compartment beneath the jewelry. So Grandma Mart had not known to watch out for Jessie. How ironic. All that she went through to save Neely and here she had put her right back in harm's way.

Mysterious ways.

Bella, Violet, Jolene, Caitlin, Shelby and Sorina sat around the table in the cottage sipping wine. It wasn't a chilly night, but as usual, Sorina wanted a fire in the fireplace anyway. Even before Violet could get the complaining words out, Sorina had stopped her. "Fire is closer to spirit," she insisted.

So an unseasonable fire roared in the picturesque, historic home.

Shelby looked around at these women who were her family now. It was strange, Jessie not being with them. It was stranger still to think they had all known her, liked her, trusted her. How disturbing to realize how deep those still waters ran and how polluted they were. And it hadn't been easy to fill her shoes. Shelby was far from a domestic goddess and she was going to need a lot of help with keeping things the way Jessie had them. But Sorina hadn't seemed to mind at all. She had been so sweet and understanding as she walked Shelby through the basics of how to live and care for a blind person. It would take patience, but that was not going to be a problem for Shelby.

She couldn't stop staring at Sorina and trying to find her mother there. The face was so different after all the surgeries, but something in her eyes when she took off her shaded glasses reminded Shelby that Neely was in there somewhere. But Sorina didn't know it. Probably never would. And it was okay. She was so happy being who she had created that nobody saw any reason to upset that cart. Shelby decided it was enough to have her mother again, no matter how compromised.

"What is that wonderful perfume?" Sorina asked.

"Caitlin brought you a bouquet of lilies, Sorina. They're stargazers from Grandma Mart's garden. They were sorely neglected, but she nursed them back."

"Well, I bet they are lovely. Their fragrance is powerful. I'm surprised that Jessie didn't plant..." She stopped herself in mid sentence. "Shelby Jean, I have somethin' to give to you, too." She reached into her pocket and pulled out a turquoise and crystal bracelet. "Do you recognize this?"

Shelby examined the jewelry and realized it was the bracelet she had worn the night Jessie abducted her. "How in the world?"

"Lucas found it in the woods. He wanted me to have it, and now I'm so glad to give it back to you."

"Thank you, Sorina. I will never lose this again. What a reminder of how precious life is." Shelby wiped a tear from her eye and then looked around the table. "I am so glad you guys are here with Sorina and I tonight. I wanted you here because I think I need some therapy. I have been having these awful recurring dreams of the shed and my time there. I doubt that I will ever get over it, you know? I can still feel it. And I can't get Jessie's face out of my mind either. I just can't understand how someone that gifted could feel she had no worth? Even after her horrible experiences, Martha gave her the tools she needed to move on. Why couldn't she?"

"She was ruined, plain and simple," Bella spoke. "And Shelby, it would stand to reason that she put some blame on you and Neely (all eyes went to the blind woman) for Lester takin' her unborn baby out of anger. It's all so twisted! And Martha wasn't here to keep her doin' right, so her own dark nature musta took over. She just didn't have the strength of character to share you with Sorina. Right?"

Sorina answered, "I don't know, Bella. I keep goin' over it in my head. What did I do or not do that made that girl think I cared for her less once Shelby showed up. I must have done somethin' to have brought all this on. Shelby and I mostly had our sharin' of the slave vision that tied us together. And I admit that thrilled me beyond belief and I was fascinated by it. I must have went on too much about it. Jessie and I always had a wonderful time, and I can't believe she would think I would replace her. And I will miss her somethin' terrible. But through all this horror I thought…we all thought Martha would help lead us to Shelby. But she was silent as she never was in her physical life."

"Maybe Grandma Mart hasn't been so silent?" Shelby corrected her. "I think she might have been working through Rory. Look at how that little bunny rabbit played a part in all this."

"You know, that's true." Bella agreed. "It makes perfect sense. I kept thinkin' little Rory was one of Martha's fairies. But she always did say that sometimes it was easiest for bein's in the nonphysical world to manipulate the little creatures in the physical world. So Martha just took him over. Why else was Rory always leadin' to clues?"

"Good gravy!" Jolene laughed and exclaimed, "Y'all are gonna have to take darn good care of little Rory rabbit!"

Shelby nodded. "Another thing that "haunts" me is my dream of the Banshee in the shed. Grandma always said the legend went that if you saw her, you died. If you heard her, someone else died. And I *saw* her."

Sorina answered, "But, hon, didn't you say the hag pointed her finger at Jessie?"

"Yes. But still…"

"Well, with your strong beliefs, you manifested her and she let you know she was meant for Jessie. The fairies were protectin' you, darlin'." Sorina smiled sweetly.

"But the really disturbing thing was that the Banshee appeared as a woman dying in childbirth, like your Sori did?" Shelby raised an eyebrow.

Sorina explained, "Oh, hon, the legend is older than time. Women dyin' in childbirth was a natural fit for the Banshee's wailin'. But there are many tales told on that subject. You were raised on the stories and legends, so whatever Martha told you helped you create your own version. The Banshee is the Scotch/Irish equivalent of the Grim Reaper, and it's very personal. But, Shelby, I *feel* Sori Duncan McBride and her spirit is all beauty and light. You must believe that."

Shelby smiled. "Okay. But whatever all that was, fantasy or fact, I pray I don't see that badass Banshee in my dreams again, at least not for a very long time."

"We'll drink to that!" Bella led in a toast.

Shelby continued, "But I am seeing Grandma Mart in my dreams every night. It's the same thing that was happening to me in the hospital after the car wreck. She and Neely (again, all eyes went to the blind woman), well, they both came to me, telling me to open my eyes. Just open my eyes. I figured then I was just missing them both so much that I conjured them in my sleep. But now Martha is coming back strong and telling me to 'open my eyes' again. I'm not sure what to make of it, but it seems to mean something."

"She must have somethin' more to show you," Violet added.

The women all shook their heads in agreement.

"I don't think she will ever stop showing me things. Grandma Mart lives in me so much. And now that I have made the decision to make this my home, I feel so blessed to live here with Sorina." She reached over and took Sorina's hand. "So blessed, and so glad she decided to share the diary with me. Talk about showing me things? I am amazed by the woman who lived in this cottage all those years ago, the woman who made "Sori's Run" symbolic with a quest for freedom.

"And maybe my captive time with Jessie has shown me that I am stronger than I realized. That I am a survivor. That somehow my eyes were opened by that experience. Maybe that's what Martha is referring to by 'open your eyes.'" Shelby stared into her wine glass before adding, "More than anything, I learned up close and personal that life is a gift and we must not squander a moment of it." She felt the bracelet she had just put on her wrist.

Bella lifted her glass in another toast.

As the glasses lifted, Shelby's spirits lifted, too. She experienced a dramatic emotional release, like the burden she had been carrying since her return to Kentucky had just moved on. She knew in that moment she was finally free to be happy. It had truly been her own *Sori's Run*.

Unbridled joy washed over her.

She reached across the table and squeezed Sorina's hand, and was literally shocked by a familiar jolt—like electricity running through her palm. It was the same sensation as suddenly having her hand held over a hot flame. Shelby closed her eyes to try to stop the strange burning.

Then she opened her eyes. And she knew what Martha meant. "Oh, my god." Shelby got up from the table and stood behind Sorina.

"Shelby Jean? What are you doin'?"

"Just sit still, Sorina. Don't be afraid. I just want you to relax." Shelby reached around and removed Sorina's glasses from her face and sat them on the table. Then she placed her hands over Sorina's eyes, completely covering them.

Nobody at the table moved or spoke. Sorina was visibly shaking as Shelby's hands got hotter. A wave of nausea racked Shelby's abdomen, but she held her position. She closed her eyes tightly, grimacing from the heat that was radiating through every nerve ending. Her conscious mind thought her fingers were on fire. Her unconscious mind knew better. At last, she felt the fire being released through her fingertips, like tiny flames. And next, in one impossible heated moment, the fire left her hands completely and Sorina screamed in pain.

"God, Shelby, what are you doing?" Caitlin jumped up from her chair, but Bella stopped her.

"She's all right, Cait. Just give them a moment."

Shelby never moved her hands from Sorina's eyes and Sorina just hung her head in submission. In another minute it was over.

The room was silent except for the crackling and popping from the fireplace. Slowly, Shelby backed away and Sorina raised her head. Her face was wet with tears and she was still shaking.

Then she—*opened her eyes.*

Sorina threw her hands up to her face in sheer disbelief. "Bella? Is that you? Jolene, Violet, Caitlin?" She looked from each face to the next, slowly.

The women were dumbfounded and speechless. At last it was Jolene who spoke, "Sorina, honey, are you seein' us? Darlin', can you see?"

Sorina smiled, then, and laughed out loud. "Yes! I am seein' you. I can see you all!"

Shelby sat back down. She looked ashen in color and her breathing was ragged.

Caitlin went over and knelt beside her. "Shel, are you all right?"

"Yes, Cait, I am. I really am." She raised her head, then, and looked at Sorina. Sorina stared back at her.

"Shelby Jean?"

Shelby nodded yes, as happy tears washed her cheeks.

EPILOGUE

"DO YOU THINK SHE WILL EVER REMEMBER?" Caitlin asked Shelby just as the plane's landing gear jerked to let them know they were about to be back in New York.

"I don't know, Cait. Sometimes I catch her staring at me in a different way, you know, like maybe I'm starting to look familiar to her, but I can't be sure. She's so fascinated with everything she's seeing. It's probably just my imagination."

"Well, it's only been a couple weeks. Bella swears it will take time, but it will happen. And then she says a whole new can of worms will open up, depending on how Wesley takes it."

"I know. And things are going so well between us right now. I really don't want anything to mess that up. But he is so different. Maybe now he could actually handle it?"

"Hey, anything can happen. Look at Bella and Lucas, shacking up at Lucas', and Bella putting her house on the market."

"Yeah, and look at you and Russell?" Shelby winked at her best friend.

"I know, right?"

"You're going to miss your job?"

"True, but I think a garden center will be perfect for Sorry's Run. I'm already working on a business plan and Russell says he knows of the perfect space."

"You guys are awesome. But I feel sorry for Tommy."

"Yeah, I hated telling him all this stuff about us moving, but he is so excited about planning the wedding. Do you think Greenup County is ready for the likes of him?"

Shelby laughed. "I'm fairly certain Greenup County can handle anything."

"Well, at least Sorry's Run sure can. Everything seems to converge there. Must be one of those hot spots on the planet."

The plane rolled to a stop and Shelby and Caitlin stood up with the rest of the passengers and got their carry-on luggage. They didn't even notice as all eyes watched the two stunners get in line in the aisle. Cait led the way.

"Tommy is going to meet us at the apartment to help pack. He says Jeremiah has already arranged for a moving van. God, you think we can really do this in a week?"

"Sure. We'll have lots of help. Besides, Caitlin Sotheby, we've got the luck of the Irish, don't you know?" Shelby winked as they de-boarded the plane.

Outside of JFK, Cait hailed a cab, and Shelby hailed another one right behind her.

"What are you doing, Shel?"

"I'm gonna meet you later. I have some unfinished business."

"Shelby Jean?"

"Don't worry, Cait. Nothing stupid. I'll tell you all about it. I swear I'll be fine. I'll hook up with you in a little bit."

Cait's blue eyes flashed and then she put her arms around her friend. "Okay. You have your cell phone?"

"Yes."

"Well, use it if you need me."

They parted ways in two separate taxies. Shelby gave the driver the address and sat back to enjoy the ride. She was surprised that she had butterflies in her stomach. *That's just silly*, she thought.

She watched out the cab's window as New York flew by, surprised at how it felt being back. It had been so long. Her entire life had changed, and now she knew it for sure. She no longer belonged in the big city. Kentucky had her heart and that's where she wanted to live out her life.

She motioned for the cabbie to stop.

"It's up one more block, Miss?"

"I know. I want to get out here for just a second. Wait on me?"

He nodded and she got out of the cab. A newspaper stand sat on the corner. Next to it, a small woman was selling flowers. Shelby went over to her and bought a bouquet. The vendor gave the beautiful woman her change. "This will bring happiness, lady," she said in a heavy European accent and smiled.

Shelby smiled back. "I hope so."

She got back in the taxi for the short ride to Bellevue. As she left the cab a second time, she handed the driver cash and asked once again, "Wait on me?"

"Sure thing. I'm glad you ain't stayin'." The cabbie grinned. He rarely had such lookers in his cab and he would have been glad to drive this one all over town.

As Shelby went through the door of the infamous institution, she felt nervous and hoped she was doing the right thing. At the information desk she was directed to the right unit. Entering his room, she found a little gray-haired man sitting all alone, staring out the window with his back to the door.

"Carny?" she asked.

He didn't reply, but she could tell he heard her. His shoulders stiffened up just slightly. She crossed the room and stood in front of him. He didn't look up. She held out the bouquet of carnations. He looked, then, at the flowers. He didn't raise his head, but he took the flowers. He appeared childlike to Shelby as he put the flowers to his face and held them there. Then he finally looked up and he saw her.

A look of disbelief crossed his old weathered face. For a moment, Shelby thought maybe she shouldn't have come.

But then a huge smile replaced the look of confusion and Shelby knew.

She had brought happiness…

THE END